LION
of
JUDAH

LION
&
JUDAH

THE SONG OF PROPHETS AND KINGS

LION *of* JUDAH

HENRY O. ARNOLD

WhiteFire
— PUBLISHING —

LION OF JUDAH

Cover design and typesetting by Roseanna White Designs
Author photo by Ben Pearson

Published in association with the literary agency, WTA Media, LLC, Franklin, TN

WhiteFire Publishing
13607 Bedford Rd NE
Cumberland, MD 21502

ISBN: 979-8-88709-104-4 (print)
        979-8-88709-105-1 (digital)

For…
Nan, Cris, Tim…
Best siblings ever.

PART ONE

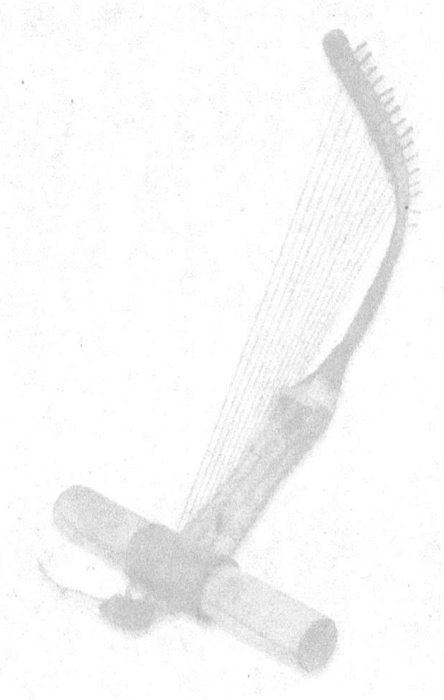

Prologue

MIKAL LEANED OVER THE BALUSTRADE OF THE ROOFTOP TER-
race, her chin resting on top of her folded arms. From this height she could
see the surrounding hills of Hebron stretching beyond the city to include the
fields and pastures. The hour was late, and the dwellings in the city reflected
little light. The shadowy outlines of the structures were illuminated from
above by the multitude of stars and the fingernail moon.

Mikal took a deep breath. The cool breeze had cleansed much of the air
created by the concentrated population. Still, the scent of fires, of corrals
and stables, of outdoor markets, and eating establishments lingered. She had
returned to city life, and she began to awaken out of the dream of her long
sorrow.

For so long she had been content to live on her family property in Gibeah
away from all contact with the outside world. Mikal knew isolation and exile.
She understood what it meant to fall prey to the evil of the world through
no fault of her own. Through an act of sheer will she had kept the grief from
hardening her heart. Now, after so long a time, a living stream was washing
away her coarsened sorrow. But she would not allow herself to cry, not on
this night. She could not permit the trickle of happiness, this new stream
bubbling in the depths of her heart, to make its joyful way to her eyes.

Mikal had spent many hours with her new handmaidens preparing herself
for this night of reunion. Tears would destroy her face, dilute her eyes, soil her

skin, weaken her muscles. She wanted her full beauty to please her husband and needed her full strength to enjoy the pleasure she anticipated.

Discipline was how she had survived these many years, and it had produced within her a kind of serenity. Like the warrior's discipline to prepare for battle, Mikal had established daily routines. She had turned her attention to the simple life of a gardener raising produce to live, to sustain life when the life she had known was torn from her with such cruelty. Her dreams and longings had died when her true husband had been forced to flee and, out of spite, a second husband had been imposed upon her by her father, the mad king.

So long ago. So many ghosts. So few pleasant memories.

Mikal turned from the raised stone barrier around the open perimeter. She stepped onto the beautiful carpet in the center of the terrace and rubbed her bare feet over the fine weaving. The space had been designed for seclusion, for quiet conversations, for the privacy of tender affections. A four-post canopy was raised in the center of the balcony with scattered cushions, quilts, and fur blankets beneath it. To one side stretched a long table covered in trays of fruit, cheeses, slices of wild game, and honey cakes. At the end of the table were two jeweled goblets. Mikal was struck by the sparkle of the light from the small firepit flickering off the gemstones embedded into the goblets, recent plunder from Canaanite tribes.

She lifted both goblets and held them above the firelight. Only two residents would be on this terrace tonight. They had enough food and drink to satiate appetite and thirst for several days and nights without being disturbed.

So much time had been lost. So much to restore.

This elaborate setting was not her doing. Mikal had not ordered servants or handmaidens to decorate this balcony and prepare this feast. She did not have servants. She could not claim the handmaidens who had bathed and dressed her as hers to beckon or command. This terrace had been prepared for her by the one with whom she would share it. He had thought through this evening, down to the last detail. He had been thinking of her.

The harshness of long years of separation were receding as she gave herself over to the fantasy of what the rest of the evening could be—all pleasure, all delight, the luxuriant warmth of her husband, the satisfied tenderness of his love.

Mikal might have to share him with others, but she was the first among his wives. She would be dearer to him than them all. The other women in her husband's growing family would provide children and secure alliances with Israel's elite. She, of course, would provide her share of children, but her sons would be heirs to the throne and her daughters would be true princesses.

The thought of multiple princes and princesses running around the palace tickled her. Mikal would see to their upbringing, their education, their training in service to the king with special attention to her firstborn son, for one day he would assume the throne. Her son would inherit the kingdom, her son would carry the name of David and that of her father into the future. Her son would be the son and grandson of kings, the first two kings of Yahweh's chosen.

Her reverie broke when she heard her name called from the steps below. Mikal placed the goblets onto the table and dashed to the top step of the terrace. One flight below David leaned against the outside wall panting. He held a torch with its light beaming down upon his head, a head that would soon wear the golden crown of a king.

The king had been running, racing up flights of stairs to her. The king had one desire in his heart…her.

Mikal raised her arms to him. "Take me, I am yours," she whispered, the words spoken only for his ears.

She had waited so long to say them to the only man she had ever desired. They must be spoken gently. Layers of wounds in her heart had to be removed, and it would begin this night with these words, whispered under the stars of Hebron.

Chapter 1

MIKAL ROLLED OVER ON THE CUSHIONS, AND DAVID WAS NOT beside her. She raised her head off the pillow and saw him standing on the first steps descending from the terrace. He wore only his undergarment, but he was speaking with someone.

The sun had risen. Loud voices rose from below, not the general hubbub of the streets and marketplace, but voices of alarm, cries of murder, howls of death at the gate of the lion.

"Mikal, it's Abner." David rushed back under the canopy. "He never made it home. He never made it out of the city. And my nephews are to blame."

"What are you saying?" Mikal sat up with a start. "What has happened?"

"Come with me." He started for the stairs.

Mikal threw on her robe, grabbed David's robe, and raced after him. Wherever he was going he needed more covering than just his undergarment.

"David, you need more clothes." She descended the steps after him. "You are indecent."

"They have seen me in less," he shouted, hardly breaking his stride.

Mikal could barely keep pace as her husband raced down the covered promenade toward the hall of tribal chieftains, where they had feasted the day before. A rage had spilled over him. She could hear it in his questions to Benaiah, his chief bodyguard jogging alongside. She could hear it in his curses when Benaiah gave him the answers. She could hear it in his outburst when he stormed into the hall shouting the names of his nephews.

The swords of David's men held the nephews in place. If they feared her husband's wrath, their faces did not show it. Rather, a surly contempt for those who held them at sword point, and there was no flicker of change as her husband approached. Not until David grabbed each one by the throat and slammed them against the wall did their faces reflect any alarm. The change was instant, from sullen to panic, their eyes bulging from near strangulation.

"Joab, is it true?" David asked. "Did you and Abishai murder Commander Abner?"

Both nephews pulled desperately at David's fingers gripping their necks.

"Uncle. Uncle," gasped Joab.

The familial term caused her husband to loosen his grip and allow them some breath, but his strong hands held their necks pinned to the solid wall.

"He opposed you from the beginning." Joab's lips gasped like a fish starved for more air. "For years he tried to kill you, then when Saul died, he tried to set up his only son as king to keep you from the throne."

"That does not give you cause to commit murder." David barely contained his fury, that, if unleashed, Mikal would witness the snapping of the necks of his nephews. "You had no authority for such action. I had given my word to Abner. He brought me my wife, and in return I gave him immunity from retribution."

"He would be a threat to your kingdom," Abishai said.

"Who made you a judge?" David shouted. "Who raised you up to make decisions of who shall live and who shall die? I know who my enemies are. Abner was not one. I sent him off in peace. He had safe conduct by my authority. He was to return and live here in Hebron, a city of refuge, with his family. And you—both of you—defied me and murdered an innocent man. You are the ones who deserve to die."

The rage that once gripped her husband abruptly turned into profound grief, and he howled like a wounded beast.

Mikal beheld the horror on the faces of the crowded banquet hall, chieftains she recognized from the tribes of Benjamin and Judah who had gathered the evening before to celebrate her arrival and a newly formed alliance between the two tribes. Most averted their eyes from the scene between the king and his nephews, something that should have been done in private, but because of her husband's anger and the severity of the crime, it had become public.

No one moved toward an exit. All remained still, and Mikal became embarrassed for herself and for her husband. He was too exposed, his rage, his murderous threats against his nephews, his bare skin. Her husband was too vulnerable before his followers.

"Cover him," she whispered handing her husband's robe to Benaiah.

Benaiah took the robe, but he seemed hesitant to approach her husband for fear of David possibly turning his wrath upon him.

"Our brother died at Abner's hand," Abishai croaked.

"He killed our brother, Unc—"

David yanked them away from the wall and then threw them back against it as he released them.

The two men dropped to the floor clutching their damaged throats, desperately sucking in as much air as possible.

"Asahel was killed in battle," David said. "Abner killed your brother in self-defense. Asahel was a fool for pursuing him. Yours was not an act of blood-revenge. Yours was a treacherous deed of assassination."

David kicked his nephews in their sides, knocking any air out of their starving lungs.

Mikal had only ever seen such rage from her father, and it had been directed toward her and anyone who had aided her husband's escape from his murderous obsession. Now, she witnessed the same uncontrolled behavior in her husband, and it terrified her.

Was this the same man who had brought her such joy beneath the canopy last night? Could such an explosive temper ever be turned against her?

"I am innocent of your wickedness," David shouted. He bent to catch his breath after such violent exhilaration. "My kingdom will be forever innocent of the blood of Abner. May the blood of the commander whirl around you to your dying day. May the blood of Abner fall upon your heads and upon the house of your father since both of you are guilty. And you, Joab, may your house always be unclean because of running sores and infections and cut off from Yahweh. May all in your house have to walk with a crutch because they are feeble or blind or cowards in battle or insane."

Her husband was exhausting himself by the curses he uttered. Spittle ran over his lips and onto his beard, the vicious spray of curses landing upon his broken nephews. His gasping was so violent Mikal could not tell if he was weeping from his grief for Abner or groaning from his fury.

Mikal motioned for Benaiah to offer the robe to her husband while bent over trying to regain his lost composure.

"My lord, your robe," Benaiah said quietly.

David snatched the robe out of Benaiah's hands then yanked the dagger from its sheath fastened to Benaiah's side.

Mikal felt her knees give way at the horrible thought her husband might strike down his nephews with the eyes of the tribal chieftains from Judah and Benjamin watching. Shedding blood, however guilty, before her husband's kingdom was fully established was a dangerous move. This action would endanger solidifying his rule.

Instead of slitting the throats of his nephews, her husband held up his robe and slashed the front. Then he dropped the dagger to the floor and ripped apart his robe from top to bottom.

"Tear your robes, O Israel," he cried. "Tear your robes and lament. Should Abner have died as the fool dies? Your hands were not bound, your feet were not fettered. You fell as one falls before wicked men."

To Mikal's amazement, every man in the hall began to wail and cut the front of their robes, exposing their fronts and falling to their knees. No one was standing except her husband. Then like her and all the men in the hall, David dropped to his knees.

"A great prince has fallen today. A great prince in Israel has fallen. I am weakened on this day by this evil deed. Though I am anointed king, I am weak. These nephews, the sons of my sister Zeruiah, have brought me to my knees. They are too fierce for me. May Yahweh repay the doer of evil according to his evil."

The two doers of evil slunk from the great hall through a side entrance, the same ingress Mikal had used to make her entrance for the feast the night before.

All these men had torn their robes, lamenting the loss of this great prince, the faithful commander of her father's army. The day before was a gathering to celebrate the beginning of a new era, and today the gladness in the hearts of these men had turned to sorrow, a sorrow that took over her heart.

First, her cousin, and then her brother. One on the heels of the other. Abner had no more been laid in his tomb when news came that her youngest and only remaining brother, Ish-bosheth, had been murdered in his sleep by two wicked men. Two men to kill her cousin. Two men to kill her brother.

All male heirs of the first king of Israel were no more. She and her sister Merab were the last of the generation of children from the house of Saul and Ahinoam.

"May I take that for you, my lady?"

Mikal looked into the solemn face of Gad the prophet. She held in her lap the sealed clay jar that contained the head of her brother.

"Oh, Gad, what has happened to us?" Mikal sobbed. "What has happened to my family? Little Ishie is gone."

When Gad gently lifted the clay jar from Mikal's lap it allowed her to give full vent to her grief. Mikal was not entirely sure what had happened, but she knew she had been uprooted and scattered. The demands of alliances had pulled her from her quiet life. She had hoped the love of her husband would bring revival to her spirit, but this double death of her cousin and brother had splintered her heart. Hers was a consuming pain. How could she ever survive? She was certain she would never be free of the sorrow brought upon her.

None of these memories would ever vanish. They would remain raw, unhealed, resistant to any future heart-stopping joys. She had known some pleasurable moments, but those moments of delight had been dislodged by larger sorrows, permanent fractures inside her broken heart. These hardened memories had taken grotesque shapes, sculptures of pain that neither time's erosion nor any future happiness could ever eclipse. Two more shapes were added to her gallery of affliction.

"I am so sorry, my lady," Gad said.

"This all feels like a punishment for something I took no part in," Mikal said. "I asked for none of this. I did nothing to cause any of this. I am cursed by the choices of men. At least they got to die while I remain to carry the grief."

"May I help you to your feet, my lady?" Gad extended his hand.

"I used to think of myself as a princess. That the house of Saul would have generations of kings and princes and princesses. That I would give joy to my husband and bear sons and daughters to the glory of Israel. But now I do not wish to bring children into this world." Mikal extended her hand toward the clay jar and looked into Gad's kind face. "What would I tell them, Gad? How would I teach them? I do not want them to witness the brutality I have seen. I do not want them to bear such sorrow."

"Come, my lady." Gad opened his hand to her. "Let us lay your brother next to Abner. They shall rest together in Sheol."

"Rest. Yes, they shall rest," Mikal whispered. "I too long for my rest."

Mikal placed her hand inside Gad's palm.

His grip was firm but tender and he helped her to her feet.

Gad would walk with her, accompany her to the burial site. The prophet would pray for her, offer comfort. He would shed his own unbearable tears on her behalf and then remind her that there were times when her family had known joy. That there had been a taste of heaven to savor. That all of her life had not been spilt upon the ground. That there was the possibility of future joy.

Gad must help her to find it.

Chapter 2

DAVID WANTED ONLY A FEW PEOPLE TO ACCOMPANY HIM INTO the cave of the ancestors. He and Benaiah slipped out of Hebron late at night. The prophets Nathan and Gad and three other trusted men waited for him at the cave of Machpelah.

Day after day, leaders from the tribes of Israel arrived in Hebron. Representatives and ambassadors from cities as far north as Tyre and Sidon were sending blessings and greetings, words of honor and recognition for his elevation as the king of Israel. The pressure was mounting for David to declare his acceptance, a growing sense of urgency to announce.

Yet David had lost his footing. For too long he had lived as a man hunted and singled out as an enemy of Israel. Now he was to be king.

He had to be convinced again deep within his heart. Treasures filling his coffers was not enough. Tribal leaders swearing allegiance was not enough. Mighty men and warriors who once fought for Saul under the command of Abner were arriving in Hebron ready to take an oath of military service. Even this was not enough. People referred to him not as the king of Judah, but as King as if now it was a foregone conclusion. That he, a herder of sheep, a poet and composer, a captain turned outlaw, a man on the run, was now the king of Yahweh's chosen.

Just to be called "King" did not make it so, not in his heart.

David needed a sense of history and his place within it. He knew his tumultuous history on this earth—filled with constant danger and few pleasures—was not enough to give him the confidence to be a king. He needed to understand the foundation of the ages before. Long before his time upon the earth, before his call by the prophet Samuel out of the hills, there were earlier calls for men and women to leave what they knew and enter the mystery of fellowship with the Almighty. For it was the Almighty who had called, and it was the ancestors of the chosen who had obeyed. David too must obey, but he did not understand why. He did not understand how the eighth son of a sheepherder would now be a king.

Jashar greeted David and Benaiah as they dismounted from their horses.

"My lord, all are here," Jashar said taking the reins of each horse.

Shadows of men standing at the mouth of the cave came into focus as David approached. From the entrance, David saw light flickering deep inside accompanied by voices.

"The ancestors have not awakened, have they?" he asked with a nervous chuckle.

"It is Abiathar, my lord," Nathan answered. "He brought Zadok with him, the priest who served the first king. They are praying and blessing the tomb for your arrival."

"This is like the cave in Ramah where the scrolls are stored. I was frightened to enter that sacred cavern, and I am frightened to enter now," David admitted.

Benaiah was the first to place his hand upon David's shoulder. Eleazar, Uriah, and Jozabad quickly added their grip of support. The hands of these staunch friends helped calm David's heart. These friends were closer than the brothers of his blood.

"This is not a place of death, my lord," Nathan said. "Like the cave of scrolls, this is a place of honor, for the ancestors of our nation rest here. These early sojourners provide a sacredness to this land. They heard the call of Yahweh. They left everything and followed the voice of Yahweh. They are buried here to remind Israel of the covenant established with Abraham."

"Here is the beginning of our history in this land, my lord." Gad cradled a small clay jar under one arm with a scroll inside it while holding a torch in his other hand. "This is a fitting place to hear the blessing our father Jacob pronounced over his son Judah, the father of your tribe. And the blessing Moses gave over Judah before he ascended the mountain and was no more."

"My lord, if you are looking for a new beginning, this is the resting place of our original fathers and mothers." Nathan pointed inside the cave. "Yahweh confided in these who sleep here. Yahweh made Himself known to these humble people who all had one thing in common. They heard the voice of Yahweh and chose to obey."

"It is more than Yahweh's voice I seek," David replied. "It is Yahweh Himself. I want the Presence. I want to be in the Presence. I never want to leave the Presence."

"Yes, my lord." Nathan raised his arm for David to enter the tomb.

The hands of his friends gave him a final squeeze and pat before releasing him.

"We will wait for you here, my lord," Benaiah said. "We will stand guard."

"Thank you, faithful friends."

Nathan and Gad led David into the burial cavern, each one carrying a torch.

David was here to do one thing. He had been on the run so long he had no sense of place, no sense of peace. David desired a connection with the sojourners of the chosen. If he was to be king, then it must begin here with those whom Yahweh first called out of their everyday lives to follow the Almighty into…into what exactly?

He knew the place of his origin, the life of a shepherd, a warrior, a composer, a leader of rogues. But now the time was upon him to become the king of a nation, a nation over one thousand years in the making.

David moved past the wrapped shrouds of human dust inserted into the crevices of cut rock and breathed in centuries of the encased earth.

Abiathar and Zadok stood at the far end of the cave. Each one held a torch. The space became ablaze with light revealing the cave's widened throat. It opened to make room for the rocky furrows cut into the walls, the resting beds of the fathers and mothers of Israel.

Abiathar bowed before David. "My lord, we serve the Almighty, Yahweh, the God of all creation."

"Praise to the Almighty," David said then turned to face Zadok who stood nervously beside Abiathar. David smiled at the young man. "Abiathar tells me you are a direct descendant from the male line of Aaron, and you served the king before me."

"Yes, my lord," Zadok answered. "I was conscripted in his last days just before the end. I did not know how to function. We lived in fear. It was a bewildering time."

"You should fit quite well into our lot, Zadok." David placed his hand upon the young man's shoulder. "We are all a little bewildered. Abiathar will tell you how he learned to serve while we were on the run. Now we stop running and serve Yahweh together. You will assist me and my house. Priests and Levites will no longer live in fear."

"Yes, my lord." Zadok bowed his head. "May Yahweh make His face to shine upon the king."

"I need the blessing of the priests and the prophets," David said. "I need the blessings of our ancestors who worshipped and followed the Almighty before me."

David bent his knee upon the ground as the two priests and the two prophets gathered around.

"My lord." Nathan handed Abiathar his torch. "Yahweh is not the God of the dead, but the God of the living, the God of our ancestors Abraham and Sarah, Isaac and Rebekah, of Jacob and the sons Leah and Rachel bore for him."

"Our father Abraham purchased this tomb from Ephron the Hittite for his wife Sarah upon her death," Gad said. "This is sacred ground for the people of Israel. This is where we remember the call of the chosen by the Almighty."

Nathan reached inside the clay jar tucked in the crook of Gad's arm and removed the scroll. He loosened the ties, unrolled the scroll, and held it before the light.

"This is the account of Judah, the son of our father Jacob," Nathan said. "This is the blessing he gave to the fourth son of Leah, Jacob's first wife. Leah did not enjoy her husband's affection. With each son she bore him, Leah hoped to earn the love of her husband. With each birth she was dismayed, finally giving up all hope of ever brightening the eyes of her husband with delight. When her fourth son was delivered, she gave him the name of Judah, praise to Yahweh, for she had turned all her hope to the Almighty.

"You, my lord, are the descendant of the fourth son, the son of praise, the son that praises and receives praise from his brothers. The son who will put the enemies of Israel to flight. You are like the lion, O Judah, not one that rages and quells, but one in the full majesty of repose. The scepter of the king will be established in the line of Judah and the nations will fall sway to his sovereignty. The prosperity of nations will flock to you. The richness of the vines, the soil, and the livestock will invigorate your heart and enhance the brilliance of your eyes and face.

"And finally, my lord, hear the blessing of Moses: with the scepter between your feet, be the voice of Judah, defend Yahweh's chosen, bring Yahweh's chosen back to the Almighty and let the kingdom of Israel be a blessing to the nations."

Abiathar raised his head. "Hear, O Israel, The Lord our God, the Lord is one!"

Zadok continued the command, "Love the Lord your God with all your heart and with all your soul and with all your strength."

David breathed the air of the ancestors. The invisible features of the patriarchs and matriarchs of Isarel surrounded him filling the secret currents of the atmosphere and bringing to bear one thousand years of connection to the chosen, to the heart of Yahweh. The priests and prophets of Yahweh stood over him calling on the name of Yahweh, calling on David to rise and take the scepter. To walk in the holiness of Yahweh.

David had to be lifted to his feet. A priest and a prophet had to hold on to each side of David to support his feeble legs while a prophet and a priest walked before and behind him. He was enfolded by the living and the dead, the past and the present. He was stumbling toward the future bolstered on the prayers and prophesies of Yahweh.

"Remain faithful, my lord," Nathan said as he ushered David out of the mouth of the tomb and into the early light of the dawn.

Outside the tomb, David collapsed into the arms of his most trusted and loyal friends. Benaiah, Eleazar, Uriah, and Jozabad held David until his limp body began to flow with strength. He had emerged from the wonder of centuries with the power of a new identity, a sure footing upon this sacred ground, and a tongue that could not be silenced. His heart burst like a reed mat put to the torch.

"I will extol the Lord at all times. His praise will always be on my lips."

Chapter 3

DAVID RODE HIS HORSE, ARDON, IN THE MIDDLE OF THE GROUP
as they traveled single file along the eastern road between the city of Jebus
and the Kidron Valley. No one in the small company spoke. The cover of a
cloudy night was to their advantage, and he and his friends did not want to
be seen or heard.

Hebron was overwhelmed with visitors arriving every day from across Israel, burdening the resources of the town. Anticipation was building among
the people of Israel. The citizenry longed for leadership and expected the new
king to declare himself in public.

David remained slow to publicly acknowledge the purpose for this re-
markable gathering in Hebron. Once he was told the chieftains from the ten
wealthy northern tribes had arrived with caravans of treasures for the king's
coffers and that elite warriors from each tribe were ready to join in military
service, David began to see his sovereignty as inevitable fact. All the rulers and
clan leaders were encouraging him to come out of the shadows and receive
the blessing and anointing from the prophets. Israel was ready to accept his
sovereign rule.

Though David kept putting off all requests for public display, he could
not wait forever. He had to get out of the city and think. He had to return to
the open landscape away from the lights and bustle of the city, from the com-
motion of the hordes and get back under the stars, into the wilderness, with
lifelong companions. With these friends he could be forthright and vulner-

able, he could be himself, as they could with him. No king and subject roles to play. So, a short but important scouting mission provided a good excuse to get away from Hebron for a night and a day.

His only concern was leaving Mikal behind. She had barely come out of her seven-day mourning period after the death of Abner when news of the murder of her last remaining brother came to her ears. She remained sheltered in isolation on the rooftop beneath the canopy he had erected for them when she had first arrived in Hebron. David spent his nights with her and attended her when not called away for assemblies with each new emissary arriving from the length and breadth of Israel. He had stood by her in honor of Abner and would have willingly done so for Ish-bosheth, but Mikal had released him of any obligation to grieve at her side.

In the cool night air, David and his companions heard chatter and laughter from the Jebusite guards stationed along the eastern wall of the city. The guards' casual merriment and dialogue came from overconfidence. The Jebusites boasted that their settlement could not be breached, that even the blind and the lame citizens of Jebus could thwart any attack. Situated on a hill well above the surrounding valleys and forests, David saw how the Jebusites could make their boast. But his friends had discovered a potential weakness and wanted David to assess it himself.

Before they left Hebron, Jashar had shared a brief history lesson on the city of Jebus. Centuries before, Jebus had been overrun by the Israelites under the command of Joshua who had been appointed by Moses to lead the chosen into the land of promise. But as the tribes scattered throughout the territory, Israel lost her way and her power. During the troubled times of the judges, Jebus repopulated with a diverse group of Canaanites and built up the walls around the city situated on its high promontory.

The sound of human voices faded as David's company rode beyond the city gates and into the Kidron Valley. Uriah led the party, and he signaled for everyone to follow as he took a spur trail off the main road.

Uriah motion for everyone to dismount. He led them along a path into the dense woods until they came into an opening with two large tamarisk trees in the center. Once their horses were tied to a low limb of a tree, Uriah and Jozabad moved some of the underbrush to the side behind the two trees.

A few days before, David had given Uriah, Jozabad, and Eleazar permission to spy out Jebus and the surrounding countryside. When they returned to give their report, David looked to Benaiah and said, "Why not go see for ourselves?"

Benaiah smiled and said, "Like the old days, my lord."

The next morning in the predawn light they had slipped out of the city. David requested Jashar accompany them to keep record of the mission. It only took a half day to ride from Hebron to Jebus, so they had hidden in the forest south of Jebus to rest the horses and waited until dark.

Once the underbrush had been cleared away, Uriah squatted and scooped his hands into a bubbling spring and playfully tossed the refreshing water onto David and the others. Muffled curses quickly ensued, much to Uriah's amusement.

"This spring is the main water supply for the city." Uriah motioned to the clear flowing water. "The source had been camouflaged with underbrush, but we were able to find it."

"Are there other sources for water?" asked David.

"We did not find any, but Kidron is lush" Jozabad replied. "There should be plenty of reservoirs just below ground."

"You three have done well." David nodded to his friends.

Eleazar grinned. "We would have spent more time, but this one here had to get back to his new wife." He gave Uriah a good-natured shove.

"A wife?" David asked.

"A few days in bed with his bride and he has gone soft." Jozabad added his own lighthearted shove of the docile Uriah.

"You knew about this?" David looked at Benaiah. "And you said nothing?"

"You have been busy, my lord," Benaiah answered. "Uriah should have the honor of telling the king his good news."

"I am not into my crown just yet, Benaiah. Do not be hasty." David bent, cupped his hands in the water, and brought them to his mouth.

He drank quietly allowing his silence to build an eagerness within the others. David finished drinking then dipped his hands into the cool water again. But this time he splashed the liquid on Uriah who lost his balance and fell into the stream.

David reached out his hand to lift Uriah to his feet but found himself yanked into the stream.

Benaiah and Jashar grabbed the reins of the horses tied to the branches of the tamarisk tree to keep them from bolting out of the forest.

"How could you do this and not tell me?" David asked, pulling Uriah to his feet.

"Benaiah is correct, my lord," Uriah answered. "You have so many demands now. These wags were there." He pointed to the others as he and David sloshed out of the water onto solid ground. "It was a quiet occasion, just a few members of my clan and hers were gathered."

"Tell me of her." David raised his foot to let the water drain from his sandal. "What is her name?"

"Bathsheba," Uriah answered. "She is the daughter of Eliam."

"Who is Eliam?" David asked.

"A valiant warrior, my lord," said Benaiah. "He and his clan have joined our forces."

"Eliam is from my part of the world," Uriah said. "Our families are connected. During our time of wanderings in flight from the mad king, I would visit the family of Eliam on occasion. He supported our cause, and once I caught sight of his daughter, I could not get her out of my heart."

"Is she fair?" David pulled on Uriah's beard. "I mean, considering who she married. How much did you have to pay?"

"All the spoils we ever gathered would not be worthy of her," Jozabad said.

"So, that beautiful, you say. I look forward to meeting her. Her name again?"

"Bathsheba," Uriah answered. "It means 'daughter of the oath.'"

"Good name," David affirmed. "Good strong name."

"Our friend has gotten more than he deserves." Eleazar grabbed Uriah's wet hair and wiggled his head.

"Yahweh has blessed me, my lord," Uriah responded. "I am truly happy."

"Now, my lord, we did not come here to discuss Uriah's marital happiness." Benaiah waved his hands to collect everyone's attention.

"Yes, there will be time enough in the future to celebrate Uriah's marriage to Bathsheba," David said.

"You sent us to scout Jebus and the countryside," Jozabad said. "You must have a capital city in which to rule."

"Hebron is too small and too far to the south for the northern tribal leaders to travel," Uriah continued. "They are coming now for your expected coronation and to pledge their support."

"Your capital city should be more central to all the tribes," Benaiah added. "You are more than just the king of the tribes of Judah and Benjamin."

"Yet your main strength comes from these two southern tribes, my lord," Jashar said. "So, you do not want to relocate too far from your primary support."

"Hebron is overrun with the tribes from all across the country," Jozabad said.

"Everyone is ready for you to take the throne," Eleazar added. "Everyone is ready to give their allegiance to you, my lord."

"We believe Jebus is the perfect location for you to establish yourself." Uriah gestured to include the group.

"My friends are looking after me, Yahweh." David raised his head in thanks toward the sky. "The city looks impregnable."

Benaiah pointed back toward Jebus. "The city has a rock girt strength for a base supporting its high walls. On three sides are deep ravines with steep inclines."

"We posed as merchants," Eleazar said. "And soon discovered that the city gets its water through a shaft leading to this source where we now stand."

"There are tunnels, some steep, others gradual, leading to a central location in the city where the citizens collect their water," Uriah added. "The night before the attack, we enter the city from the water shaft using ropes and grappling hooks."

"How many warriors would be needed?" Benaiah asked.

"No more than fifty," Eleazar suggested. "That would be about all who could safely climb the shafts in one night."

"We did notice only a few Jebusite men dressed out as soldiers," Uriah said. "They believe their city is sound and unassailable, and we know of their boasting."

"Once the guards are subdued and the gates are open, I believe we will meet little resistance," Jozabad offered.

"And what of the north side of the city?" Benaiah asked. "The natural landscape is high making the city walls more vulnerable. With such high ground we could attack from a position of strength."

"That ground is sacred, Benaiah." Jashar held up his hand as a sign of caution. "Be wary about trampling that terrain with the feet of soldiers and shedding blood."

"Explain, Jashar," David stated.

"The high ground above the city is called the hill of 'Yahweh will see to it.' Our fathers, Abraham and Isaac, climbed that hill a thousand years ago.

Yahweh had asked the impossible of Abraham, but Yahweh provided a ram for the sacrifice when Isaac was the intended one."

"A faith tested. A faith rewarded." David bowed his head pondering their forefather's greatest moment of obedience. David then motioned for them to form a tight circle. "Do a little more exploration and come back with a plan to take a city. Thank you for your faithfulness."

"We believe you are the king of Yahweh's choosing, my lord," Benaiah professed. "We believe you are to wear the crown."

Every voice softly echoed Benaiah's words.

David took a deep breath of the night air and released it above the heads of his friends as if breathing a blessing upon them. But it was these faithful ones who were breathing a unified blessing upon his soul with their affirming words.

"With such friends, I will wear the crown in strength," David declared. "Should Yahweh give us the city of Jebus, you will each be given your own dwelling next to the palace. You will settle down and stock your homes with wives and children."

"Even Benaiah gets a house?" Uriah slapped Benaiah's shoulder in jest.

"Oh, he gets to live with me in the palace," David said.

Groans of annoyance and complaints of favoritism quickly followed David's promise of rewards, all expressed in good humor.

"Now, we must return to Hebron before Uriah starts sniveling about missing his new bride."

David slung his arm around Uriah's neck. He felt so thankful for this small band of brothers. Yahweh had woven these flawed but faithful men into the plot of his life, and he could never imagine their fraternal bond ever being broken.

Chapter 4

NATHAN UNFOLDED THE LINEN CLOTH COVERING THE OX horn that lay upon the pedestal. The king had asked Nathan to use the same receptacle for this public anointing that Samuel had used when the two prophets had come to David's home in Bethlehem. That stealthy mission to anoint David as the future king was done in secret for fear of the wrath of Saul.

Nathan ran his fingers over the gemstones attached to the ox horn. His delicate touching of these precious stones caused him to tremble, and he stepped back.

"What is the matter?" Gad asked.

"The horn and stones spark with memories. I wish you had been with us, Gad. David's family had gathered in the common room. Our master instructed me to take the holy oil and pour it upon the head of the future king, and not just in sprinkling drops, but all the contents poured out like a fountain."

"What was first done in secret will no longer be a secret," Gad said.

"So many years ago." Nathan pondered his memory.

Nathan and Gad had separate memories of distant time. Each had followed separate paths after they served together in the court of King Saul. Gad continued to serve in the house of the king while Nathan returned to Ramah as overseer of the prophet's school presiding over the copying of the sacred words of Yahweh. This ox horn and the scrolls of Yahweh's words had been kept hidden in the cave of Ramah beneath the *nevayoth*, the house of study Samuel had built.

"What has been kept in darkness is now coming into the light," Gad said. "Your faithfulness has allowed it so."

"It is Yahweh's faithfulness," Nathan responded. "For both of us to have endured and survived in our split worlds could only have happened by Yahweh's protective hand."

"Yes, and amen," Gad replied. "A sting comes into my heart whenever I remember how we parted the morning we buried the wife of King Saul. I thought our friendship might have ended with our separate choices."

"There were no wrong choices that day." Nathan smiled at his friend. "The will of Yahweh is often a painful and bewildering path. But after regular defeats and failures, we are still here."

"Indeed, we are." Gad stepped closer to Nathan. "Could the nation be unified again, like in the early days of Saul?"

Nathan again lightly caressed the ox horn. "I pray to the Almighty it will be so."

The flap of the sheltering tent was pulled back, and Abiathar entered carrying the holy vessel that contained the anointing oil.

"All the priests and prophets and the chieftains from the twelve tribes have gathered in the city center," Abiathar announced. "Zadok is with the king supervising his ritual bath before the ceremony. He will accompany the king in the procession from the baths to meet us here."

"Very good." Nathan extended his trembling hands in front of Abiathar and Gad. "Gad, would you hold the ox horn while Abiathar fills it with the sacred oil? I fear I am not able to control my quivering fingers."

Nathan positioned himself between the priest and prophet placing a hand on a shoulder of each man. This act of pouring Yahweh's oil from one receptacle to another would be a connecting bond, a private memory they would always share.

"Fill it to the brim, Abiathar," Nathan instructed. "I want to pour this ointment over the head of the king like a waterfall."

Gad carefully lifted the ox horn from its pedestal and removed the cap. He lowered it so the oil could easily flow from one vessel into the other. Abiathar removed the covering from the brass ewer and placed it upon the pedestal. When the lip of the priestly vessel touched the lip of the ox horn, the liquid flowed from one into the other filling the tent with the perfume of Yahweh.

"Blessed be the name of the Almighty, Maker of heaven and earth," Nathan whispered. "Blessed be His holy name forever and forever."

The scent of myrrh, cinnamon, the cane of calamus, cassia spice, and olive oil saturated the inside of the tent with a bouquet so pungent Nathan could feel the pores of his skin opening and drinking in the fragrance. He was immediately transported back to the common room in Bethlehem when he poured this same blend of oil and spices upon the head of David for the first time. Now the past had become the present as he prepared to anoint this king a second time.

"Hear, O Israel. The Lord our God. The Lord is one," Nathan said once the liquid reached the top of the ox horn.

Gad placed the cap on top of the horn just as the shofars began to blare.

"The king is coming," Nathan said. "Abiathar, why not leave the ewer on the pedestal until after the ceremony."

Abiathar re-covered the brass ewer with the cloth and set it on the pedestal.

"Gad, once I anoint the king, would you place the crown upon his head?"

Gad's silence puzzled Nathan. The face of his friend trembled as if he dreaded the thought.

"What is the matter?" asked Nathan.

"I placed the crown atop the head of Saul twice, once after the queen died and then on the day of Saul's death. Those memories still weigh upon me. May I defer the task to Abiathar?"

"I anointed the king when the chieftains of Judah proclaimed David king over the house of Judah," Abiathar said. "This moment is much greater. I am not sure of myself."

"I have witnessed you seek the will of Yahweh for our king using the ephod of the High Priest and the sacred Urim and Thummim," Gad assured him. "I think you are capable."

"Then so be it," Nathan said. "Let us go out and meet the king."

Nathan led them out of the tent into the brilliant light of the midday sun. The city center was as full as the inside of the ox horn he carried. To crowd another human being into the town center would require dismantling the outside walls. The representatives from the twelve tribes stood beneath their tribal banners forming a circle around the tent that had been set up per Nathan's instructions to shelter the holy anointing oil until time. Soldiers from the tribe of Judah held back the crowds for the king and his procession to have a clear path leading up to the shelter.

Nathan took his position in front of the shelter with Abiathar and Gad flanking each side. He pressed the ox horn against his chest, which helped to calm his nerves. He held the oil of Yahweh's spirit. He would pour out Yahweh's spirit upon the head of the king. He would release Yahweh's spirit into the air of Hebron for all to inhale the fragrance of the Almighty.

Nathan smiled when he spotted Zadok at the head of the procession. He was adorned in the full wardrobe of the High Priest, the turban with its gold plate, the breastplate bearing the twelve precious stones representing the twelve tribes, the ephod of heavenly glory over the dark robe hemmed with bells. He held the chains attached to the golden incense bowl swinging the puffs of aromatic white smoke from side to side as he walked up the incline toward Nathan repeating prayers and blessings to Yahweh.

Behind the High Priest walked David, buoyant with such a joyful expression it seemed the king might break rank and dance ahead of Zadok's slow gait. Mikal held steady by David's side carrying the king's crown resting upon a cushion covered in purple linen with golden tassels hanging from the four corners. Her expression was more somber as she carried her husband's newly minted crown.

When Zadok stepped aside for David to take his place in front of Nathan, he removed the cap from the ox horn, handing it to Gad. Once David knelt down, Nathan raised the ox horn above his head. He closed his eyes and could hear the words spoken by Samuel, his master, at the first anointing, for they were the words of Yahweh. He would repeat the blessed prophesy first uttered to only a small number of listeners, but now to be shouted into the heavens for the ears of all Israel.

"Hear, O Israel. I have made a covenant with My chosen one," Nathan cried and began pouring the holy oil onto the head of the king. "With My sacred oil I have anointed him. I have sworn to David, My servant. I will establish his line forever and make his throne firm through all generations. My hand will sustain him, surely My arm will strengthen him. My faithful love will be with him, and through My name his horn will be exalted. He will call out to Me, 'You are my Father, my God, the Rock, my Savior.'"

The oil streamed down upon David's head with the aroma wafting up into Nathan's nostrils. A purifying rapture, an ecstasy raced through his heart.

"I will appoint him the most exalted of the kings of the earth," Nathan continued. "I will maintain My love to him forever and My covenant with him will never fail. His throne shall be established forever. Once for all, I have sworn by My holiness. David's throne will endure before Me like the sun."

When the last drop of ointment fell upon David's head, Nathan raised the ox horn back to the heavens and exclaimed, "Hear, O Israel. The Lord our God. The Lord is one."

Nathan motioned for Abiathar to place the crown upon the king, and Mikal raised the cushion bowing her head in deference. The crown was a woven pattern of three gold cords with the face of a lion embossed on the front. Abiathar lifted the crown from the cushion and placed it upon David's drenched head.

Nathan handed Gad the ox horn and reached down and took David's hands.

"My lord, Yahweh is the God of the promise, the promise to our fathers, the promise to His chosen people, and the promise to His appointed king. You are the king by Yahweh's promise. What my master was commanded to do years ago has now come into the fullness of being. Arise, my king, and receive the oath of your people."

Nathan helped David to his feet. The quaking in his body could be his own or the king's. He could not tell. The Presence was having its way with both prophet and king, and Nathan could only yield to its powerful sway. David's face and head and beard glistened reflecting the sunlight. Nathan turned David to face the people of the chosen and hear them advance their support to him and to his kingdom.

Zadok stepped forward and opened the scroll of the people's covenant. "We the people of Israel are bone of your bone. We are your own flesh and blood. While Saul was king over us, you led us out to war and brought us back from battle. We declare that Yahweh, the Almighty, has raised you up and said to you that you will be the one to lead us. Like a shepherd who tends his flock, you will lead the people of Israel and be our king. We recognize you, David, son of the house of Jesse, lord of the tribe of Judah, as monarch over all of Israel. Before Yahweh, we make this compact with you to serve you to the end of your days. May the king live forever."

Nathan had first met David when he was summoned from the hills of Bethlehem, ruddy of complexion and reeking of sheep and raw earth. Now, the holy oil of Yahweh covered him, and the fragrant confection rose into the air like a sacred veil. The people recognized what Nathan had witnessed that day, that Yahweh had raised up a shepherd to the nobler office of king.

Nathan lifted his arms and the shofars blared, the people roared, and the sky above Hebron was blasted with praises to Yahweh for the shepherd who would be king.

Chapter 5

DAVID REGRETTED THE WORDS THE MOMENT HE SPOKE. IF HE had not been standing before a crowd mashed together in the city center of Hebron. If he had not been celebrating his recent victory over the Philistines or his recent coronation with the tribal chieftains and the generals and captains of his army. If his wives and young children had not been present. If he had not overindulged in eating and drinking, David might not have said those exact words. But there was no denying it, and he could not pretend he had not spoken them. He could not retract them. He must honor his declaration. It was not fitting for a new king to go back on his word especially so new into his crown.

"Whoever leads the attack against Jebus, the city of the Jebusites, I shall put him in command of my whole army."

The crowds roared in approval.

So, it had to be done. David had just not counted on Joab, taking up the challenge. David's fury with Joab and his brother, Abishai, for murdering Abner had not subsided. Since the killing, his two nephews had been smart to make themselves scarce, but now Joab had stepped out of the shadows to lead the attack. David suspected this was a cunning move on Joab's part to get back into the good graces of his uncle, but it was a calculation David did not trust. But if Joab should die in the attack, it would quiet his desire for justice.

Everyone agreed on Jebus as the perfect location for David to rule. Thousands had descended on Hebron for his crowning and thousands more had come to join his army. The Philistines were testing his new kingdom, mustering its military forces in the Valley of Rephaim to strike David before he even entered the gates of Jebus in triumph. It was unanimous among David's military leaders; the Philistines must be taught a lesson. David asked Abiathar and Zadok to inquire of Yahweh, and with the promise of the Almighty that he would defeat the Philistines, David went out to battle.

"Yahweh is the Lord of the breaches," David bellowed before his army after his victory over the perennial foes of Israel. "Like the bursting forth of great waters, Yahweh has broken upon my enemies before my face."

The battle had been quick and the victory decisive. Those Philistine soldiers who survived the rout fled leaving behind their weapons and their idols. The Philistines never went into battle without carrying the idols of Baal and Ashtaroth, and David ordered the false gods put to the flames.

After the fires of the Philistine idols had cooled in the Valley of Rephaim, Joab led the attack against Jebus. David had to grit his teeth when Joab jumped at the chance to prove himself, but what could he do?

The night before the attack, Joab stole into Jebus through the water shaft with Uriah, Eleazar, Jozabad, and fifty of David's elite force. Once the Jebusite guards were dispatched, Joab dashed through the city gates at first light waving his sword and motioning for the army to advance. David did not bother to lead his men into the city. He let the captains of the twelve tribes have the honor of securing Jebus. It would give them a greater sense of pride in their capital city were they to advance before the king. David waited in the Kidron Valley until the victory flag was hoisted upon the city gates heralding the all clear.

David and Mikal entered Jebus riding in a chariot. As David guided the team of horses through the gates of the city, the army burst into a frenzy of cheering.

"Did we not do something like this before?" David had to yell so Mikal could hear him above the rumbling of the horses and chariot and welcoming soldiers. "Did we not ride in a chariot through the streets of Gibeah on the day of our wedding?"

Mikal gripped the chariot's side with one hand and David's arm with the other and leaned toward his ear. "That was my sister Merab and her husband Adriel who took a ride in my father's chariot," Mikal shouted. "We had other things on our minds."

David laughed when Mikal gave him an amorous pinch, and he almost slipped off the chariot. After regaining his balance, he steered along the walls of the city waving to the soldiers standing on the fortified landings and ramparts.

When David turned onto the main street, Benaiah was waiting for him mounted upon his horse.

"This way, my lord." Benaiah led them toward the assembly at the top of the street.

Lining the street up to the city center were more of his army guarding the subdued citizens and military leaders of Jebus. The Jebusite city council had been separated from the rest of the people and were corralled inside the portico encompassed by statues of their Canaanite gods.

David pulled into the city center, and Jozabad and Eleazar took hold of the harness of the team of horses. Uriah came around behind the chariot ready to offer his hand to help Mikal step out, but David leapt to the ground and took her by the waist lifting her from the chariot.

"This will be our new home, my lady," David whispered into Mikal's ear, which made her smile. "No more sleeping in tents and caves."

"We shall make it a city fit for the king of Israel," Mikal said.

"This way, my lord." Uriah motioned David toward the portico of idols where Joab and Abishai stood in front of the haughty Jebusite rulers.

David ignored his nephews and the rulers, striding right by them onto the portico of idols. In front of each idol was a large brass basin for the purpose of sacrificing to an individual god or goddess. Every basin still smoldered, the last futile offering in hopes that their gods would favor the citizens of Jebus over the Israelites.

"Where is Jashar?" David called from the middle of the portico.

"Here, my lord." Jashar dashed toward the portico but stopped short of stepping onto the stony flooring.

"Do not be afraid, Jashar." David was amused by Jashar's apprehension. "These idols are deaf, dumb, and blind. Come, I need you to translate this Canaanite tongue."

Jashar took a tentative step onto the portico then crept toward David.

"You see how ineffective these gods were," David declared. "Nothing to fear."

"It is not the Canaanite gods I fear, my lord, but Yahweh," Jashar replied.

"As you should. But today, Yahweh has given us victory, and we shall destroy these gods just as we destroyed the gods of the Philistines."

David moved to the Jebusite lords standing with insolent poses, dressed in the finery of city magistrates, and bedecked with jewels. He paced in front of them nodding and smiling, then turned and began to pace in front of the wide circle of pedestals supporting a variety of deities.

"Jashar, I recognize some of these gods. Baal, of course, with his bull face and horns holding his lightning bolt, and Astarte, goddess of war with her crescent moon headdress. But these two are new to me." David pointed toward a statue of two deities.

Jashar read the inscription on the pedestal. "My lord, they are twins, one is Shalin, the god of the dusk, and the other is Shahar, the god of the dawn."

David approached another statue also with the face of a horned bull but with arms outstretched toward its personal basin of hot ashes.

"Molech, my lord," Jashar said. "The god of fire."

"Today we have put out your fire." David spit into the basin causing it to hiss and sizzle, then spun to face the dour city fathers. After instructing Jashar to translate, David waved his arm over the panoply of idols. "Are these your protectors? The ones you bragged would make it so the blind and lame citizens of Jebus would keep my army from breaching the gates? It is your gods who are blind and lame."

While Jashar translated the words, David strode to each stand holding the basin of sacrifice of the respective idol and kicked them over one after another. Once he had toppled the basins around the circle, he had to bend over to catch his breath. When he straightened up, the horrified faces of the Jebusite rulers drew his attention. A few were brave enough to rage at David in their native tongue. Once Jashar translated the Jebusite curses, David only laughed.

"Now, Jashar, tell these lords I am in a charitable mood. Instead of mounting their heads on a spike, tell them they may keep their heads and fine clothes, but they will be escorted out of the city and banished forever from these walls. They may test the benevolence of their gods by wandering the earth. The same offer is given to all citizens of Jebus, but all who remain will become servants to the people of Israel."

As Jashar rendered the pronouncement into the Canaanite language, David motioned for Joab and Abishai to come forward. He gripped his nephews by the back of their heads and brought them into his chest so they might hear the words meant only for their ears.

"You killed a great commander who was under my protection," David snarled. "I should have cut off your heads like I did to the two assassins who murdered my wife's little brother, but I did not want to disgrace my sister and the rest of our family. Now, do not make me regret my decision."

David did not care if he saw any expression of contrition on the faces of his nephews. He wanted to see that they both understood his blunt meaning.

"Yes, my lord," each one replied.

"And remember that I am your lord and king till the day Yahweh snatches away my last breath." David pointed to the crown on his head. "Now, Joab, let me keep my word and reward you for your victory."

David spun Joab to face the triumphant army.

"This day Yahweh has established my kingdom." David's voice echoed through the city center for all to hear. "You witnessed my anointing and pledged yourselves to me. Together, we have routed the Philistines who dared to challenge our sovereignty, and now we have captured the city of the Jebusites. In days to come we will turn this hilltop into the capital city for all of Israel."

David slipped in front of Joab untying the scarlet sash around his middle. He held up the cloth for all to see, and then he draped it over Joab's neck.

"After our victories over the Philistines and before we marched to the city, I proclaimed whoever leads the attack on Jebus will become commander of the army."

David then removed from his left arm the brass armband bearing the face of a lion engraved on the front and the name of the tribe of Judah written above it. He lifted Joab's right arm and slipped the armband over his nephew's wrist.

"The Almighty has kept His promise to make me king. On this day, I keep my promise to make the one who captured the fortress of the Jebusites the new commander of my army."

David then untied the leather belt strapped onto his waist that secured his sheath and sword. He raised the armaments into the air.

"This day I give the weapons of my strength to my nephew, Joab, son of my sister, Zeruiah, from the household of my father, Jesse of Bethlehem of Judea. Look upon the new commander of the mighty army of Israel."

When David handed Joab his sword and sheath, the Israelites erupted with shouts of honor and praise to the king, the new commander of the host, and the Almighty.

The day began with a swift victory and ended with David and Mikal hosting a feast under the stars with the tribal leaders and families of his mighty men who had arrived with the priests and prophets once the city had been secured. They celebrated on the very portico that had once been dedicated to the Canaanite gods whose blind and lame carved figures were roasting in a pit of their own sacrificial fires outside the city.

"My lord, what shall we call the new city?" Uriah raised his goblet of wine.

David did not initially respond to Uriah's question. His eyes were struck by the presence of the woman at his friend's side. *This must be Uriah's new wife. The one the others teased him about. This must be… What was her name?*

Her beauty in the firelight snatched his ability to respond to Uriah's question.

"My lord, if this location is to be the capital of Israel, we need to give it a proper name," Nathan said.

"Ah, what?" David snapped out of his trance. "Yes, I was trying to think of her name, or rather think of a name. You are right, Nathan. We need a name."

David hoped his distraction and momentary confusion was not obvious to everyone. He had been taken by surprise by the unexpected loveliness of Uriah's bride.

"My lord." Gad rose from his seat of cushions. "I have a suggestion for a name that comes from an ancient story of our father Abraham."

"Please, Gad, give us this story." David slid his arm across Mikal's shoulder and pulled her closer to his side. He was glad for her eager snuggling, which indicated she had not noticed his wandering eyes.

"The story goes that our father Abraham was returning home by the great trees of Mamre after defeating a pagan war lord who had pillaged from his family. As he passed through this area, the king of Salem came out to meet our great patriarch offering bread and wine to Abraham and his company. This was King Melchizedek, and he blessed Abraham saying, 'Blessed be Abram by God Most High, Creator of heaven and earth. And blessed be God Most High who delivered your enemies into your hands.' In response, our father gave one tenth of his plunder to the king of Salem."

"What are you suggesting, Gad?" David asked. "How do we name our city?"

"My lord, Melchizedek was the king of Salem and priest of Yahweh Most High." Gad raised his goblet toward David. "May I be bold and suggest we combine the name of Yahweh and the king of Salem and call our capital, 'Jerusalem,' the City of David."

David allowed the name to settle. Jerusalem, the City of David. The weight of such a name stirred his soul. The faces in the crowd glowed in the crackling firelight, all silent, all staring at him, none raising an objection to Gad's proposal, their silence affirming the sound of the name mulling inside his mouth and taking shape on his tongue.

He rose to his feet and offered his hand for Mikal to rise beside him. When she stood, everyone around the large fire also came to their feet.

David extended his arm to Gad and then raised his goblet to the heavens. "So let it be called Jerusalem, the City of David."

A rolling rumble of voices tested the sound of the naming on their lips, repeating the phrase and raising their goblets and drinking in approval of the king, to Yahweh Most High, to the city of Jerusalem, to the City of David.

As the name of the city and the people's praises filled the air, Mikal leaned into David's ear. "Lie with me tonight," she whispered. "Give me a child. Let me bear you a son, a prince for the king in the City of David."

David pressed Mikal against his chest and kissed her, but his gaze darted in the direction of Uriah, who also embraced his wife in the joy of celebration.

What was her name? He must find out her name.

Chapter 6

MIKAL'S HANDS TREMBLED AS SHE HELD THE SEALED SCROLL. It was delivered in secret so as not to arouse suspicion or hostility from those of her husband's inner circle.

While Mikal might have been David's first wife, she was viewed with mistrust by most everyone in court. She was the daughter of the first king, the one who had gone mad, who had slaughtered the priests of Nob, and who had relentlessly pursued her husband to kill him. No one seemed to consider her innocent in all of this. No one seemed to care that she too had suffered from her father's madness. She was the daughter of the mad king, therefore, guilty by association. It did not matter that David had taken the initiative to have her rejoin him and publicly made his affections known. Few in the king's court treated Mikal with any favor except one person who appreciated her situation and offered comfort in her isolation. The prophet Gad.

"I fear what is written inside this scroll." Mikal handed it back to Gad.

"My lady, the courier claimed not to know who had written it." Gad took the scroll from her trembling hands. "He feared there might be some danger and sought me out privately. When he gave me this letter, he said I was the only one to know of it other than my lady."

"How could the courier not know who wrote this letter?"

"He was a Gibeonite, a merchant traveling from Gibeah. My guess is that the letter was given to him secretly, and he was charged not to inform me. He did say he was compensated for its safe delivery. His only other words were, 'For the queen.'"

"You and I both know that I am not a queen." Mikal let out a scornful laugh. "The one and only queen Israel has ever known was my mother. I am not certain I will follow in her footsteps. Being first wife to a king has given me no status. I am lodged in the house of wives and children and have hardly seen my husband since the capture of Jerusalem. He is too busy building his palace."

"My lady, I believe your current situation is temporary. Once the palace is complete, I am sure—"

"I am sure he will find other projects to occupy his time." Mikal stopped Gad from perjuring himself. From the window she looked upon the City of David. "If not another building program, then another war or another wife or concubine to bear him children. Seems our king must have flocks of children. You can take him out of the hills, but he will always be a shepherd. How many Jebusite women has he conscripted now?"

"I am sorry for your distress, my lady."

"His heart, Gad. His heart is all I ever desired," Mikal said. "I could have lived with him all those years he was a fugitive if I knew he loved me."

"The king's life was dangerous, my lady. He lived in constant privation and peril."

"All because of my father. You do not have to say it, Gad, but I too was in constant privation. I had to live alone without the love of my true husband."

"What of the letter, my lady?" Gad extended the scroll toward her.

Mikal turned from the window and faced Gad. "Break the seal and read it, please, Gad. Whatever the news, it will go easier on my heart if you read the words."

"As you wish." Gad unsheathed the small knife attached to the belt around his waist and carefully broke open the seal.

Mikal braced her back against the wall as Gad silently read over the written words on the scroll. His grave expression confirmed what she feared. Whatever the news from this author, it would not be good.

"It is from your sister, Merab, my lady. She and her five sons have returned to your home in Gibeah along with Rizpah and her two sons."

"This is good, is it not, Gad?" Perhaps she had misread the prophet's somber expression. "Our home should not be empty, but a dwelling once again for our family."

"There is more, my lady."

"Read the letter, Gad. Read it from beginning to end. Omit nothing." Mikal felt a chill coming on and folded her arms around herself.

"May I?" Gad nodded toward the open window. "The light is better." Mikal motioned for Gad to move.

Once he took his place, he cleared his throat and began reading.

> *My dearest sister. I do not want to think of the time and distance that has separated us for so long. We have had so little control over our fortunes. Life events overwhelmed us. How could our lives been so full of turmoil? I long for peace and quiet, and so I have returned to our home with my boys. Rizpah and her two sons journeyed with me. She is from Gibeah, and her family is nearby, though she will live with me in our home. There is room for all, and having seven strong, rambunctious boys will liven the house. We intend to work the land and make it productive again.*
>
> *We chose to leave Mahanaim where our brother was murdered. With Abner and Ishie both dead, no one was left to protect us. We hired a few tribal kinsmen from Benjamin still loyal to our father to safeguard our journey home. We traveled at night so as not to draw attention, and now we are safely back in Gibeah with plans to make a new life for my boys. I have become dear to Rizpah. She has become my closest companion since I do not have you with me. She has proven faithful. What a strange bond. The concubine of our father and the wife of our cousin is now like a sister.*
>
> *I understand our father and brothers who died in their last battle are buried in Jabesh Gilead. I never learned what happened to Adriel. I am sure my husband died bravely by Jonathan's side, his faithful armor-bearer to the end. I hope someday our father and brothers may be returned to our family tomb here at home. This is why I am writing. There is no way to say this except that I am going the way of all the earth. I can feel the remaining time for my life can be numbered in a season or two.*

Mikal's legs gave out, and she slid down the wall onto the floor. She clasped her hands over her mouth, but this did not stop the sobbing.

Gad lowered the scroll and extended his hand to help her back onto her feet, but she refused. He waited until Mikal gained some control.

After wiping her eyes and taking a deep breath, she said, "Finish the letter, Gad."

Gad sat beside her on the floor and leaned against the wall. "There is not much left to read, my lady."

"Continue, please. I must hear everything."

Gad raised the scroll toward the light coming from the window.

> *I spent all my time and strength getting us back home and helping Rizpah and the boys get established to carry on with their lives. My older boys can sense something is wrong, that I am not the same, weaker and more tired than normal, but I do my best to wear a brave face. We are daughters of a king, after all. Bravery is expected.*
>
> *We may never again see each other in this life, my dear, dear sister, but as I sit by the hearth fire in our common room, the memories of growing up together in this house flood back. Sharing our stories and dreams at night in bed. Those days when all was peaceful, filled with family joy and laughter. I am remembering only the good. I refuse to allow the darker recollections to creep in. Watching my boys romp around the house brings me delight and reminds me of our childhood days.*
>
> *We were girls, and then we were women. And then we were wives, but through it all, we were sisters. How the time flew. I hold you close inside my heart along with all the memories of our loved ones.*

Mikal dropped her head upon her arms braced across her knees. She could only moan, only feel an emptiness, a merciless gnawing in her soul. To expel her full grief would only create a deep scar in her heart. She was grateful to have Gad beside her. Hearing his compatible weeping was one thread of comfort she could hold. The prophet had remained true—true to her father, true to Jonathan, and now to her. He bore witness to all the sorrow of her family, and he remained. She knew he would always remain.

As she gradually came to herself, Mikal leaned against Gad, rested her head upon his shoulder, and whispered, "Say nothing of this to the king."

Chapter 7

MIKAL HAD TO GET OUT OF THE FAMILY DWELLINGS. THE RESIdence had become overcrowded with wives, concubines, children, and those women fortunate enough to have been impregnated by the king. The constant bustle of females and children and expectant mothers all through the household was too noisy, too smelly, and too much of a reminder of her own isolation

It was the deeper isolation of her barrenness that Mikal found overwhelming. David was not the problem. Mikal could not escape the evidence of his fertility. Every room in the family lodging was filling up with his offspring.

She was the only inhabitant of her private chamber. Her womb was fallow ground. Had she become too old? No, other matriarchs of the chosen who were much older than she bore children.

Had Yahweh singled her out for unfruitfulness? It was as if the Almighty held it against her that she was the daughter of Saul, like everyone else. That there was to be no carryover of progeny from one king to the next broke her heart.

Mikal had no one to confess her sense of desperation. She was a wife in name only, one of many.

How many females did she share the title with now? Difficult to count.

Her one friend was busy, setting up the prophet's school and new library in the heart of the city. Gad was overseeing the transport of all the sacred scrolls and materials from the school established by Samuel and his wife Shira in Ramah. He made frequent journeys back and forth bringing everything to Jerusalem.

Mikal had not seen Gad since the day he came to her with Merab's letter. How could she confide in him anyway? He was single and a man. How would a prophet of Yahweh ever understand the emptiness she felt?

Being the first wife of the king brought no special privileges, no honors or respect. The only designation that set her apart from the other females in David's stable was her childlessness, and it was not for lack of trying. Mikal found it difficult not to be jealous of the others or become bitter. It all felt like a punishment, and for what purpose? If her reality never changed, she would be forced to embrace the bitterness in her heart till the end of her days.

Each morning, Mikal found excuses to escape the confines of the multi-level structure located in the heart of the city that had come to be called the home of the king's "private stock." The temporary housing was well-guarded and well-staffed. The plan was for the "private stock" to move into the palace once it was complete. Mikal had the freedom to take her leave whenever she pleased. She needed no one to attend her as she strolled through the streets and markets. She did not want to draw attention, so she dressed in the modest apparel of a conventional wife with a hood covering her head, a discreet disguise.

Mikal had been seen in public only a few times since Jerusalem had been captured, but the population had proliferated since then with citizens from across Israel coming to serve the king. Few of these arrivals would recognize her.

Ambassadors and representatives from the twelve tribes arrived in the city week after week. Not only were these tribal envoys bringing caravans of tribute in support of the king, but they also were purchasing buildings for embassies and constructing houses for personal family dwellings.

The city was undergoing major restoration. David had put Joab in charge of fortifying and renovating the city's infrastructure, including the construction of a military compound with barracks and training grounds. Warriors from every tribe were joining her husband's army.

Meantime, David focused his attention on building the palace with all the materials and manual workers sent him from the king of Tyre. The city was alive with momentum and growth, and few, if any, would give her their attention. Mikal was a person in name only, known more for being the daughter of the mad king, not the first wife of the reigning king. Neither distinction pleased her.

Mikal could not remember the last time David had called for her, dined with her, or slept with her. After weeks of only hearing gossip and rumors of her husband's whereabouts and his activities, she was determined to seek him out. If he would not come to her, then Mikal would go to him. She made her way to the stepping stones on the eastern side of the new edifice. The massive size of the palace being built into the northern wall and the swiftness of the progress of construction was difficult to comprehend for one who had always lived in a modest home.

From the staircase Mikal could see very little of the city. At the top of the flat stepping stones, scaffolding had been built into the corner where the palace and the city wall converged. Workers climbed up and down the staircase inside the cage of scaffolding carrying loads of materials to laborers on top of the wall. Mikal could not see David from where she stood, but if he was not up there, she could at least gain a much better view of the city from the high point of the walls.

No one bothered her as she made her way up the stairs. No one stopped her and asked her purpose. Mikal was prepared to explain that she was there to see her husband, but she was completely ignored from the moment she began to climb the stairs until she stood on the solid landing that was part of the thick wall encircling the city. A raised extension on the edge of the wall came up to her middle. The landing itself was wide enough for several men to stand shoulder to shoulder. Guards would be posted along this wall day and night.

Mikal looked back over the city. From this height, the city appeared to stretch all the way to the southern horizon. The Kidron Valley to the east and the rolling hills to the west were lush with forests, pastures, and farmland. To the north she could see the hill of sacrifice. The top was crawling with laborers like a colony of ants. They were waxing the swaths of dyed wool and linen stretched over tentpoles. Stacks of cedar beams were used as supports beneath the tent.

The rumors Mikal had heard must be true. Her husband intended to reestablish the worship of Yahweh. He had captured a city and made it his capital. The national religion for all of Israel would be centrally located here, and her husband was preparing for the arrival of Yahweh.

Then she heard his voice. Just a stone's throw away, David stood precariously on the parapet extension along the walkway of the wall. He cupped his hands around his mouth and shouted at someone on the hill. People around him were holding onto his legs. If he lost his balance and fell forward, he would plummet to his death. Barely into his crown and residing in the capital city, and her husband risks his life shouting to people on the next hill.

Mikal kept her hand on the parapet to steady her tread as she moved toward David and those clinging to his legs. No one noticed her approach.

"You need more support in the middle," David shouted. "Put extra beams in the middle of the tent and work out. I want to see the Ark from where I am standing."

A shudder of fear went through Mikal like the bolt of an arrow. He *was* planning on bringing the sacred relic into the city.

"No, no, no." Her breath grew shallow as the men stretched the linen on top of the hill. The tent would shelter the Ark. This Tabernacle would be located on the mount overlooking the palace.

Yahweh was close, too close.

"No," she cried. "It is too close to the city. Too close to the palace."

Mikal did intend to speak with such force, she did not mean for her words to be heard by everyone. This was an impulsive response, a reaction borne out of fear, and all eyes, including her husband's turned in her direction.

"Mikal, what are you doing here?" David jumped from the parapet and moved swiftly toward her.

Mikal immediately began to back away, but David grabbed her arm. "What are you doing here?" he asked again.

"Do not do this," she cried. "Do not bring the Ark so close to the palace."

"Why not?" David asked. "What is wrong with you? How did you get up here?"

Mikal did her best not to become hysterical but knowing the Ark of the Covenant would be located right outside the palace windows caused her to shake wildly. So much so that her husband led her back toward the staircase.

"You need to go back to the family house," he insisted. "This is no place for you."

"Wait, David." Mikal yanked her arm from his tight grip. A strength surged through her body in part from fear, but also in anger at being ignored for so many weeks. "Listen to me, David. Please. I regret coming here. I am sorry for any shame my presence has caused you, but do not be hasty in bringing the Ark to your city."

"What are you talking about?" he said. "The Ark needs to be in my city. I want the Ark here."

Mikal inhaled a few deep breaths to regain control. She felt the lightheadedness from the height of the wall and the wreak of emotions.

"I do not mean to humiliate you or anger you," Mikal said. "But I fear what you are planning is dangerous. It could be a danger to your city, the people, and to you."

"You are making no sense," David blurted. "What are you talking about?"

"The Ark is a dangerous force. I do not know all the stories from the ancient days. Gad can teach you its history. But we know the Ark brought plague and destruction to the Philistines. When it was returned to Israel, the Ark's uncanny power killed dozens of men from Beth Shemesh just for getting too close and looking inside. Yahweh dealt our people a heavy blow. My father never wanted to be near the Ark. He kept it far from our home. He was afraid of it. I am afraid of it. My father would never—"

"I am not your father." David's words were like the growl of a beast. "I am not your father. I am king. This is my decision. Now, do you want an escort home?"

"No, my lord. I found my way here. I will find my way home."

Mikal began to descend the stairs. She would say no more. She had spoken her mind. She had given her warning.

After several steps she paused to see if David was watching, if he might speak a last word, perhaps from regret for his harsh tone. When she heard nothing, she turned to find he was gone, no longer in view on the wall.

Mikal grabbed the railing to keep from crumpling on the staircase. She would not lose strength, not on these stairs, not in public view.

Mikal rose from her bed and went to her window. From the height of her private chamber atop the family dwelling she could view the streets below. Small crowds of people milled about in the city center, and a larger crowd waited at the southern gates. In the golden hue of the sunset, she saw the guards stationed along the wall above the gates. For the size of the crowd, Mikal could detect little movement, the city eerily quiet. Given the purpose of the gathering it was unusual to hear so little sound coming from the people. Was this not to be a joyous occasion?

Messengers had been sent throughout the city and surrounding villages announcing that Yahweh was coming to Jerusalem. All the citizens of Israel had been invited to celebrate with the king as he accompanied the Ark of Yahweh. Crowds gathered along the parade route from Kiriath Jearim into the city to watch the spectacle, but Mikal could not see much of a celebration.

The day before the event, the chief steward of the house gathered her husband's entire family in the common room. The king's wives, concubines, and offspring would be driven in a special wagon in the parade. Mikal had feigned illness and remained at home. She could watch the spectacle from the window of her bedchamber, but there was no spectacle. In the fading twilight, Mikal witnessed a subdued and bewildered crowd. Something had gone wrong.

She moved from her window to the table. Before she could ignite the flame of her oil lamp, she was startled by the wraith-like figure standing at her door.

"Please, do not light the lamp. I do not wish to be seen."

By the sound of her husband's grating voice, she knew he was shattered and broken.

Mikal set down the oil lamp but did not move straightaway to her husband. She allowed him to explain his disheveled appearance, his weak voice, and the cause for his distress.

He leaned heavily against the doorframe and raised his limp arm to her. "I should have listened to you. That day you came to the wall."

Mikal did not wait for him to finish but tucked her body underneath his outstretched arm and helped him to the edge of her bed. He was almost dead weight, and he groaned wearily as he sat.

Mikal knelt in front of him. "What happened, my lord?"

David was like a frightened creature agitated by the slightest sound or movement. "Yahweh is fearsome. I thought the Almighty would be pleased. I thought…I only wished to please Yahweh." David dropped his head into his hands and sobbed.

Mikal ran her fingers over his head. His hair was plastered to his scalp with dried sweat and hardened grime. She was startled that he was not wearing his crown. *Has he lost it?* This was not the time to ask.

"A man died today, right in front of me, right in front of everyone."

"How, my lord?"

"The Ark was riding in the cart. The road should have been smoothed. They should have removed the stones and filled in the ruts. When the oxen stumbled, one of the men in charge walking beside the cart reached out to stop the Ark from sliding onto the road. The moment he took hold of the Ark, his whole body began to convulse, and he collapsed onto the ground. Then he dissolved inside his robes like oil or hot wax until nothing remained but his wet garments."

David fretfully rubbed his hands over the tops of his legs.

"I have seen many men die in my lifetime, but not like this man. I was terrified and angry, and in my shame, I panicked and ran."

"Did you abandon the Ark?"

"If I had not commanded for this day to happen, that man would still be alive."

"My lord, what happened to the Ark?" Mikal insisted for an answer.

"There was a home of a Levite in a nearby village. I ordered the Ark taken there, and then…and then I fled like a terrified child."

"How did you get through the city gates without being seen?"

"I was unrecognizable." He reached inside his torn garments, covered in dirt and reeking of human dampness, and removed his crown from a pouch. He handed it to her.

Mikal exhaled a sigh of relief when she took the crown. This royal artifact she understood. The Ark of Yahweh, its holy and invisible power that could kill in an instant, she could not fathom, but the royal diadem, the crown of a king and the power it represented, she understood.

"Who will save me from myself?" David hung his head, his voice raw from exhaustion. "Who will protect me?"

Mikal lifted her arms and gently laid the crown on David's bent head.

"You are the giant-slayer, the poet-warrior, the slayer of ten thousand, the king of the chosen, the Lion of Judah," she whispered. "Yahweh has saved you. Yahweh will protect you. You are to wear the crown…the crown of the Almighty."

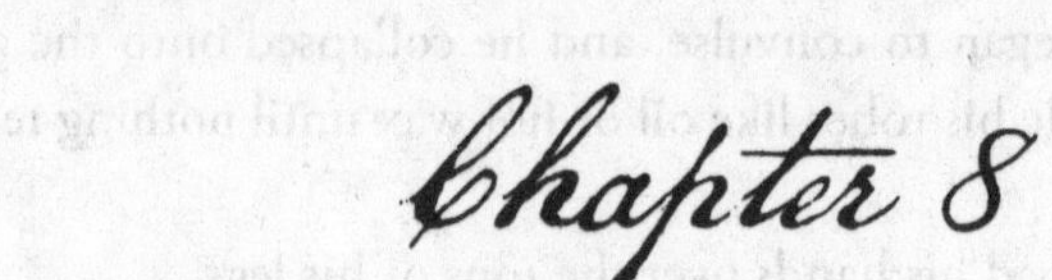

DAVID LOST INTEREST IN THE PALACE. HE LOST INTEREST IN RE-building the city. Those projects could be done without his input or supervision.

He was preoccupied with one thing. David did not care if those closest to him did not understand. It did not bother him what they thought of his constant brooding. He was obsessed, perhaps slightly crazed, but he would no longer engage in conversation on subjects that would slow the process of repairing his bemused heart.

Each day, he rode Ardon into the Kidron Valley and the surrounding hills. He refused Benaiah's urging to have a protection detail accompany him. Bodyguards would be a distraction. Solitude was required for his soul to regain any feeling of calm.

What had Yahweh done and why had He done it? That question overshadowed everything. David had come to accept that Yahweh had chosen him king, even when forced to flee and live for years on the run from the relentless pursuit of the mad king. He did not believe Yahweh would ever turn against him, but with the death of the Levite, everything changed. Had the Almighty shifted His favor away from him?

David did not even know the man who died. He had just met Uzzah the Levite on the day of his death. Now, he could never forget his name. And so he decreed the very spot where Uzzah melted into the earth would be called "Perez Uzzah, the outbreak of Uzzah." Like the outbreaking of waters, Yahweh was the Lord of outbreaking. There was no taming Yahweh, no understanding the Almighty.

These disturbing thoughts drove David into the wilderness, forcing him to confront his fears, his anger, his disgrace. He would end each daily sojourn on Mount Moriah, the mount of sacrifice, ambling along the edges of the deflated tent stretched out on the ground. Piles of tent poles lay around the perimeter. Stacks of cedar beams were set at different points. The preparations for the arrival of the Ark were abandoned and the laborers and Levites assigned other tasks until a later time, a time David had not yet determined. The tent had been dismantled in the days after Uzzah's death and allowed to lay on the crest of the hill. His heart felt like the collapsed Tabernacle spread across the land, shrunken and dispirited.

Before returning to the city, David would kneel and place his hands on the sacred covering as if feeling for a pulse. Could there be any sign of life flickering through the dense wool and fabrics, a sign of Yahweh's Presence? Just a faint glint of strength that might reveal a trace of life within the waxed linen could bring him hope. When would this tent be raised to receive the holy relic of Israel? What must happen to revive the immediate Presence of the Almighty on this place? The materials were ready. He need only to give the command for the Tabernacle of Yahweh to be reassembled and secured on this hill, but David could not find it in his heart to issue the order.

The one order he had passed along to Zadok and Abiathar before he fell into his time of introspection was for them to seek and find the best singers and musicians from among the Levites. He also instructed Joab to build housing for the influx of singers, composers, and musicians. Included in these plans were designs for the new prophet's school that Nathan would oversee and a library for Gad to house the sacred words of Yahweh and the histories and stories of the chosen. He wanted priests and prophets, musicians and composers all residing in Jerusalem.

David did not know when, but deep within him, beyond the levels of despair and darkness, he hoped, he believed, joy would return. The Tabernacle would rise from the ground, and the glory of Yahweh would come to reside beneath the shelter of this cover. When that moment happened, he wanted to be ready. It would happen swiftly and would be a new outbreaking of Yahweh.

One afternoon when David invited Nathan to join him on the mount, he sensed the time was near, that recovery was at hand. He watched the prophet trudging up the hill as the sun shed its golden light upon the city. A crowd had gathered along the northern wall, larger than usual. The area normally bustled with laborers and guards going about their assigned jobs. This time the crowd did not move. All eyes watched the prophet ascend the hill to join the king.

"We have an audience." David pointed to the northern wall.

Just below where David stood, Nathan paused to catch his breath before he glanced back toward the city. "Everyone is anxious about the king's well-being."

"I too have been anxious. These last few months have been unsettling for me."

Nathan removed the wineskin and satchel he carried and held them up to David. "Are you hungry, my lord?"

"Famished," David replied.

Nathan and David straddled a large cedar beam that would be used as one of the center posts of the Tabernacle. David could feel a growing appetite in his belly as the prophet spread the small feast of mutton, cheeses, bread, and raw vegetables on the beam. David removed the top from the wineskin and offered it to Nathan.

"Please, my lord." Nathan raised his hand. "You have borne the heat of the day. Take the first swallow."

David did not argue and took a large drink, swished the sweet taste inside his mouth before swallowing, and instantly felt the livening effect.

"How is Joab coming along with the prophet's school?" David replaced the top into the neck of the wineskin.

"The renovations are nearing completion, my lord. Students are coming from across the country."

"I want Jerusalem filled with prophets and Levites, priests and musicians and poets." David gazed upon the city below. "My city will not just be a capital of commerce, military complex, or affairs of state, but the center of the worship of Yahweh."

"Shiloh used to be the center of worship," Nathan said. "All of Israel would come to Shiloh for festivals and the worship of Yahweh at the Tabernacle. When Gad and I studied with our master, he would tell us of growing up under the tutelage of Eli, the High Priest, and of hearing the voice of Yahweh inside the Tabernacle. The great prophet often said those were days of hardship, but they forged his character and devotion to Yahweh."

"When I fled from Saul, I took refuge with Samuel and Shira," David said. "The great prophet shared with me how hard it had been to be left in Shiloh as a child and rarely see his family."

"You and the great prophet had to learn the hardship of Yahweh's call. There was suffering and there was blessing, but out of the depths of your souls, your faith blossomed." Nathan waved his hand over the deflated tent. "Now I believe Jerusalem will become the new Shiloh."

"Yes, the Ark must have a sacred location for Yahweh to dwell and not the common room in the home of a priest or Levite." David nibbled on some bread. "I believe this hill where Father Abraham was tested by Yahweh must be the resting place for the Ark."

"It is the place of testing, my lord."

"I too feel as though I have been tested for years, Nathan, and especially since the death of Uzzah. The ways of Yahweh, who can know them? Only in these last few days have I felt the beginning of revival in my heart."

"Perhaps the chaff around your heart is falling away, my lord," Nathan suggested. "And grains of wheat are beginning to flourish."

"What do you mean?" David asked, intrigued by the prophet's notion.

"Before Abraham and Isaac climbed this mountain to sacrifice to Yahweh, it was a threshing floor. Harvesters would crush and break the sheaves of wheat upon makeshift wooden planks to separate the husks from the grain. The final winnowing came when the harvesters would toss the grain and husks into the air allowing the breezes to separate the weightier husks from the lighter grains."

"This hill is one of separating and testing," David mused. "It is a wonder."

"Indeed, a wonder, my lord."

David stood from the cedar beam and went over to Ardon grazing close by. He rummaged through a sheepskin pouch, then returned to Nathan with a scroll.

"I have written a few lines recalling Abraham and Isaac," David said. "It is not finished. There is more. Would you please read it aloud? I want to hear how it sounds coming from someone else's lips."

"I am no singer, my lord. The lyrics would trip off my blundering tongue."

"No singing required, Nathan." David chuckled. "Just speak the words. Let them flow naturally and see how they may touch your heart."

Nathan opened the scroll and glanced up.

David nodded to him.

> *"Give thanks to the Lord, call on His name;*
> *Make known among the nations what He has done.*
> *Sing to Him, sing praise to Him;*
> *Tell of all His wonderful acts.*
> *Glory in His holy name;*
> *Let the hearts of those who seek Yahweh rejoice.*
> *Look to Yahweh and His strength;*
> *Seek His face always.*
> *Remember the wonders He has done,*
> *His miracles, and the judgments He pronounced.*
> *He is the Lord our God;*
> *His judgments are in all the earth.*
> *Yahweh remembers His covenant forever,*
> *The word He commanded, for a thousand generations,*
> *The covenant He made with Abraham,*
> *The oath He swore to Isaac.*
> *He confirmed it to Jacob as a decree,*
> *To Israel as an everlasting covenant."*

Nathan lowered the scroll but did not look up from the writing. He stared at the words, silently repeating some of the phrases.

"As I said, it is not finished." A level of anxiety bubbled up as David waited for Nathan's reaction. "I have not written any psalms or poems since…I do not remember. I know there is more to be written. Perhaps you might help me."

"I would not know where to begin, my lord." Nathan lifted his eyes to David. "This is a beautiful call for us to remember Yahweh as He remembers His covenant all the way back to our first ancestors of Abraham and Sarah."

"So, you think this is a good opening, Nathan?"

"Your thoughts reestablish one thousand years of our history, my lord." Nathan swung his leg over the cedar beam and handed the scroll back to David.

To David's surprise, Nathan knelt before him.

"My lord, the chaff has flown from your heart and the grain remains." Nathan took the hem of David's garment and brought it to his lips. "Your words of remembrance have set in motion the return of the weight and glory that once descended upon this mountain when Abraham prepared to sacrifice his only son, Isaac. May Yahweh bless you, my lord."

David took a step back. He had not expected Nathan's humble response to his authority. He had not expected the spark of revival he had been feeling in the last days to ignite the flame burning inside him. His whole body quaked. His fingers lost their strength. He could not hold on to the scroll and let it fall to the ground.

Nathan was quick to retrieve it as he rose to his feet. "Let us make ready the return of Yahweh to this mountain."

David felt the firm grip of Nathan's hands upon his trembling shoulders.

"Is this the beginning then, Nathan?" David's words rattled out of his quivering mouth. "The beginning of rebirth?"

"I believe it is, my lord. A new beginning for the king and for the nation."

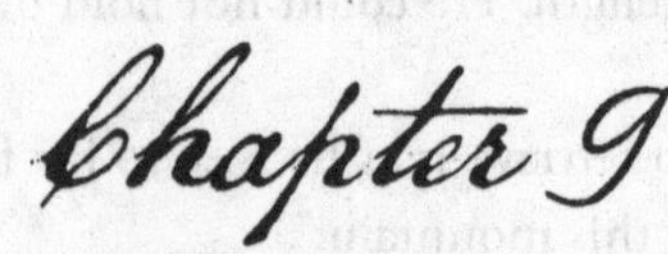

Chapter 9

THE COMMAND WAS GIVEN, AND WORD WAS SENT OUT TO ALL of Israel that the king was bringing the Ark of the Covenant to Jerusalem. Because David had assembled all the materials for his earlier attempt to bring the Ark into the city, it did not take long to set the pillars in the ground and raise the drapery barriers of fine linens to encompass the site of the Tabernacle.

David could oversee that work, but as for the interior work and furnishings, that had to be done by the Levites and priests. David had to stand outside the barrier for the placement of Altar and Laver in the outer court area. Abiathar and Zadok took charge of the raising of the interior tent and arranging the altar of incense, the table of the bread of Presence, and golden lampstand in their proper places in honor of Yahweh. The interior veil was hung inside the tent that would house the Ark in the Holy of Holies and then the outer veil. Day and night, the work did not stop. David took little time to eat and sleep, and the whirlwind of labor brought a speedy completion to all the preparations.

David slept under the stars on the last night. He camped in front of the home of Obed-Edom, who had housed the Ark for the last three months, refusing the kind invitation to sleep indoors. When the morning light began to brighten the eastern sky, a holy delirium seized David. It seized all of Jerusalem. It seized all of Israel.

The ninety-day boon enjoyed by the devout Levite proved to David that there was blessing and joy to be had in the mystery surrounding the Ark. It was not only to be feared but celebrated. The holiness of Yahweh was to be expressed as rejoicing with trembling. David was trembling. He felt he had never stopped trembling from the moment Nathan confirmed what he believed when the two of them were alone on the mount of sacrifice. That it was time for the Ark of the Covenant to be brought into the city and set inside the Tabernacle as constructed to the specifications documented by Moses in the sacred writings.

David kept a respectful distance from the Ark as it left the home of Obed-Edom. He kept a respectful distance from the Levites who had been consecrated and assigned to carry the Ark on poles along the parade route. He kept a respectful distance when every six steps the musicians played their instruments, the singers sang their choruses, and the priests offered their sacrifices. However, once the Ark broke through the gates of the City of David, the king was no longer able to keep his joy under control.

His lungs were infused with the holy breath of Yahweh, the very breath that brought to life the first beings to inhabit Eden's lush gardens. The divine breath filled every space in his body—those hidden places, the shadowed ones, spaces he did not even know could exist inside—and brought all of his being to a radiance that lifted him off the ground. He leapt with such passion he shed his royal robes, leaving him in only his linen ephod and sandals. He leapt so high it was as if he had taken flight and had the clear vision of an eagle soaring above the clouds.

David danced before the multitudes in honor of the ancestors chosen by Yahweh as a people for Himself. He danced through the streets of the city in honor of the multitudes gathered from the four corners of Israel to join the king in celebration. But above all as the procession began to ascend the mountain of sacrifice where the Tabernacle awaited to receive the sacred Mercy Seat of Yahweh, David danced for the Almighty, the Creator of heaven and earth. He could not believe he had the breath to sing and dance at the same time.

> *"Sing to the Lord all the earth;*
> *Proclaim His salvation day after day.*
> *Declare His glory among the nations,*
> *His marvelous deeds among all peoples.*
> *For great is the Lord and most worthy of praise.*

Splendor and majesty are before Him;
Strength and joy in His dwelling place.
Ascribe to the Lord, O families of nations,
Ascribe to the Lord glory and strength,
Ascribe to the Lord the glory due His name.
Worship the Lord in the splendor of His holiness."

When David reached the crest of the mountain, he was met by Zadok and Abiathar who stood on either side of the entrance into the outer court of the Tabernacle. Levites posted at the entryway pulled back the curtains. Levites with their shofars blasted the air. Levites stationed at the altars of sacrifice built outside the Tabernacle grounds set the offerings ablaze. David fell on his face away from the entrance as the Ark passed through the doors of the outer court. He did not rise from his prostrate position until Zadok and Abiathar came back outside and announced the Ark was placed safely behind the veil in the Holy of Holies.

David leapt to his feet and raised his arms to the crowd and shouted:

"Let the heavens rejoice, let the earth be glad;
Let them say among the nations, 'The Lord reigns!'
Give thanks to the Lord for He is good;
His love endures forever.
Praise be to the Lord, the God of Israel,
From everlasting to everlasting."

The roar of the crowd split the air. The blasting of the shofars pierced the blue sky. The trumpets and cymbals, the lyres and harps, the chorus of singers carried the adorations of the people into the highest heavens.

Once the echoes of praise began to fade, David raised his voice to the people.

"Open the storehouses," he shouted. "Let every man and woman in Jerusalem be given a loaf of bread and cakes of raisins and dates. Feast on this day. Feast on the bounty of Yahweh, the Almighty. Feast on the love of your king."

David was never so thankful to see Benaiah lead Ardon toward him. He had kept the fatigue of the last days at arm's length, but it consumed him.

"My lord, there is a feast at the family residence." Benaiah handed him the reins. "The wives and mothers and your children await you."

"Thank you, dear friend," David said, embracing Benaiah.

"My lord!" Nathan hurried up to David holding the royal robe he had discarded somewhere along the parade route through the city.

Only now was David aware he wore so little covering. He slipped his arms through the sleeves. "I do not remember taking this off, Nathan."

"You were dancing before Yahweh, my lord." Nathan helped David tie the tassels around his waist. "You were in the heat and light of Yahweh."

David threw his arms around Nathan. "And Yahweh is home in Jerusalem."

"Indeed, my lord. Yahweh is home."

David climbed upon Ardon's back and tucked the reins beneath the covering under his legs. His faithful steed did not need his guidance. Ardon had free rein.

David had touched the hearts of his people. Now, as he rode into the city, he extended his arms gripping the people's outstretched arms and hands.

Once he passed through the city center, he led Ardon to the family dwellings. His offspring surrounded him the moment he dismounted, wrapping their arms around him, clasping his robe in their fingers. David playfully dragged them through the gardens into the portals of the house where the mothers and wives snatched the children off their father like insects, giving him freedom to move.

"Begin the feast," he said. "I will join you soon."

David bounded up the stairs to the top floor and found Mikal looking out the window. "Come, Mikal," he said breathlessly. "Everyone has gathered. The feast is—"

"How the king distinguished himself today." Mikal whirled around to face him. "I saw you from my window. I watched you disrobe before the hordes of Israel."

"I do not remember losing my robe, Mikal," he said with a light chuckle. "I was in a joyous mood celebrating the arrival of Yahweh. It must have just fallen off."

"You humiliated yourself performing for an audience of slave girls and servants."

"I do not know what to say." David did not grasp her unexpected vitriol.

"When my father was king there were never such vulgar displays of such heathen behavior," Mikal sneered. "My father would have never allowed it."

A bolt of shock stabbed his heart.

Out of hateful spite the house of Saul had been resurrected. In the body of his wife, the house of Saul had risen from the dust, mocking him, cursing him, detesting him for having taken the crown from her family, for boldly expressing his love and passion for the God of Israel whom her father had despised.

David had sought her comfort after the disaster of a few months ago. He had sought her out now to share his joy, but her verbal arrows pierced deep, and now his tongue had no pity.

"It was before Yahweh that I danced," David began. "My audience was Yahweh, and if I humiliated myself, I will do so again and again. Yahweh chose me as king, and I will dance before the Almighty anytime, anywhere. Yahweh chose me over your father to be king to the people of Israel. Your father's bones rot in the ground while the people look upon me with honor because I am king, the king of Israel, the king of the chosen."

He had to grip the doorframe to keep from falling, but his fury propelled him from Mikal's room and down the flights of stairs back into the gathering room on the ground floor.

The room was now empty. He was thankful to hear wives and concubines, mothers and children enjoying the feast behind the walled garden. There would be no feasting for him. He had lost all appetite. He had enough energy to run down the garden path, climb upon the back of Ardon, and ride straight to the palace just as the stars were appearing in the night sky.

Mikal took nothing. She wanted nothing. She had changed out of the fine robes she wore that morning in preparation for the celebration and into the common clothes of a house servant. She tossed her jewelry on the bed, including those items given her by the king, blew out the oil lamp, and tiptoed down the stairs.

She stopped in the gathering room and listened. Not a sound. She was thankful for the heavy exhaustion that lay over the city. No one would be aware of her departure. She slipped down the garden path and entered the street where Gad waited with a donkey.

"This is all that was available, my lady," he whispered.

"I rode into Jerusalem in a chariot and exit on a donkey. How fitting," she replied.

"I am surprised, my lady. You are leaving in such haste. What of the king?"

"I doubt the king will notice my absence."

"Shall I tell him you are visiting your sister?" asked Gad.

"You may tell him whatever you like. Now, give me the rope to this beast."

"Forgive me, my lady, but you are acting very strange. I am concerned. Will you not allow me to travel to Gibeah with you?"

Mikal leaned forward and gave Gad a gentle kiss on his cheek. "I will travel alone. I understand being alone," she said, and then cupped her hand on Gad's cheek, the one she had graced with a kiss. "You have been so kind to me. You served my father even at his worst. Thank you for your faithfulness."

"Shall I tell the king when to expect your return, my lady?"

Mikal dropped her hand from Gad's cheek and inhaled the cool night air deep into her lungs. She almost began to weep when she exhaled but controlled herself. She would not be returning, and she would not allow herself to weep about her choice.

"I should have known this would never work," Mikal said. "A union of the old kingdom with the new would only happen in dreams…my dreams. This is for the best. Good-bye, old friend."

"Yahweh be with you, my lady."

"I am sure Yahweh is quite comfortable remaining here in the City of David."

Mikal led the donkey from the family dwelling and down the street. The city center was deserted, the streets empty. The guards at the gates were either asleep or indifferent as she passed beneath them and onto the road to Gibeah, the road back home.

PART TWO

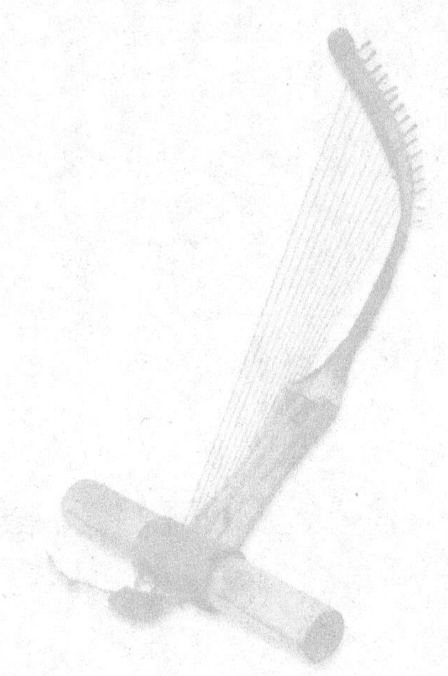

Chapter 10

DAVID ALWAYS TOOK HIS WALKS IN THE EARLY MORNING hours, but these strolls were never beyond the city walls or out in the fields and forests. The path he took was along the balcony that encircled his entire dwelling. The terrace began in the courtyard and wound along the high walls of his palace.

The palace was still under construction. David wanted multiple rooms including a great hall in the center of the structure. From meetings with military and tribal leaders to receiving foreign ambassadors and dignitaries to giving lavish banquets at festivals and holidays, David wanted a gathering hall large enough to accommodate scores of people.

From the height of his balcony, he could view the entire city and the surrounding countryside and observe the rapid expansion of growth. Personal dwellings were sprouting up throughout the city. The military and merchant classes were constructing family homes of stone and cedar financed in large part from the treasure plundered from his conquered enemies. The riches of the caravans traveling from all directions and always stopping in the City of David to do business only fattened his treasure houses. David made sure his commander and his captains were well housed and in close proximity to the palace. Many had built homes just across the street below the upper tier of the palace courtyard with its southern view of the city.

David delighted in rewarding his most faithful followers. The ones who never left his side during the years of his flight from Saul. They had shared hideouts of caves and mountain ravines. Now, he wanted his companions to enjoy what city life would provide. Living across the street from the palace was the highest reward he could bestow.

As good as this was for David, he could not ignore a level of personal discomfort. The transition from being a hunted outlaw to becoming the king of Israel living in luxury was not easy. The purpose of his daily walks along the circumference of his palace helped him become more grounded in his new life.

"I find it difficult to be walking on man-made surfaces," David said to Benaiah and Joab as they completed their first loop along the high walls.

"You could rejoin us on the battlefield, my lord," Joab suggested. "That would get you out of the palace and your feet back on hard earth."

"Routing the mercenaries of the Ammonites was enough," David said. "I am thankful for the victories, but the many battles are beginning to take a toll on my body."

They paused at the front terrace in the main courtyard and took some refreshment set out on a portable table.

"But we are enjoying the rich bounty these victories afford." Joab lifted a goblet of wine off the golden tray and waved it over the city.

"Yes, Commander, we are." David lifted his own goblet to his lips. "You and Abishai have done well. When my sister hears of her sons' exploits, she will be proud."

"And you, my lord, are you proud?" Joab asked.

His nephew's question caught him by surprise. David had tried to keep all dealings with Joab on a level that did not require familial affection. David had no trust in either of his nephews. Their wicked plot to assassinate Abner was unforgivable. But Joab proved capable of leading men into battle, yet when it came to bestowing praise on his nephew for his increasing victories over the enemies of Israel, his heart was far from it.

"You are worthy of the honor and reward you receive for your triumphs," David demurred, and it was all he could say. An uncle's pride in his nephew's heroics was not possible, warm affection for Joab might never be possible.

"Thank you, my lord." Joab returned the empty goblet to the tray. "Now that the king has been successful in routing the mercenaries hired by the Ammonites, we are preparing to lay siege to Rabbah in the spring."

"You and the army have done well and deserve this respite from war," David said. "We can talk strategies for besieging the capital of Ammon another time."

Joab bowed and took his leave.

David waited until his nephew descended the outside staircase along the southern wall before he spoke. "Why is it I am unable to feel any fondness for my nephew?" David looked at Benaiah, but his dear friend and chief bodyguard did not give a response. "Your silence is not a sufficient answer to my question, Benaiah."

"My lord, I understand why you are unable to muster affection, but Joab has proven capable. The men respect him for his military skills and bravery in battle."

"And yet…," David sensed Benaiah may have more to say.

"My lord, we have been together since the early days. In all these years I have never known you to guard your heart with anyone except the commander."

"Am I that obvious, Benaiah?"

"It is because you are a man of truth, my lord. You cannot play the deceitful fool."

"I do feel some guilt at my inability to muster *affection*, as you say, for Joab."

"You do not get to choose your family, my lord," Benaiah offered.

"I do have a large family, but must I like every member? I do not believe any of them care for me. I have always been the runt in their estimation."

"My lord, you have far exceeded their low estimation. Even if some in your family do not serve you well, even thwarted your wishes and done evil, I believe they should receive mercy and benevolence from the king."

David smiled at Benaiah's truthful words even if they did not tickle his ears. "You speak as a friend not the captain of my bodyguard."

"I am both, my lord, but I am mostly your friend." Benaiah bowed his head.

"This is true." David gave Benaiah's arm a firm grip. "This is true."

Laughter and squealing came out of thin air, and both David and Benaiah looked around for the source. The terrace bustled with palace servants going about their tasks, but none looked jovial. Too early in the morning for that. But when they heard the laughter a second time, Benaiah pointed to a possible source. They approached the raised wall of the balcony and saw Uriah chasing his wife around the potted plants and cushions on the roof of their house across the street. The wife threw a cushion at the husband in a playful game of the hunter and the prey.

"Is this how you spend your time when you come home from the wars?" David shouted at Uriah from his balcony.

"Does not every husband do so, my lord?" Uriah answered, out of breath. Uriah tossed the pillow back to his wife who was also out of breath. The couple tried to offer David the courtesy of a bow, but they lost their balance. Trying to recover from this awkward misstep only caused more laughter.

David adjusted his crown and brushed away the residue of wine from his beard as he whispered into Benaiah's ear from the side of his mouth. "What is her name?"

"Bathsheba, my lord."

"I see you have building materials on your roof." David pointed to a pile of cedar logs and masonry tools beside some potted plants.

"I go away to war and come home to a list of tasks, my lord," Uriah replied, wrapping his arms around his wife.

"What is this project?" David asked.

"A rooftop garden with a modest pool, my lord."

"Lady Bathsheba, I promise not to send your husband off to battle again until he completes your project."

"Thank you, my lord." Bathsheba bowed again, this time with steadier legs.

"Uriah, you know you are exempt from military service for a year after you are married," David said. "You are free to stay home and bring happiness to your wife. Just say the word, and I will inform Joab."

Uriah appeared stumped by this news.

David could not believe Uriah would not take advantage of this marital exemption from military service.

"My lord, may I speak?" Bathsheba slipped out of Uriah's arms and took a step forward.

"Please." David motioned for her to continue.

"My husband is a great warrior, my lord," she began. "You know this from his long years of friendship and faithful service to you."

"I hope you have not told her all the stories, Uriah," David interrupted, and Uriah and Benaiah laughed at the shared joke.

"Not all, my lord," Uriah responded. "We are bound by the brothers' pact of silence."

"But when it comes to the demands of the army of Israel," Bathsheba continued, ignoring the bawdy male humor. "I would never keep my husband from his place at the king's side. He will always serve you when and where you require him. I will see to it."

Bathsheba spoke with quiet confidence yet with humility. She did not plead in favor of the marriage furlough from military service. She merely expressed the pride she had in her husband.

"May all the wives and mothers of my warriors be so devoted," David declared.

David was struck by the sway of her words that matched her beauty. In the morning sunlight, she had the bewitching presence of a deity, and he felt the animal strength rise in his blood and rush through his body.

"I see why you married this woman, Uriah." David sensed the craving awakening inside him. He needed to withdraw before he made a fool of himself, so he waved them good-bye.

David went straight back to the tray and swiped a neatly cut piece of honey and raisin cake from the top of the stack stuffing the whole piece into his mouth. Then he refilled his goblet. The robust surge of strength needed to be fed. Though this stirring in his body was a natural reaction, it was unnaturally focused, and he needed to restrain it. He must avert his eyes and occupy his mind with other thoughts than those of another man's wife.

"My lord," Gad shouted. He came running toward David waving a scroll.

David took a swallow of wine to wash down the sweet cake. As Gad staggered up to David, he handed him his goblet of wine.

"Thank you, my lord, but no," Gad wheezed, waving away the offered goblet.

Benaiah gripped Gad's shoulder to help stabilize him as he struggled for breath. "What is the matter, Gad?"

"Yahweh has spoken to Nathan, my lord." Gad held Benaiah's arm in one hand while showing David the scroll in the other. "It has happened. We never expected the Almighty…we spent all night writing down the sacred words, copying them onto several scrolls. Our master Samuel said this might happen. We have not slept. We raced from the hall of the prophets to the palace…Jashar and I…Nathan…we—"

"Gad, please slow down," David implored. "I do not understand you."

"Come with me, my lord." Gad finally was able to draw a deep breath. "Nathan and Jashar await us on the north wall."

Gad broke free from Benaiah's hand and marched along the balcony. He did not wait for David to follow as he disappeared around the corner of the palace for the northern wall.

"I have never seen the prophet in such a dither," David chuckled.

"Perhaps we should follow, my lord." Benaiah motioned toward the back of the departing Gad.

David and Benaiah caught up with Gad and, when they rounded the corner of the palace, saw Jashar and Nathan braced against the balcony wall facing the Tabernacle on Mount Moriah. Both prophets were shouting praises to Yahweh.

"Gad, what is the cause of this praise to the Almighty?" David came to a stop. He could not believe what he heard and saw coming from these prophets.

Gad slipped his arm around David's waist and led him toward the two prophets.

When David approached, Nathan fell to his knees before him. "My sovereign lord," Nathan gushed. "On this very spot before the evening sun had set on the day, you said to me, 'How can I live in a palace of cedar while the Ark of Yahweh lives in a tent? We should build a house for the Almighty to dwell in.' And I told you to do whatever you had in mind for Yahweh was with you. But my lord, I spoke in haste for this is not the desire of Yahweh."

"Nathan, please rise." David offered the prophet his hand.

When Nathan gripped David's hand a jolt of energy rush into his arm. It was not the power of a human grip, but a divine force that made him break into a sweat. Nathan did not need David's help to stand. He needed Nathan's help to keep from falling.

"My lord, it has happened. Yahweh has spoken to me." Nathan's eyes were misting with tears. "Countless times, I witnessed the spiritual toil my master experienced when Yahweh descended upon his heart, but this was different."

"Tell me everything." David and Nathan leaned into the parapet wall.

"I call it a vision, my lord, for indeed I know not what else to name it," Nathan began. "We had finished the evening meal. I was sharing with Gad and Jashar what we had discussed right here the day before. When I rose from the dining table, I became immobilized for it had come upon me."

"What came upon you?" David asked.

"Divine communication, my lord," Nathan answered, but he did not continue. His eyes glazed over as if reliving that moment of stunned ecstasy.

David looked to Gad.

"I heard him gasp, my lord, and then I heard him moan just as he dropped to his knees. Fearful of the worst, I rushed to his side. Jashar and I helped him to bed, but there was no sleeping for him or either of us."

"Nothing appeared to my natural eye." Nathan reemerged from his memory.

"But his gaze was fixed, my lord," Gad interjected.

"His eyes were unmoved, my lord," Jashar added. "It was as if he were looking into a faraway world."

"I saw nothing, but I felt a rigor in my loins." Nathan held his hand tight to his belly. "As the feeling intensified, what I thought might be an oncoming illness was in truth an intense focus of spiritual sight. I had been subdued by the power of Yahweh, and I had no liberty to move other than to speak."

"There was dye and parchment on the desk in his room," Jashar said. "I sat down immediately and wrote all that Nathan said."

Gad offered a scroll to David. "Here is the king's copy."

"Slumber fled, my lord," Nathan gasped. "We spent the night recording and copying everything. We did not want to lose or forget one word from the lips of Yahweh."

"We waited until the morning light to share with you, my lord," Gad said.

"I am fearful of the words of Yahweh." David inched away from Gad.

"Do not be, my lord, for they are proclamations of grace and mercy." Nathan returned to his knees and placed his hands upon David's feet. "The word is clear. You are not to build a temple for Yahweh. That honor will go to the one who is next in line. But Yahweh will establish your house so that, when you rest with your fathers, Yahweh will raise up an heir to succeed you. Yahweh will establish your kingdom forever. You are not to build a Temple for the Almighty. That task belongs to your offspring. It is all there. It is all written, and the words of Yahweh will be fulfilled. Your house and your kingdom will endure before Yahweh; your throne will be established forevermore."

"Who am I?" David sank to his knees in front of Nathan. "Who am I? Who am I before the God of all creation?"

David's hands trembled as he reached for the scroll, but he could not clasp it. How could he take these sacred words into his hands let alone absorb them into his heart?

"How can I ever divine Yahweh's plan and purpose for me?" David groaned.

Nathan sat up on his knees and took the scroll from Gad. Holding it in both hands, Nathan extended the written words of Yahweh to David.

"My lord, do not be afraid," Nathan reassured him. "Read of the compassion of Yahweh extended to you and to your house for the length of your days and to all who spring forth from your own flesh and blood."

David took the scroll and unfurled it. His eyes ran wildly over the words and lettering. He was at play, pure abandon in the lettered fields of Yahweh's promises. At play, as a young son with his father, in the great light that flowed over and around and through him. He was anointed again. He was held in stunned reverie before the written word of the Presence. "How great You are, O sovereign Lord. There is no one like You, and there is no God but You."

Chapter 11

BATHSHEBA COULD NOT STEADY HER HANDS. SHE HAD BROKEN the dry reed stalk when she pressed too hard on the papyrus sheet. She had blotched the paper with the dye mixed with burnt linseed oil and melted gum from Arabia.

She ripped up the ruined papyrus and broken reed stalks and tossed them into the fire. As the writing utensils were devoured by flames, Bathsheba wished the same for herself, be devoured by fire.

She held up her hands. The sight of her tremulous fingers made her light-headed and faint. She had suffered several days of nausea, and looking at her quivering hands made it worse. A wave of nausea struck, and she crawled to the large clay pot next to the fireplace and wretched. Bathsheba did not trust her legs for they too were unsteady. She crawled back to the table and pulled herself upon the stool to make another attempt at writing.

The letter she wished to compose should be addressed to her husband, the news she wished to tell, should be for his ears alone. Israel had enjoyed a winter of peace, but as soon as the spring rains had ceased, Joab, the commander, called up the army of Israel. The elite force was sent to the city of Rabbah with orders from the king to finish the war with the Ammonites once and for all.

There was never a doubt that her husband would go when called. Bathsheba would never even hint any displeasure or complain to Uriah of his long absence. This was the way of military life, the way of their married life.

Bathsheba had written Uriah while he was stationed at the camp besieging the city of Rabbah. Her letters were delivered by the military courier who made bimonthly trips to the front bringing written messages from mothers and wives to the men in the king's army. Bathsheba described her mundane routines knowing Uriah would love to hear all the details of daily life and her longing for him to return to her welcoming arms. In a previous letter, she told him of her excitement when taking her first bath in the pool he had completed for her right before he departed for the front. How the pitch he used to seal the cracks in the beams had held the water, and for him to hurry home so they could bathe together under the stars of heaven.

But the last bath she had taken on the rooftop might well be the last she would ever take in the new pool. How to write these words? How could she convey the unimaginable to her dear husband?

Bathsheba pressed her hands upon the fresh sheet of papyrus to steady herself. The flow of her blood should have come and gone by this time, and she should have done her ritual cleaning, but instead, a waning appetite had replaced her monthly cycle followed by nausea at the sight and smell of food. She wished to tell Uriah of this joyous news, but the news was not joyous, and the letter was not for him.

Weeks earlier, after her last ritual bath, she barely had time to dry off and put on her robes before she heard quiet knocking. She cracked the door just enough to see soldiers standing in the threshold of her house. One held an oil lamp up to his face so that she could see they were members of the palace guards.

Bathsheba might have been frightened but she recognized some of the faces. These were military men of whom she was familiar. It came as a surprise when she was told the king desired her presence. Perhaps he wished to tell her some news of the war or relate a specific detail regarding Uriah. She remembered a tremor of fear at the thought that this might be dire, and the king wanted to personally deliver such a message. But she did not hesitate and left immediately with the palace guards.

She made the short walk from her door down the street to the outside gate on the southern end of the palace wall. Two sentries stood at the base of the steps and opened the gate for her to enter. As she began to climb the staircase, she realized her escort remained behind. When Bathsheba paused her ascent, the palace guard with the oil lamp said for her to continue, that the king awaited her at the top on the terrace.

Her heart quickened. *The news the king had to tell must be dire if the guards have been instructed to remain behind.*

Bathsheba lifted her robes and hastened up the stairs. When she reached the top step, she paused to recover her breath. She expected to see more palace guards to direct her to the king, but the terrace was deserted. It was as though she had stepped into a dream. Except for the torchlight on either side of the large doors of the great Hall of the Lion, the other torches on the surrounding columns above the terrace floor had been extinguished. In the half-moon and starry sky, Bathsheba saw only shadows. Then a voice called her name, a low raspy growl, a hoarse whisper as if spoken by a wild beast.

She spun around. Perhaps the palace guard was now coming up the outside steps, but there was no one. She looked around the empty terrace, colonnade steps, the covered walkway behind the columns, all vacant of human presence.

Bathsheba took a few tentative steps forward, then waited and listened. The flames of the torches beside the doors of the great Hall snapped in the breeze. There was shadowed darkness and quiet and emptiness. Perhaps she had been dreaming or walking in her sleep.

Now she was frightened. What if this was not a dream? What if she were brought to the palace under false pretense? Were she caught on the premises, she might be thought a criminal and unjustly maltreated.

"Bathsheba," the voice said. "You have come."

The voice was more distinct, the human voice of the king.

"My lord," Bathsheba responded, yet she still did not see anyone. The king had summoned her, or so she had been told, but where was the king?

"Come to me," commanded the voice.

Bathsheba peered into the shadows of the upper arcade behind the columns. "My lord, I do not see you." There was a chill in the air, and she wrapped her arms around her middle or was it a sudden apprehension descending upon her heart? "You summoned me, my lord?"

"Indeed, you were summoned. Take my hand."

It was the king. She was sure of it. His voice still bore a low growl but was recognizable. From around the center column in front of the Hall of the Lion an arm and hand appeared motioning for her to step forward.

Bathsheba lifted her garments as she walked up the steps. When she took his hand, she went to bow, but the strength of his grip prevented her from doing so. This was the clutch of a different intent, not one to aid or guide her around the column. This was the painful grasp of an aggressor. This had not been a summons to hear any news of her husband. This was a summons to capture, to seize her in the shadows out of sight of all human eyes, out of sight of heaven, out of sight of Yahweh.

"I saw you in the starlight as you bathed, and I beheld a goddess."

Bathsheba flinched and tried to remove her hand. This was not appropriate praise from the king or any man. These words should only come from the lips of her husband.

The king tightened his grip and pulled her into his arms. He breathed deeply of her hair, her neck, but when he pressed his lips to hers, she placed her arms firmly against his chest to push him away.

"My lord, please do not do this," she pleaded. "You should not have looked upon me while I bathed. You should not touch me in this manner. Think of my husband, Uriah, your loyal subject and friend."

"Tonight, think of me as your husband." David pushed her back against the doors of the Hall of the Lion.

The darkness and obstructions of the pillars barred anyone from viewing this show of unwanted and unwarranted aggression. The absent sentries and the deserted terrace meant there was no chance anyone would come upon this terrible moment.

"I must have you. I must know you. I must know you utterly."

There was only one thought in the king's mind. His superior strength and the force of his lust was no match for Bathsheba to resist. Even when he pinned her against the door, when he placed his forearm beneath her chin and against her throat, lenient enough to allow her to breathe yet forcefully enough to keep her from crying out, when he tore open the front of her robe, there was little she could do.

Her mind promptly disintegrated, her sight became obscured, what strength she could muster, she used to push and twist and delay the inevitable. But it was not enough.

When the king had finished, he collapsed as if the air had gone out of his whole body. He stumbled back against the column he had hidden behind when Bathsheba first approached, but his feet slid out from under him. He leaned against the column panting, wheezing like a brute, making a sound she had never heard, not one of satisfaction, but of guttural fatigue, of a beast yielding its life to the brutality of an unexpected death. The king was in a weakened state, but to her surprise a strength rushed into her body, the power to strike in retribution for the king's brutal assault.

Instead, she ran.

Bathsheba took the shreds of her ripped garments and folded them tightly around her before bolting down the steps of the colonnade. The weak voice of the king called her name, whimpering something that may have sounded like the words of a stricken conscience, but she could not decipher the meaning.

She ran across the terrace with such speed, there was no chance to reverse course for the stairs. The gate at the bottom of the staircase was abandoned. The street to her house, deserted. There were no palace guards to escort her home. She wanted no escort. She wished she would be attacked in the street and left for dead before arriving at her threshold never to face her shame.

Nothing would do but a second cleansing, a second bathing, but not in the rooftop pool. Bathsheba would not defile its waters. It would be a cleansing with rags, with a liniment of stale oils and bitter herbs, with an immersion of rancid rainwater from an old pot that she would toss into the street for the dogs to lap. She would not wash her robes or mend them. All evidence of the assault must be destroyed. She would burn her garments along with the rags she had used to wash her body from the stain of the king's depravity.

How would she ever cleanse the stain from her memory? How would she ever face her husband? How would she ever face her future?

A wave of sickness rose in Bathsheba's throat, and she jumped up from her writing table to relieve her nausea. What she had lived through should have been a terrible dream, but it was not a dream, and the turmoil in her inward parts was proof of the reality.

No one but her knew of this second life she carried. Once it came to light, the calculation of days would begin, and the numbering would not be in her favor. Uriah had been absent too long to claim fatherhood. She had not been with him since he left for the front. For this act she could be put to death, her life and the child's forfeited. In more than a month, she had hardly been out of her house except to shop at the market. She had heard no word from the king. No word of regret, of concern, or even to express a desire to see her again, perhaps this time with her consent, which she would never give.

She was utterly alone.

After a few sips of water to settle her stomach, Bathsheba returned to the table and once again stared at the blank papyrus. The boisterous rumble in her belly was a constant reminder of how broken she was, how fragmented her mind and heart. She had to take the risk. She must tell her assailant.

What would he do? How would he react? He was the king and could deny it had ever happened. One word from him, and everyone would be silent.

She would write the truth, and her future and that of the child would rest in the reaction of the king.

She placed both hands on top of the papyrus and whispered, "O Yahweh. O Yahweh, I commit my life and the life of my child into Your hands."

Bathsheba lifted her writing hand off the papyrus, took a fresh-cut reed stalk, dipped the tip into the bowl of burnt oil and resin, and wrote two words, "With child."

Chapter 12

AFTER A LONG DAY LISTENING TO REPORTS OF THE PROGRESS of the war at Rabbah against the Ammonites, reviewing construction plans for a wall around the base of Mount Moriah to protect the Tabernacle and Levitical compound, and interviewing candidates for positions in his court, the doors to the Hall of the Lion were opened and David ushered his guests onto the terrace. The Jerusalem summer was blistering, but the heat of the day had dissipated, a pleasant breeze reducing the temperature of the palace courtyard. It was a mild summer night, perfect for a banquet under the stars.

David had called for this celebration to welcome the only surviving son of Jonathan. For the sake of his covenant with Jonathan, David let it be known his wish to show kindness to anyone in Saul's house who might be alive. When David heard his dear friend had one son, Mephibosheth, and that he had a son of his own, Mica, the king sent an envoy to bring the grandson and great-grandson of King Saul to Jerusalem.

Had Mikal stayed in the city, she would have been at David's side. As the aunt and great-aunt of this father and son, Mikal's position at the banquet would have been a place of honor. It surprised him to learn Mikal had returned to her home in Gibeah. David had not seen her since the Ark came into Jerusalem, but he was relieved to no longer face her. So much had gone wrong in their life, so much to overcome. Mikal's place in his kingdom was more a burden than a blessing. Wondering what might have happened had they not been forced to separate so long ago was a waste of time. He doubted they could have ever really loved each other, had children, or reared a future king.

Pondering such options proved useless. What was done, was done, and there was a nation to rule. In bringing Mikal to Hebron and then Jerusalem, while it had not been all for show, their reunion was a public statement of unity and healing for the nation. The purpose was served. Now, by extending kindness to the son and grandson of Jonathan, heirs of the first king of Israel, David had done all he could to mend the frayed relationship he had with the house of Saul and the tribe of Benjamin.

The guest list included not only members of David's inner circle, but he expanded it to include ambassadors and chieftains of the tribe of Benjamin. David had everyone rise to greet the guest of honor when father and son made their entrance. Mephibosheth was carried on a covered seat by four men with young Mica walking beside his father.

David burst out in song as the procession made its way to the place designated at the right hand of the king.

> *"May the righteous be glad and rejoice before Yahweh;*
> *May they be happy and joyful.*
> *Sing to Yahweh, sing praise to His name,*
> *Extol Him who rides on the clouds—*
> *His name is the Lord the Almighty—*
> *And rejoice before Him.*
> *A father to the fatherless, defender of widows*
> *Is God in His holy dwelling.*
> *God sets the lonely in families,*
> *He leads forth the prisoners with singing.*
> *From Your bounty, O Yahweh, You provide for Your people."*

David raised his goblet as Mephibosheth was lifted from the litter and set in the place of honor. "Welcome, Mephibosheth and Mica. Welcome to the City of David. You and your son shall live in Jerusalem and always eat at the king's table."

Mephibosheth began to weep as he tucked Mica under his arm.

"If I could rise, my lord, I would do so, and lay my face before you, for you are worthy of all honor," Mephibosheth exclaimed. "You have taken your servant, one despised and undeserving, and raised him up in honor of my father, Jonathan. May Yahweh bless the king and his court, his heirs and all his kingdom."

Those gathered elevated their voices to echo their praises of the king and his guest.

"Mephibosheth, from this day forward, you and Mica are to be considered like sons," David declared before the gathering. "Now, let us feast in honor of the heirs of my brother, Jonathan, first prince of Israel."

The feasting went well into the night with David sharing heroic stories of Jonathan. Of that day when David slew the giant and he and Jonathan became covenant brothers. Of how brave Jonathan was, with the reputation of a great warrior, "a deadly shot with a sling or bow," David said. And of that last time they had been together, how David and Jonathan renewed their covenant to include the promise that David would always care for Jonathan's survivors.

When the night drew to a close, David watched with pleasure as Mephibosheth and his son, Mica, fast asleep in his father's lap, were transported on the litter to their private quarters.

"A covenant made. A covenant fulfilled," David whispered to himself.

While saying his farewells to the last of his guests and with the servants busy cleaning the terrace, David noticed Benaiah approaching with a small silver tray. Upon it lay a folded parchment.

"My lord, how was it the son of Jonathan lost the use of his legs?" asked Benaiah.

"He was a young boy at the time," David answered, his gaze darting from the letter to Benaiah. "When word was brought to his nurse that Mephibosheth's father and grandfather were killed by the Philistines in the battle at Mount Gilboa, she panicked. As they fled, she dropped him from the wagon and the wheel crushed his legs. Does he not look like his father, Jonathan?"

"Indeed, my lord," Benaiah replied, offering the tray to David. "This arrived earlier in the evening, but I waited to give it to you. It did not seem urgent."

David reached for the letter with its burnt wax seal. "Who is this from?"

"I was told, the lady Bathsheba, my lord."

"She came to the palace?" David's hand hovered above the tray.

"No, my lord. A captain in the palace barracks delivered the letter. He received it from the hand of Bathsheba. Probably a request regarding Uriah."

David's hand became rigid, his fingers frozen. They were not flexible enough to grasp the letter. He kept fumbling with the folded parchment trying to lift it from the tray. He laughed at his clumsiness, but it was a false laugh. He withdrew his hand and massaged it, blowing on his fingers to loosen them.

"Shall I open it for you, my lord?"

"No, no," David replied. "Just set the tray on my cushions. I will get to it. I must have drank too much wine, or this chill in the air has disabled my fingers."

"Is there anything else, my lord, before I retire?" asked Benaiah.

David stared at the letter while vigorously rubbing his hands.

"My lord?" Benaiah said, redirecting David's attention. "Is anything the matter?"

"No, no. I am weary. It has been a long day and longer evening." This time, when David reached for the parchment, his fingers bent to hold it. "I will read this in my chambers. I am sure she is requesting I bring her man home from the front for a little comfort time."

Benaiah gave a polite smile at the king's coarse inference.

"I will let you know in the morning." David hoped his feigned humor shielded his fear as he ambled toward his chambers adjacent to the Hall of the Lion.

Once he slipped around the column he braced his back against it. A sharp pain rose in his chest. His heart beat rapidly. His brain began floating inside his skull. It was not with an anticipation of joy, of hoping to read amorous words of missing him and desirous for another meeting. His instinct at the true contents of this letter denied him that pleasure. What he held in his trembling fingers contained not sweet words, but dangerous and damning words.

David leaned around the column and looked across the terrace. Benaiah was gone, but the servants were still clearing away the remnants of the banquet. Was this not the very column he had taken cover behind when he lured Bathsheba with his hand? Was this not the very spot where he had his way with her, without her consent or affection?

He broke the waxed seal, unfolded the papyrus, and raised it to catch the reflected light from the torch attached to the opposite wall.

"With child."

She had not signed it, had written no other words. She gave no indication how she felt about him or this new predicament. Just "With child."

I am the one. There is no way I am not *the one.*

The two words lit inside his head like the blaze of a torchlight kindled by the wind, yet the radiance of those two words only enhanced the darkness of his mind. His memories went from image to image of encounters with Bathsheba, stunned by her beauty, admiring her poise and dignity, and then abandoning himself to the scrambling weight of unbridled lust when viewing her bathing from his balcony. He had lost control and given in to passion. Yet in truth it was unfair to call this a passionate encounter. Passion implied a mutual giving over to desire, and David knew beneath the layers of all rationalization Bathsheba had no choice in the matter of satisfying his craven appetite.

He leaned around the column again and found the terrace deserted, all evidence of a feast cleared away. David slipped down the steps of the colonnade, across the terrace, and to the edge of his balcony. He looked upon the darkened houses across the street, all quiet, the inhabitants fast asleep. Was Bathsheba asleep? How had she fared since that night? What thoughts might she have of him?

David could summon her again. It was his discretion, his pleasure, his whim. He was the king. He could summon who he wanted when he wanted. He was the king. He could take who he wanted when he wanted. He was king, by Yahweh's decree. Was he not entitled?

The solution was simple. Bring Uriah home from the front. David raced across the terrace to a sentry posted at the top of the staircase leading to the barracks of the palace guard below on street level. He ordered the soldier to summon Benaiah.

When he darted down the staircase, David moved to the nearest torch attached to a column. He glanced over the terrace and courtyard. No other sentries, no other servants, no one was about, no one was watching. He did not bother to read Bathsheba's two-word letter again but held it to the flame pinching a corner of the letter as the fire consumed the papyrus until it singed his fingers. He dropped the last of the letter as it turned to ash. He ground the soot into the terrace stone with his foot. Then he scraped the bottom of his sandal on the edge of the steps to remove the grime.

Written incrimination destroyed. The truth ground into the stone. Remove all taint from his person. The blackness of time would conceal his actions. He was king.

"My lord, you summoned me?" Benaiah arrived breathless from racing from the palace barracks back up the staircase.

"Yes, sorry to have disturbed you, but I am feeling benevolent and desire to take swift action."

"What is it, my lord?"

"How long would it take to bring Uriah home from the front?"

"A few days for the message to arrive at the camp. A few days for Uriah to arrive home," Benaiah answered.

"If Uriah knows he is summoned home with an opportunity to see his wife, I am sure he will ride through the night," David said, amused by his ploy for Uriah's return.

"He will leave the moment he receives your message," Benaiah affirmed.

"Then at first light send a messenger to the front and bring Uriah home. I am impatient, no, rather, the lady Bathsheba is impatient."

"Is that all, my lord?"

"Yes, Benaiah, thank you." David clapped his hands together. "I promise not to disturb you again tonight. Sleep well, my friend."

Benaiah bowed and departed.

Yes, sleep well. With Uriah's return all will be concealed, all will be forgotten, and I will sleep well again.

Chapter 13

DAVID KEPT BUSY ENTERTAINING FOREIGN DIGNITARIES AND tribal chieftains to thank them for their consistent and generous provisions to his coffers of coin, gold, precious stones and livestock and crops. Then there were the numerous caravans to welcome all loaded down with tribute from other nations. Gone were the days when he lay awake wondering how he would care for the people aligned with him while he lived in hiding from King Saul. The days of raiding and gathering plunder just to survive were ended. The wealth of the tribes of Israel and the surrounding countries were a constant stream of revenue.

Teams of workers labored constantly to keep up with the abundance pouring into the City of David. No sooner were the old storehouses filled, larger ones were constructed. David was thrilled to offer employment to so many. People throughout the nation were moving to Jerusalem for the improved prospect of a better life.

At the same time, David was gathering the material for the house of Yahweh. Whenever he needed to escape, he would sneak into the royal stables, saddle Ardon, and ride to where the walls were being built along the base of Mount Moriah. The Ark was safe inside the Tabernacle, but this was housing similar to the days of the wanderings, and while David wished to build a permanent house for Yahweh, the Almighty had denied him that honor. One of his progeny would bear that responsibility. But which? His wives and concubines were giving him children. His quiver was filling with sons and daughters, a rambunctious lot, always eager for his attention when he visited the family dwellings, but they were still young and none of the sons showed promise as a future king.

Except maybe Absalom. The boy had a flare about him, an exuberance that needed to be tempered, but David would keep a watchful eye. Eventually one would rise, and David would have the materials ready when the time came for the task of building a house for Yahweh whoever the heir.

The great wall was attached to either end of the city's northern wall and completely encircling the Levitical compound. The wall was designed to protect the sacred site. David could view the construction from his palace. All construction inside the walls would be devoted to the service of Yahweh. There was housing for the priests and Levites and student scholars and scribes, those in permanent residence and those Levites who came to Jerusalem from around the country for their rotation of service.

A new archive was under construction that would house the sacred texts of Yahweh and the writings of the chosen. The first of its kind. David insisted the histories of the chosen were recorded and in safekeeping. The people of Israel were people of the Word. As far back as the great prophet Moses, Yahweh had initiated the writing of stories and instructions, commandments and laws for the people Yahweh had called His own. David would see that what had previously been passed down orally for generations would be recorded and copied. All future writings would no longer be stored in caves. Priest and prophet and any who wished could access the great storehouse of the words of Yahweh.

What excited David most about all this construction and new life streaming into Jerusalem was the development of the school for musicians and composers. The call had gone out to all of Israel that the king would fill his court with singers, composers, musicians, and dancers commissioned to create music and songs. They would be trained in the arts of worship and praise of the Almighty. This investment of the nation's time and treasure was of utmost importance. The artists David employed would be housed in the walled compound of Mount Moriah. Instruction halls and rehearsal spaces were built. At certain times of the day, David could stroll along the northern walkway of his palace and listen to the guilds of musicians and singers rehearsing.

Such creative activity stirred David to write more psalms and give them to Asaph, the head of the new music school. This talented Levite musician could arrange psalms into compositions for multiple voices and instruments, creating an awe-inspiring sound.

When David made the offer to Nathan and Gad to build a new prophet's conservatory inside the compound and get out of the old building in the heart of the city, the two prophets were gracious but firm in refusing. From the day Nathan had presented him the scroll of Yahweh's words regarding his kingdom, David had kept the scroll near him. The declaration was a source of comfort and inspiration, but of late, David could not remember where he had placed the scroll. It was not in his chambers, and he could not find it among the documents he kept beside his throne in the Hall of the Lion. He could have misplaced it among the growing piles of scrolls he received. From the reports from the battle front, to petitions and tributes were presented to him daily. It was impossible for him to organize so many documents, and David was embarrassed to ask Nathan for another copy. It would turn up somewhere, sometime.

Benaiah had made the not-so gentle suggestion that he employ a secretary and personal assistants to help structure his life. His dear friend was a soldier and David's chief bodyguard but overseeing his administrative life was not Benaiah's strength or responsibility. For so long, David had been either a renegade captain of a company of a few hundred or king of one tribe, neither of which had required a large managerial staff. Now, times had changed, and David had begun interviewing candidates who would soon become his administrative laborers.

Evening had fallen when David returned from his inspection of the wall around Mount Moriah. The torches were being lit by the servants across the terrace. As he moved toward his chambers he kept smelling a foul odor and thought it must be him. He might have stepped in horse droppings leaving the stables. He paused in the middle of the terrace to check the soles of his riding sandals, but other than some straw and street grime, they were clean. He sniffed under his robes, but there was not the foul smell that permeated the terrace.

Then he heard laughter and familiar voices. He turned to see Benaiah escorting Uriah from the palace barracks.

"My lord, look who just arrived." Benaiah shouted with delight.

"I could smell you before I saw you," David laughed, opening his arms to his old friend as he welcomed Uriah into his embrace.

"I do smell, my lord." Uriah brushed away any grime that might have rubbed onto David's garments. He hastily bent on one knee. "I came straight from the front lines as soon as your messenger arrived with word for my return."

"Get up. Get up." David motioned for Uriah to rise.

Uriah sprang to his feet. His arms, legs, and feet were streaked with dirt. Blood was splattered over his battle garments.

"Is that your blood?" David asked in surprise.

"No, my lord." Uriah nonchalantly looked down at the front of his protective leather covering. "Must be from my last kills."

David burst into laughter. "You never change, my friend. A wild ass of a man."

"I tried to get him to go home and clean up before coming to the palace." Benaiah lifted his arms in a gesture of helplessness.

"And you, you old scoundrel." Uriah slapped Benaiah on his belly. "You are getting fat. My lord, send him back with me. We will work off the pounds by killing the Ammonites."

"How is the war progressing?" asked David. "How are Joab and the soldiers?"

"You want a full report, my lord?" Uriah asked. "I would need time to tell you."

"That can wait," David said. "In brief, how soon will this be over?"

"Your nephew is a good commander, my lord," Uriah began. "The soldiers are in good spirits overall."

Uriah dropped his head, his face falling slack, something David was unaccustomed to witnessing. He knew Uriah had more to say.

"Go on, Uriah. Speak plainly."

"My lord, the Ammonite city is well-fortified, but I believe we could have sacked Rabbah by now. Joab seems timid and reluctant to press the attack."

"I see. I see," David responded. "This will require more time, but tonight, go home to your wife, if she can stand the smell of you. Come back tomorrow and give me a thorough report."

David watched the two friends make their way across the terrace.

"Benaiah, on your way out, go by the kitchen," David called after them. "Tell the cooks to prepare an extra ration of meat and roasted vegetables from my table and send it home with Uriah. Husband and wife should enjoy feasting tonight."

Uriah bowed, offering his thanks to the king.

David held this man in high esteem, honorable and honest. Uriah might be unruly and coarse, but he would always be faithful. However, his regard for Uriah did not change the present reality. David stood alone on the terrace as night began to fall. He waited for any sense of misgiving to creep into his heart by how easily his plan was taking shape, but he felt no unease. No prick of guilt at what he had contrived. He had devised was a good plan, the details falling neatly into place and known only to himself. One night at home, and Uriah would provide him the covering he required, cleared of all misdeeds. No light would be shed upon that moment when he became dispossessed of his soul and lured this man's unsuspecting wife to the palace.

What surprised him as he lay awake most of that night was a roused jealousy at the idea of husband and wife enjoying the pleasures of reunion after a long absence. He had thought little about Bathsheba after the incident. Now, he had reunited this couple, and it angered him that he had brought these two back together by his own command.

David had to force his rational mind to override his heart and remember why he had brought Uriah home. The purpose was clear, the mission explicit. He could not lose sight of that fact even if his lust burned at the thought of these two enjoying this night.

The next day when word came to David that Uriah did not go home but, instead, spent the night in the palace barracks with Benaiah regaling the soldiers with stories of their exploits, David felt a peculiar mixture of irritation and relief. At least Uriah had not slept with her. But that was a foolish fantasy. That was the whole point of his return.

David could not show his vexation with Benaiah the next morning. Nor could he let on to Uriah that he had been told such. This was an unexpected development, but he had to remain calm and focused in order to devise a new approach.

David delayed the start of his busy day at court and had Benaiah summon Uriah. Instead of meeting on the terrace or in the Hall of the Lion, he instructed that Uriah was to join him behind the palace on the balcony of the north wall. He preferred the two of them taking a casual stroll along the upper tier.

When Uriah appeared around the corner of the back wall of the palace, David was leaning over the parapet watching the bustle of activity inside the Levitical compound. David smiled and opened his arms to receive him. He had to maintain a jovial mood. He could not slip and let Uriah suspect anything was amiss.

"I see you took a bath and put on fresh clothes." David gripped Uriah's shoulders and prevented him from taking a knee.

"Even I could no longer stand myself." Uriah waved his hand under his nose.

"And your wife…" David gave a spicy chuckle as he wagged his finger at his friend, pretending he did not know precisely how Uriah had passed the night. "I am sure it was filled with pleasure."

Uriah did not try to break free from David's hold on his shoulders, but his gaze dropped, and he winced as if from a slight internal pain.

David did not let go but bent his knees to look into the downcast eyes of his friend. "You did go home last night, did you not?"

It was not an inquiry but a stated assumption.

"My lord…" Uriah began, but then he wavered.

"The food I sent home with you." David had to tamp down his frustration at Uriah's hesitancy. "Was it not delivered?"

"My lord, the food was superb, but I did not partake of it at home with my wife."

"I do not understand." David took a step back. He must remain calm. He must not reveal a hint of irritation. "Please explain."

"I shared the portion with my lord's servants and fellow soldiers."

"Well and good. Just like you, but you did go home," David said. "You have the clean smell and the fresh clothes to prove it."

"My lord, I did not go home last night." Uriah raised his hands to affirm the truth.

"What is the matter with you?" David blurted, but then immediately restrained his annoyance. "I mean, you have been at the front for months, traveled a long distance to get here and…and you do not go home?"

David was dumbfounded, not by the oddity of Uriah missing out on a night home from the front, but that his perfect plan was foiled. He took a step toward the balcony wall and placed a hand on the protective barrier. He needed to steady himself, needed a moment to think. He would give Uriah a chance to explain himself.

"Why ever did you not go home and enjoy your wife's company?"

Uriah eased beside David. Side by side they looked out over the compound.

"My lord, you see the Tabernacle on top of Mount Mariah." Uriah direct-ed David's attention to the dwelling of Yahweh. "The Ark of the Covenant, the Mercy Seat where Yahweh rests is housed in a tent. For generations Israel and Judah sheltered in tents. The king's army now lies on the face of the field and sleeps in the open exposed to the elements as we lay siege to Rabbah. I could not in good conscience go to my house, eat and drink with my wife, and take pleasure with her. Upon the life of the king. Upon the life of my soul, I could not do such a thing."

In all conscience. In all good conscience.

David could not believe what Uriah had said. He faced the compound digging his fingers into the stone parapet. If he turned to Uriah, he was liable to strike him. He must collect himself. He must adjust to this new predica-ment. A new option must be devised.

"Stay one more day." David threw up his arms in a moment of inspiration. "I have a busy day ahead, but return to the palace this evening, and we shall dine together. You, me, Benaiah, just like old times. I wish Jozabad and Elea-zar could join us, but they are at the front. Come back tonight, and we will eat and drink and drink some more."

David could not help his jabbering. His nervous tongue spilled words, hoping to latch onto a coherent thought. He put one hand back on the wall to stabilize himself.

"Yes, my lord," Uriah said. "Like old times."

The moment Uriah disappeared around the corner of the palace wall Da-vid began gulping down big breaths. He did not let go of the top of the wall. Had he done so, he would have crumpled to his knees. He had to regain his composure. He could not waver. He must use all his human faculties to en-sure the desired outcome.

Chapter 14

DAVID SPENT HIS AFTERNOON IN THE HALL OF THE LION. HE endured listening to appeals from city leaders to finance public service projects in Jerusalem and the interviewing of candidates for a personal secretary. When Benaiah escorted the last of the people from the Hall, David slipped off his throne and went to the large cabinet with its open shelving crammed with documents. He pulled out random scrolls scanning the contents then piling them on the table beside the cabinet.

"What are your thoughts of these young men?" Benaiah asked.

"I like them. I like them all." David paid little attention to Benaiah while he discarded one scroll and opened another. "It has to be here."

"What are you looking for?"

"Nothing. Just a scroll Nathan gave me."

"The one with the oracle of Yahweh written out for you?"

"Yes. Yes, that one," David cried unable to hide his irritation at the question and of his own carelessness for losing it. "It must be here somewhere."

"May I suggest Seraiah as secretary and Jehoshaphat for your recordkeeping," Benaiah said. "They could help you arrange the scrolls in a proper order."

David stopped his futile search. The scroll might not even be in this shelving among the hundreds of documents. It might be anywhere, or it might be lost forever.

He pressed his hands against the table in front of the large cabinet.

"Yes, Benaiah. You are correct. You always are." It was a concession to his disorderly habits and easy distraction. "Appoint them both. They may begin immediately, with this mess." David waved his hand over the shelving.

"Wise of you, my lord. I shall make the arrangements."

"Then you will be free just to protect me." David pushed off the table and faced Benaiah with his hands upraised. "Protect me from myself."

Desperation edged into his mind. Attempts to be humorous were his only defense.

"It is what I am best at doing, my lord. I am organizing an elite group from outside the military ranks to be your protection detail."

"Brilliant," David said. "I look forward to a review of this group. Anything else?"

"Uriah is waiting for us on the terrace. The evening meal is prepared."

The whole point of this day had arrived. David must use all his skills to cajole and prevail upon Uriah to go home and sleep with his wife. A simple thing. It should not be that hard to appeal to a man's carnal appetite especially after so long an interval from such pleasures.

The dishes were savory. The wine flowed. The stars were in full splendor as the three men reclined on the cushions and ate and drank off the tables covered in the finest cuisine. The conversation flowed as freely as the sweet wine, reminiscences of past glories, of battles won, of plunder taken, of narrow escapes, of miserable conditions while living on the run from the mad king.

"After all these years, is it not a blessing to finally have a roof over your head and a wife to keep you warm?" David refilled Uriah's goblet with more wine. There had been enough talk of the past. The night was waning. David needed to direct the attention of his inebriated guest of honor toward home, a comfortable bed, and the pleasure that awaited.

"Yes. I never dreamed a man like me would have such good fortune." Uriah's speech was as sloppy as the wine that spilled down his beard after a dripping swallow.

David had pretended to drink as much as Uriah, but he only sipped from his goblet, only nibbled at his food. He wanted to remain sober and watchful, his mind clear enough to advance every incentive to go home. When he signaled the servants that it was the end of the evening, the sleeve of his robe slipped down and revealed his gold bracelet with the face of a lion on the front.

A new idea. A gift. A final reward.

"Take this, my friend." David removed the gold band and handed it to Uriah. "Let this wristlet always remind you of our evening together."

"It will remind me of our life together, my lord," Uriah garbled as he extended his unsteady hand toward the golden gift, his glassy eyes trying to bring the object into focus. "Thank you, my lord. This is a great treasure."

"Now, off to bed with you." David pointed to the night sky. "There is not much left of this night for you to enjoy your…enjoy a time of pleasure."

Benaiah rose from the table and lifted Uriah's limp body to his feet.

"Time to go home, Uriah." Benaiah slung Uriah's arm across his shoulder and led him from the table.

David rose to watch the two men stumble across the terrace.

Uriah waved the arm newly swathed with David's gift and started singing…one of his songs, one of his praises of triumph over his enemies.

David cringed at the slobbery rendition of his psalm.

Then Uriah pulled away from Benaiah. "I know the way, you old scoundrel. I know the way." Then he stumbled down the staircase to the palace barracks.

Yes, you do know the way, and you had best take it.

David slipped to the edge of his balcony and looked across the street. A light shone in the front window of Uriah's house. Bathsheba must have placed it there to guide her husband home. David had avoided looking across the street from his balcony since receiving word from Bathsheba of her current condition. His gazing down upon her rooftop had brought him to this dreadful state in the first place. He did not wish to be reminded of his rutting desires when he had seen her bathing in the pool. He did not want to be reminded of any portion of that night. Now, if the wine and food and the gift and this light in the window all wove their seductive spell, then he would never have to be reminded again. Life could go back to normal.

The last of the moon's tarnished brilliance was enough for David to see the street below. Even drunk, Uriah had time to descend the stairs, exit through the barracks of the palace guards, and lurch along the street to his house. He needed an end to this. He needed Uriah to do his part, but the man was nowhere in sight.

David leaned over the edge of the balcony for a better view. Perhaps he had missed Uriah. Perhaps he had staggered home concealed in shadow. Then he saw Bathsheba in the window looking in the direction she expected to see her husband.

David had not bothered to inform Bathsheba that he was bringing her husband home. That was a surprise visit he would allow Uriah to spring on her. By the light in the window and her expectant gaze, David surmised she had gotten word of Uriah's return from the front. But her husband did not appear, and Bathsheba withdrew from the window and extinguished the light of the lamp.

The window turned black, and David's heart sank. All his efforts to adjust the course of his past actions had been in vain. "What a fool I have been," David mumbled.

He drew his robes around him against the chilly air. He felt his wrist where the golden band had been. Its absence caused an itch. He scratched at the bare skin, and then a nauseating sensation as though a creature began rising from a dark region he never knew existed. A new thought, a new plan, a new alternative to this whole sordid circumstance was needed. Perhaps this disturbance below his heart was the rumbling of another course of action.

He felt he might retch, and he braced his hands on the balcony wall. As the bilious wave passed through him, it left behind a vision of a battlefield, of an army, his army, of men lying slain on the field, his men, of one man in particular, his guest of honor at tonight's dinner, dead by a thousand cuts.

David spun around pressing his back against the parapet for support. He gasped for air as if a great weight pushed all the wind out of his chest. He could not wish for this outcome. He could not wait or hope for this vision to be reality. It had to be a certainty, and it was within his power to make it so.

David left the balcony and dashed across the terrace into the Hall of the Lion.

"I should have thought of this earlier and not wasted these last two nights," he grumbled while rummaging through shelves of scrolls, looking for clean papyrus, a stylus, a small pot of colorant, and a stick of wax. Scrolls fell from the shelving and dropped onto the table until he found the materials needed to write to Joab, his commander in the field.

He ignited a straw stem from a torch mounted next to the cabinet then lit the oil lamp on the table drawing it close to the clean papyrus. Good light was required for his words to take proper shape. He yanked a stool from underneath the table and sat.

He had no need to compose himself to organize his thoughts. He just needed to issue the order, scribed by his hand, sealed with his seal. Uriah had every chance to save himself. Now, a heartless decision was made and a cruel order written. He whispered the words as he wrote waving his other hand over the wet coloring hastening the drying of this death sentence.

"Place Uriah at the front lines where the fighting is fiercest. Then withdraw from him, so he will be struck down and die."

The spoken and written word set in motion the brutal reality.

David blew his breath on the papyrus drying the letters. When he reached for the wax stick to leave his seal upon the order, he saw an open scroll lying on the table.

Nathan's scroll.

David rolled it up and placed it to the side. The first order of business for the new secretary was to organize this untidy cabinet.

Satisfied his words would not smudge, he heated the wax stick in the flame of the oil lamp and dropped a blot beneath the order. He took his signet and plunged the embossed face of the lion into the warm wax, then removed it to watch the fierce expression harden into shape. After allowing it to cool, he folded the papyrus to a quarter of its size sealing it shut with a thick line of hot wax.

A judgment made. A death warrant written. Permission to execute, granted.

When Uriah came to him, he was in a pitiful state, apologizing for the disorder of his foggy brain.

David almost felt sorry for him. If he had just gone home and spent the night at his house. In his drunken condition, there was little expectation Uriah would have been able to take pleasure with his wife, but David cared nothing for that. All he had to do was spend one night at home and all the talk of Bathsheba expecting a child would be explained. David would not have been forced into this drastic decision.

Hungover and pale, Uriah struggled to stand straight when David handed him the letter for Joab. Uriah gave it a brief glance before stuffing it inside his leather pouch. Then he raised his arm with the gift of the king's bracelet around his wrist. "My lord, we miss you out there with us in the field," Uriah said, his voice turning quivery. "Like the old days when we were scrambling for our lives."

"Well, it is no longer like the old days." David forced a smile. "Now, off with you. Tell Joab to hasten a victory."

Uriah hesitated as if confused about what else he might say or if David needed to add more instructions for the commander, but David had nothing else to express, his impatience and temper rising with every heartbeat.

"May Yahweh be with you, my lord," Uriah said before stumbling back across the terrace, his legs not yet functioning after last night's indulgence.

David watched Uriah depart the palace. *Men die in battle all the time.* One life must be forfeited to protect him, the king.

He was king.

Chapter 15

DAVID REACHED INSIDE HIS ROBE AND REMOVED NATHAN'S scroll. He was relieved to have found it before anyone knew he had misplaced it. He held a direct word from Yahweh. "Go and tell my servant David," it began. Yahweh was paying attention to him. Such a word was both a comfort and cause for disquiet. In his wilderness years, he had so often begged for Yahweh to make Himself known to him. He held written proof that the Almighty was a constant in his life.

"My lord, do you wish for us to add that scroll to the inventories?"

David looked up from his throne startled to see Seraiah and Jehoshaphat standing in front of his desk and open shelving. The studious young men were studying the scrolls and tablets for their proper categorization. The mess he had made of all his documents was finally becoming organized. It had taken days, but progress was being made, and soon all these records would be sorted and in the proper cubicle.

Seraiah and Jehoshaphat were eager to please, but David was reluctant to part with the scroll after it had gone missing.

"These are important words for me." David pressed the scroll against his chest. "Important words the prophet Nathan conveyed to me directly from Yahweh."

"They are of the utmost importance, my lord." Seraiah bowed his head, a reverent tone in his voice. "The words of Yahweh to the king."

David held out the scroll and read aloud. "I took you from the pasture and from following the flock to be ruler over My people Israel." David lowered his hand. "You know I was a shepherd, lived out in the hills and pastures of Bethlehem tending sheep?"

The two men exchanged puzzled glances as if unsure how they should answer.

These young men were from wealthy families and had never known hardship. They were trained in letters and the mercantile trade. Their clothes were designed and fashioned from the finest material and by the finest tailors. Their fathers had made significant contributions to the king's treasury, and thus there was access to royal opportunities. David could not fault them for being born into privilege. He could not fault them for their soft physical features, their aromatic smells, and latest styles of fashion. He could not fault them for having excellent minds and willing natures to help organize the life of their disorganized king.

David marveled at such efficient and quiet work reading over the documents. It made him feel useful when asked for clarification of a word or phrase. Once this clerical work was completed, David would transfer the bulk of these accounts to the department of historical records. He could not help a twinge of resentment at the thought of his uncommon life becoming a written record to be stored on a shelf.

"Have either of you slept outside on hard ground under the stars?" David asked.

His question appeared to stump them, and David knew that neither of them had never entertained such an idea.

"My lord?" asked Seraiah.

"Never mind." David rolled up the scroll and handed it to Seraiah. "After you make copies, find a special place on my shelving for this scroll."

"Yes, my lord." Seraiah took the scroll and returned to the task at hand.

David nestled into the comfort of his cushioned throne. He stared in wonder and amusement at the ease and efficiency of the two men reshuffling and reshaping copies of stories and archives compiled since establishing Jerusalem as the capital city.

How far David had come from the hills of Bethlehem, from being a soldier and a captain, from living off the land. He placed his hands on his belly. It jiggled instead of remaining firm. He raised his arm and flexed. The skin was pale and leathery, the battle scars whitening, and the muscles strained only to form the shape of a small hill. When was the last time he had held a spear? When was the last time he had gripped his sword and sliced the air let alone the head of an enemy? How long had it been since he had known any form of hardship?

David never dreamed he might miss his former life, of nights under the stars, of composing songs with his old kinnor wrapped in a lion's pelt, a lion he had killed. He could not remember the last time he saw it or played it.

"If you find any copies of my songs and poems in that clutter, set them aside," David said. "I want to revise them before giving them to Asaph to arrange for the musicians and vocal troupes."

"Yes, my lord." They spoke together without breaking concentration.

David lifted his crown from his head and held it in front of him. He had been a good and conscientious shepherd, a good soldier, slain a giant, followed by "tens of thousands," as the song went. Israel had suffered under the mad king, and David had restored her, made her whole. David had brought low the enemies of the nation, had conquered Jerusalem, and was now transforming it into the center of the world with its beautiful new buildings and residences, lush gardens, and, of course, his palace. He had brought the Ark of Yahweh into the City of David and was gathering the materials for its future permanent housing, built one day by an heir of his loins. The psalms and poems he had composed were being recorded and performed by the Levite singers and musicians.

As he looked through the empty space inside the oval of his crown, he yearned for a deeper sense of purpose. The signs of his mortality were creeping into his body, and he had to tamp down a rising panic. David was not ready to accept any notion of his own decay and death, not ready to be forgotten, shut up in the darkness of Sheol, his life and songs becoming legends or bedtime stories. He was a man of action. He would not tolerate thoughts of self-pity.

"My lord," Benaiah said as he rushed into the Hall of the Lion ahead of Abishai, David's nephew and brother of Joab, commander of the army laying siege to the Ammonite city of Rabbah.

David returned the crown to his head and stood. For Joab to send Abishai home from the front carried more meaning than an ordinary messenger.

"My lord, Abishai has arrived from the siege of Rabbah." Benaiah motioned for Abishai to step forward.

Abishai bowed low before David, knees and head on the floor, a more than normal show of respect. This was a sign his nephew carried a burden of news.

"Rise, nephew," David said. "What news do you bring from Joab?"

"My lord, Joab your commander sends his greetings to the king, and he desires for me to relate an urgent report of the siege of the Ammonite capital."

Abishai remained on his knees until David reaffirmed his command to rise, and then Abishai got to his feet.

Abishai removed a letter from his pouch and held it out to David. The papyrus was wrinkled and smeared with dirt, but it had been folded into quarters. Joab had sealed it with the signet mark of the commander. The instant he recognized it was the same one he wrote to Joab, the blood froze in his veins. Why had his letter been returned? It was obvious it had been opened and read. Had anyone other than Joab read the contents of his order?

"This letter...from Joab..." The moisture in his mouth evaporated and his tongue thickened. He did not reach to take the letter. "How is it with the commander? How is it with the army?"

"My lord, I am to tell you that we were unable to find a breach into the city of Rabbah. The walls of the city are high and well-fortified, and the citizens are supplied and able to endure a long siege. The Ammonite warriors are fierce defenders of their city. In the last few days, the commander of the king's army chose to strike Rabbah hoping to capture the royal citadel and cut off the water supply. We struck at first light and were successful in drawing the Ammonites outside the city gates. The fighting turned fierce, but we were able to drive them back. As we neared the gates, the archers shot arrows down upon us from the city walls and some of the king's men fell in battle. Moreover, the king's servant, Uriah the Hittite, is dead."

It was time for the hypocrisy of emotion, time to show a flare of anger.

David snatched the letter from Abishai's hand. "Why did Joab allow the army to be drawn back to the city gates? Has he lost his mind? He should have known they would shoot arrows from the walls."

David waved the letter in the air, a continued feint of wrath. "Joab should have learned from history when that woman threw a rock down upon someone's head when he was storming a tower or something. Jehoshaphat, help me here. I know I read it in one of the records."

"Yes, my lord," Jehoshaphat replied. "The prophet Samuel and his students recorded the story in a collection from the time of our judges. There was civil unrest in Israel. Abimelech, son of Gideon, a great warrior, wished to be a king. He led attacks on different villages. When he tried to capture the city of Thebez, he got too close to the citadel and a woman dropped a stone upon his head. Abimelech had his armor-bearer run him through with his sword so it would not be said he was slain by a woman."

"There, you see?" David turned back to Abishai. "Lessons from history."

No one in the Hall reacted and the steam went out of his rant. The letter trembled in his hand. He did not want to reveal the wave of his anxiety, so he broke the seal on the letter and opened it. That David would read this message from his commander in the field was a show of control, but the words he read were his own words, his order for Joab to do the very thing that had just been reported. He braced himself against his throne glancing at the others trying to judge the faces of those standing silently before him. No one viewed him with concern or suspicion, so he refocused his eyes on the bottom of the page beneath the waxed seal of the king.

Written below the seal of the Lion of Judah were the gut-wrenching words scribed in Joab's bold hand, "Your servant, Uriah the Hittite, is dead." There it was on the same papyrus, the written order, the written result, sealed with the commander's official signet.

His stomach hardened into a knot, and his lungs expelled a blast of air. He had to slap his hand over his lips to keep the air from completely escaping. This reaction was not feigned. This grief was real, sharper and more intense than he ever expected. The power of his written words now manifested in the stark reality of blood and death by his secret order. He gripped the arm of his throne and fell into the seat. He was alone, his mind adrift, floating over a battlefield covered in bodies, his eye finally settling upon the blood-soaked corpse of Uriah.

David knew he had to speak, but the words refused to come. He stared at the letter and refolded it along its natural creases closing out the reproving words. This letter could not find its way into the king's archives. These words would be hidden, his guilt never brought to the light. He stuffed the papyrus into the inside pocket of his robes.

"Say this…" David instantly became choked on the salty rheum gathering in his throat. He swallowed hard and took a deep breath. "Say this to encourage Joab: 'Do not let this upset you; in battle the sword devours one as well as another. Now strengthen your attack against the city and destroy it.'"

There it was; his assault on both husband and wife, one sent to Sheol, the other…he did not know what to do with the other. Death had covered one secret, but could there be a reckoning beyond death?

"I want Uriah brought home, and I want him buried in Abner's tomb, a warrior's tomb, with all honors due him. Now leave me."

Everyone bowed and immediately cleared the room.

"Benaiah, not you," David said. "Please stay."

Once it was just the two of them, David grabbed Benaiah and began to weep. The king's tears brought Benaiah to weeping. David was no longer king, Benaiah no longer his chief bodyguard. They were two friends grieving the death of their companion.

"I must go to the lady Bathsheba." David pulled away from Benaiah's embrace and sat back down on his throne.

"May I summon her to the palace instead?" Benaiah asked as he wiped his eyes.

"No," David replied. "I shall go to her."

"But, my lord, this is unusual."

"This is our friend, Benaiah. This is his wife. I shall go to her."

"I shall arrange an escort."

"No, only you must bear witness," David insisted. "Just the two of us and under the cover of darkness, so as not to draw attention. You may send word ahead for her to expect a visit in the evening, but do not tell her it will be the king. Leave me until then."

Benaiah plodded out of the Hall of the Lion under the burden of grief.

David waited until Benaiah had closed the large doors behind him. The hall was empty. His table and cabinet shelves were in order, the documents arranged. He reached inside his robe and removed the crumpled papyrus. There was no place for this document, no clean slot to store this written order. He crammed it back into his pocket. He stretched over the surface of his table and pressed his hands upon it. In the light from the oil lamp, he saw his shadowy reflection on the clean tabletop.

He extended his head toward the lamp and blew out the light.

"I am king," he whispered.

David lifted the hood of his robe over his head when Benaiah knocked softly on the door of the home of Uriah and Bathsheba.

He had not seen her since that night she came to him. He had thought of her a thousand times, but the pleasures of remembering her beauty could not change what he had done. No matter how he preferred to imagine a more pleasing scenario of the two of them, he could not wipe away the stain of his assault. It would always blemish the conscience and sully future encounters.

"My lady, it is Benaiah, friend to your husband, Uriah," he said when the voice coming through the door asked to identify himself. "I come in the name of the king. We have a report of your husband. We mean you no harm."

The door opened only a crack. The light from the lamp revealed a haggard, fearful face. The beauty David remembered was absent.

"My lady, may we enter?" asked Benaiah. "We have news from the front."

"We?" She raised her lamp to see who might be in company with Benaiah.

When David pulled back the hood of his robe she gasped, a natural reaction, but David knew it came from a place of fear, not a pleasant surprise.

"I am sorry for this late hour, my lady," David said. "I…we mean no harm."

David wanted Benaiah at his side when he told Bathsheba that Uriah was dead. He needed a protector. He was not sure how he might react after not seeing her for so long. Could he control himself?

He had lost control over to his base compulsions once before, and the consequences had brought him to her door, the bearer of news of her husband's death by his own order. The killing of Uriah on the battlefield was his effort to acquit his conscience and cover his sin. He may as well have shot the arrows himself.

Bathsheba retreated giving quick glances around her common room as if looking for a way to escape.

David paused at her threshold. "May we enter, my lady?"

Bathsheba nodded, and David stepped into the common room.

"Shall I wait in the street, my lord?" Benaiah asked.

"No," Bathsheba blurted, then placed her hand to her mouth. "I am sorry, my lord. This is so unexpected."

"I understand, my lady. Let me reassure you, I mean no harm."

"Thank you, my lord." She kept her eyes downcast, avoiding his gaze.

"Just remain in the threshold, Benaiah," David said. "Keep the door open."

David looked about the modest room, sparsely furnished with a table and two stools, the cooking fire in the open oven smoldering with an orange glow. A bowl of mutton and flatbread sat half eaten on the table. His arrival had interrupted her supper. His choices had more than interrupted her life, they had upended her life.

David felt treasonous in her presence. He had committed multiple treasons—her assault, her husband's murder, even the deaths of other warriors in his army. His order for Joab to lead an attack on Rabbah could all be used to establish his guilt. Being king was now a feeble argument as he looked upon her pitiful state.

The hand that held the lamp began to quiver, and she placed her other hand beneath the bowl to hold it steady.

"My lady, I wanted to be the one to give you this news," David began. "I did not want you to think that I was calloused in any way by sending a stranger to deliver it."

"What is the news, my lord?" asked Bathsheba.

"Your husband, my friend, our friend," he said, glancing back at Benaiah. "Uriah has died in battle. I regret telling you this. I regret his loss. I regret everything."

While he did feel regret, he could change nothing. All he could do was control the damage done to others and keep his actions concealed from the populace. If any other man had done what he had done, his life would be cut down the moment it was discovered. That would be justice, but he had set himself beyond justice.

Bathsheba did not speak, did not collapse, nor wail or moan, nor did her eyes fill with tears, all reactions David expected to witness. She leaned against the interior wall, balled her hand into a fist, and gently began to rap her chest, a single gesture of grief.

David did not expect her subdued reaction when he delivered his news.

In that quiet moment of her restrained grief, it came to him that he should offer more than condolences. He should let her know he had received her note informing him of his fatherhood to the child she carried, and that in the midst of her grief an offer, no, rather a solution he would extend to her. He would suggest a way out of this trying situation that would answer all public doubts and conceal all transgressions—his transgressions, for there was no other party to this predicament.

"I have sent instructions to my commander in the field to bring home the body of your husband, along with the others who died in the recent battle.

Uriah will be buried with honors in Abner's tomb. He shall rest beside Israel's first, great commander."

"Thank you, my lord," she said.

"I will send servants to your house to serve you during the days of mourning."

"That is not necessary, my lord."

"I understand your current state." David paused and gave a sidelong glance at Benaiah. He saw no look of suspicion flickering in his eyes that David might be expressing any other awareness besides understanding her state of grief. He returned to Bathsheba to see if she grasped his deeper meaning.

She had stopped the gentle, repetitive beating of her breast. The quivering of her other hand holding the vessel had ceased. She appeared ready to receive any offer he might tender.

"I am aware of your current state, my lady, and I wish to propose a remedy, one I hope will not be an offense to you. After your days of mourning are ended, I wish to invite you to the palace and live with me as my wife."

That did come as a surprise to Benaiah.

David raised his arm for him to not speak, then he extended his hand toward Bathsheba. She looked at the opened hand, then into David's eyes. If she clasped his hand, he would take that as a sign of accord, that she would not scorn his forthright offer.

She unfurled the fingers of her grieving fist and slipped them into his hand.

It was a pact.

"My lady," he whispered. "May Yahweh give you comfort."

She did not flinch when he tenderly kissed her hand, a second sign that they were in league together and that their shared secrets would remain in darkness.

Chapter 16

NATHAN LIFTED THE MENORAH OF PURE GOLD ABOVE HIS HEAD to brighten the darkness. The tips of the seven branches were a blossoming almond flower that held the oil. The seven lights provided the only illumination inside the cave. The prophet Samuel had assigned Nathan the task of proofing all the scrolls that were copied before storing them in the underground room beneath the archival building of the prophet's school.

Each time Nathan descended the stairs from his workplace with a new batch of scrolls, it was as if he descended into a holy chamber scented with the aroma of the dank earth. It was difficult to leave this sublime depository, but the shelves were empty, the jars had been removed, the last of the parchments and scrolls with the sacred writings had been carried out of the cave and were being prepared for transport to Jerusalem. The stories, the histories, the laws, the Ten Sayings of Yahweh were coming out of the bowels of the lair. These texts had been stored in the protective darkness of the earth when Samuel brought them from Shiloh after escaping its destruction at the hands of the Philistines. The blessed words no longer needed to remain in shadows. By order of the king, they were to be housed in the new archive in the safety of the City of David.

"Nathan, are you coming?"

He could not respond to Gad's question. Though empty, the space still contained the authority of the ancient writings, its hold on his heart had not set him free. If he answered Gad, then it was final. If he left the cave and climbed the staircase into his old study, his life would never be the same. He would never be the same.

He had lost count of how many times he had entered this cavern with copies of fresh parchments and spools of gevil containing the words of Yahweh. This was the only life he had ever known—coming to live in Ramah from Bethlehem first as a young student of Samuel, then becoming a scribe and teacher, and finally taking over supervision of the prophet's school once Samuel wished to devote his remaining years to write, to be with his beloved wife, Shira, and be in quiet communion with Yahweh. The master had passed the prophet's mantle to Gad and him, his true sons, he had called them. Nathan knew he was unworthy of such trust, but the mantle was passed, and his future was determined.

"The sun is setting behind the hills, and I am starving," Gad shouted. "Nathan, can you hear me?"

"Yes, yes. I can hear you," Nathan shouted in return.

Gad did not have the same attachment to this place. How could he? There was the brief stint he and Gad shared in service to King Saul in the early years of residence in Gibeah, but Nathan chose to return to Ramah and work in the prophet's school while Gad remained in service to the house of Saul. Now, Nathan had to leave. His world was changing, and he did not care for it. He was moving from the country to the city, and he did not care for that either. This was a difficult transition. The home and property of Samuel and Shira would always stay within the holdings of the prophet's school, but all the scholarly work would continue in Jerusalem. This property they would keep as a place for retreat.

Before he set the menorah down at the opening into the storage room, he gave one last look around the cave. He was saying good-bye to all the characters he had come to know and love in the histories of the chosen. Beginning with creation and on through the centuries with their array of ancestors, Nathan had given his imagination over to these people, their stories, and to the Almighty who had participated in the twists and turns of Israel's history. Except for copies dispersed to the local Levitical schools and priests throughout Israel, all of these writings had rested here, in the dark, waiting to come into the light.

It was time. The sacred words of Yahweh were on the move. It was no different than the exodus and the wanderings of the chosen. Yahweh and the people of Israel were always on the move.

He set the menorah at the entrance into the cave. It could be required again to bring light to the impenetrable blackness. Given the unpredictability of life, Nathan could foresee this small cavern beneath the *nevayoth* once again used to store and protect the words of the Almighty. He blew out the flame of each blossom one at a time until he was absorbed by the empty darkness.

Nathan made his way through the tight walls of the short passageway from the storage room into the anteroom with the staircase leading up to his old workspace. By the light coming from the opening in the floor above, he moved to the ladder and slipped into his sandals. Only bare feet were allowed to enter the sacred chamber. He could see Gad standing at the top holding a torch.

"Come up, my friend. I need to eat." Gad rubbed his belly.

Nathan did not have much of an appetite. He had been feasting on the memories of his life and work here in the *nevayoth* of the prophet's school. He was quite full.

Once he climbed out, Gad and Nathan closed the trapdoor, rolled the thick goat hide carpet over it, and then placed Nathan's old writing table and stool on top of the carpet. Nathan took the torch from Gad's hand and gave one last look at his working area, the space where he sat each day poring over copies of the writings. He had done this task for so long the words he had revised and copied day after day had attached themselves to his muscles and bones, their mysteries flowed through his blood and the meanings absorbed into his heart. There was no way to scour them from his soul.

"Jashar is serving our supper on the roof of the house." Gad stood at the door anxious to leave. "We can watch the sunset as we eat."

Nathan and Gad crossed the open area in front of the devotional center, descended the sloping hillside, and began walking the road back to the house of Samuel and Shira. They saw Jashar on the roof waving at them as they approached.

"He is a good man, our Jashar." Gad waved back in response.

"I agree," Nathan said. "He served the king well while he was in exile."

"Those were difficult years, and Jashar proved himself worthy."

"Do you think Jashar would like to remain here and manage this property as a haven for prophets and priests?" asked Nathan. "It could also be a place to withdraw for anyone who would like to devote time for study and quiet reflection."

"A prophet's school in the city and a place to retreat in the country," Gad mused. "I applaud your notion."

"We can ask him at supper," Nathan said.

"I do believe Jashar might enjoy a more contemplative existence after years on the run with the king," Gad mused. "And he could live in the master's house."

"I would like to see the house of our master and his wife inhabited once again," Nathan responded. "It does not feel right to have it empty."

"We must ask the king's blessing," Gad said. "He grew fond of Jashar and came to rely on him for many things during a very trying time."

"Let us approach the king after the wedding," Nathan suggested as they walked through the courtyard of the house.

"You have not said much about the wedding," Gad said. "Is it not generous of the king to take Bathsheba as his wife after the death of Uriah, and she great with his child?"

"The king is a force of nature." Nathan began to feel lightheaded, a reaction from an empty stomach. "He is a man of strong will. I know he is appointed by Yahweh, but my concern is the taking of too many wives and concubines. His heart could be led astray."

When they reached the outside stairs up to the rooftop, Nathan felt a sharp abdominal pain. Gad had taken a few steps ahead and turned back to Nathan bracing himself against the wall.

"What is the matter?" Gad asked, a note of concern in the voice of his dear friend.

"I am unsure." Nathan rubbed his belly. "A sudden pain."

"Well, that is easily explained." Gad chuckled. "Your belly is empty and sending its complaints. Now come. I can smell the lamb roasting on the fire."

"Must be." Nathan groaned. He watched Gad bound up the steps, his appetite spurring him forward. The pain subsided, but Nathan kept his hand against the outside wall of the house as he ascended the staircase with faltering steps. Once he reached the roof, he saw Gad and Jashar before the metal basin dishing roasted vegetables and lamb medallions into a bowl. The scent of the food wafting into his nostrils did not incite his taste buds. Rather, he was struck with nausea as he approached his friends.

When Jashar offered a bowl full of food, Nathan did not take it. He stood before the firepit, entranced by the flames.

"You both have served kings in your time as prophets," Nathan began. "I have little experience with such matters. My time has been spent with our master and among the prophets and priests with studious pursuits, writing and copying the words of Yahweh. I sense there is a new beckoning, a summoning of my life requiring more of me than I am capable. I had a taste of it when we wrote down Yahweh's words declaring the Almighty's intention to establish King David's house. I confess, all of it frightens me. How did you both do it? How did you serve the kings of Israel?"

Nathan lifted his eyes from the flames and looked into the bemused faces of his friends. They had not expected such a question, and Nathan, too, was surprised by his asking, but the need to know suddenly became critical.

"A sense of resolve propelled my life," Gad answered. "I always encouraged King Saul to follow Yahweh. No matter the circumstances or state of his heart. Until the end when the spirit of Yahweh departed and it was too late."

"I served only King David and saw many things that were painful to watch and record, yet I did not judge," Jashar said. "I learned from our master and from both of you that whether or not you are able to influence the king to keep his heart bent toward Yahweh, it is not my responsibility to see that he does. I have concluded that the role of prophet is to bear witness, to be truthful with what I record. The stories of the kings and the prophets and the people of Israel must be recorded so they might be remembered. Yahweh has given me no other task."

Nathan returned his gaze to the flames. The pain in his stomach had become a pressure on his heart, and he massaged his chest and groaned.

"Eat something, Nathan." Gad extended a bowl of food toward him. "You need to fill your belly with—"

Nathan cried out and bent double as if snapped in two. His heart was fragmenting. He fell to his knees. The invisible weight pressed down upon him making it impossible to rise. This was not like the first time. This was not the temperate visitation back in Jerusalem that caused him to be still and know that Yahweh was God, that Yahweh was present, that Yahweh was making contact and desired to convey a message. This was an intrusion, one born from impatience and divine purpose, of displeasure and resolve, an urgency that could not be ignored.

"Not the king, Yahweh. Not the king." As Nathan spoke these words an invisible power rushed through his body. He gripped the top of his robe, and with one surge of strength, ripped the garment from collar to hem. The moment he exposed his flesh to the elements and to his fellow prophets, the heat of the fire, the chill of the wind, the fingers of Yahweh pressed into his chest.

"No, Yahweh. Not the king." Nathan cried out with such force as to rend the sky as he had his robe. "Not the man after Your heart, O Yahweh. Not the one You plucked from the shadows to make him Your own. Not the king. Not the king. Not the king."

Chapter 17

GAD HAD NEVER WITNESSED THE POWERFUL IMPOSITION OF Yahweh upon another human. Samuel had such encounters, but he had no firsthand experience with such marvels. His only witness of such an incident was when Nathan had been subjected to the divine outpouring of Yahweh in Jerusalem when the king needed a message delivered. His friend had fallen into a quiet daze at the wonder of the Almighty, listening to the words of Yahweh in his heart and speaking them as Gad and Jashar wrote them down.

This night on the roof was nothing like that moment in the prophet's quarters in Jerusalem. This night on the rooftop was heartrending, almost combative, as if Nathan wrestled with Yahweh, unable to comprehend what was being required of him, even daring to refuse the will of the Almighty because it was too painful to comprehend, too painful to bear.

The will of the Almighty was too powerful to resist. The will of the Almighty carried a burning content that would consume all who bore witness to the fulfillment. The will of the Almighty was to break the heart of the king, and by Gad's observation, the message of Yahweh had broken the heart of his dear friend.

Gad and Jashar remained with Nathan throughout the night. Gad did not want to move Nathan until Yahweh had finished, but Yahweh did not relinquish Nathan's soul. Nathan was not to be a simple courier. This was a lamentation, a pouring out of sorrowfulness, Yahweh's sorrow, drenching the soul of his friend. He could not leave Nathan's side. The weight of such an outpouring of grief from the Creator of heaven and earth was too much to bear alone.

Gad instructed Jashar to keep the fire going in the metal basin, but the flames did not provide enough warmth. Gad wrapped Nathan in blankets and clung to his friend while in his fevered state, but Nathan's body continued its uncontrolled tremors. The fire, the blankets, the heat from Gad's own body could not calm his friend or bring him warmth. It was as though Nathan might shatter or burst into flame. Whatever his friend was experiencing originated out of the dark foreboding of the heart of his friend.

Yahweh was sharing the grief He bore with the one who must speak on His behalf. Before Nathan could say the words, the prophet must bear the weight of Yahweh's anguish and displeasure.

At first light, Gad helped Nathan descend the outside steps of the house while Jashar hitched a team of fresh horses to the wagon loaded down with baskets and clay jars full of scrolls and writing supplies. It was fitting that they should ride back to Jerusalem carrying the word of Yahweh in the wagon and in the heart of Nathan.

Gad had been able to get a little food down Nathan and some sips of water. His friend had refused the offer of wine, though Gad thought it a mistake. After such a troubling and exhausting night, Gad felt Nathan needed his strength restored.

Nathan spit out the fermented wine when it had touched his lips. "I must not. I must speak to the king with a sober heart. We must leave at once. I must speak to the king before the wedding."

"We will never make it in time," Gad replied. "You are in no condition to travel at a hard pace."

"Then we will speak with the king once we arrive," Nathan said, and then gripped Gad's arm with a forcefulness that made his knees buckle. "And you must go with me. I cannot do this without you."

"I will never leave you," Gad answered slowly getting back to his feet.

"And Jashar, you must stay behind," Nathan said, his voice beginning to quiver. "What we must do is…is beyond my ability to control. I do not know how the king will react. The consequences could be dire. You must live to bear witness. You must carry on if we are no longer able."

Before leaving Ramah, Gad and Jashar unloaded several of the clay jars and baskets of parchments and scrolls and stored them in the home of Samuel and Shira. Gad would take only copies of the divine manuscripts back to the conservatory in Jerusalem. Should anything happen to Gad and Nathan, Jashar would carry on the mission of the prophets within the kingdom of Israel.

Gad did not push the team of horses. He did not push Nathan to tell what he had experienced or what Yahweh might have spoken. It was unimaginable what terrible words his friend had to carry in his heart and deliver to the king. He only saw the results, the words striking deep, and Gad thought it best to let Nathan remain quiet and try to restore his strength on their return to Jerusalem.

Gad arranged a mattress of straw and quilts inside the wagon bed for Nathan to rest while he drove, but there was no resting for Nathan. Though he spoke during the trip, it was not to Gad. Nathan spoke to himself, to the Almighty, repeating words and phrases that Gad was unable to put into a logical context. Words that, at first, sounded as if they were shaping into a narrative he might follow, that Nathan might be rehearsing a tale to perform for an audience, then he would veer off into moans or cries.

The outbursts frightened Gad the most.

"You are the man," Nathan would shout. "You murdered Uriah. You took his wife. You are the man…the man after Yahweh's own heart. I gave you so much. I would have given you more. You despised Me. Why? Why? Why? Your secret has come to light."

What was Nathan saying?

These words were for the king, and when these accusations were spoken it could mean a death sentence. Gad had seen King Saul's murderous reactions to Yahweh's words spoken through the prophet Samuel. His master knew his life was in jeopardy whenever he had to deliver such messages. But his master feared Yahweh more. Not to be faithful with the divine oracles of Yahweh was indeed more fearful than the reaction of any man, even a king.

At midday, Gad parked the wagon at the front doors of the prophet's conservatory in Jerusalem. He instructed the students to unload the jars and baskets and store them in the reference room to be sorted later. He did not bother to explain Nathan's curious state to the students who were baffled by the disheveled appearance of their master. Gad simply told them to go about their business as he helped Nathan from the wagon and brushed the loose straw from his robe and out of his matted hair.

"We must leave at once for the palace," Nathan insisted.

"Would you like to eat something? At least change your garments?" Gad asked.

"We must go now." The lack of sleep, an empty stomach, a parched throat, the hard travel, nothing would deter his friend from going to the palace at once to face the king. It was the urgency of Yahweh.

Gad would go with Nathan, and if they should die on the spot after his oration to the king, so be it. He would die with his dear friend.

He did not have to help Nathan along the streets to the palace. He had to take two steps to his one just to keep up. Gad could not imagine such strength and determination in his friend. It had to be the force of Yahweh propelling him. Up the palace stairs, two at a time, along the walkway of the balcony, and into the open courtyard where he and Nathan were met with wedding guests applauding King David and Lady Bathsheba.

If his friend had intended to stop the marriage, he was too late. The king and his new wife had emerged from the Hall of the Lion where Zadok, the High Priest, had just officiated the ceremony.

The country was still at war with the Ammonites, and this wedding was not meant to be a spectacle. There were representatives from all twelve tribes, leaders of commerce and trade, civic leaders, a small chorus of singers and musicians, and a few retired military captains present in honor of Bathsheba's fallen husband. But the courtyard was not swarming with people. Several dining stations all faced the king's banquet table set at the base of the steps leading up to the Hall of the Lion. The bridal robe Bathsheba wore could not conceal the physical sign that she was near her time of giving birth.

Gad was met with perplexing looks from the people and heard their murmuring and whispered comments as he led his friend through the dining stations to stand before the king's table. The respectful applause for the new husband and wife died out once King David and Lady Bathsheba stood beside their seats of honor. The king took his goblet, raised it, and thanked the guests for their attendance, then saluted his new wife.

It was a surprise at the lack of real joy in the king's speech of thanks or praise of his bride. They both lacked the excitement of an eager couple. The smile on Bathsheba's face was strained. She was great with child, so Gad allowed this reality might hamper the joy of being married, even to the king.

Yet, Gad could not dispel the uneasy feeling that this wedding was nothing but a dutiful exercise, a display for appearance sake, the king's goodwill toward the wife of one of Israel's fallen heroes.

"Nathan. Gad. My two favorite prophets," David cried, raising a salute to them standing in the middle of the courtyard. "So glad you were able to attend the wedding, even if you are late and did not bother to change your clothes."

A polite jitter of laughter came from the crowd at the king's humor.

"My lord, I have come to tell you a story." Nathan ignored the king's greeting.

"Well, make it a good one. We are about to feast. And I hope you will give a prophetic blessing for the king and his new bride." David held out his hand to Bathsheba.

Gad caught Bathsheba's flinch as David clasped her hand, but he focused his attention on Nathan and his forthcoming story.

The king and his bride took their seats, which signaled to the guests they too could sit or recline before their tables laden with food.

"There were two men who lived in the same city, one rich and the other was poor," Nathan began, a voice clear and strong, echoing through the courtyard.

As Nathan moved toward the king's table, Gad fought the impulse to restrain him.

"The rich man had great numbers of flocks and herds, but the poor man had nothing except one little ewe lamb he had bought and reared."

Nathan began to turn in a circle, engaging the crowd with the illustration of a stark difference between the two men in this tale.

"The ewe lamb grew up with the poor man and his children. He loved this lamb so much he would share his food with it. The lamb would drink from his cup, even sleep in his arms. In this man's family, the ewe lamb was like that of a daughter."

Once Nathan made a complete circle, he began to inch his way toward the king.

Gad wondered where his friend was going with this story. Why had this narrative warranted such urgency? It seemed nothing more than a simple folktale, to be told around a campfire or to entertain children, not at the wedding feast of a king.

"Then one day a traveler came to visit the rich man, but the rich man did not wish to take a lamb or calf from one of his flocks or herds and prepare a meal for his guest. No, instead, the rich man took the ewe lamb that belonged to the poor man, he dressed and prepared it, and then served it to the traveler who had come to him."

Nathan stopped before reaching the table. Everyone including the king remained silent, waiting to see if there was more to this story, but Nathan said nothing.

Gad began to feel anxious at his friend's stillness. He took a few steps forward to pull him away from the table.

David broke the uncomfortable silence by slamming his goblet down on the table, splashing the red contents upon the robes of the bride and bridegroom. Bathsheba cringed and wrapped her arms protectively around her middle.

"I swear as Yahweh lives this rich man is a wretch who deserves to die," David exclaimed, rising to his feet. He braced his hands on the table as if it held him back from attacking the villain in the story or the teller of the tale. "Because this rich man showed no pity and did such a cruel thing, he should pay four times over for the life of the lamb he took."

Gad did not expect this outburst from the king. Such was the power of this story. The actions of the rich man had ignited David's quick temper causing him to condemn the deed with a severe sentence. A declaration with such vehemence brought the crowd back to its feet giving the king a vigorous ovation for his denunciation of the cruelty displayed in the character of the rich man.

Even Gad put his hands together to show his appreciation for the king's sound yet brutal judgment until Nathan raised his hand in the air that brought a quick end to the applause.

"You are the man," Nathan roared, dropping his arm away from heaven and pointing his splayed fingers in the direction of the king.

The boldness and sudden vehemence of Nathan's denunciation caused a collective gasp of shock, the last human sound in the courtyard. Until this moment, Gad, the king and his bride, and all the invited guests had no suspicion that Nathan would compare the rich man with David.

The next words Gad expected to hear was the king's order to expel the two prophets and put them under guard.

Instead, Nathan's voice broke the quiet. At first, Nathan was unable to speak. He only sobbed.

Gad inched closer to Nathan and laid his hands upon the shoulders of his friend. He would share the burden of delivery, the weight of Yahweh's words that Nathan had to flush out of his soul.

"This is what Yahweh, the God of Israel, says: 'I anointed you king over Israel, and I delivered you from the hand of Saul. I gave you the house of Israel and Judah. And if all this had been too little, I would have given you more. Why did you despise the word of Yahweh by doing what is evil in His eyes? You struck down Uriah the Hittite with the sword. You seized his wife to be your own. You killed him with the sword of the Ammonites. Now, therefore, the sword will never depart from your house, because you despised Me and took the wife of Uriah the Hittite to be your own.'"

Gad began to tremble. His eyes filled with tears. His own heart was breaking at Nathan's words. No wonder his friend had been so distraught at this revelation from Yahweh. He could not believe David could be guilty of such dark actions. Gad thought he knew David. He had served King Saul and witnessed the evil that consumed him. Had such blackness now consumed this king?

Gad wiped his eyes with the sleeve of his robe and saw Bathsheba clutching her armchair bent over sobbing and retching. Not only had the news of how her husband had died at the hand of the king come to light, but so had the king's assault upon her. The result of his lust was now apparent for all to see.

Gad remained attached to Nathan's shoulder as he moved closer to the king's table.

"This is what Yahweh says: 'Out of your own household I am going to bring calamity upon you. Before your very eyes I will take your wives and give them to one who is close to you, and he will lie with your wives in broad daylight. You did it in secret, but I will do this thing in broad daylight before all Israel.'"

David had been frozen until that moment, then his entire body began to shudder as if all his limbs were about to fly off into the air. Gad had gripped the back of Nathan's robes in anticipation of the king's wrath, but instead, David collapsed onto his throne.

The king opened and closed his mouth, but no words came forth, only garbled sighs and bays. He was a distressed animal, consumed by his wound.

"I have sinned against Yahweh," he finally uttered.

As if in concert with the king, Nathan also collapsed, but Gad was able to keep him from falling onto the ground. Nathan was not yet finished.

All in attendance heard the spoken truth of Yahweh and the king's response. David had sinned. He had tried to keep his crime against Bathsheba and the murder of Uriah hidden from the people of Israel, and now it had been revealed and confessed. This was not a parable. This story proved that a mighty man had become delirious with prosperity and power and had yielded to his depraved instinct for wantonness. David had been anointed king over the chosen people of Yahweh. Nathan had been present at the first anointing of David in his home in Bethlehem. Gad had been present on the other occasions, watching as the oils of Yahweh were poured out upon David's head.

The sweet scent of the holy ointments had now become a foul stench. The office of the king and the Almighty had been despoiled in the eyes of everyone.

After several heaving breaths, Nathan roused himself. He was not strong enough to stand on his own, so Gad positioned himself behind his back and wrapped his arms around his middle to hold him steady. Gad nestled his face inside Nathan's robes. He could not imagine his friend would have anything else to say, but if he did, Gad did not want to hear it. He had heard enough, seen enough. His memory would be forever seared.

"Yahweh has taken away your sin. You are not going to die," Nathan said. "Yet, because you have shown utter contempt for Yahweh, causing the enemies of Yahweh to scoff and blaspheme the name of the Almighty, the son born to you will die."

The howling from the king echoed through the courtyard rising above the sobbing of Bathsheba, the painful groans of the tribal leaders, the weeping of wives and servants, even the horrified grumbling of the military men, shocked that their king had acted with utter lack of conscience. Gad stuck his head around Nathan's shoulder and saw the king collapse over the table, scattering the food and drink that had been set before him. Bathsheba had fallen to the ground, her frantic handmaidens trying to comfort her. Nathan's prophesy had brought a great sorrow upon the courtyard.

The king of Israel, the giant-slayer, the poet and composer of songs, the one who had conquered his enemies, the one who had captured the heart of Yahweh and adored by the nation of Israel was slumped over his table racked by uncontrollable weeping.

"We must leave now," Nathan uttered, his strength depleted. "But I cannot walk."

Gad maneuvered beneath Nathan's arm draping it over his shoulder. It was as if his friend's legs had turned to stone. Gad had to buttress his heart against this scene of grief as they limped out of the courtyard.

"I am broken. My heart is broken," Nathan kept repeating as Gad led them away.

How would Gad chronicle this moment?

How would he describe the broken hearts of Yahweh, of his friend, his king and his new bride, his nation? How would his own heart ever be made whole again?

Chapter 18

DAVID ROLLED ONTO HIS STOMACH AND STRETCHED OUT HIS legs and arms releasing energy through his fingers and toes in short bursts as if flinging and kicking away unwanted objects. With each expelling of energy, he heaved a bestial groan, exorcising a demon that had slipped inside his soul. Every muscle in his body ached and burned. If he burst into flames, it would be a welcomed conflagration, but there was no blaze, not even a spark.

I must be like the burning bush Moses saw on the mountain. Burning but not consumed.

David placed the palms of his hands onto the chamber floor and forced his knees beneath his middle. He pushed up into the position of a child on all fours, old enough to test his mobility before taking his first steps.

The child.

That was why he was here in his dim chamber, lying on the hard surface, not in his bed. He knew too well what it was like to lie on the ground, to have a fitful sleep on the cold hard earth, but there was no sleep or rest. His chamber floor provided no comfort. Its firm surface was indifferent to his agony.

If their child had been born dead it would have been easier to bear. When the midwives washed the boy and wrapped him in a blanket, David was handed a child that appeared healthy, perfect in every way. Then Bathsheba insisted he hand over her son. But was it not his son as well? Her face was exhausted by hard labor, but she was fierce in her insistence, even fearful he might hurt the child.

He would never hurt this child.

"We must give him a name," David said as he handed over the boy.

"No," she blurted, and immediately attached her son to her breast.

David remained bent over and traced a finger down the boy's arm and into his little hand. He needled his finger into the tiny palm and the boy's fingers curled around the finger of the king. When David tried to gently remove his finger, he felt the tremors in the little hand and a clasp that was more from pain and terror. David placed his hand upon the boy's chest and head. His skin burned. The fevers began to rack his little body. He pulled away from his mother's breast and gave a violent howl. He viciously kicked his feet and waved his arm as if fighting off an assailant.

"Please leave," Bathsheba said as she rocked the child in her arms.

The moment David stepped away from the foul bed, soiled with the blood and water of mother and son, the midwives went into action. David backed out of the birthing chamber pausing long enough to see the midwives trying to take the boy from his mother and Bathsheba refusing. The screams of mother and child burst upon his ears, the desperate echoes pummeling his brain.

The child's fever had been transferred to David. The tiny fingers of his son had been a conduit of fire. It had happened so quickly, the birth, the cleansing, the swaddling, the tender passing of his son to his mother, and then the fever's lightning strike. The twisted pain that distorted his face. The violent strength of the body trying to cast off the agony. The howls of rage. How could all this be expressed in a newborn? How could he come into the world raging against the curse of his doom?

Did the child somehow know he was innocent, that he was paying a price for a debt he had not incurred? Did he know he had gripped the finger of the one who was guilty? Who could not save him? Whose actions had brought on this terror?

David staggered across the courtyard to his private chambers. He ordered Benaiah to keep out all who might enter. He refused to see anyone. He would have no audience with court assistants, tribal nobles, dignitaries, or priests. He would not dine at the king's table with invited guests. No onlookers would observe his private agony.

David requested Gad to come to the palace. He wanted the prophet near him, and for he and Benaiah to remain just beyond the door. He wanted the comfort of knowing they were within the sound of his agonized voice should he need to summon them.

He lost track of time. There was no day or night. There was only his chamber with its hard flooring and the weak light from a single oil lamp, the flame sputtering when David heaved his heavy breath in sobs and gasps. The entire world was confined inside this chamber, and there was no relenting from the torment of the emptiness of his belly, the parchedness of his throat, the hollowness of his soul. He was naked except for a rank loin cloth. The fire of his skin made it impossible for him to be clothed. He never knew so much grief could pour out of a human being.

David had grieved before. The death of his dear friend Jonathan had brought him to his knees in despair. But this was a different grief brought on by exposed truth of his iniquity, and it was brutal and unrelenting. If Nathan's verdict came to pass, that his newborn son must die, then he wished Yahweh would take him as well.

"The child. The child. O Yahweh, have mercy on the child, this innocent child," David pleaded. It was all he could do, plead for mercy.

David was aware of the presence of others but unable to comprehend their whispered communications. Benaiah, Gad, and the servants were concerned for his well-being, wanting him to eat and drink, bathe and put on fresh clothing, but he refused. This was not a time for normal routines. This was a time out of joint, a time when complete attention was to be paid to the child. Nothing else existed, and if at any moment his attention would stray, the painful shrieks of the infant and a mother's wailing heard from across the courtyard brought his focus back to his chambers and its hard floor.

It was the silence that finally drew him out of the agony of his suffering.

The shrieks had ceased. A loud final wail followed and then a chorus of moans and keening from all who attended mother and child. Then silence.

He knew. He knew the end had come, yet he had to ask. He must have it confirmed from those he trusted, who had stood near for all the days of his agony.

"Is the child dead?"

An answer was not forthcoming, and the silence continued. He could hear the beating of his heart increasing. He could hear the final echoes of a mother's sorrow inside his head. He could hear the sputtering of the flame in the oil lamp as a slight breeze blew through the sheer curtains of his chambers. He could hear the whispering.

"Speak to me, Benaiah." David turned his head and looked at Benaiah and Gad standing at the entrance into his chamber. "Is the child dead?"

"Yes, my lord. He is dead."

The end had come. The intercession had failed. Continued pleas for mercy on behalf of the child were now vain.

He should have expected this end. How could he be a proper advocate for the child, one to plead the case of the innocent? He was not innocent. He was steeped in his own guilt, so why would the Almighty pay attention?

David rolled onto his stomach, gradually rising to his feet. His head was spinning, and he faltered.

Benaiah and Gad rushed to catch him. "You must eat something, my lord," Gad implored. "You have gone too long with only broth and a few crumbs—"

"I cannot eat and drink." David's throat was raw, his voice the rasp of an old man. "Not yet. I must bathe and put on fresh clothing. I must go to the house of Yahweh. I have failed in swaying Yahweh, but the justice of the Almighty has been met, and I am compelled to worship."

"It is a cruel justice, my lord," Benaiah said.

"And shrouded in mystery," added Gad.

"My guilt has fallen on the innocent," David said. "How this can be is a wonder."

It was a wonder. He had lured Bathsheba to the palace on false pretenses. He had assaulted her behind the colonnades and ignored her afterward until he received word she was with child, the child that was now dead. He had ordered her husband, his loyal friend and subject, home from war with similar false pretenses, and after two days of coercion that failed to entice his friend to go home and enjoy the pleasures of his wife, he ordered this honorable man to be killed.

He wrote out those orders with his own hand.

That he had stooped so low to cover his lust was the true wonder, not Yahweh's reaction as portrayed by Nathan. The man after Yahweh's own heart had assaulted the woman who was now his wife, had murdered her former husband, and now had been responsible for the death of an innocent child. All three were innocent, victims of his pride, his power, his sense of entitlement, his lechery.

There was nothing left for him to do but repent.

He did not drive to the house of Yahweh in his chariot, nor was he driven in a carriage. He did not order the stable master to saddle Ardon. He did not try to covertly slip out of the city and up the mountain to the Tabernacle with the hope of being unseen. All he had done he had tried to keep hidden, but his dark actions had been brought into the light. What was the use of hiding?

After his bath, after applying olive oil to his dry skin, and after changing into fresh garments, he walked through the streets of the City of David in full daylight, the eyes of its citizens staring at him in the disquieting spectacle of their broken king. He walked with no protection detail. He walked alone, legs and body weakened from lack of food and drink, through the streets, out of the city gate. He kept his eyes fixed as he passed through the crowds who reacted in silent reverence bowing before their shattered monarch.

When he reached the Tabernacle, Abiathar and Zadok opened the curtains for him to enter then closed them once he passed through. The Levites and priests in the outer courtyard came to a standstill.

David walked past the slaughter tables and stopped between the Altar and the Laver. He gazed at the closed curtains that concealed the Holy Place and its sacred furnishings. Just beyond was the Holy of Holies where that most sacred of objects resided, the Ark of the Covenant with the winged cherubim of the Mercy Seat that fashioned the throne of Yahweh.

David had danced before the Ark while it was paraded through his city and upon the mountain of Yahweh where Abraham had come to sacrifice his son Isaac. He was now the sacrifice. He was now the one who would willingly throw himself upon the altar. He was the one in need of mercy, forgiveness, of the great compassion of Yahweh if only it might be available. He had thrown off all restraint and broken covenant. What he had done could not vanish like a mist by the divine breath of Yahweh just by rote confession.

David raised his arms, but that was not enough. He took the crown from his head and tossed it to the ground, but that was not enough. He rent his garment, but that was not enough. He dropped to his knees, but that was not enough. He began to weep, but that was not enough. He fell upon his face digging his fingers into the earth and pouring the dirt granules upon his head, but that was not enough.

Nothing was enough. Nothing he could do was enough.

Only Yahweh was enough.

> *"Have mercy on me, O Yahweh,*
> *According to Your loving kindness;*

According to the multitude of Your tender mercies
Blot out my transgressions.
Wash away my wickedness, cleanse me from my sin.
I know my transgressions. My sin is always in front of me.
Against You, only You have I done this evil in Your sight.
So You are proved right in Your sentence
And justified when You judge.
I was born in guilt and sinful since my mother conceived me.
Yet You desired faithfulness even in the womb;
You taught me wisdom in that secret place.
Purify me with hyssop, and I will be clean;
Wash me, and I will be whiter than snow.
Let me hear once again joy and gladness.
You have crushed my bones; let them rejoice and dance again.
Hide Your face from my sins and blot out my iniquity.
Create in me a pure heart, O Yahweh,
And renew a right spirit within me.
Do not banish me from Your presence
Or take Your Holy Spirit from me.
Restore to me the joy of Your salvation
And grant me a willing spirit to sustain me.
Then I will teach sinners Your ways
So they will turn back to You.
Save me from the guilt of bloodshed, O Yahweh,
The Lord of my salvation.
Then my tongue will sing of Your righteousness.
Open my lips, O Yahweh that I might sing Your praise.
You do not delight in sacrifice, or I would bring it;
You take no pleasure in burnt offerings.
My sacrifice, O Yahweh, is a broken spirit;
O Yahweh, You will not despise a broken and contrite heart."

When David returned to the palace, he did not bother to change his garments, filthy from lying prostrate on the ground in the courtyard of the Tabernacle. He did tie a sash around his robe, torn asunder by his sorrow and repentance, to cover his exposure. While he was at the Tabernacle, the child had been prepared for burial to be laid in a tomb dug out of a cave in the Tyropoeon Valley just beyond the western wall of the city. It was designated the King's Tomb, a resting place for members of the royal family when their life came to an end. The child, the nameless child, was the first to be buried in the King's Tomb.

The small procession that accompanied David and Bathsheba was instructed to remain silent. David did not want any vocal mourning as they trudged out of the city and into the valley. Bathsheba carried the wrapped body of their son all the way before handing the body to David. When he asked if she would go inside the tomb, she declined.

Once they returned to the palace David instructed the servants to set up a table in the courtyard and prepare something to eat. He had sequestered himself in his chamber for seven days refraining from the king's table, and he was ready to eat. He invited Bathsheba to join him, but she refused, and he did not insist. He watched her return to the room where she had given birth and had remained with her son until he died in her arms.

David wanted company, and he invited Gad and Benaiah to sit and eat. The two men had watched over him in his days of intercession for his son, they had accompanied him to bury the child, and now the three of them sat together and ate a simple meal of vegetables and mutton.

It took David to break the silence. "Gad, will Nathan come back to the palace?"

Gad stopped eating but did not immediately answer. He stared into his plate and slowly chewed his last bite of food.

"He need not fear me, my friend. Neither of you," David added.

"I have not seen him myself, my lord," Gad replied. "I have remained here with you at the palace since you summoned me."

"I believe the prophet does fear you, my lord," Benaiah offered. "His words were punishing."

"Brutally punishing. But true," David admitted.

"I have never heard the like before." Benaiah shook his head. "I hope never to hear such words again."

"I know what it is like to incur the wrath of a king," David said. "But I am not like my predecessor. I hold no anger toward Nathan or anyone else. I am too broken and empty to be provoked. I want only peace."

David placed his hand upon Gad's arm and gave it a reassuring squeeze which caused tears to appear in the prophet's eyes.

"Thank you, my lord," Gad said. "I shall tell my friend."

David removed his hand and took some mutton, sopping it in the juices of the cooked vegetables before putting it into his mouth.

"Something does puzzle me, my lord," Benaiah said. "A reverse order of things that I find strange."

"What is that, my friend?" asked David.

"Why are we eating and drinking?" Benaiah asked. "While the child lived, you fasted and wept, but now he is dead, and you eat and drink. We should be in mourning. He was your son. We just laid him in the King's Tomb. Should not the whole palace be in mourning? Should not you and all of us be sharing our grief by fasting and prayer?"

David looked at Gad to see if he might add a word.

"It is true, my lord," Gad said. "I do feel uncomfortable eating and drinking at this moment of grief even though you did invite us to your table."

David wiped his lips with a damp cloth and glanced toward Bathsheba's chamber. The curtains concealed the entrance. He wondered what she might be thinking. She had to be in such pain. She must be so bewildered by all that had happened to her because of his actions and frightened by the prospects of her future with him. He had to comfort her, to reassure her that all would be well. She need not be afraid.

"I pleaded with Yahweh for my innocent son," David began. "During those days he was alive, painful as they were for the lad, I fasted and wept. I thought who could know the mind of Yahweh. Perhaps the Almighty would pity me and have compassion on the child and allow him to live. But this was not to be. He is dead now, and I ask you, what is the purpose of my fasting? Do my prayers and fasting have the power to bring him back? I am the cause of all of this, and one day I will go to where my son now rests. He will never come back to me."

David stretched out his arms, placing a hand on the shoulders of Gad and Benaiah. "Thank you, my friends. Thank you for bearing witness. Thank you for breaking with tradition and sharing this simple meal. Thank you for your faithfulness to me."

He cast his eyes away from his friends.

"I now must try and bring comfort to my wife," he said.

David rose from his seat and walked toward Bathsheba's chambers.

Chapter 19

BATHSHEBA STOOD ON THE BALCONY OF THE COURTYARD OF the palace looking out over the City of David. The torchlight along the main streets gave Jerusalem a rosy glow like embers of a fire while the night sky was a gallery of stars circling the endless moonlight. She looked down upon the house she shared with Uriah, now inhabited by a new family, a reward to another of the king's mighty men who had distinguished himself in military service. She had been startled the first time she saw young children playing on the rooftop, splashing in the pool Uriah had assembled for her. These children might have been her own were it not for the all-consuming turn of events; the swooping in of a king hurtling her life into its long plummet. Only now had she begun to feel the volatile world around her was softening enough to break her fall.

Bathsheba had aged in such a short time, not in chronology, but by life-altering hardships beyond her control. She tried to remember the last time she had taken a conscious action of her own free will. She had chosen to marry Uriah. Was that the last choice she had made? It was the first that came to mind. Bathsheba had chosen to be happy with this man until he had been taken from her.

So much had been taken from her. She leaned over the edge of the balcony. The sound of sobbing burst from her throat followed by the pungent queasiness of her unsettled stomach, which reminded her of her last act of free will.

Not long after she and the king had carried their child to the King's Tomb, he had come to her. David entered her chamber, but neither spoke. They sat in silence until the king asked if there was anything he might do for her. She did not look into his face, but kept her head bowed, not out of respect, but in shame and sorrow. When she did not respond, he quietly slipped out of her chamber.

Each day afterward he returned. Each day he brought her food and drink and took her tray from the day before as he made his exit. Each day he brought her clean robes with lotions and perfumes. Once, he surprised her with flowers he had gathered during a ride into the Kidron Valley. One day, he came to her carrying two basins of warm water. He got down on his hands and knees and scrubbed the floor of the entire chamber. She sat on her bed while he worked. When finished, he left.

She swiped a finger along the floor examining it for a proper grade of his domestic work, but no residue darkened the tip of her finger. In the reflected light from the oil lamps, her ghostly image was mirrored upon the floor.

They rarely spoke during these visits. There was little need for words. He never asked anything of her, made no demand or gave any instruction. He was simply present, until the day when without words, she tugged on his sleeve as he scooted past where she sat. The moment she touched his palm David began to weep. It was her choice to clasp the hand of the king, and her action brought him to his knees. She laid his head upon her lap and ran her fingers through his hair as the grief flowed from his heart.

The quiet intimacy that followed brought on the same unsettling in her belly that she had known before. It frightened her the first time, and it frightened her now. This time she kept the secret, not sharing what she knew to be true, allowing the king and the servants to assume she was still in mourning for her first child. Bathsheba would always mourn her firstborn, only seven days old when he took his last breath.

She pushed away from the parapet and wiped her mouth with the sleeve of her robe. Her legs were weak, and she braced a hand upon the ledge until the stars behind her eyes dissolved and were replaced by the stars in the dark canopy above where she stood.

"Are you unwell, my lady?"

Bathsheba turned her head in the king's direction but did not release her grip on the ledge. She bowed her head in respect but did not bend her legs for fear of lacking the strength to rise.

"Sleep eludes me," she responded. "I thought the night air might do me good."

David eased next to her, and they both gazed at the city.

"I love this view of Jerusalem in the high middle of the night under the light of a full moon," he said.

"It is a beautiful city, my lord. One worthy of a great king."

The king trembled as if a chill had come upon him. He leaned over the parapet of the balcony, taking several deep breaths before he stood straight again.

"I am not worthy, nor am I a great king. I have begged the forgiveness of the Almighty," he said as he turned to face her. "But I have not begged your forgiveness."

The king knelt before her and took her hand. "I have sinned against Yahweh. I have sinned against Uriah, my friend and your husband. And I have sinned against you. I cannot live the rest of my life without asking for your forgiveness."

David kissed her hand, then released it.

The king remained kneeling before her. His arms hung limp at his sides, and he slumped back upon his knees with his head bowed low. He showed no sign he intended to rise but was prepared to wait in this humble posture. Bathsheba now had a sovereign's power, not the power to wield control over a nation with all its resources, but the control over a human heart, the heart of a king. She looked across the City of David. The king of this city, the king of all Israel, knelt at her feet waiting her response. She had never been asked such a question, but then she had never gone through such trauma. She had been broken by this man, and now he knelt before her broken himself, broken and contrite.

The memory of the evil done to her would never be completely banished from her mind, but by her choice to forgive, the sharp power of its puncture could be removed. No power on earth was its equal.

Bathsheba set her hand above the head of the kneeling king and let it gently rest upon his thick, wavy hair. "You are forgiven, my lord. You are forgiven."

David began to gasp, the air around him suddenly unbreathable. He rocked back and forth on his knees like a flagged beast after an exhaustive chase.

Bathsheba would have to help him to his feet. He was unable to rise on his own. She waited until the relief of his heart had been expelled before she took his hands and helped him to stand. The strength pulsating through her came as a surprise, but once the king was steady, he opened his arms to her. He did not pull her into his embrace but waited for her to step into his encompassing arms.

She would have to choose, and her choice would finish the request to forgive. She inched forward and laid her head upon his chest. The rapid beating of his heart sparked her own, and she curled her arms around his back. When the king's arms enveloped her, it was as if their combined warmth was enough to lift them off the terrace floor.

"Thank you. Thank you. Thank you," he said softly.

Resting in this embrace, Bathsheba found that her heart could find a future, both of them newly made that could fashion a fresh beginning.

"I could not leave without seeing you, without my attempt to put things right with you," David said. "I want a new future with you, with you alone."

"Why must you leave, my lord?" Bathsheba pulled away slightly so she could look into his face. "Where are you going?"

"Word has come that Joab has captured the royal citadel of Rabbah. I must go there and claim the victory."

"How long will you be gone?"

"I do not know," David answered. "The water supply has been cut off, and it is only a matter of time before the Ammonites must surrender."

Bathsheba now had a second choice before her. She had given her forgiveness, which had brought her an unexpected release from a burden she knew she could not carry alone. Her next choice was a test for them both. His reaction might not be one of relief or thankfulness, but he should know before he departed what lay ahead for both of them once he returned.

"My lord, you must come back alive. You must come back…to me."

"After all I have done, you would wish for my return? You would wish me such favor?" David was unable to conceal his astonishment.

"I ask not only for myself, but for our child," she said.

Her news forced David back against the protective wall of the balcony. He braced his hands against it and looked up into the sky.

> *"Yahweh is the portion of my heritage.*
> *Yahweh is the blessing of my cup,*
> *Yahweh holds my future secure.*

> *The boundary lines of my life have fallen in pleasant places;*
> *You have given me a delightful inheritance.*
> *I will praise Yahweh, who counsels me;*
> *Even at night my heart instructs me.*
> *I have set Yahweh always before me.*
> *Because Yahweh is at my right hand,*
> *I will not be shaken."*

Bathsheba did not wait to be invited back into his embrace, but boldly took him into her arms. "Return to me and our child," she said with an insistence, not a plea.

"This will be my last battle." He wrapped his arms around her. "I have no more heart for war. And when I return, it will be announced that you shall be at my side. I shall care for the others of my family, but you will have prominence. You shall help me rule. You shall be my only love. We shall begin anew."

Bathsheba had to be sure before Nathan returned to the palace. She had to be sure her son was healthy and that he would live, to see the scrunched face of surprise at being forced into the light. She had to see him twist his little head, raise his arms in defiance, not pain, at such rough handling, to hear the defiant cry of so small a creature that meant he was here for good. She needed to lift the child to her breast and feel the tug of deep hunger not the clamp of desperate pain. Only then would she feel safe to name her son. Only then would she feel safe enough for David to ask the prophet to return.

And when the prophet did return, he brought a favorable word, that Solomon was beloved of Yahweh, a son of peace. David's wars were ended. An era of quiet had begun. The divine favor of Yahweh for her son made Bathsheba's heart swell with hope, softening her memory of the dark visions of her past burdens.

PART THREE

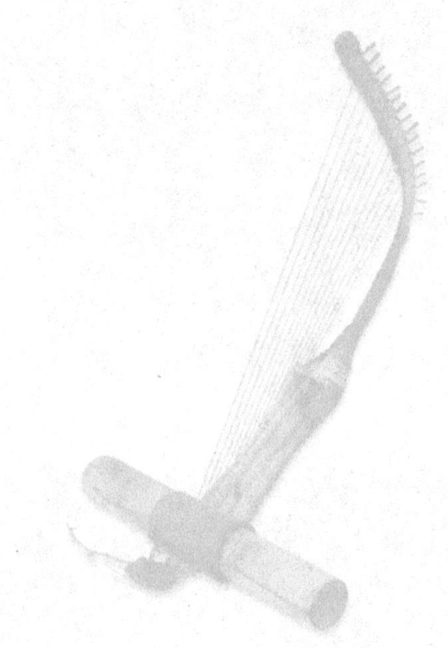

Chapter 20

DAVID INSISTED EVERYONE MEET EARLY AT THE ROYAL STABLES. He wanted to move through the streets before the city roused itself from slumber. Jerusalem had nearly doubled in population in the last year, and the people had become more unruly and unpredictable. Famine and starvation had created erratic behavior, which is why Benaiah insisted on a protection detail that David thought excessive. David understood that if privation came to a whole nation, the effects could be devastating. He had lived through years of meager sustainability while fleeing from King Saul and having the burdensome task of caring for his followers and their families when there was so little to be had.

In those desperate times, David's followers often threatened to turn against him. This current circumstance was far greater than anything he had ever experienced, and the results were both dangerous and deadly. Drastic action was needed before the national trauma of food shortage turned into national chaos. So, he did not complain to Benaiah about the extra bodyguards.

Mephibosheth was waiting for him, seated in his single donkey cart outside the royal stables. David had assigned Mephibosheth the task of managing the city storehouses. This son of Jonathan had refused to be the passive beneficiary of David's kindness. He wanted a duty in the ongoing administration of the kingdom. "My legs are crippled, but my mind functions quite well, my lord," Mephibosheth told David once he and Mica had been welcomed into the royal household.

"I was hoping I would arrive before you," David said as he approached the cart.

"I never want anyone to have to wait on me, especially the king," Mephibosheth replied. "I left the palace as soon as Mica went to the Levitical academy."

"The boy's studies going well?" asked David while tickling behind the donkey's ears. "He adjusting to court life?"

"Yes, my lord. I believe I am watching a budding scholar grow before my eyes."

"Israel needs all the scholars she can produce," David said. "At present, we are unable to grow crops or enjoy the bounty of fertile herds and flocks, so we might as well be cultivating scholars."

From the corner of his eye, David saw Benaiah nod his satisfaction with the formation of his security detail before he approached.

"My lord, do you wish to ride?" Benaiah asked. "We have a busy day ahead."

"I know, Benaiah, but I do not wish to be rushed," David replied, yet he was unable to question Benaiah's judgment. "Do we really need such an escort?"

"My lord, the number of bodyguards is fitting with the need. If you insist on walking through the streets, I must insist on the size of the protection detail."

"And I thought I was king." David smiled at Mephibosheth, though Benaiah did not appear amused. "Thank you, Benaiah. I will walk though. My legs need the exercise."

"Shall we go then, my lord?" Mephibosheth asked.

When David stepped back, he noticed Mephibosheth barely had enough room for himself and his crutches inside his small cart.

"What are all these?" David pointed to the stuffed bags around his feet and stacked in an open crate attached to the back of the cart.

"Every few days, I collect leftovers from the palace guards and servants," he answered. "I try to distribute the food before it spoils."

"I have noticed you scraping the uneaten food off the plates of my children when we are finished at the table. Now I understand why."

"The servants have been helpful in the effort, my lord. I do not wish to be wasteful in this difficult time."

"Nor do I," replied David.

David did not wish to be surrounded by Benaiah's guards, so they were positioned in front and behind giving David access to either side of the street. Along the route to the central storehouse, he allowed for Mephibosheth to stop anytime to give out the bags of food. In every street, in every alleyway, in the city center, in the doorways of homes, the sick and starving were hunkered and hiding, their gaunt faces drawn with fear and creased with desperation.

In the first year of the famine, the families living in the surrounding towns and villages were able to survive from the harvest yields of the previous year. The second year of the famine if a village was to survive, then families had to communally share what they had, but it was not enough to sustain the life of the village. Livestock could not be fed for lack of grain and were butchered. Soon, the corrals and pens in all the towns were empty. David received frequent reports of starvation and people abandoning their homes to forage in the wilderness. Then the wild game became scarce. By the third year, panic set in. People moved to the city as their last hope against the scarcity of food.

This was not the City of David from those early days when David's cup brimmed with goodness and mercy and abundance. This was not the table ladened to the breaking point with the bounty of harvests and herds, vineyards and wild game. This was his city, but in its current impoverished state, it was rapidly becoming a charnel house.

When Benaiah ordered the column to stop at a crossing for a wagon overflowing with the dead citizens of Israel to pass by, David gripped Benaiah's arm to keep from faltering. He had seen so much death from wars and battles, but never from the ravages of starvation. This vision of the dead and dying, these living wraiths with barely enough flesh on their bodies to cover their bones, barely enough energy to beg for crumbs, pierced his heart. And the lack of audible sounds coming from these hordes astounded him. The people were too weak from the pangs of hunger to even groan.

When they arrived at the central storehouse, a ring of soldiers surrounded the building with a double row standing guard before the only entrance. Crowds of hungry people had collected in front of the building hoping for any distribution of the remaining goods kept inside. From this central location, foodstuffs were dispersed to other storage locations throughout the city until there was too little to apportion. David ordered those satellite locations closed and everything to be mete out from this one location.

"Do not make a fuss, Benaiah." David pointed to the huddled souls in the street camped around fires so small they would barely warm the hands.

"We do not need them to move. We can slip inside the building to see what remains."

Mephibosheth stopped near the front door. The guards formed a cluster in front of David as he waited for Mephibosheth to get out of his cart and grab his crutches.

"You look so much like your father," David said as Mephibosheth fit his crutch pads beneath his arms then swung his legs in front of him. He had just enough strength in his legs to use them to aid in balance as he managed a hobbling forward movement with the crutches.

"I was so young when my father died. I barely remember him, my lord."

"Not only do you have his looks, but his good heart as well. He would be proud of you," David said as they paused at the entrance of the double doors of the storehouse. "Have I ever told you the story of how your father and I cut the covenant of friendship?"

"I never tire of hearing stories about my father, my lord."

"He was closer to me than blood kin." David smiled at the flash of memories of his dear friend.

"Thank you, my lord. Shall we go in?"

Once David and Mephibosheth entered the building, the guards formed a tight rank in front of the door. Benaiah positioned himself at the entrance while David and Mephibosheth went into the interior. Most of the stalls and bins were empty with rats and mice scurrying about in frantic search for crumbs. Those bins that contained any grain and flour and wheat had dwindled down to a quarter of what had been delivered by caravan weeks ago. The soil had lost its rich nutrients. Most of the herds and flocks had been devoured. That first year, the olive trees produced fruit the size of grapes until they had stopped producing altogether. The ground was so hard from lack of rain that a man with a pickax risked breaking his blade when he struck the earth.

"Why would the Almighty bring such terrible affliction upon us, my lord?"

David stopped in the center of the building and stared at the near-empty stalls in front of them. These stalls were as vacant as his heart. He had no answer to Mephibosheth's question. Why would the Almighty allow his kingdom to become fraught with hunger and suffering?

As he looked over his shoulder and through the open doors of the building, the soldiers held back the crowds. The people were not belligerent, they were too weak to storm the food center, but David could see the desperation on their faces and their open hands stretching in his direction. They were his flocks of sheep bleating for him to find those green pastures.

David then placed his hands upon Mephibosheth's shoulders. They were strong, and David could feel the muscles in his arms. This son of Jonathan must be strong enough to hear what he had to tell him.

"We have walked the streets and witnessed the misery of the people," David began. "The whole country is suffering and dying. The survival of the nation is at stake. I have begged Yahweh for an answer like these miserable creatures outside the door beg for a bite of bread."

David tightened his grip on Mephibosheth's arms so much so that his crutches became useless. "Mephibosheth, I fear we suffer from an old crime. We suffer because men's hearts are hardened by ethnic discrimination and distrust. We suffer because your grandfather gave in to his darker nature and decided that a race of people must be extinguished from the earth."

Mephibosheth began to tremble. The man's face cracking under the realization of a bitter truth.

"It is my grandfather's house that is stained with the blood of the Gibeonites." He dropped his head in shame. "I know this history, and it is true."

"It is our history," David was quick to point out. "Not just the personal liability of your grandfather, but it is our collective responsibility."

"It happened such a long time ago, my lord," Mephibosheth said.

"Yes, it was in the long ago, before I ever met your father or married into the house of Saul." David wrapped his arms around Mephibosheth hoping to console and reassure this broken man. "Your father had nothing to do with your grandfather's genocide against the Gibeonites, and he could not have prevented this terrible tragedy even if he tried. But we now bear the responsibility of continuing the bigotry. Our conduct toward these poor people has only gotten worse throughout the years borne out of hard hearts that hold longtime prejudices. I believe Yahweh has had enough of our evil treatment of this race of people."

"What must be done, my lord?" Mephibosheth pulled his head back from David's chest to look at him. "If the house of Saul is stained with innocent blood, then what must I do to make amends?"

"Just like your father, ready to right every wrong." David kissed Mephibosheth on both cheeks. "It is impossible to comprehend what I believe must be done to make amends. I thought in time the famine would pass, but it has not. I have sought the face of Yahweh night and day for an answer. I had Zadok and Abiathar cast the sacred stones. When an answer came, it was terrible to imagine. I intend to give Yahweh one last time to confirm the answer given or offer a different solution before I meet with the Gibeonites this morning. When I face them, I want you with me. I want you at my side to hear their request and my response."

"Of course, my lord. I will stand with you and accept any ruling you deem just."

"Thank you, dear friend." David bent and retrieved the crutch that had fallen to the floor. He tucked the pad underneath Mephibosheth's arm then pointed to the front three stalls that contained the last of the supplies. "We have little left to distribute. Give it all out, empty the stalls, and once you have completed the task, join me at the city gates, and we shall walk together to meet the Gibeonite delegation outside the city."

"They are not coming to the palace, my lord?" asked Mephibosheth.

"I do not want them to enter Jerusalem. I do not want them to see what we have seen today and have seen for too long."

"I understand," Mephibosheth said.

"My lord, we must leave for the prophet's school," Benaiah said as he stepped inside the open doors.

"Nathan and Gad are walking with me up the hill of olive groves east of the city," David explained to Mephibosheth. "Zadok and Abiathar are joining us and will cast the sacred stones one last time before the Almighty. I want multiple pairs of eyes to bear witness to Yahweh's answer. Once that is done, I will join you at the city gates."

David departed the storehouse with Benaiah. He set a quick pace, his face like flint as he made his way past the starving people. His only priority was to save his people. But at what cost? What price would be paid by those who might have to die for the sake of another's crime?

It was too bitter to contemplate, but so was the sight of waste and hunger on the faces of the people. The heavy weight of his sovereignty sunk deep into his soul.

Chapter 21

DAVID MARCHED UP THE HILL OF OLIVE TREES AHEAD OF THE others. The sense of urgency boosted his legs, but it was not an urgency for something he anticipated with joy. David knew the answer Yahweh would give, and once David gave the command to abide by the will of the Almighty, he knew the deep cost that lay ahead. There would be no joy.

The consequence was bloodshed. David had been treading upstream through a river of blood most of his life and, after today, the flow would become a little deeper.

There were no simple answers to the cause of the famine and drought. Capricious weather patterns, a mere fluke of agriculture, a poor farming season in isolated areas. Nothing could explain this nationwide crisis. Every city and town in every tribe suffered. There had to be a deeper reason for three successive years of this dearth in harvests.

The pivotal answer would be confirmed at the top of the Hill of Olives where Zadok and Abiathar awaited him.

"Quicken your pace," David said over his shoulder.

Nathan and Gad huffed and wheezed behind him while Benaiah tried to shepherd them up the steep grade. David was impatient. He was ready to take action, and these out-of-shape prophets were slowing him down. Yet he was wise enough to know the insight these prophets provided was vitally important in confirming the will of Yahweh.

Days before, Gad had pulled David aside to give his reason for the possible cause. "Seek the face of Yahweh, my lord, to confirm my belief," Gad said. "This famine could be the result of our poor treatment of the original peoples before us."

"What do you mean?" asked David.

"When I served in the house of Saul, the king gave the full weight of his authority to the extermination of the Gibeonites. Nathan had returned to Ramah to serve Samuel at the prophet's school, but I remained in Gibeah to serve the king. The night of the killings, I was told to lock myself inside my dwelling. The horrors of mass slaughter were evident the following day."

"I have seen such horrors in my life, Gad."

"My lord, I know the weight of our present grief lies heavy on your shoulders. When our forefathers entered the land of promise, they cut a covenant with the Gibeonites to spare and protect them. Even though the Gibeonites used deception and flattery to make an oath with our ancestors, the covenant remains to this day. It forbids their extinction and requires they be treated with fairness. We have ignored their right to exist and plundered their land. This could be a reckoning for our sin against them."

David had great difficulty accepting Gad's argument that there might be divine condemnation upon a nation for the past crime of a king. And any solution might be even more difficult. Yet, he could not rest until he had exhausted all possible causes for the disaster that had fallen upon the kingdom.

After Gad's private counsel, David arranged to meet with Abiathar and Zadok. Late at night, he slipped out of the palace and went to the Tabernacle. He wanted to be as close to Yahweh as possible to hear what the Almighty had to say on such a terrible matter. Zadok and Abiathar stood outside the curtained entrance into the Tabernacle as David approached. He brought no one with him, not even Benaiah. He would face this moment with the High Priests alone.

The Levite guards pulled back the curtains for the three men to enter the outer court area of the Tabernacle. They stopped between the Laver and Brazen Altar. In the firelight, David viewed the entrance into the Holy Place where only priests and Levites were permitted. He longed to enter that sacred space, but knew it was off limits.

Abiathar unrolled the dark coverlet onto the hard ground.

"Is this the same coverlet we had when we were fleeing Saul?" David asked.

"No, my lord," answered Abiathar. "That was linen, and it became worn with time and use. This is made of goat skin dyed with hyacinth blue. More durable."

"Very well. The prophet Gad encouraged me to seek the face of Yahweh," David said to the priests. "I must know the cause and the solution for this famine."

"What is the question for the Almighty, my lord?" asked Zadok.

David looked into the faces of the two priests and then turned to the Levite guards stationed around them holding torches to provide sufficient light.

"You are to say nothing of this night," David commanded. "I charge all of you that what you witness tonight will not be spoken of beyond this sacred place."

Silence followed his directive. No one moved. It was as if the order had paralyzed them. The fires from the torches flickered and snapped in the slight breeze.

"We shall honor your request, my lord." Abiathar answered for the group.

"Good," David responded. "Then I am ready to inquire of Yahweh."

Zadok removed the pouch containing the Urim and Thummim from behind his breastplate and dropped the stones into his open hand.

"Is this three-year famine a direct result of Yahweh's disfavor with his people?" David asked.

Zadok tossed the stones onto the sacred mantle, and both priests leaned in to study and interpret the reading.

"Yahweh says 'yes,' my lord," Zadok said, his face somber after his reading.

"Is the cause of Yahweh's disfavor on account of King Saul's crime of putting the Gibeonites to the sword?"

Zadok tossed the stones. Again, both priests conferred about the result.

"Yes, my lord," Zadok replied. "The house of Saul is stained by this bloodshed."

"One final question. Will the Gibeonites demand blood in return, and will this lift the burden of the famine?"

Zadok rattled the stones in his hand and was about to toss them onto the coverlet.

"Stay your hand, Zadok," David blurted, then he moved around the circle of Levites. He scrutinized each face, testing their character. "Remember your loyalty. The answer given by the Almighty must not be spoken beyond this circle."

Each Levite guard bowed his head in agreement with their king.

"Continue, Zadok. Let us know the will of Yahweh."

When Zadok threw the stones and both priests confirmed the results, David could feel his soul draining out of his body.

"In three days we are to meet with the prophets on the Hill of Olives," David said. "We shall cast the sacred stones one last time so all can bear witness to the will of the Almighty."

He left the Tabernacle without saying another word. What was there to say?

The answer was his to carry. The burden was his to bear. When he got back to the palace, he summoned Benaiah and instructed him to send for the delegation of the Gibeonites to come to Jerusalem.

Now the day for action had arrived and David was impatient to get on with the fulfilment of this grave burden.

"Pick them up, Benaiah." David neared the top of the Hill of Olives. He shouted back down the path. "The priests await, and the day is getting away from us."

When Benaiah secured each prophet by the arm, David went on up the path. Once he reached the top of the hill, he was stunned by the sight of the withering grove of olive trees. The limbs drooped, and the leaves hung brown and wilted. The bark peeled from the trunk and the ground around the base was hard and dry. If there was no rain soon, this entire grove would die.

When David approached Abiathar and Zadock sheltering in what little shade was available, Abiathar handed David a full waterskin. He guzzled down the warm liquid.

"Do you have another skin?" David asked. "The prophets will be thirsty."

Abiathar removed a second water sack from his shoulder. David stepped back to the crest of the hill. Benaiah was holding an arm of each prophet, pulling Nathan and Gad up the hill. He needed these faithful men to be alert and attentive to the will of Yahweh.

When they reached the top, David handed Gad and Nathan the waterskins. Once they drank their fill, Benaiah took his turn.

"Climbing this mount reminds me of our days in the desert wilderness," Gad wheezed, finally able to take a deep breath.

"I prefer never to return to those days," David mused. "Yet it feels as if we are still pursued by crimes of the house of Saul. Come, Abiathar and Zadok are waiting."

David requested that Abiathar cast the stones this time instead of Zadok, but it mattered not which priest performed the ritual. The answers were the same. The same questions were asked, and the same affirmative answers given. In the full light of day, not by torchlight under the night sky, the interpretation of priests and prophets alike was that the Almighty held the house of Saul accountable for the attempted decimation of the Gibeonite people and that the famine was the consequence.

No one expressed relief at this confirmation. No one was pleased with this knowledge. David looked into each sober face, awed by the divination of the Urim and Thummim, awed by the Almighty, and there was no need for further deliberation.

"If possible, I want to avoid more bloodshed." David stared at his outstretched hands. "We are not to say anything to the delegation about our findings. I know we are required to make amends with the Gibeonite people, and we will do so. Perhaps silver and gold from the treasury will satisfy. But I shall first hear their demands, and if they confirm these results, then we know we have heard from Yahweh."

"My lord, I fear the sin of the house of Saul is deeper than what any recompense from the nation's coffers might provide," Gad said.

"You may be right, Gad, but we will not manipulate the Gibeonite elders in any way. I will test Yahweh one last time. If the Gibeonites accept financial restitution for the blood guilt from the house of Saul, then we are free. If they demand blood for blood, then the will of the Almighty is complete."

No one spoke as they descended the hill and met Mephibosheth at the city gates. They marched the northern road in silence beyond the Levite compound to the crossroad where the Gibeonite delegation waited. Joab and Abishai assembled a cohort of soldiers at the intersection, but David had instructed Joab to have no interaction with the Gibeonites.

No tent shielded them from the sun. No refreshments. David could offer this group of representatives nothing except an ear to listen and abide by their demands. This was a council meeting to mend a broken covenant, a formal face-to-face to bear out the terms of restitution. This was not a gathering for enjoyment.

This group was not impressive. If these were the Gibeonite elders, David saw nothing that distinguished them. They wore no finery in clothing or jewelry but dressed in the wardrobe of laborers. Their sandals were worn. Their leggings and tunics were covered in patches and double stitching. Their wineskins cracked and withered. This shabby faction looked as poor as the people in the streets of his city.

"All are assembled," Joab said, as he and the soldiers bowed before David.

"Thank you, Commander." David then studied the faces of the elders. *How had the nation of Israel been brought to its knees by such a ragtag band?*

"Who stands before me? Who is the one who speaks for the Gibeonites?"

"I, my lord. Zakariya, of Gibeon, appointed by my people to bring our petition before the king," Zakariya said as he stepped forward and took a knee before David.

David looked at Mephibosheth sitting in his donkey cart and nodded.

"The kingdom of Israel suffers from the cruelties of famine," David said. "We sought the Almighty and summoned you here to seek your direction on these matters."

"My lord, the Gibeonites are humbled by your summons for our counsel," Zakariya began as he rose to his feet. "We all suffer and want to restore the blessing of Yahweh to the king and his kingdom. The covenant our ancestors made together when the people of the chosen entered the land of promise was broken by the Wolf King long ago, and his posterity continued to trod upon us with bloody footsteps. One act of cruelty followed another intending to extinguish the flame of the Gibeonites."

"Then how shall we respond, Zakariya?" David asked. "What may I offer to make restitution for the crime done so long ago against your people?"

"My lord, time does not wear out the guilt of sin," Zakariya answered. "Yahweh looks to bygone days and brings to remembrance past iniquities."

"My storehouses of food are empty, Zakariya." David held up open palms as proof. "But my treasury I gladly open to you. My supply of gold and silver is plentiful."

"I am but a humble servant of the covenant made between our ancestors, my lord," Zakariya responded, bowing again as did the others. "The Gibeonites have no right to demand silver or gold from the king's treasury or from the heirs of the Wolf King. But a storehouse brimming with treasure is no satisfaction for blood though we have no right to put anyone to death in Israel."

"So, it is blood for blood that you require?" David asked.

"The Wolf King broke covenant with the Gibeonite people. We were decimated and have no place in Israel. We then require blood of the house of Saul."

David had his answer. The sacred stones of Yahweh had been confirmed through the mouth of Zakariya with no prompting from David. He had done all he could to seek the will of Yahweh. He offered to open the doors of his treasury to appease the Gibeonites but in vain. There was no lifting the curse of the famine until the curse of the mad king's action had been atoned for by the shedding of blood. How did it come to this?

Mephibosheth scrambled out of his cart. He did not bother with his crutches but dropped to the ground at David's feet. "My lord, send me with the Gibeonites to make amends for my grandfather's sin."

"Joab, your sword." David extended his hand to his commander.

"My lord? Are you sure?" Joab was stunned by the king's request.

"Do as I say," David demanded. He took the sword from Joab, and then David stepped forward and struck the hard ground in front of Mephibosheth. Leaving the point of the sword in the ground, he walked in a full circle around Mephibosheth digging a trench in the hard soil before returning the sword to Joab.

"Hear me now, Zakariya. It is true our ancestors cut a covenant not to harm the Gibeonites when they entered the land of promise. It is true the house of Saul pressed its foot upon the neck of the Gibeonites in an effort to wipe out your people. But I too cut a covenant. I made an oath within the oath. I stand before you now as a keeper of that oath. The man kneeling before me is the son of my covenant blood brother. I cut a covenant with his father, the son of the Wolf King, to protect the heirs of Jonathan with my life. You go through me and my kingdom to get to this man and his son."

Mephibosheth burst into tears, and David knelt and wrapped his arms around the weeping man. He did not rise when Zakariya stepped forward.

"My lord, may the son and grandson of Prince Jonathan live forever in the favor of the king," Zakariya said. "We honor your oath within the oath. But the blood debt remains as does the famine that ravages the land."

"What is to be done, Zakariya?" David asked.

"There are seven male descendants residing in the home of Saul in Gibeah. Two sons and five grandsons. Give them to us. They must be hung on the gibbet before the eyes of man and the Almighty to bear witness that the blood debt was paid for the crime of the Wolf King against our people."

David rose and turned his back to Zakariya and faced his priests and prophets.

"Yahweh has spoken," he whispered, his words for their ears only.

They nodded in silence. What David had required of the Almighty had been spoken by the wronged party. It must be done.

"Go back to Gibeon, Zakariya," David said. "My commander will oversee the executions but will not lift a finger to facilitate them. The death sentence is your responsibility. While those young men are male heirs in the house of Saul, they did not raise the sword against you. Show mercy even though none was shown to you."

David lifted Mephibosheth from the ground and carried him to his donkey cart. He helped him into his seat, and they returned to the city.

Chapter 22

MIKAL LOOKED INTO THE BRIGHT BLUE SKY WHILE SHE AND
Rizpah waited for the boys to come to the garden with their yokes of water.
Each morning it was the same survivor's routine, dress, eat a bite of leftover food from last night's meager dinner, draw water from the well, fill the
troughs for the livestock, and then water the garden.

Throughout the famine, Mikal was able to maintain a limited number of
sheep and goats for food and milk and two mules for plowing and pulling the
wagons. The amount of productive land she could manage had shrunk to a
sustainable patch, enough to assist in feeding her family and what could be
sold at the market in Gibeah. The famine had taken its toll on her livestock
and crops just as it had devastated the rest of the country.

It was hard to remember how verdant and abundant their family property
had been in the long ago. How it had flourished before her father became
king. How exciting and full of promise it had been when the house of Saul
rose to prominence. But that family was no more, leaving behind only a trace
of their existence. Mikal could never allow herself to drift back and linger in
the happiness of that distant time. Her present reality was too demanding.

"Not a cloud to be seen." Mikal wiped her forehead with the dirty rag she
pulled from the leather strap tied around her waist.

"We have not seen a rain cloud in months," Rizpah said as she plopped
on the ground, shielding her eyes with her hands to block the glare of the
sunlight.

"What I would give to be doused in water," Mikal said followed by a long sigh.

When the clouds had last appeared and formed a mass large enough to offer the promise of rain, they only produced so small an amount it barely tamped down the top layer of dust. The family had to rely on the well to water the gardens, the livestock, and themselves, always fearful it would run dry.

Her father and brothers and cousin Abner had spent weeks digging this well deep into the earth until they hit an underground aquifer. It had never run dry, but it had never been tested for three straight years of famine and little rain. For months, the water level steadily dropped. More rope was used to lower the buckets before they heard the splash once it reached the water surface.

She was always thankful to hear a splash and not a splat of the bucket hitting the muddy bottom of the well. That would be a dreadful sound.

Mikal and Rizpah would take the full buckets of water the boys carried from the well and carefully pour the precious liquid among the barley plants. Because of the drought, the stalks had leafed early, the heads had appeared early, and if they had any hope of a small harvest, the plants had to be kept watered before she and Rizpah and the boys cut down the stalks for the spring harvest. Mikal was thankful there *was* a harvest this year, though a poor one.

"When the boys go to bed tonight, we can pour a bucket of water over each other," Rizpah said. "Get a sponge bath and water the barley wheat at the same time."

"So tempting," Mikal said, and they both snickered at the idea.

Mikal took her hoe and began to widen the trench along a row of barley in preparation for the water.

"When do you expect Paltiel to return from his home place?" Rizpah scooped the top layer of dirt away from the water trench with her hands.

"Not for several days," Mikal replied. "His mother has needed more help after his father's death. Now, with the famine, she is barely able to manage."

"He is a good man." Rizpah brushed the dirt from her hands.

"He is indeed," Mikal said.

When Mikal had returned from Jerusalem, Paltiel welcomed her back, no questions asked, no resentment expressed, no effort to make her feel guilty for her choice to leave him and go to the king. Mikal was shocked by Paltiel's acceptance. She was not worthy of this man's steadfastness.

Though she had never been in love with him and knew her heart was incapable of any amorous affection for him, she could honor and respect him. He followed Mikal when David had summoned her to Hebron. He wept and begged her to return with him. He so humiliated himself that Abner, who had been sent to bring her to the king, threatened to kill him if he did not stop his sniveling and return home. She deeply appreciate what no one had ever done for her, debase themselves on her account.

Paltiel's show of devotion carried more heroic qualities than her only true love. The Lion of Judah had not pursued her and begged her to come back when she left. The king's last hateful words still felt like knife blades that could not be removed from her heart. For the preservation of her heart, Mikal had left behind a life at court. When she returned home, she found Paltiel working in the garden. He was busy trenching around the base of new plantings. She did not speak as she approached, and it took a moment for him to realize she stood before him. When he did feel her presence, he stopped and straightened, and his eyes began to water. Paltiel's emotions were always accessible.

Mikal would never again be disdainful of this quality. She would never again leave him.

"You have come home?" The hesitancy in his voice meant he did not wish to relive what he had gone through when she left the first time.

"I have," Mikal said. "And for good."

"Come inside. I will make us some breakfast."

Once Mikal reconciled with Paltiel, she gave her attention to her sister, Merab. She was so grateful to have arrived home and found Merab had not yet succumbed to death. She had lost weight, and her strength and stamina were diminished, but Merab lived for several months. Before she gave in to the disease, Mikal had promised her sister to raise her five boys as her own.

"I wonder what is taking the boys so long?" Mikal leaned on the hoe. She looked in the direction of the well, but the crumbling wall built around the house after her father became king blocked her view. "They have had enough time to get the water."

"I fear they are getting weaker," Rizpah suggested. "Growing boys need more sustenance than we are able to provide."

"I do see a lethargy in them from lack of food." Mikal waved her hand to encompass her surroundings. "This famine has got to end soon."

"Should I go and hurry them along?" Rizpah asked.

"No, no," Mikal replied. "They do not need to be scolded."

Violent rumblings, human screams, pounding, and the earth shaking came all at once. Mikal could not sort the clamorous dissonance of noises except for the human screams. Those she could identify. They were the shrieks of the boys.

One of them has fallen into the well.

When Rizpah scrambled to her feet and took off around the compound wall, Mikal knew a mother's instinct had been quickened by the terrified screams of her boys. Her own legs were not as fast as Rizpah's, but Mikal felt a strength rushing through her body she thought had been extinguished long ago.

When she raced around the corner of the wall, Mikal stopped in her tracks at the appalling sight of a horde of men surrounding the seven boys, pummeling them with their fists and kicking them with their feet. The water buckets drawn from the well were knocked over saturating the ground where this mob had ambushed the boys and were brutalizing them.

Rizpah had thrown herself upon one of the attackers clawing his face with her fingernails until she was thrown to the ground, and her victim began to kick her.

Mikal had no comprehension of what was going on or why. She saw only this vicious attack upon her defenseless boys. Her garden hoe transformed into a weapon, and she struck Rizpah's attacker across the face with the full force of her strength, knocking him out cold. Mikal gave no consideration whether or not she struck a death blow to the man lying on the wet ground. She only swung the hoe again and again, striking whoever was in front of her.

The only thing that paused the assault was the arrival of a large contingent of the king's soldiers. Thrilled to see armed men, Mikal expected them to slay the attackers, but they did not draw their weapons. They did not dismount. They watched.

A greater horror than seeing her boys beaten senseless was the horror that Joab gave no order to stop this violence. Her heart split in two.

"What in the name of the Almighty are you doing?" Mikal screamed as she rushed toward Joab. "These men are attacking my boys. Stop them."

Only then did Joab raise his hand in the air and shout for everyone to stop.

In the stillness Mikal heard the faint whimpering from the boys and grumbling from the attackers at being forced to pause.

"Abishai, read the king's edict," Joab said. He glared down upon Mikal as his brother unfurled the scroll and read the words of the king to the crowd.

"By order of King David and following the will of the Almighty, the king has decreed that the seven heirs of the house of Saul, the five sons of Merab, daughter of King Saul, and the two sons of Rizpah, concubine of King Saul, are to be executed at the hands of the Gibeonites to satisfy the blood guilt against the house of Saul for King Saul's massacre against the Gibeonites."

When Abishai finished reading the king's decree, the mob of Gibeonites picked up the limp bodies of the seven heirs and marched up the hill behind the compound where two wagons were parked and waiting.

Mikal dropped the hoe and fell upon all fours. The power to wield this garden weapon now heaved out of her body in wave after wave of sobs. How could this horror be unfolding right before her eyes? How could this be the will of the Almighty? How could this be the will of the king, her husband?

She could absorb his loathing and scorn against her, his curses against her family, against her barrenness, but this…this slaughter of innocents? Had everyone lost their minds? Had the famine and drought driven everyone to madness…this madness?

Or had she alone suddenly lost her mind? She had lost everything else in her life.

Through her burning eyes Mikal saw Rizpah crawling up the hill after the mob. Much of Rizpah's clothing was torn and covered in blood, her blood since she had no weapon other than the fury of her body to hurl against this deranged horde. This hill and grounds behind the compound had once been a training area. In the long ago, she and Merab would sneak onto the balcony to watch the young men train for Israel's first standing army, her father's army. The memories of this ground were being transformed into a cruel site of execution.

Mikal struggled to her feet and staggered to Rizpah, who had collapsed in exhaustion upon the ground halfway up the hill.

Joab's men remained atop their horses observing from a distance.

She knelt beside Rizpah whose face was buried in the dirt unable to watch. Mikal was amazed to see seven gibbets inside the wagon beds. These cages had been constructed ahead of time. This was all preplanned. This plot upon the weak and unsuspecting had been well thought out.

"What are they doing to our sons?" Rizpah asked, her voice broken and cracked with grief.

Mikal cupped her hands on her brow to shield her eyes from the sun. She had a clear view from the base of the hill. The neck of each boy was broken before being stuffed into a cage then hung onto the main support beams of scaffolding. One by one, all seven cages were suspended in the air, each containing an heir of the house of Saul.

The efficiency of man when the mind is set on evil. Mikal dropped to her knees.

"I cannot see for the horde around our boys." Mikal chose to lie. She chose to give Rizpah a little more time before she was forced to behold the horrors.

The Gibeonite murderers stood back to observe their handiwork.

A cool northern breeze picked up causing the treetops to come alive with the rustling of the wind blowing through the branches. The wind grew stronger, and the hanging cages began to swing back and forth. Mikal could not remember the last time such a cool breeze dried her wet face and damp skin.

She stretched across Rizpah's back. Perhaps if she might only fall asleep, when she awakened, the horrors before her would have vanished and life would go back to normal. But she could not sleep, and she could not hear any recognizable call or boyish clatter from the seven sons. The screaming had stopped. The whimpering and crying had stopped.

Mercy. What a vile word in the face of this dreadful vision?

The rain started falling in hard droplets hitting Mikal in rapid splashes until her clothes became soaked.

May this rain refresh the earth. May this rain wash the soil clean of this innocent blood. May this rain cleanse this day from my memory.

David stood alone on the roof of the citadel on the back side of the palace overlooking the Tabernacle and Levitical compound. Bathsheba waited below at the head of the staircase leading down into the compound. She was expecting another of David's children and did not wish to descend the steps to meet her son returning from school. Solomon would come to her.

Solomon was proving to be a little scholar. His Levitical teachers praised the agility of the boy's mind capable of grasping some of the deeper complexities of the laws of Moses. David expected it would not be long before the young boy would join Nathan and Gad at the prophet's school to continue his education.

From his vantage point on the roof of the citadel, David could see the countryside to the north. His skin shivered when the cool wind pushed the stagnant air away. The atmosphere had been dry and hot for so long this cooldown came as a surprise. Clouds were forming in the northeast, and the speed with which they turned dark and flew in his direction came as a shock. He had never seen such a wonder. The first few drops of rain pelted his face as if hurled from a slingshot.

> *"The Almighty has heard our prayer.*
> *To You, O Yahweh, all people will come.*
> *When we were overwhelmed by our sin,*
> *You forgave our transgressions.*
> *Blessed are those who live in Your courts.*
> *We are filled with the good things of Your house."*

"Abba. Abba."

David heard the high-pitched voice of his young son and spotted Solomon running up the outside steps of the palace below. He waved for the boy to join him on the rooftop. There was no sound of fierce thunder or jagged lightning cutting across the dark sky. But the belly of the clouds had been sundered and the rain poured out of the sky as if dispensed from wine vats.

His clothes were drenched, so David disrobed down to his leggings and raised his arms to the heavens.

> *"O Yahweh our Savior, the hope of all the ends of the earth*
> *You care for the land and water it;*
> *You enrich it abundantly.*
> *The streams of Yahweh are filled with water*
> *To provide the people with grain,*
> *For so You have ordained it.*
> *You drench its furrows and level its ridges;*
> *You soften it with showers and bless its crops.*
> *You crown the year with Your bounty*
> *And Your carts overflow with abundance.*
> *The grasslands of the desert overflow;*
> *The hills are clothed with gladness.*
> *The meadows are covered with flocks*

> *And the valleys are mantled with grain;*
> *They shout for joy and sing."*

"Abba. Abba," Solomon shouted as he pulled on David's soaked leggings. "Why are you naked in the rain?"

"Worshipping Yahweh," David cried as he scooped Solomon into his arms.

"Is the famine over?" Solomon embraced his father's neck.

"The famine is over." David whirled the two of them in a circle.

"We are getting wet, Abba," Solomon said, his laughing voice matching the joy of his father.

"Yes, is it not wonderful? Yahweh is giving us a bath."

Chapter 23

DAVID PICKED UP THE LAST BUNDLE OF BARLEY STALKS AND carried them over to the large pile at the end of his row. He dropped it onto the pile and began to clean the grime from the blade of his sickle. He looked on with pleasure as his sons worked down their individual rows. Amnon, Absalom, Adonijah, even young Solomon had his own sickle, and after instruction from the local farmers on how to cut and stack the barley stalks, they were assigned their row and told to commence work.

David wanted his sons to experience the hard labor of those who supplied the king's tables and storehouses. Three months of listening to lectures from prophets and Levites and straining their eyes studying the scrolls was time well spent. But his sons also needed to get out of the classrooms and work up a sweat under a hot sun.

David watched with pride as his sons groaned and complained and teased each other as they made their way down their rows. Solomon was too young to keep pace with his older brothers, but he hacked away with all his might. David went to lend a hand, but Solomon refused his father's offer. His son had his pride to maintain.

The farmland, the livestock, the wild game in the forests, partridge and pheasant, stag, the streams teaming with fish, the vineyards heavy with grape clusters, all of life had surged back since the rains. It was unnatural, a miracle of overabundance after three years of want. Since the land began to thrive and the bounty began flowing into the city, David kept a low profile, not wanting to express public exuberance at this flourishing. To survive three years of famine with such depravation had exhausted the nation. It would take time for the souls of the people to recover, for the country to feel it had resumed the rhythms and balance of life.

David needed to regain confidence in his ability to lead a people who had suffered this oppressive famine under his kingship. He did not call for national celebrations or for the Levites to assemble a corporate time of worship and sacrifice. He remained pensive and kept his interactions to a minimum. He had not come to terms with the terrible suffering during the famine, the crime that had brought it about, or how he chose to resolve it. After he had given the order for Joab to oversee the executions, he became physically ill. He remained aloof and alone, and each day climbed the stairs of the citadel to wait and watch.

The day the rains came, he knew the death sentence had been carried out. David did not need a special messenger to bring him the news. He was thankful once the rains arrived and the country began to blossom and prosper, but his initial joy did not last, and a melancholy crept into his heart. To help settle his mind, he chose hard labor, to sweat alongside farmers and shepherds, vineyard keepers and livestock wranglers, woodcutters and carpenters. He wanted his sons to have the same experience. Out of the Levitical classrooms and rubbing shoulders with the people who worked by the sweat of the brow.

"You boys will sleep well tonight," David said to his sons whacking at the thick barley stalks with their sickles.

His words brought groans of complaint.

"My lord. My lord," Mephibosheth shouted. His cart was parked on the eastern road of the Kidron Valley. He pointed a crutch up the road. A caravan of ox-drawn carts, camels, and mules pulling wagons ladened with goods was lumbering down the road.

David dropped his sickle and ran down the hillside to join Mephibosheth. The line of the column extended north as far as he could see.

"From the northern tribes, my lord." Mephibosheth used his crutches to lift himself from the cart seat for a better view of the caravan. "The fourth supply train in under a fortnight, and by all accounts, the most bountiful. I cannot see the end."

"Mephibosheth, would you like to escort this convoy into the city?"

"It would be an honor, my lord."

"My boys and I will join you once they finish cutting their rows."

Mephibosheth tapped the donkey's behind and turned the cart around in the road, signaling for the convoy leader to follow him through the eastern gates.

For a time, David stood at the side of the road marveling at the number of wagons and beasts of burden rumbling by him. The largess was beyond his grasp, and he could not help himself and began to dance with delight. When the last wagon passed by, he waved to the driver and trudged back up the hill to join his boys.

In spite of his great joy at the arrival of this caravan, he still wrestled with how to explain this glut of blessing. His sons were young and not all that curious how the years of famine and the events of the last month were related. The particulars of the how and what and why of the matter eluded him as well. David was just glad that he and the kingdom could begin a renewed life.

Once David was satisfied with the work his boys had accomplished in the field, he announced they were going to the main storehouse in the central part of the city to help unload the supplies from this latest caravan. It surprised him that his boys did not protest this new chore. David expected adolescent grumbles from his sons and a desire to return to the palace, but they were eager to take part in the work. During the years of famine, the population of Jerusalem had multiplied because people had fled to the city desperate to find some food source however sparse. Now, they stayed because of large quantities of provisions coming into the city. He hoped, as the summer progressed, that many of these people would return to their towns and villages to begin anew.

The crowds around the entrance of the storehouse, while eager to receive their allotment, were not unruly and demanding. The guards did not have to act as barriers but were part of the assembly line handing out the supplies. Since this was the fourth caravan in as many weeks, Mephibosheth had a distribution system in place both orderly and impartial for all the citizens. David and his sons were incorporated into the line with the soldiers and storehouse workers.

David caught sight of Gad and Nathan standing to the side observing the orderly proceedings of the bread lines, speaking with the people, and blessing them as they walked past, their arms weighed down with generous portions of the newly arrived bounty. He was determined never to act toward these prophets as his predecessor had done and lost his mind in the process. The bond between prophet and king might be tested and strained, but David trusted their faithfulness to Yahweh, and by being faithful to the Almighty, they were faithful to him.

When the sky began to lose its light, it became apparent that it would be impossible to unload all the surplus of goods before dark. David walked through the storehouse taking inventory. The remainder from the last caravan still had not yet gone out the doors. A blessing and a challenge David gladly welcomed.

The baggage carried by the camels and mules would have to be removed so they could be stabled for the night. The teams of oxen would need to be unyoked and given the same care. The public stables would be full, and the stable hands would be working extra hours required for this influx of beasts. The inns also would be full with all those weary travelers ready to pay for food and lodging. This was powerful evidence of a great rekindling of life in the city and the country.

"Our cup fills to the brim and pours over the lip," David whispered, looking into the sky at twilight. "Yahweh, You care for the land and water it. You enrich it abundantly. O Yahweh, our Savior, the hope of all the ends of the earth and of the farthest seas. You are like the brightness after the rain that brings prosperity from the earth."

Mephibosheth pulled his donkey cart to a stop in front of the storehouse. "My lord, I have instructed the workers to unload the baggage and place it along the storehouse walls, so the drivers can stable their animals."

"I shall order a guard stationed around the storehouse for the night," David said.

"Excellent, my lord. Then we can continue where we left off at first light."

Once the crowds in front of the storehouse began to disperse, David noticed Gad and Nathan were waving to him with a sense of urgency. David waved in returned and then gathered his boys around him and praised them for their hard work. Mephibosheth added his praise before David sent the boys back home with their guard detail.

"Straight back to the palace now." David feigned sternness. "I need to finish here with Mephibosheth."

"Do we really need the palace guards, Abba?" Absalom asked. "We are not children any longer, well, except for Solomon."

Absalom slung his arm around Solomon's head and pulled him into his side.

"Look at you, my golden child." David playfully tugged on Absalom's long gilded hair. "Thinking you are all grown-up. I want you home before dark."

"Will you be with us for supper, Abba?" Solomon asked, his head pressed into his brother's side.

"Yes, but have your mother tell the cooks vegetables for me. Now, off you go."

David allowed the boys to head up the street toward the palace by themselves before waving over the sergeant of the palace guard.

"Give them a little distance, Sergeant," David said. "Close, but not too close."

"Yes, my lord." The sergeant stepped away to recruit a few soldiers for this close-but-not-too-close security detail.

The storehouse workers remained busy inside the building sorting the various goods and placing them in separate stalls while the soldiers took their posts in front of all the containers and crates stacked against the outside wall.

"There will be days of sorting such abundance, my lord," Mephibosheth said.

"Praise be to the Almighty. I hope this means that those who came to the city during the famine will be able to pick up life again in their own villages."

"The barley harvest is coming in long after the spring rains," Mephibosheth said. "By all indications, the country should be restored by summer's end."

"Yes, let us hope." David turned to see Nathan and Gad approaching. He stretched out a hand to each prophet. "The tide of life is coming back to us and bringing the prophets of Yahweh with it."

While the two prophets agreed with David's assessment of Israel's improving fortunes, their grave expressions troubled him.

"I have missed seeing you both at my table," David said.

"We have been shuttling back and forth from the city to the retreat center in Ramah." Nathan took David's hand.

"We just returned last evening," Gad continued, taking David's other hand. "Neither of us have been able to eat or sleep since."

"We cannot remove the sight from our eyes," Nathan added.

"Or the stink from our nostrils," offered Gad.

"My lord, perhaps I should not be present for this conversation," Mephibosheth interjected. "I shall continue to work inside the storehouse."

David grabbed Mephibosheth's arm before he reached for his crutches. "Stay, friend. I fear what the prophets must tell involves the house of Saul."

Was not the business with the house of Saul finished? Had he not satisfied the will of Yahweh by giving justice to the Gibeonites?

The famine was lifted, the summer fruitful. Surely nothing was left to be done.

"What have you to tell me?" David braced himself prepared to receive an ominous word from the prophets.

"For near three months, we have been traveling back and forth to Ramah," Nathan began. "Since the famine ceased, we chose to avoid Gibeah altogether, but rumors persist regarding the executions."

"What rumors?" David asked. "Why have I not heard anything? Joab reported they were carried out efficiently."

"The commander's report is true, my lord," Gad was quick to say. "It is the aftermath we witnessed that we are here to tell."

David gave a wary look to Mephibosheth before telling the prophets to continue.

"We drove our wagon through Gibeah and took the side road toward the family dwelling of the former king," Nathan said. "As we approached the compound, we first noticed flocks of ravens and vultures circling the field behind the compound."

"Where Abner would train the military and practice their war games," Gad said.

"I remember it well," David responded. "Go on."

"We drove around the compound, and…and…" Nathan faltered, so Gad put his hand on Nathan's shoulder and continued.

"My lord, the stench made us retch, and the sight made our eyes flow with tears."

Remembering the dreadful moment rendered both prophets speechless, but David was impatient to hear the rest. "Get yourselves under control and tell me what you saw."

"On the hill above the compound, open before the heavens and in clear view of all who might pass by, were seven rancid gibbets suspended from the scaffolding, each containing the body of a male heir of the house of Saul," Nathan said.

"Lady Rizpah protects the cages night and day from the carrion eaters," Gad interjected. "Feathered carcasses cover the hillside."

"The seven heirs of Saul are not yet buried?" David gripped the wooden siding of the cart to keep from falling. "Why?"

From his sitting position inside his cart, Mephibosheth wrapped his strong arms around David's chest and held his heaving body preventing him from pitching forward onto the ground. Gad and Nathan quickly formed ranks around David lending support to their distraught king.

"My lord, there are none to bury them, but I believe a deeper connection exists between Saul and his heirs," Gad said.

"Please tell me. The results of this terrible famine have not ended until there is a proper burial for these seven. I want no enmity between our two houses." David gripped the hand of Mephibosheth.

"Nor I, my lord," Mephibosheth said.

"The bodies of King Saul and his sons were hung from the walls of Beth Shan by the Philistines after they defeated our army at Mount Gilboa. Do you remember Jarib, King Saul's secretary?" asked Gad.

"I do, yes. A good and loyal servant," David replied.

"He was indeed, to the end. Even though he could no longer serve in the court of the king after the massacre of the priests at Nob, Jarib remained loyal," Gad continued. "When I learned the Philistines intended to expose the bodies of King Saul and his sons on the walls, I fled to Jabesh Gilead and recruited Jarib and a contingent of warriors to retrieve the bodies. The bones of King Saul and his sons are buried in Jabesh Gilead."

"Your grandfather, father, and uncles were hung from a Philistine stronghold," David said, feeling a renewed strength coming back into his legs. "Now seven of his heirs are exposed to the same disgrace."

Mephibosheth's comforting embrace had bolstered David, and he now stood firm, a surge of conviction rushing through him clearing his mind and bringing resolve.

"We will end the dishonor of Saul's house," David announced. "We must bring home the bones of the king and his sons and my beloved Jonathan."

David cupped his hands around the face of the son of his dearest friend. "They must all be buried together in one tomb. King Saul and his family must all rest together."

Chapter 24

JOAB AND ABISHAI WERE DISPATCHED TO COLLECT THE BONES of Saul and his sons from Jabesh Gilead. David could have ordered Joab to provide a large contingent of soldiers. He could have made a public spectacle of returning the former king and his sons to their home place to be laid in the tomb of their ancestors. But to do so would be a dishonor to the dead and could draw public criticism as a reminder for the cause of the famine.

Once Joab and Abishai returned to Jerusalem, David made plans to slip out of the city with this secret cargo and travel to Gibeah. On the designated day, David and Mephibosheth left the palace before dawn and went to the royal stables. When they entered the stables, Nathan and Gad, Benaiah, Joab, and Abishai awaited them. David wanted only family, the prophets, and the faithful Benaiah to accompany him and Mephibosheth on this quiet mission to reunite the House of Saul in one burial site.

"Everything is ready, my lord." Joab pointed to the wagon and mule team.

Gad held a torch and led David and Mephibosheth around to the back of the wagon and removed the large cloth covering from four wooden boxes.

"The king and the three princes, my lord," Gad spoke quietly. "Jarib identified each box with a copper name plate. The lids are not sealed if you care to see inside."

David allowed Mephibosheth to crawl onto the back of the wagon to examine the row of containers. He rubbed his fingers over each plate, and then he carefully removed the lids of each container. He motioned for David to witness with him the royal contents. The bones of Saul and his sons were each wrapped in woolen blankets with their skulls resting on top of each blanket.

"My father. My father," gasped Mephibosheth, laying his hand upon his father's skull. "I barely remember him, my lord."

David opened his right hand to Mephibosheth and pointed to the long scar running along the center of his palm.

"This is the cut of the covenant I made with your father in the Valley of Elah. This is how much I loved your father." David drew the tip of his finger along the scar tissue. "This was the sign of our eternal brotherhood that extended to our offspring. You are under that bond, and I see the heart of your father within you."

"My lord." Mephibosheth pressed David's hand upon his chest.

"My lord, we must depart if we are to leave Jerusalem before sunrise," Joab said.

"Yes. I do not want the unwelcomed attention of curious eyes."

David drove the mule team while the others rode their mounts in front of the wagon. Mephibosheth remained in the back of the wagon, nestled among the boxes of his ancestors. He had spent so little time among the men of his family when he was a lad, and this would be the last time he would ever be this close to them. David glanced over his shoulder to see Mephibosheth stroking the top of his father's crate, his lips quietly moving as if conveying all the thoughts and feelings he was never able to express to his father. David understood. He too wished to converse with his dear friend like they once did in the long ago when their friendship was not restrained by the madness of the king.

There were no travelers on the northern road to Gibeah, but in the pre-dawn darkness, David observed campfires flickering in the fields and valleys. The fieldhands would soon be rising from their tents preparing for work.

The full moon shone above, the third one since the rains had stopped. If it was true that Rizpah had been protecting the bodies of the seven heirs from scavengers and carrion eaters since the spring rains ended, then the devotion and conduct of this gallant woman was beyond his grasp. No one he knew, man nor woman, would have such endurance or show such fearlessness for as long as this noble woman had done.

David could not pinpoint the last time he was in Gibeah.

Was it the night he fled from Saul when Mikal had to let him down with a rope out of the window of their dwelling as the soldiers pounded on their door? That felt like a lifetime ago, or perhaps it was another life altogether.

Joab guided them through the woods on the outskirts of Gibeah so they would not go through the town.

When they came out of the forest and onto the road leading up to the front of the compound, David could not believe the disrepair of the Hall of the Wolf King. As the sun peeked through the trees, the light revealed the decay time had wrought on the magnificent structure. The roof had fallen in, and rafters were gone as well as the support beams. The great doors had rotted and fallen from the frames onto the floor of the hall.

This was where he had stood before the king. This was where he and Mikal had been wed along with her sister and husband. This was where the king had hurled a spear at him while he sang during the family meal. The house inside the compound fallen victim to time and the elements. The rock wall encircling the house had crumbled in several spots. It could be breached by rambunctious children. The royal stables and barracks had tumbled in on themselves. A few sheep and goats bleating from their corrals appeared indifferent to the arrival of strangers.

Had they all mysteriously entered a dream?

If this was a shared nightmare, it came with a horrible odor. More shocking than the sight of the poor conditions of the structures, was the putrid smell of decomposition. As David followed the others around the side of the house their horses became skittish and resisted the direction their riders were forcing them to take.

Gad turned back to David. "My lord, we forgot to warn you."

David's mule team came to an abrupt stop, both shook their heads in refusal to move forward.

Before David could snap the reins upon the rumps of the mules, he was knocked back into his seat by the thick stench that buffeted his face and flowed into his mouth and nostrils. His eyes felt as if they were melting.

In the wagon bed, Mephibosheth gagged and spit. David turned to see him hanging over the side of the wagon retching.

Benaiah tossed the reins of his horse to Abishai and jumped to the ground.

He walked to the mule team, took the harness of the lead mule. "Just a little farther and we can park the wagon, my lord."

"Thank you, Benaiah." David took a swig from the waterskin and tossed it back to Mephibosheth, who had begun to recover.

"Why is the air so foul?" Mephibosheth wiped his mouth before he drank.

"I have never smelled a battlefield so rank." David held tightly to the reins as Benaiah guided the team around to the side of the compound and stopped. Once he locked the front wheels of the wagon, David jumped out and moved to the edge of the overgrown garden.

"If I remember, the family tomb is on top of the hill tucked inside the tree line," David said. "We must clear a path through this foliage, wide enough for our wagon."

The garden plants were lush and green, but nothing had been harvested. The fat stalks of barley were spread over with the plump heads of wheat disintegrating into the soil. The weight of the vegetables had bent the plants nearly in two leaving the unpicked yield to rot on the ground. The smell of decay was everywhere.

"Gad, you and Nathan stay with the wagon." David drew his sickle-shaped sword from the wagon seat and began to hack through the thick vegetation. His nephews and Benaiah followed behind, clearing a wider space for the wagon to get through to the open ground beyond.

The morning sun was beginning to radiate its bright yellow glow warming the earth, but also intensifying the terrible stench. Feathered creatures circled above, casting dark shadows over the earth and screeching in rattling cries.

Then came a human howl.

David first thought it a soaring bird or four-legged beast. It sounded human yet not human, otherworldly, out of the depths of Sheol uttered from a tormented soul. The muscles in his legs and arms quivered. The fear unleashed in him was something he had never felt, not even before a battle. The sword fell from his hand, but instead of reaching down to retrieve it, he was propelled forward through the verdant thickness until he stepped out upon the barren hill.

He had trod into the valley of the shadow of death.

Carrion eaters hovered in the air above or perched in the dead branches of the surrounding trees, all looking down upon the thick carpet of vultures, buzzards, crows, and ravens strewn across the ground. Scattered among the dead were the carcasses of wild dogs and boars, even a few wolves. This layer of fowl and beast were not huddled together waiting for death to offer a meal. This flooring was a lifeless gathering, a rotting ground cover.

"Away! Away!" shrieked the phantom dressed in ragged sackcloth and wielding a sword at the carrion eaters foolish enough to swoop within the length of her blade. The strike of the sword was true. Another vulture dropped, flopping about in the throes of death until it became as lifeless as the others.

The phantom had established her position upon a flat rock protruding from the ground. A small tent sheltered her from the elements. Just above her crude dwelling, the seven cages were suspended from the scaffolding with thick rope. Inside the seven cages were the withered bodies of Saul's sons and grandsons.

Here was death and wrath. Here was the stark rebuke. Here was a brutal judgment that he had approved. The innocents had died for the guilty. The natural world of David's memories of this place had become unnatural by this evil vision and wretched smells. The vision David had entered must come to a final end here, with the burial of the house of Saul, and never, ever be repeated.

"These boys never had the chance to become grown men. Never had the chance to fall in love and bring children into the world. What a terrible world it has become."

David recognized the voice, and though it pierced his heart to hear it, this voice was a welcome sound. He turned to see Mikal holding a bowl of porridge and a water sack strapped across her front.

"I cannot eat," he said.

"Not for you." Mikal motioned the bowl toward the phantom. "For her."

"Is that Rizpah?" David squint his eyes for better focus.

"The bravest, most honorable man or woman I have ever known," Mikal said.

"This is my doing," David confessed. "Do not blame Yahweh for this."

"I do not blame Yahweh," she replied. "How can I blame someone I never knew?"

"How can you stand this stench?" David raised a hand to his mouth and nose. "Or this field of carnage?"

"My senses adapted months ago when there was no way to escape," Mikal replied. "Now, may I pass?"

David stood still, not to block her way up the hill, he just could not move his legs.

"We did not part well," David said. "Not on good terms."

"They were your terms," Mikal replied. "A life at court as the spurned and barren wife of the king would have been too agonizing."

"I have brought the bones of your father and brothers. We had them unearthed and brought from Jabesh Gilead, where they had been buried."

Mikal became visibly shaken.

David stepped forward and slipped his hands beneath hers that held the bowl.

"My father and brothers are home?" Her voice became fragile.

"In the wagon parked beside the compound wall with Nathan and Gad."

"Gad also?" she asked. "Gad is with you?"

"He and Nathan stand guard over the four crates of remains." David watched Mikal's eyes fill with tears. "There is a surprise as well. Jonathan's son is with them, your nephew, Mephibosheth."

"He is alive?" Mikal asked. She kept shaking her head as if refusing to believe David's words.

"My vow to your brother exceeds any agreement with the Gibeonites. I am here now to bury the dead. All the members of the house of Saul shall rest together in the tomb of their ancestors."

"My lady," Benaiah greeted Mikal as he stopped beside David.

Mikal looked as if she did not recognize him and stepped back.

"My lord, we have cleared the foliage for the wagon to drive through," he said.

"Thank you, Benaiah. Would you escort Lady Mikal to the wagon?"

"Yes, my lord," replied Benaiah, and he raised his arm to receive Mikal's hand.

But she hesitated, her face pinched with anxiety and bewilderment.

"You must see Mephibosheth, Mikal. You will be so proud of your nephew. I will take the bowl and waterskin to Lady Rizpah."

Mikal relinquished the dish and the waterskin to David before taking Benaiah's arm, allowing him to lead her gently to the wagon.

David trudged up the hill of the dead to offer this simple breakfast to Lady Rizpah. She had never wavered. She had never fled. He would rank this valiant guardian of Saul's heirs among his mightiest of warriors.

PART FOUR

Chapter 25

SOLOMON BELIEVED SHE WALKED ON AIR. *HOW COULD ANYONE so beautiful ever touch the ground?*

The world parted before her. Songs were composed praising her beauty. The king and his court, indeed all in the royal household, doted on her. When she entered the gardened courtyard or the Hall of the Lion or any chamber in the palace, conversations paused and heads swiveled in her direction. When she walked through the streets of Jerusalem, children skipped behind her, women joyfully waved, and men marveled that such splendor could be captured in one human form.

She needed no guardian from the crowds. Her beauty was protection enough. One glance from her bright eyes, one smile, one nod of her head, one pleasing word of gratitude for a kind word spoken in her honor, and whoever was before her melted away, their heart quenched with a memory of the grace given to them. For the nation of Israel had claimed Princess Tamar as their own. She was the pure bride of the chosen.

Solomon was unsure how to act around his older sister, the ineptness of middle adolescence gave him no confidence in her presence. No one quite knew what to do with her. It was not as if she were fragile and might break at the slightest touch like a delicate piece of pottery. Yet who would risk blemishing such an exquisite creature by mere human contact?

There had been suitors, but none found worthy. Each arrived with wagons full of treasures and an overconfidence that the king's daughter would be unable to resist. To woo this prize away from King David's royal house to accept a new role as wife to the son of a noble tribal lord, or better, become a wife to some foreign prince seeking alliances with Israel was a daunting challenge. After an audience with the king, a banquet with the royal family, and a private sitting with the princess, each hopeful departed without a bride. The wagons of treasure brought to entice the princess remained behind, filling storerooms with the gifts of the rebuffed. When the dejected wooer made his exit from the city, the nation breathed a sigh of relief. Israel could keep this beauty to themselves a little longer.

His father did not seem to mind the steady flow of hopeful-turned-melancholic courters. Rather, the king seemed to relish the consternation caused by his daughter's reluctance to marry. His father was proud of his lineage and took joy in the company of his offspring. Dinners were lively affairs. Holidays were celebrated with gusto. When his father grew restless and wanted to get out of the city, Solomon and the whole family loaded into wagons and carriages, and the large caravan traveled throughout the land so the king could show off his brood.

The nation had been at peace for many years, and "what good is peace if you are unable to go out into the country and enjoy it," his father would say.

There had not been a war since the defeat of the Ammonites and the sacking of the capital city of Rabbah, the same year Solomon had been born. It was as if his birth ushered in a time of tranquility. At least, that was how his father conveyed it to him. He was proud to be the son of David and Bathsheba, the son of peace—a fitting description of his nature.

With peace and prosperity, the people of Israel had the liberty to travel without fear. When his father's advisors suggested he visit the capital city of each of the twelve tribes, the king embraced the proposal. Such excursions were not quiet visits when the king and his court paid homage to the tribal elite. They were elaborate undertakings with musical performances and dances, bazaars lining the streets, exhibits and competitions, and a full day devoted to military games and exercises. It was an economic windfall for the host city, and no expense was spared to lavish honor upon the king and his family.

Solomon loved these trips as a young boy. These jubilees were thrilling spectacles, but as he grew older, he saw how such events benefited his father. These trips were an opportunity for the chosen to celebrate the bounty and blessing of the Almighty during peacetime, and with such unity among the tribes, his kingdom grew stronger.

Like a shooting star, his father did not shy away from a chance to dazzle the crowds on these occasions. The first day of every festival, the king drove his chariot into each host city with great fanfare. Solomon was most proud to see his mother riding in the chariot at the king's side. Bathsheba might not have been the king's first wife, but she was his last. His father had not taken any additional women into the family dwelling after marrying his mother, not even additional concubines. While his father saw to it that his wives and concubines and his heirs were well cared for, his mother was elevated to the status of queen. Solomon had lived in the palace with his parents since his birth. Life at court was all he knew.

While the king and queen enjoyed the cheering crowds of the host city as they rode the chariot at the head of the parade, they were not the main attractions. That honor went to his older sister, Tamar, and her twin brother. Absalom was as blessed with handsomeness and physical prowess as Tamar was with natural beauty. The twins were born to his father from a marriage to Maacah, daughter of the king of Geshur during his time of exile fleeing the mad king.

Absalom and Tamar rode in their own chariot and the soldiers lining the parade route had to link arms as they drove into the host city. Solomon and the rest of his siblings and their mothers traveled together in large family wagons behind the twins. Watching the people's reaction to his parents and the twins, Solomon learned early on this was what the citizens of Israel wanted in their leaders, an attractive and self-confident outward appearance more than what quality of character might reside inside the soul.

Solomon could never confess to anyone his secret infatuation with his older sister. All he could do was languish, daydream, and write verses. He was too nervous around Tamar. On the rare occasion they might be placed next to each other at the king's table, Solomon only nibbled at his food and hardly spoke. Tamar would try to engage him in conversation, asking after his studies at the prophet's school and what he was learning, but his youthful uneasiness made it impossible to give her a thoughtful answer.

She confided how she wished to attend the prophet's school with Solomon and the rest of her brothers and cousins along with the young men from wealthy families and those of high military rank. "Women should not be denied the study of the sacred texts," she whispered one evening at table.

Solomon almost choked on his wine. He believed Yahweh would not prohibit any woman studying these revered stories and instructions, but Tamar was not any woman. Were she to sit at the prophet's table with the other students, their ears would go deaf, their eyes glaze over, and their tongues would turn to stone from staring at her beauty.

Solomon bent over his desk, one hand rubbing his forehead while the other struggled to write the perfect words of his newest verse describing Tamar. "Your eyes behind your veil are the eyes of a dove. Your flowing hair is like a flock of goats as they descend the mountain, your teeth are like shorn sheep fresh from washing, your lips are like a scarlet ribbon, your mouth is lovely, your neck is like a tower built in elegance, your…your…"

He sighed. Even with his gift of language, Solomon was never satisfied with his odes. And what did it matter?

He could never give these love songs to Tamar nor show them to anyone. He would burn this newest one just as he had all the others. As soon as the ink had dried on the parchment, he would toss these scribbles into the fire. They must never be read.

"Jedidiah."

The name was spoken from just outside the discourse room.

"Jedidiah, what are you still doing here?"

Solomon startled out of his trance.

"Everyone has finished the lesson and gone to the games. What are you doing?"

"Nothing, Master Nathan," Solomon sputtered. "Nothing."

"You still copying the assigned text?"

"No, my lord. Just practicing my lettering. It is nothing." The dye had not dried on the parchment, and he wiped the words with his sleeve.

"Well, come with me." Nathan motioned for Solomon to stand and follow. "The games will begin soon, and I am sure the family is gathering in the royal box. Hurry now. You do not want to miss your brother's shearing."

"Absalom and his hair," Solomon said as he stood. "What a spectacle."

"Now, now. It is for a worthy cause," Nathan chided.

"The cause is always about Absalom." Solomon folded the smeared parchment and tossed it into the brazier used to heat the lecture room of the prophet's school. "Whether selling his beautiful hair to the highest bidder or winning the gilded olive branch, again, my older brother is always his own best cause."

"You drone like a younger brother," Nathan said, a slight grin on his lips. "It is unbecoming of you, Jedidiah. So, gird up your loins, young man. We must depart."

Nathan was the only person allowed to call him by the name "Jedidiah." Solomon was a little perplexed about the circumstances around his birth. His parents were always evasive with the details. All they ever told him was that he had a brother who died only a few days after being born and his parents were grief-stricken until he came along. When he pressed for more details, both reassured him of their love, and that after he was born, Nathan had come to the palace to say their son was beloved of Yahweh. When Nathan referred to Solomon as "Jedidiah" it was always with affection even when chiding him.

When his older brothers spoke the name, it was pronounced with derision. His father had to intervene to stop the teasing, which only made it worse for Solomon.

No guard detail escorted Nathan and Solomon from the prophet's school to the city center. A prophet and a young prince attracted no attention. The focus of the crowd was directed to where the royal family was ensconced on the platforms towering above the city center. These rostrums were built for the royals and invited guests to observe the celebrations and friendly competitions among the military elite. The rest of the people were jammed around the open center or took positions on the rooftops and windows of the surrounding buildings.

After years of traveling to all the capital cities of every tribe, his father announced he wanted the celebrations and the games to be held in Jerusalem. These festivities followed the Day of Atonement when citizens from around the country came to Jerusalem. After ten days of worship and sacrifice at the Tabernacle, the High Priest made the final atoning sacrifice for the sins of the nation sprinkling blood on the Mercy Seat of the Ark. The time of repentance was complete, and what better way to celebrate than with a festival of music, dances, and games?

Solomon and Nathan took seats among the royal family. His father jumped to his feet the moment Absalom entered the city center that had been transformed into an arena. The rest of the throng burst into frenzied cheering and applause.

Absalom was flanked by three of his brothers—Amnon, Daniel, and

Adonijah. Daniel held Absalom's glistening raven hair like a royal cape to keep it from dragging the ground. Amnon clasped a sword before him, and Adonijah carried a wide golden tray. The rest of David's sons marched in step toward the podium with a staircase of a dozen steps to reach the top. A table was placed on the platform at the top of the stairs.

Only the sibling honor guard escorted Absalom up the steps while the other brothers remained below. The quartet of unsmiling faces, stern with single purpose, inspired the crowds into greater frenzy.

Solomon laughed at the theatre of it all and received a knobby prophet's elbow in his ribs for his trouble.

"I thought Israel was to have no other God but Yahweh," Solomon said, rubbing his side where Nathan's blow had struck.

Nathan pointed to the platform, indicating for Solomon to hush.

Solomon had declined the invitation to be a part of the brotherly entourage. Such public glaring was not to his liking.

Absalom took the long rope of his hair from Daniel. When he raised it into the air, the city center fell silent.

"The days of repentance have come to an end." Absalom began to turn in a full circle on top of the platform. "The skies above the City of David are scented with offerings to Yahweh. But one more sacrifice is to be made, and it is my honor to offer it."

Solomon could not ignore the obvious. By such an outward show, Absalom proved to be every inch a king. Amnon and Daniel were ahead of him in age and rank, but the unspoken truth was that David preferred Absalom to the others. Aside from his eye-catching presence, he excelled in his military training and took the top prizes in nearly every competition. However, given the long-extended peace enjoyed by the nation, Absalom's soldierly skills, had yet to be tested in battle.

Solomon was too far back in the pack to even consider becoming king, so he did not blame his father for doting on his older brother.

Absalom was not just a handsome face. He was becoming a perfect candidate to be the next king, gaining respect among the people as someone who could settle disagreements and equitably resolve legal disputes. If the king was too busy or disinterested in a minor squabble between two parties, then the complaint or petition could be brought to Prince Absalom, and it was quickly expedited. He performed this duty not just for the wealthy classes or tribal leaders, all of whom poured vast amounts into the treasury of the king. Everyone was treated with equal status.

Neither Amnon nor Daniel displayed the physical prowess and mental acuity to become king. Nor did they possess the mesmerism of their brother. Those assets had not passed through the bloodline. Absalom horded those qualities for himself.

His father cupped his hands over his mouth and shouted down to his sons. "And where will the money collected from your sacrifice be spent?"

"We will build a new addition to the school of the prophets," Absalom replied. "There is a need for more room to store the records of our great nation."

Absalom saluted the adoring crowd before handing his hair back to Daniel.

"Did you know about this?" Solomon leaned toward Nathan and spoke into his ear. He had to shout to be heard.

"Only rumors," Nathan replied, and then offered a helpless shrug.

Solomon was impressed with Absalom's innate skills of diplomacy. Donating his hair to raise financial support for the school of the prophets only enhanced his reputation.

Absalom knelt before the table. He leaned back as Daniel scooted around to the other side and stretched out the long plait funnel across the top like a great snake uncoiling itself in the warmth of the sun. Amnon then raised his sword.

The blow would be struck within a few inches of Absalom's head, and here the drama could take a tragic turn. If Amnon miscalculated or flinched as he brought down the sharp blade, he could easily lop off Absalom's head and not the intended coil of thick hair. Such was the purpose of the spectacle, to emphasize the bravery of the king's son. The stagecraft of this sacrifice had been carefully produced and, Solomon hoped, carefully executed.

He scanned the crowd, many of whom were looking away or covering their eyes. Not Tamar. She sat at the feet of the king and his mother, leaning forward, hands folded as if in prayer and tucked beneath her chin, her complete attention on her brother.

Tamar had never looked at him this way. If she ever did, Solomon would disintegrate.

He looked back just as Amnon brought the sword down upon the thick lock of Absalom's hair. The cut was swift and clean, and Absalom leapt to his feet yanking the severed hair off the table and raising it into the sky.

His brother's identity was wrapped up in outward appearance, and Solomon was shocked to see him without his famous locks. The crowd did not seem to mind such a drastic alteration to his handsome stature. They loved him all the more.

Tamar sprang to her feet blowing kisses to her brother. She was the first to toss shekels into the enclosure. She grabbed two leather pouches off a tray and hurled them into the air. What followed was a hailstorm of coinage and jewels. It was as if the Almighty were pouring riches from the sky.

Solomon leaned back to Nathan and shouted, "You could build a whole new school with this deluge." He pointed to the airborne wealth covering the arena floor.

The prophet was too captivated by the spectacle to respond.

Solomon could never compete for such adoration. He could never receive such sisterly affection from Tamar. He could never be worthy of such greatness.

Chapter 26

TAMAR WAS PUT OUT BY THE REQUEST BUT CHOSE TO HONOR it. She preferred to remain at the banquet tables in the Hall of the Lion with her family and other guests of the court. Her older brother, Amnon, had taken ill after a long day at the festival games—perhaps too much sun, the king surmised—and Amnon requested their father send Tamar to his chambers.

For what? Prepare him some food? What an absurd request. *What are the servants for if not to cater to my brother's whims?*

The firstborn, the heir to the throne, was the pampered one, and Amnon always knew how to manipulate their father.

The evening had been devoted to celebrating the end of the Day of Atonement, and Tamar did not want to miss any of this joyous time with her family.

"I have just returned from his chambers," her father told her. "Amnon is ill."

"But Abba, he is always ill," Tamar had protested. "We are celebrating. I want to remain with you and the family. Send one of the servants to feed him."

The king wrapped his arms around Tamar, pulling her into his chest. "Amnon has not been the same since his mother died," said her father as he stroked the back of her hair. "I know he is mopey, but perhaps you can cheer him up and both of you return here with us. He just wants you to bake him some of your famous honey cakes. When I left, the servants were setting out everything you will need in his chambers: the baking oven, honey and nuts, pot of dough. Bake a few cakes then hurry back. I promise you, we will be celebrating well into the night."

Her father kissed her forehead and sent her off.

Tamar could not refuse him. She traipsed behind Jonadab, her cousin, who had been assigned to befriend Amnon when he came to the city for his court appointment. Tamar could not remember when Jonadab had first arrived. She could not keep track of the number of cousins flowing in and out of court, all looking for placements in the kingdom, all expecting favors because of the bloodline association to her father. As a clan, the king's extended family was large enough to qualify as a separate tribe had not the number been set at twelve long ago.

The king felt obligated to keep ties with his brothers and sisters even though he rarely saw them. "You are born into a particular family not of your choosing," her father told her. "But you can choose the distance you keep."

Right now, Tamar wished for a mountain range between her and her faint-hearted brother.

"Jonadab, what is wrong with Amnon?" Tamar asked, barely disguising her irritation as she followed her cousin down the long corridor to her brother's chambers.

"Oh, you know," Jonadab said in his wispy voice with a hand whirling around the top of his head signaling an invisible confusion inside Amnon's brain. "Chills and fever. An ague that seems to come and go."

Jonadab's slippery answer was typical. His evasiveness was not a playful mischief cousins might engage in, but more subtle from a scheming personality that felt manipulative.

She had little contact with him, but whenever he was near, Tamar felt her body temperature drop. Her vexation at leaving the feast turned more sour just by having Jonadab as her escort. She wanted this drudgery over quick.

Tamar had visited her brother's chambers only once, and in the company of Absalom. Her twin trusted Amnon even less than she did. He had cautioned her never to count on such an inept person.

When the construction of the palace was completed and rooms assigned to the king's offspring, Amnon got first choice. Tamar's compartment, as well as the other adult children, was located in the upper levels of the palace. However, she preferred spending much of her time at Absalom's house which was built on top of the high interior wall at the base of the Stepped Stone staircase below the east wall of the palace.

Absalom had insisted on living away from the intrigues of court and from pesky siblings. Tamar, of course, was the exception. The twins loved to host the young men and women their age, the next-generation courtiers of a future king, at Absalom's house for entertainment. Tamar felt most at ease with her twin brother in his home with its view of the Kidron Valley, and she escaped to its solace as often as possible.

One of the servants drew aside the curtains surrounding the bed when Jonadab ushered Tamar into Amnon's chamber. A small oven was set beside the bed with a tray for the ingredients required for her honey cakes on the table beside it. The coals smoldered inside the oven. Two other servants were stationed behind the table awaiting instructions. The bedchamber was shadowy and scented with the oven fire and wafts of incense.

In spite of the warmth in the room, a chill ran along the top of Tamar's shoulders. She folded her arms around her middle to keep from shivering.

"You have come," Amnon said. "Oh, dear sister, you are here. My spirits are coming around just by the sight of you."

"Yes, I am here." Tamar looked suspiciously at Jonadab whose focus darted between her and Amnon. She sensed the web of plotting between them to lure her here to play some practical joke. "Abba said you were ill and wanted some of my honey cakes."

"The heat of the day's sun has sapped my strength." Amnon pressed his fingers into his forehead as if relieving lingering pain from the heat. "All food is repugnant. The wine tastes bitter. Only one thing that can revive me—honey cakes prepared by my sister and given me by her hand."

"It might do you some good if you got out of bed and came back with me to the feast." Tamar tried to keep her frustration from sounding like a scolding. "I…we…are missing all the merriment here in your musty room. We could use more light."

One of the servants made a move to bring oil lamps to the table, but Amnon held up his hand. "Sister, my head," Amnon whined, his face a grimace of discomfort. "The shadows help diminish the pain."

"Very well then." Tamar went to the table and began to tie the cloth apron around her waist. If she were not so annoyed at being sent away from the feast, she would find her whimsical brother pitifully humorous. She could not wait to tell Absalom. They would enjoy a derisive laugh at Amnon's expense, but for now, she found no humor in fulfilling this silly caprice.

She made quick work of kneading the ingredients, flattening a few patties, and dropping them onto the heated pan before placing it inside the mouth of the oven. Tamar was so absorbed in her baking activity that it was not until she placed the pan inside the oven that she realized Jonadab and the servants were absent.

"We need a few moments for the cakes to bake." She sat down on the end of the bed and looked about the room. "Where is everyone?"

"Sent away." Amnon waved a limp hand toward the exit. "They were moving about too much. It made my eyes blurry."

Tamar let the excuse satisfy. She had heard so many of his explanations for bodily infirmities and how each ailment hamstrung his ability to do much of anything. Cutting Absalom's hair today was the most physical exertion she had seen from Amnon since she could remember, and just the latest excuse for his malady.

How could he ever be king? Tamar wondered as they sat in the long silence, waiting for the honey cakes.

"Do not let them burn, sister." Amnon adjusted the cushions in his bed.

"Who is doing this job of baking?" Tamar snapped.

Amnon held up his hands in apology for his interference.

Tamar rose and went around the table and began to stack the leftover fixings back into the wooden kneading bowl.

"Why have you not married?" Amnon tossed aside a cushion and maneuvered himself into a kneeling position on the bed. "Tell me the real reason. In this parade of suitors, have you not found one man who caught your fancy? Was there no one that sharpened your desire to be wed?"

Tamar wiped her hands upon her apron before untying it and tossing it into the bowl. "I find your questions inappropriate. I will keep my own counsel regarding my plans of whom to wed. He will be of my own choosing, and I will not require your involvement on the matter."

Amnon chuckled as Tamar retrieved the apron from the bowl and knelt in front of the oven. She wrapped the apron around her hand before taking the handle of the pan and removing it from the warm fire.

"Just the smell of your honey cakes intoxicates me," Amnon said. "I feel my blood simmering and my body regaining its strength. Please take one of those sweet morsels and put it into my mouth."

Tamar sighed at the absurdity of this reaction to her simple baked patties and fought the impulse to toss them back into the oven and walk out. This was for her father, she reminded herself, and it would be over soon. Tamar held onto the handle and blew her breath on the cakes to cool them. She placed a finger on top of one to check the temperature then pinched off a bite to test. It tasted acceptable, and then she offered one to her brother for him to take one.

"I do not care for your cakes, Sister." Amnon's voice had transformed from weak and feathery to that of an animal growling over the death of its prey. "Good as they are, they are not why you are here."

Amnon rose up on his knees, snatched a cushion, and knocked the pan from Tamar's hands. The cushion and pan smashed against the brazier scattering the warm coals and ash onto the floor. Then he grabbed her hands.

"It is you I want. You that I crave. You are the honey cake to satisfy my desire."

He reached beneath her arms and yanked her onto the bed.

"No. Do not humble me by this evil." Tamar tried desperately to draw back.

Amnon only tightened his grip. She could plead, she could beg for him to restrain himself, but he was past reasoning. He kept clawing at her robe trying to remove it.

She could feel the white heat off his body and was shocked at how her weakling brother had become a ravenous beast. Still, she might be able to prevent this folly. She might fight back. Tamar slammed her fists into his chest pushing him away.

"Amnon, listen to me. This is a wicked thing you are trying to do. Such evil should not be done in Israel. And what about me? I would never be rid of my disgrace."

But there was no stopping him. Amnon gripped her shoulders forcing his kisses upon her. All reasoning had given way to licentious folly.

"You are a caught dove, my sister," Amnon said. "Yield."

Tamar would not yield. She twisted and turned inside the arms of her captor.

"What about you?" she gasped. "You will be remembered as one of the wicked fools in Israel for the rest of your days. Is this what you want people to think when the throne is given you? Talk to my father. He will not keep me from marrying you."

"You think I wish to marry you." Amnon's derisive laugh revealed his utter depravity. "I only want the pleasure of subduing you."

Tamar was pinned between his arms and chest, but she fought hard enough to free one arm, and with all her might slammed her balled fist into the side of his face. The blow only perturbed Amnon. The strike against the side of his head brought a momentary pause before he resumed his brutality.

"Speak to the king," she begged. "Please, speak to the king."

Her words did nothing to sober him.

"This is your marriage bed." Amnon forced her down upon the cushions and smothered her cries with his lips.

Her heart was destroyed. Her body was broken. Her mind fragmented. Was this the wrath of Yahweh poured out upon her?

What had brought on such judgment? With her eyes clamped shut, Tamar could not imagine how she might have offended her brother, what she had done to incur this maltreatment. She had no anticipation of Amnon's brutal action, no expectation of intent. She was taken completely by surprise. She had thought him incapable of most anything and certainly not this vile deed.

Whatever the reason, she could now see her end. She could see the emptiness before her, her life shut out, her body shut up in darkness, the slow rot of her soul preparing her for the burial cave.

When she found herself on the floor, she did not know how she had gotten there. Had she fallen? Had he tossed her from the bed?

She did not want to turn her head. She did not want to open her eyes, to ever open her eyes again and see the faces of others staring back in horror.

"Get up." The voice rose from beneath the cushions and blankets. "Get out."

By the snarling command Tamar understood that Amnon's gratification had turned to hatred. She stretched the hem of her robe over her bare legs and feet smeared by the ashes from the oven scattered across the floor beside the bed.

"No. No," Tamar moaned. She would plead for milder treatment. "Sending me away would be more disgraceful than this evil you have inflicted upon me."

The moment Amnon shouted their cousin's name, Jonadab stood before her. He did not reach out his hand as an offering of aid. His face was rigid as hard stone. His grip on her wrists was only a continuation of the rough handling she had endured.

"Throw this woman out of my sight and fasten the door behind her."

This woman. He did not refer to her by name.

Amnon did not even call her sister. *This woman.*

This woman. Her new identity.

By casting her out, by hurling her into the dark corridor, by shutting his chamber door upon her pitiful shape sprawled upon the floor, all the world would believe she was the guilty party, that her despicable brother had fallen victim to her enticements.

This woman had become untouchable.

Tamar struggled to her knees. She felt a warmth in one of her hands. When she curled back her fingers, she found her palm covered in ash from the brazier. She rubbed her palms together then wiped the ash over her hair and face.

A sudden strength coursed through her arms and into her hands as she tightened her fingers onto the neckline of her multicolored robe with its long purple sleeves and gold embroidery sewn onto the cuffs. This ornamental robe was given to her by her father, a sign of his pride and affection, a sign that she was a princess, a sign that she was, no, had been, a virgin daughter of the king, a virgin daughter of Israel.

With the muscle of a warrior, she ripped her beautiful robe from top to bottom. Why had not this power come to her before now?

Tamar could not return to the feast, not in this condition, not with the aftermath of her turmoil so obvious.

Her father would know. Absalom would know. Everyone in the Hall of the Lion would know. She would wait. She would find a place of darkness and wait, a darkness so deep it would match the darkness of her heart.

Chapter 27

SOLOMON WAS SLOW TO AWAKEN. HE HEARD HIS NAME BEING called, but not with an urgency or with a tenderness as if waking a sleeping infant. The name he heard was the name only used by the prophet Nathan, but it was not his voice.

The voice that spoke was in pain, the sound of deep mourning, a grief so abysmal it was uttered in the whole tone of despair.

"Jedidiah," the voice moaned. "Jedidiah."

Solomon did not want to move from his bed. He did not want to open his eyes to find the source. Could this be some disembodied spirit come to trouble him, he wondered? Was this spirit from the underworld of Sheol, or did it inhabit his dreams?

His heart quickened, and with each utterance of his name, he was drawn from the layers of slumber into the dim light of the room.

"Jedidiah," the voice spoke, this time as if in lamentation. "Jedidiah."

He rubbed his face, quickening wakefulness, then his eyes to wipe away the fog. Might this be Yahweh speaking his name, beloved of Yahweh?

One oil lamp burned at his bedside, the small flame struggling against the full darkness in his bedchambers. "I am here," he whispered. "Who is this?"

He turned his head and stared through the curtains surrounding his bed. He could see no divine shadow, no human form. Perhaps someone was playing a prank, one of his siblings trying to frighten him by altering their voice into ghostly sounds.

"Jedidiah. Jedidiah."

His name was all the voice kept repeating, in grating pleas.

"I am here," Solomon replied.

He sat up and took his oil lamp from the bedside stand. Then he pulled back the bed curtain and swung his bare feet onto the floor. He lifted the oil lamp above his head.

No one was in the room. No one was standing or sitting. No one was at the door. It must be a spirit, he surmised, and not siblings enjoying a hoax.

"Jedidiah."

His name never sounded so pitiful in the voice of this spirit, and his blood surged throughout his body.

"I am here," he said, rising to his feet. He extended his arm and waved the lamp as he took his first steps into the open space of his room.

When the voice spoke again, the sound stopped him in his tracks.

"Jedidiah," the voice now sobbed.

Here was the source. Not a spirit. Not a mischievous sibling. His name was being called by a berobed lump of flesh lying prostrate at his feet, calling his name from a wound so deep it took all the strength it had just to speak it.

Solomon did not bend. He lowered the lamp over the body and waved the flame along its full length.

"I am ruined. Jedidiah, I am ruined," the voice cried like an ancient expression of grief for an act of judgment from the Almighty.

Solomon had heard this voice before, but never in such turmoil of the soul. He did not want to believe it might be her, but no one else was present. He bent beside the prone form, heaving in painful sobs. He placed his hand upon a shoulder.

The reaction was immediate. The shoulder stiffened and jerked free, the whole body frantically crawling away as if in terror of another touch, less gentle, fiercer.

"Forgive me," he said. "I did not mean to frighten you."

The body stopped crawling and slowly rose to its knees as if carrying a great weight upon its shoulders. Her balled fists beat her breast pounding out her breath in heaves and cries. "I am ruined. I am ruined."

"Tamar? Is that you?" Solomon did not want to believe this disheveled figure on her knees in front of him was his sister. He stretched the lamp toward her to be sure of the identity. In the full light of the flame, he saw a head covered in ashes, a face streaked with soot and tears, eyes swollen, a beautiful robe torn asunder.

This could not be Tamar. This evil apparition arrived without invitation.

"What has happened to you?"

"Help me. Take me to my brother's house while it is still night," she pleaded. "No one must see me like this. No one must look upon my shame."

Solomon did look upon her shame. The woeful echoes of her shame filled his ears. He tried to orient his mind around this despairing vision of his sister. This angel, this untouchable goddess, this idol of purity praised and adored by all of Israel was a freakish hunk of agony begging him for aid. He had last seen her squealing with delight at the trophy of her brother's hair hoisted before the crowds at the festival games. Now, her broken soul was half-clothed in shredded purple rags.

It was not far to Absalom's dwelling, but no matter how late the hour, they could not leave the palace and risk being seen. Not with Tamar in this condition.

Whatever the cause for her unhappy state, he did not want to inflict further sorrow if seen by friend or family or stranger. He set the oil lamp on the floor, yanked his robe off the foot of his bed, and draped it over Tamar's shoulders.

"Come," he said, and tenderly lifted Tamar to her feet.

Solomon looked outside his entrance. It was still night, though he could not tell the hour. He leaned his head around the threshold.

The sentries clumped together between the columns near the entryway of the private compartments the king shared with Solomon's mother. The courtyard was empty. The doors of the Hall of the Lion were closed, the feasting finished.

"Are you ready?" Solomon whispered.

Tamar nodded.

Solomon folded his arm over her shoulders and tucked her into his side. He had never been this close before. He had never touched her. Now, she was attached to him, like a breastplate. He was her protective covering.

They saw no one in the short distance between the palace and the wide Stepped Stone staircase on the eastern side of the palace. As they descended the steps, Tamar was unable to keep from sobbing, at times crying out so forcefully the dogs barked in response. Solomon could not imagine what tragic event had brought her to this state of uncontrollable sorrow.

When they reached the bottom, Solomon guided them to a gated entrance that opened onto the stairs to Absalom's private quarters. The stairs were built into the towering interior city wall separating the palace from the military housing. These dwellings were given to those who had distinguished themselves in service to the king. Absalom's quarters were situated on the uppermost section of the eastern wall. As they stumbled up the winding steps, Solomon prayed Absalom had not brought his young friends home to continue celebrating once leaving the palace. The twins were known for hosting revelries well into the night. Titled courtiers from the twelve tribes and military leaders with promising careers vied for coveted invitations. If there were overnight guests in her brother's house, it would only make Tamar more distraught.

Solomon paused for Tamar to catch her breath once they reached the top of the stairs. She was exhausted from expelling her grief, and the vigorous ascent had winded them both. He looked around the outside of the house while Tamar recovered. It appeared no one was on the premises, not even sprawled on the cushions and couches in the garden terrace overlooking the Kidron Valley. No oil lamps burned inside the dwelling. Was Absalom even home, he wondered?

Tamar began to squirm before bolting free of Solomon's tight hold. He felt a sudden coolness in the vacancy where he had pressed Tamar into his side to comfort and protect. In an instant she was gone, disappearing through the entryway calling her brother's name.

He did not follow, but through a window saw a flickering light and then a shadow emerging from an interior room.

The moment he heard Absalom cry out in horror, Solomon felt an icy coldness seize his heart. He cocked his ear toward the front entrance, listening for what might happen next, waiting to see if he was required. But no immediate summons came.

He remained at the front entrance as the duet of wailing, a sister's sorrow echoed by her twin brother continued. Solomon might be moved by this grief, but he could not share its burden. Whatever had attacked Tamar, possessed her, broken her, only Absalom could find out the truth.

The night sky was yielding its darkness to the predawn light. Solomon had never been invited to this house. He knew the twins thought him too youthful and too studious to associate with their friends. It was not that they looked down upon Solomon, they had never paid much attention to him, the little brother, one of a score of children sired by their father. He understood that the quiver full of the king's children was too much to keep up with, and he did not blame them for ignoring him. But now he had been brought in. He had borne witness to the aftermath of something horrible inflicted upon a delicate creature.

"Solomon, are you still on the terrace?" Absalom asked from inside his dwelling.

"I am," Solomon replied.

"I need your help."

Solomon did not hesitate, and he went straight into the house.

There in the common room, Absalom held Tamar in his arms. "I need you to light the way to the guest room." Absalom stepped aside for Solomon to come forward and take the oil lamp sitting on the table.

Solomon raised the oil lamp. The dwelling's spacious interior was beautifully decorated with nice furnishings, tables set for dining with fine pottery, and embroidered hangings covering the walls. The impressive home was designed for entertainment.

"Her room is on the right." Absalom nodded for him to lead the way.

Solomon slipped into a hallway then into the room ahead of Absalom. He raised the lamp above his head, so Absalom could lay Tamar on her bed.

"On the table there is a pitcher and bowl. Pour her some water," Absalom said before covering his sister with a quilt.

Solomon set down the lamp and poured water into a clay bowl then handed it to Absalom.

Absalom removed a cloth scarf from around his neck and dipped a corner into the water. Then he began to dab away streaks of grime from his sister's face.

"Does our father know about this?" Absalom looked back at Solomon, but Tamar answered for him.

"He knows nothing," she said, her voice raw from the flow of grief.

"What do you know, Solomon?" asked Absalom.

"He knows nothing." Tamar again answered for him.

"She is correct. I was asleep in my chamber, and Tamar awoke me. We came straight here."

"Good. Good." Absalom gently pushed back the hair from Tamar's face. "My sister has been…has been…," and Absalom tried to continue, but instead lay his head upon Tamar's shoulder and wept.

Solomon could not imagine a more sorrowful moment than the one he now witnessed, a brother and sister conjoined in grief so bitter the stricken were incapable of expressing it except in wailful tears.

When Absalom regained his composure, he used the scarf to wipe his face followed by his sister's.

"Amnon has done this evil deed," Absalom said. "He has forced himself upon my sister. Do you understand, Solomon?"

Of a thousand wrongs that could be done by one human to another of its kind, why had this one been done to Tamar, and by her half-brother?

"I do," whispered Solomon.

Solomon aged into a new place of knowledge, how life in a world thought safe could turn brutal. It was a cruel wisdom. He marveled at how one mighty sin could strike down something so pure and shatter it into fragments.

Tamar suddenly sat up in bed, yanked the cloth from her brother's hand, and frantically wiped the front of her torn robe sobbing louder with each swipe.

"I can never return to the palace," she cried. "Never. Never."

Absalom clasped Tamar's wrists and brought them to his lips. "Calm yourself now," he said. "We must not torment ourselves. We must try to forget this injury, or it will stain us all as children of the king. We must bear this evil until…until…we shall be made whole again."

Absalom helped Tamar to lie back down then replaced the blanket over her. "Sleep now, for you are innocent. Sleep in your innocence. Be at peace."

Tamar complied with her brother's charge to sleep. She pressed her eyes together and tucked the blanket beneath her chin.

Absalom pointed for Solomon to exit the room with him. When they entered the common room, Absalom placed his hand upon Solomon's shoulder. "You have been witness to a great evil, my brother, from which I fear my sister will never recover," Absalom whispered. "You will carry this night with you for the rest of your days and must never forget, as horrible as it is. We must remember the beauty that was once my sister, our sister. I am thankful for your tenderness toward her, and I must ask one more thing of you. I cannot speak to the king about this. I must burden you with that message. I fear what I might say, what I might do. Can you do this for me?"

"I can. I will," Solomon answered.

Solomon returned to the palace in a daze. His heart was so heavy he felt as though he was returning from the smoldering ruins of a great city, sacked by its enemies. A city might be rebuilt to its former glory, but not a human heart after such trauma.

The sun was appearing in the east. How could it rise with such beauty and glory, when lying on a bed inside the house on the wall above him was the hollow shell of a young woman, once a beautiful star torn from the heavens and allowed to plummet to the earth burning out in a trail of dust and ash?

Chapter 28

BATHSHEBA DETECTED SUBTLE CHANGES IN THE KING'S DE-meaner. They were not apparent at first, but as time passed, she could see his gradual wariness to life, even a measured withdrawal of his affection toward her. Bathsheba wondered if it might be the number of years collecting in his soul and body, but the more she observed, the more she suspected something other than the march of time.

Her husband had lost a level of confidence.

David had always thrived in the company of others. He was a man of great passion and quick emotions, but since the incident, his interactions with others had diminished. She watched the subtle pulling away as if he was no longer sure he could trust others or himself. The duties of the king were carried out with the assistance of his aides, but Bathsheba witnessed a hesitancy to render decisions even when his worthy counselors gave good advice. He was not demonstrative in his reception of foreign dignitaries or of the tribal emissaries who came with offerings for the treasury. Feasts were always given in honor of these envoys, but her husband would soon tire of their company and feign a headache as an excuse for an early exit.

Bathsheba always looked forward to listening to the Levite choir whenever it was announced there was to be a concert. She was disappointed when she learned her husband had stopped requesting the music director to arrange recitals at court. David's visits to the Levite compound to listen to a rehearsal of one of Asaph's new compositions or one of his own submissions were rare.

She had not seen David composing for some time, and those spontaneous outbursts of praise expressing excitement by a new poetic inspiration, became fewer and fewer.

He had stopped attending the lectures of Nathan and Gad at the prophet's school or studying the ancient writings with Solomon. But when she heard her husband ask the servants to take his collection of musical instruments out of their bedchamber and put them in storage, Bathsheba knew her husband's soul was out of balance.

The assault could not be kept secret for long. Bathsheba expected retribution once it reached the ears of the king. He became enraged, but the outburst was a brief storm that dissipated like a summer squall. This man of action took no action.

The king did not allow anyone in court to speak of the incident, no one was allowed to speak ill of Amnon. He had the immunity of the firstborn son, heir to the throne. The absence of Tamar from family meals was enough of a reminder of the evil Amnon had inflicted upon her. Her vacant seat was a judgment on the king for his acquiescence to a son's iniquity.

Absalom continued to attend the royal family meals making excuses for Tamar until excuses became redundant then irrelevant. Bathsheba was shocked that Absalom never demanded his father pronounce a harsh sentence against Amnon, nor did she ever hear of Absalom threatening revenge. In her presence, Absalom never spoke to Amnon, either good or bad. He just ignored his older brother. The jovial spirit of family gatherings departed, and Bathsheba longed for its return.

The evenings preparing for bed disturbed Bathsheba the most. Where once their conversations were jammed with news from court and juicy tidbits of gossip, they were now fact-based and terse. Where once David filled her ears with new plans for expansion in the city and showed her drawings for new architecture, now it was as if all construction stopped. Where once David asked her opinion on a recent psalm he had scribbled and played for her, now the flow of inspiration had become a dry riverbed.

There had always been cuddling after the oil lamps were extinguished and before slumber took them, but since the assault, it was as if a sickness had crept into their souls and the ordinary life routines became exhausting. When they got into bed and the oil lamps were blown out, there was no loving embrace or whispered words of affection.

One evening as Bathsheba prepared for bed, sobbing came from within

David's private bathing stall. She tiptoed to the entrance and heard weeping. She had chosen to honor her husband's request never to speak of Amnon's wickedness against Tamar and had pretended life was continuing as normal, but it was far from normal and her husband hiding in his water closet weeping was proof enough that his heart was crumbling.

Bathsheba slipped into the partition. She would no longer ignore the obvious.

David sat on the tiled floor, a towel wrapped around his middle, his back propped against the large, tiled vessel full of hot water. Steam rose from inside the bathing cask. He had not dried himself, and water formed small pools on the floor where he sat, evidence he had just emerged from his bath.

When David saw her, he brought his legs up to his chest and crossed his arms over his knees and dropped his head upon his arms.

Bathsheba knelt on the wet floor beside her husband. She did not touch him for fear of stifling his outpouring of grief. She knew this grief must be expelled before there was any hope of consolation.

"I bathe and bathe. I scrub with hyssop and spices, soak in oils, but my sin is ever before me." David's voice was a wet rasp. "I thought I might…I hoped to escape the calamities Nathan spoke of on our wedding day, but my sin is ever before me."

Bathsheba rested her hand upon David's head. He had not finished his lament, and she did not want to restrain him but wanted him to know that the mercy in her touch reflected the mercy in her heart.

"The heartbreak has begun. My firstborn has imitated my sin against you. I have shed the blood of tens of thousands, yet this is the sin for which I am to be remembered for all time. This is the sin that brings tragedy upon my house. This is the sin Yahweh has not forgotten."

Bathsheba rose and lifted David to his feet. She took a clean towel from the stand and dried him off. She replaced the damp towel around his middle with a fresh robe and led him out of his private bathing room.

He was a helpless child. He did not resist her care. He did not resist her guidance to their bed. He did not resist when she covered him with linen blankets. He did not ask her to refrain from sitting beside him in their bed or for her to stop singing a chorus from one of his songs.

> *"O Yahweh, You are my God, earnestly I seek You;*
> *My soul thirsts for You, my body longs for You,*

> *In a dry and weary land where there is no water.*
> *Trust in Yahweh at all times, O people;*
> *Pour out your hearts to Him, for Yahweh is our refuge."*

Bathsheba sang until his weeping stopped, his breathing steadied, and his eyes closed in weariness. When she knew David was sound asleep, she extinguished the oil lamps on the bedstands, slipped out of her nightclothes, and dressed in warmer attire. Bathsheba moved briskly to Solomon's chambers and saw his oil lamps still burning. She knocked on the frame of the entrance into his rooms but did not wait for him to answer. She pushed aside the curtains and found her son at his desk reading from the scrolls.

"Take me to see Tamar." It was not a request. It was a charge.

"At this hour of the night?"

"Now," she replied.

"Should we not first send word of an intended visit?"

"Stop arguing with me, Solomon."

Bathsheba did not need her son to help her down the rugged Stepped Stone staircase beside the palace or to the gate to Absalom's dwelling. Her son struggled to match his mother's determined strides, stubbing his toe a few times trying to keep pace, but she did not slow. She did not even ask about his injury as he limped beside her to the gate and up the flights of stairs to Absalom's house atop the interior eastern wall.

Bathsheba reached the top of the stairs ahead of Solomon. She expected a security detail protecting the children of the king, but there was none. Lights glowed from inside the house, so Bathsheba knocked on the front entrance. Once she identified herself, the door cracked open.

Absalom's disbelieving eyes appeared. "My lady. The hour is late. Did you come alone?"

"Solomon accompanied me. May we enter?"

Absalom glanced back into the house. Bathsheba expected him to ask Tamar if she wanted visitors. She would have been thrilled to receive an affirming answer. She would have been thrilled just to hear the sound of Tamar's voice.

"What is the purpose of your visit?" Absalom looked back through the half-open door. "The hour is late."

"Your sister needs me," Bathsheba answered. "May I enter?"

Absalom thought for a moment then opened the door.

When Bathsheba stepped inside, she saw an open courtyard on the opposite end of the common room illuminated with torchlight and oil lamps. Hanging baskets were suspended from the vine-covered rafters sheltering the portico. A table and a few chairs occupied the center of the courtyard. A low wall stood at the edge of the balcony, but the view of the Kidron Valley was unobstructed. A robed figure sat in one of the chairs wrapped in a blanket.

Absalom gripped Bathsheba's arm before she moved to the courtyard.

"You come to see my sister, but my father does not," he said, his voice a low growl, the oval snarl of his lips framing his bare teeth.

Bathsheba remained silent. She had not come for the brother. She came for the sister. Her bond was with Tamar. Her comfort and solace were to be given to Tamar. Any answer she might have for Absalom would never satisfy.

"Does he even ask after his daughter?" Absalom said.

"My husband was furious when he learned of Tamar's ill-treatment but—"

"She was raped, my lady. It goes far beyond ill-treatment," Absalom's interruption seethed with disdain. "Amnon raped my sister."

"There is hardly a day that passes that the king does not weep for his daughter." Bathsheba decided to offer some defense of her husband, however weak. "He laments for her, for the sin that was wrought upon her."

"And this is all he does…weep. It seems the only action the king is capable of is weeping. After all the time that has passed, he only weeps for the evil done to my sister. My sister is broken, and the king weeps. My sister is a desolate woman, forever stained, and the king weeps while his firstborn son, heir to the throne, remains unpunished."

Absalom kept his back to his sister and spoke in hushed tones so as not to be heard, but he could not disguise his contempt for his father's inaction.

"Your anger is justified, Absalom, but I did not leave the palace in the middle of the night to see you or be chastised by you. Apportion your wrath as you see best, but I am not here to bear the brunt. I am here for Tamar."

Absalom relaxed his furrowed brow. He expelled a great sigh and stepped aside.

"Has she eaten anything today?"

"She eats very little," Absalom confessed.

"I remember how she loved to snack on flatbread and dates with goat milk," Bathsheba said. "Do have any on hand?"

Absalom went to fetch the food, and Bathsheba moved into the courtyard. Bathsheba tried not to react at the sight of this once beautiful face that had become creased and haggard framed inside the hood covering her golden locks. The torchlight illuminated the dissipation on her face. Tamar's eyes reflected the light, but as if it were a reflection off a brass plate and not a quickened life. The eyes that had once entranced all who beheld her stared blankly at the vast openness from the balcony wall.

Absalom set a tray on the table but made no motion to leave.

"Give us some time," Bathsheba said, so he joined Solomon in the common room.

Bathsheba knelt before Tamar and took her hands. The skin of her fingers was cracked, her once manicured nails, chewed and broken. The princess would never have allowed such wasting of herself prior to the assault. When Bathsheba drew Tamar's hands to her lips, she resisted. "I am not worthy." The dry whisper of Tamar's voice was the sound of an ancient crone. "Not worthy."

Bathsheba chose to ignore Tamar's rebuff and lay her cheek upon Tamar's cold hands nuzzling her cheek against Tamar's chapped fingers until they flowered into a cupped shape beneath Bathsheba's chin.

"You are worthy, my child," Bathsheba said. "You are worthy."

Tamar looked bewildered and unsure as if doubting who was kneeling before her.

Bathsheba withdrew her hands and reached for the goat milk on the table. She brought the mug to Tamar's lips, but she did not drink until Bathsheba encouraged her to do so. They were only sips, but Bathsheba considered it a small victory.

The rest of the night Bathsheba sat beside Tamar holding her hand, caressing her arm, feeding her bits of bread and dates. They were even able to doze off while sitting in their chairs until the songbirds brought them out of a quiet slumber. The mist in the Kidron Valley hovered upon the ground enveloping the olive trees. The tree branches rose like twigs of green fungus out of the white fog.

Tamar turned her head to speak for the first time since Bathsheba began her vigil. "Will the world ever be bright again?"

Bathsheba's heart leapt. Brightness in all its forms would begin with a smile, and she curled her lips upward in radiant welcome. "I have some new foundations and blushers, a gift from the ambassador from Tyre. We could try them on together, find our colors. May I return soon?"

The slight nod Tamar gave was the answer of a princess.

Bathsheba rose from her chair and leaned close to Tamar's ear. "I love you, my child," she whispered. "And you are worthy."

Solomon was asleep on a pile of cushions. Absalom was nowhere to be seen. She tapped Solomon on his forehead, and he gradually awakened. She put a finger to her lips for him to remain silent then motioned to leave.

Once they descended the walled stairs and were out the gate, Bathsheba looked back up at Absalom's house. "I know her grief, Yahweh, the pain she harbors. Be merciful. Be merciful."

Her departing prayer was for herself.

"What do you mean, Ima?" Solomon asked. "How can you know her pain?"

"We are in no hurry to return to the palace." Bathsheba pressed her hand against her son's cheek. "There is a secret I have kept from you since the day of your birth. It has smoldered all these years until it burst into flame at the act of violence against Tamar. You are old enough now to learn the truth. Walk with me."

Chapter 29

SOLOMON STRUGGLED FOR A LONG TIME BEFORE HE COULD muster his courage. Before the lectures or after sitting through the long writing assignments at the prophet's school, Solomon would approach his master with his request on the tip of his tongue then give in to the fear.

He knew the story must be written and stored in the archives, but he had never seen or read it. The story had never been the subject of a lecture or debated among the scholars and Levites in his classes as an integral moment in the history of the prophets and kings of Israel. He had never heard a whispered rumor. No one ever spoke of it until he had taken that morning walk with his mother.

Solomon had grown up in the happiness of the palace, the child adored by his mother and indulged by his father. He had distinguished himself with his aptitude and intelligence. He was not afraid to challenge Gad and Nathan as they taught from the books of Moses and the histories. He could only learn by being inquisitive and these teachings and stories were beautiful mysteries to be explored centuries after the fact. He was not afraid to debate with the priests and Levites as they split hairs over the words of Yahweh with their varied and passionate interpretations. He took pleasure in poking holes in the theology of a haughty Levite's personal biases when condemning others with the words of the Almighty.

Solomon had an insatiable curiosity in all areas of study. He not only devoured the sacred books and scrolls in the prophet's library, but he purchased the writings of the scholars of other countries from the merchants in the traveling caravans, learning the languages and studying the cultures. He would engage with the foreign ambassadors when they came to court, keeping them up long into the night with lively conversations.

His appetite for knowledge was not confined to the library or the prophet's lecture hall or the Levite school. He spent many nights throughout the year sleeping under the stars charting the heavenly skies. He took long excursions traveling throughout Israel mapping the realm. His mind never stopped seeking truth and proof of the realities around him.

Now, he had come to an invisible barrier that had routed his soul. There was no way around this complexity. The only way was through, but his spirit had stopped. His way forward had stopped. What he imagined after learning the story had fragmented his mind, and he could think of nothing else. He needed clarity.

Knowledge was everything to Solomon, but some knowledge was a terrible thing to learn, dreadful to accept, and impossible to correct. Yet he would not, could not believe what he had been told unless he saw the writings on the parchments and interviewed the one who had spoken the terrible words. Just hearing the long-ago story even from a trustworthy source as his mother did not satisfy. Surely such a story must be chronicled. If the words had been written, then he could believe it, because after reading the story, he could look the author in the face and question the veracity of the account. Written words and the author's testimony was the true knowing.

Day after day when the lectures were done, when the other students departed, when the halls and discourse rooms sat empty, the library deserted except for those few prophets assigned to catalogue each new parchment, Solomon tried to muster his courage. Each time fear overwhelmed him. He would stand outside his master's private study, then hear Nathan and Gad talking through the thick curtains, and his heart would grow faint, and he would stumbled away.

Then, one day, he was caught by surprise. The fear that had given Solomon the energy to flee every time he prepared to enter, had now anchored his feet. Before he had time to think, Gad pulled aside the curtains. All the moisture evaporated on Solomon's tongue, and the vast vocabulary at his command for debates and conversations fled. His mind was blank.

"Prince Solomon, was there something you wanted?"

The truth, the full truth, the written truth, the truth known to many, yet unknown to him. This was what he wanted, but Solomon could not shape the words to ask, nor did he have the breath to expel them.

"You look troubled, my lord," Gad said. "Are you ill?"

Solomon cast his focus upon Nathan at his desk littered with scrolls and writing utensils, staring at him with a quizzical expression. Behind his master were built-in shelves from floor to ceiling where the parchments, scrolls, and tablets were kept. In the center of the shelving was a built-in cabinet that stored some of the oldest copies of the Ten Sayings. The top shelves were crammed with clay jars and wooden crates filled with scrolls. To reach those containers required a freestanding set of steps positioned below the shelves available when needed.

"I know." Solomon swallowed hard. He braced himself against the entrance. The strength was draining out of his legs. "I know."

Gad glanced at Nathan, then back to Solomon. "Know what, my lord?"

"Is it written?" Solomon asked. "Did you write the words of your prophesy?"

"Jedidiah, please enter." Nathan motioned for him to come in.

Should Solomon enter this inner sanctum, he would not exit as the same young man. To validate what he believed meant his view of the world would be changed forever. Did he want such confirmation?

His mother told him the two prophets stood shoulder to shoulder that day as Nathan spoke the words of Yahweh and Gad bolstered the weight of Nathan's body with his own. His mother believed seeing the two prophets standing together as a burden they both shared because the millstone of such divine truth was too much for one man to bear. If Solomon crossed this threshold, there would be no veil or shadow to hide the truth. He would now carry a portion of that prophetic burden in his soul for the rest of his life.

Gad guided him into the room, closing the curtains after him.

"Pour him a bowl of water." Nathan pointed to a pitcher and bowls on a side table.

"May I have something a little stronger, Master?" Solomon asked.

Nathan nodded to Gad, so he pushed aside a crate of scrolls from one of the shelves and removed a wineskin. He poured the wine into a bowl and handed it to Solomon, but his hands were trembling. Gad placed the bowl on Nathan's writing table instead and offered Solomon to sit on a stool.

"Before you speak, my son, take a few deep breaths." Nathan patted his chest. "Breathing in more air will clear your head better than the wine."

Solomon eased onto the stool closing his eyes until the room stopped spinning.

Gad returned the wineskin to its place on the shelf and stood beside Solomon. The prophet's hand upon his shoulder was enough reassurance for him to speak.

"My ima has told me the story. I am not her firstborn son." Solomon kept his eyes riveted upon Nathan, his quivering voice betraying the deep internal pain. "My older brother was the result of my father's aggression upon my mother. To conceal the sin, my father ordered the death of her first husband. When this was revealed, you both came to the palace and spoke of Yahweh's displeasure with my father and prophesied their unnamed child would not live. He died within a week of his birth. Is this true?"

Solomon felt Gad remove his hand from his shoulder. The prophet knelt beside him and began to weep.

Nathan stood and pulled the stepping stool from the corner of the room. He positioned it in front of the shelves and used it to take a small crate from the top shelf. After stepping down, Nathan set the crate on the table and took out a scroll tied with a strand of leather. He removed the leather band, unfurled the scroll, and showed Solomon two parchments.

"This is the only copy," Nathan said, his voice turning husky. He had to clear his throat with a sip of water from his bowl. "I knew this day would arrive. These are the words of Yahweh I spoke to the king on that day. Gad held onto me and bore witness to what was spoken. I...we believe they should be included in the annals of the prophets and kings, but I did not want to add them to the histories until you were made fully aware of the circumstances. The hour has come for you to know the truth."

Solomon read the content of the prophesy twice through; the story of the poor man and his ewe lamb; his father's reaction; the uncovering of the evil his father had done to his mother and her husband, Uriah; the heartbreak of Yahweh at what his father had perpetrated on honorable people; the pronouncement of death on his innocent older brother; and finally, the omen of calamity upon the house of David.

He read those particular words aloud one final time before lifting his eyes from the scrolls. "The sword will never depart from your house," Solomon said softly. "Out of your own household I am going to bring calamity upon you."

Solomon handed the scrolls back to Nathan then slumped over the table.

He could not contain his sorrow and did not want to drench this document with his tears.

How could this be? How could his father have acted with such heartless intent? How did his mother endure all she had carried in her memory?

"This is a cruel truth for your young heart to bear." Nathan retied the leather strap around the scrolls and placed them back into the crate.

Solomon sat up from the table and wiped his swollen eyes. "Master, you said that my father will not die, yet the righteous sword of judgment hangs over his head."

"Both are true words." Nathan took his seat on his stool. "The king will go the way of all the earth and close his eyes of natural causes, not on the battlefield."

"Once the king sleeps with his fathers, will the sword be lifted?"

"I do not know the answer to that," Nathan answered. "But a future king should know the full truth of this history if he is to become a wise ruler."

Nathan leaned over his writing table. His eyes bore into Solomon's face forcing him to lean back and rub his chest. The prophet's intense gaze caused his heart to race.

"Why are you looking at me this way? There are many sons in line before me."

"But are they qualified?" Gad asked, wiping his face with his sleeve and rising. He waved his finger before his eyes. "My young lord, these eyes have witnessed the comings and goings of men, those who strive against Yahweh and those who try to move within the flow of His will. I can say this about your father, his heart is for Yahweh. The difficulties of his life, all those who have died in the wars he has fought, and the ruinous consequences of his wicked actions have not darkened his heart against Yahweh. King Saul never learned that, and he died in the despondency of his mind estranged from the Almighty. The time may come when the throne is given to you, and…"

"Please, Master, you must not say this to me." Solomon began to rise in protest, but Gad placed his hand upon his shoulder.

"My lord, none of us can fully know the purposes of Yahweh. Neither Nathan nor I would ever assert our wills to manipulate circumstances. But we both can see the quality of character you possess, and you must be prepared for…"

"Solomon. Solomon, where are you hiding?"

The shouting of Solomon's name coming from the entrance of the prophet's school intensified as several young men marched down the main hall of the school demanding Solomon appear before them.

"Oh, I completely forgot." Solomon jumped up and knocking over his stool.

"Forgot what, my lord?" Nathan asked.

"Absalom's celebration at his country estate north of the city," Solomon explained as he picked up the stool and placed it back beneath Nathan's writing table. "It was a good year for wool, so Absalom invited the king and his sons to a feast on this last day of shearing. My father begged off, but all the brothers accepted, even Amnon, which was a surprise. Absalom put me in charge of seeing that Amnon did not back out at the last."

"Why did the king decline his son's invitation?" asked Gad.

"It would turn Absalom's purse inside out were he to host the king and his entourage. My father gave his blessing but will remain at home."

"Be careful, my lord," Nathan cautioned.

"Be careful of what, Master?" Solomon asked. "My father? My brothers? What exactly? My mind is reeling from all that I have learned from my mother and today from you. I am not sure how I am to be careful and of whom or what."

The voices reached Nathan's private entrance. One voice rose above the rest. "Solomon, are you in there?"

"Yes, Adonijah," Solomon replied. "I am finishing my lessons."

"The carriage is parked outside," Adonijah spoke through the curtains. "You have to ride with Amnon in the carriage."

There followed a chorus of playful laughter before the small herd of brothers dashed away from the door.

"My punishment for not learning to ride a mule," Solomon said with a shrug.

"You must go, my lord," Gad said. "We can return to this another time."

Solomon moved to the entrance. He looked back at his two masters. Both men loved him and his father. Solomon was confident that their devotion to following Yahweh meant they would do all within their might to encourage and support father and son. These master prophets kept the records of the chosen. From the earliest days until now, they, above all, knew the stories that revealed the heart of the Almighty and were trustworthy mouthpieces for Yahweh.

Solomon began to speak, but the words caught in his throat. A foreshadowing of fear began to rise in his heart.

"My lord, you do not have to go to Absalom's feast with your brothers," Gad said then looked at Nathan. "We can provide a reason for you to remain."

Solomon was appreciative that his masters would use their influence to shield him from his brothers, another proof of their love for him. "No, no. Absalom made me promise that I would get Amnon to this gathering. I cannot go back on my word, but that is not why I hesitate."

"Do not be dismayed, my lord," Nathan said. "I know this is troubling…"

"I do not wish to be like my father," Solomon blurted. "I do not wish to be king. I do not wish to bring calamity upon my father or my father's house."

Nathan rose from behind his writing table and moved to Solomon cupping his hands around Solomon's face. "My lord. My son. You are a complete wonder. Yahweh is with you. Whatever may happen in the future. Whatever you may become, you will be your own man, and your destiny will be a blessing to all who bear witness to your life."

"Thank you. Thank you, my lord," Solomon whispered.

Nathan dropped his hands upon Solomon's shoulders and tenderly kissed both sides of his face. "Now go," Nathan said. "Your brothers are waiting."

When Solomon exited the prophet's school and climbed into the carriage, Amnon was already in high spirits. He stood inside the carriage dancing in clumsy twirls as the sons of David sat on their mules applauding and cheering their older brother. The transport was roomy enough for multiple passengers, but Absalom had provided his personal carriage insisting he and Amnon ride in comfort and style. Solomon took his seat in the carriage opposite his older brother.

Immediately, Amnon thrust the wineskin into Solomon's face. "Why so glum, little brother?" Amnon's slurred speech was a sign of heavy consumption. "Absalom sent skins of wine for us to enjoy on the way. Cheer up. Drink."

Solomon reached for the wineskin, but when the driver of the carriage snapped the reins of the mule team, Amnon fell forward onto Solomon. All the brothers alongside the carriage burst into laughter and the goading continued as the company of David's sons rode out of the city gates and onto the highway heading north to Absalom's estate.

Solomon was thankful it was a short distance to Baal Hazor. Many of the villagers were under Absalom's employ, and it appeared the whole settlement had gathered for the celebration in front of Absalom's house. Musicians were playing and the shearers and villagers were singing and dancing around a great bonfire. Servants were emerging from the cooking tents with trays of food and carrying them to the tables.

A great pile of freshly shorn wool was stacked in front of the open doors of the storehouse. Naked sheep frantically scurried about inside the corral attached to the storage shelter bleating in frustration for the sudden loss of their wooly coats. It was indeed a plentiful year as his brother reported, and Solomon could see this bounty was reason for such festivities.

The moment the driver pulled to a stop, Absalom leapt into the carriage and helped Amnon out and into the arms of several men attending the gathering. Solomon did not recognize them but assumed they were friends or employees of his brother. They threw their arms around Amnon, and as Absalom cheered them on from the carriage, they led Amnon into the line of dancers as they circled around the great bonfire. Everyone was making merry.

Solomon was ready to join them. He was ready to put aside the written prophesies about his father. He was ready to forget. He was ready to enjoy himself and stop thinking about his studies and his uncertain future. But as he was about to step out of the carriage, Absalom slammed his forearm into his chest, knocking the breath out of his lungs, forcing him back into his seat. Solomon's eyes watered at the fierceness of the blow and the loss of air.

Absalom jumped into the driver's seat blowing a sharp whistle through his teeth. He waved his arms, and in the blink of an eye, those men dancing with Amnon, lifted him off his feet and rushed him back to the carriage tossing him into his seat. Absalom was positioned behind Amnon, and he swiftly locked his arm around Amnon's neck making it impossible for him to escape. All Amnon could do was squirm as a trio of men climbed into the carriage.

Solomon watched in horror as the three men drew daggers. Before they plunged their blades into the intended victim, Absalom raised his arm to stop them. For a moment, Solomon thought perhaps this was only a cruel merriment aimed to terrify Amnon. If that was the case, then this charade was proving true. Amnon was gasping and squealing like the naked sheep running around in the corral.

But this was not a prank. This was an act of revenge.

"This is your last breath, dear brother. At my command my assassins will be the last thing you see. But as you bleed out like a beast in the field, I want you to beg. I want you to say my sister's name and plead for her forgiveness. Say it. Say her name."

Absalom loosened his hold on Amnon's neck to allow a slight intake of breath and to squeak out Tamar's name with a plea to forgive. It was a pitiful bleat, a miserable whimper for mercy, but there was no mercy to be had.

When Absalom gave the order to strike, Amnon kicked his legs as if trying to flee.

Solomon drew in his legs to avoid being kicked as the hired killers viciously plunged their blades into Amnon's chest and belly again and again until the victim's legs stopped churning and became limp. When the final breath was expelled, the murderers leapt from the carriage and raced away.

Absalom remained in the driver's seat, his arm still locked around Amnon's neck. To keep from retching, Solomon crammed his arm over his mouth at the sight of both of his brothers covered in blood. When Absalom withdrew his arm, Amnon's lifeless body slumped to the side of the carriage. Then Absalom climbed over the seat and stood in the middle looking down at Solomon.

"Can you drive this carriage?" Absalom asked, his face covered in their brother's blood accentuated his eyes blazing with the triumph of retribution.

Solomon had never driven a carriage. He had never ridden a mule. He had never been inside the royal stables. But if there was any way to escape the presence of Absalom and his henchmen, he would assent to anything, so he nodded and agreed to drive.

Absalom reached behind him and removed a clean fabric tucked inside his belt. How it had avoided becoming soaked before now, Solomon could not imagine.

Absalom wiped his face. "Our father did nothing to avenge my sister. She may never know the jolt of a lover's kiss or feel true love blossom inside her pure heart, but she will know the villain who denied her such joy is dead. And you shall tell her."

Solomon could not move. It was Absalom who pulled his arm away from covering his lips.

"You will tell her, yes?" Absalom asked. "Say you will."

"I will tell her," Solomon eked out through his chattering teeth.

"Good," Absalom said, and then he lifted Solomon to his feet. "Look around you. Everyone has fled. The villagers are hiding. Even now, our brothers are riding for home as fast as their plodding mules can go. We have no more witnesses. You and I and our dead brother remain. So, I charge you to care for my sister. She is fragile. I must flee the country and do not know how long I will be in exile. Watch over her until I return. Will you do me this service?"

Solomon found his voice and agreed to care for Tamar until…until…only the Almighty knew for how long.

Absalom leapt from the carriage and dashed into the stables. He was only a moment before he emerged riding his mule ladened with supplies. Amnon's murder was not a sudden impulse, a spur of the moment decision. This had been premeditated, and Solomon was an unwitting player in its gruesome unfolding.

As Absalom rode past the carriage he shouted at Solomon, "I trust you!"

Solomon covered his face with his hands and sobbed, but his sobbing could not block out Nathan's righteous words echoing in his head: *the sword will never depart from your house, and out of your own household I am going to bring calamity upon you.*

Calamity had fallen, horrid and bitter, and Solomon sat quivering inside the carriage abandoned in its butchery.

PART FIVE

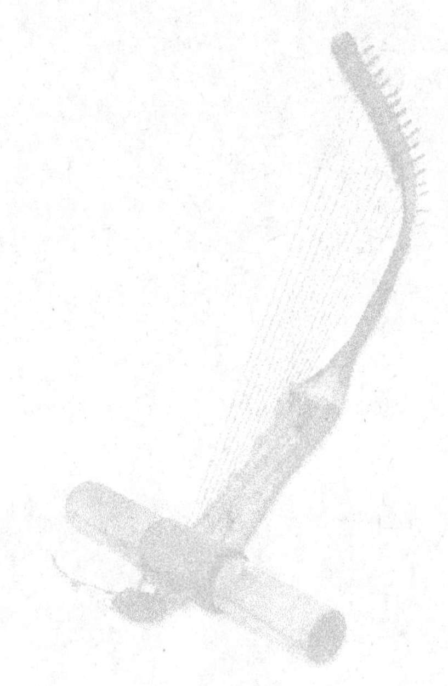

Chapter 30

SOLOMON REMOVED HIS FILTHY, SWEAT-SOAKED TUNIC AND draped it over the wooden railing on the new staircase. The sun had reached the middle of the sky above the hills of Ramah. After guzzling some water out of the dipper, he upended the bucket over his head. The cascading water was refreshing after a long morning spent in the broiling temperature. In such heat, he preferred to work in his sandals and linen skirt and leather apron with a sash around his bare middle to secure his mallets. The loose attire kept him cool and allowed him the freedom of movement in the routine of construction.

Gad stuck his head out of the doorway of the renovated prophet's hall and called out to Solomon.

"Down here." Solomon moved out of the shadows beneath the new staircase that led up to the entrance into the building. The steps of the old one were rotting away, and the railings were rickety. The workers did not like having to carry building materials up and down an unstable staircase for the interior renovations of the lecture hall along with its smaller classrooms used by the student prophets. The library also had been expanded with the shelves filled with parchments and scrolls of copies of all the writings of Moses, the laws and histories.

Solomon had made his own contributions to the library. He had copies drawn of the geographical maps he sketched on his travels around Israel, plus maps of each tribal territory as well as charts of the stars he observed in all his journeys. His newest project was the design and construction of this new staircase and securing it to the building.

Solomon had chosen to move to Ramah and had grown deeply attached to the family home and property of Samuel and Shira. This location held a special place in his lineage, a unique history that he had come to appreciate.

His father took shelter in the home of the prophet and his wife when he had to escape the pursuit of the mad king. It was here that Shira taught his father to write. It was during his stay that Samuel had taken his father into the cave of scrolls and shown him the collected words of the Almighty. It was on this land that Samuel and Shira had reaffirmed to his father that Yahweh had chosen him to be king. And when the mad king had pursued his father to this place, it was the prophet and his wife who helped him escape.

When Nathan, Gad, and Jashar made the decision to transform the property into a sanctuary for anyone wanting to spend time in study and reflection, David donated a sizeable portion of the building materials. Once Solomon made the conscious choice to no longer live in the palace, he had first taken quarters in the city near the prophet's school. But living in the shadow of the palace was still not far enough away, so Gad and Nathan invited him to come to Ramah and become a part of the community of prophets and scribes and priests who lived and worked on the property.

"Is it safe for me to step out onto the landing?" Gad shouted.

"Only one way to find out." Solomon laughed as he looked up at Gad leaning out of the entrance.

From the ground to the doorway was the height of five men. Solomon covered his brow with a scrap of wood, shielding his eyes from the sun's glare. Gad would be the first to test the sturdiness of his new build.

"I do not see the humor in me crashing down upon your head," Gad responded.

"But what a dramatic way to die," Solomon offered.

"I do not want a dramatic death. I want to die in bed after a good meal and not from a poorly assembled staircase." Gad pressed his foot onto the landing without venturing out upon it.

Solomon tossed aside the wood scrap and dashed up the first flight of steps. He paused at the landing and gripped the handrailing. He began to wobble, pretending the ground was convulsing beneath him.

His test proved the sturdiness of the structure. "You see, Master. My work will withstand the punishment of any weight." Solomon was unable to keep from gloating.

"Is that a slight against my girth?" Gad slapped his belly as he stepped out onto the top landing.

"No slight intended. Just easing your mind that you thought you might topple my creation," Solomon answered.

"Ha, I do not believe you," Gad grunted at Solomon's not so subtle insult. "Now, come up here. I found something."

At a critical moment in Solomon's life, he had chosen to exchange the luxuries of the palace for a more common existence, trade in a life overrun with servants for a life of learning to become self-sufficient. Living in Ramah, Solomon learned to plant and tend the prophet's community garden, how to husband livestock, and then how to prepare one's own meal from the harvest. Suppers were still communal but not like the more royal banquets with the king and the family who were always entertaining special dignitaries or tribal courtiers. Meals shared with student prophets, scribes and priests, farmers and herdsmen, and local citizens were more relaxed and, at times, boisterous and jovial. He might be the son of a king, but among the residents of Ramah, he was not treated as such.

Solomon followed Gad through the expansive lecture hall. Laborers were replacing a row of rotted windows. The windows provided a panorama of the hills above the lecture hall and the expanse of the valley below.

"Come with me." Gad motioned Solomon into Nathan's old office.

Nathan's desk had been shoved against the east wall of the room beneath the open window that also looked onto the valley and the road cutting through the barns and gardens leading back to the home of Samuel and Shira. Crates and jars full of scrolls we lined against the wall. Gad had removed the wooden insert that covered the secret opening down to the anteroom of the cave of scrolls.

"Now that you have completed the outside staircase you may go to work on this one." Gad pointed to the hole in the floor and the steep steps descending into the antechamber of the cave. "I nearly broke my neck climbing those stairs just now."

"Is this the last batch from the library in Jerusalem?" asked Solomon.

"For now. Jashar needs to replenish the library here in Ramah. We will transport fresh copies when they are made available."

"But why do you want these crates down in the cave?"

"With the chosen of Israel, anything could happen," Gad replied. "It is best to prepare. We never know when the winds of calamity might drive us back here."

Solomon tested the top step with his foot. "Is that what you wished to show me?"

Gad pointed to Nathan's desk. Sunlight illuminated an opened gevil scroll on top.

Gad led Solomon to the desk and tapped his finger at the top of the calf-skin scroll. "I requested this be brought back to Ramah. It is the last known document of Samuel, in his hand. He used dyes his wife Shira extracted from plants and insects. Here is the story of your forebearers two generations past, Ruth and Boaz."

"Is this the earliest version?" Solomon leaned in for a closer look.

"I believe so," Gad answered. "I was not around for much of the writing and copying. That was Nathan's task, but I know the animal skins were often used for original writings because of the lasting quality. Under Nathan's guidance the students wrote copies on parchment or thinner leathery skins for the priests, judges, tribal chieftains, military leaders, whoever expressed interest in the sacred writings. I always carried parchments when I served in the court of King Saul. From time to time, he requested I read to him, until he went… until he no longer did so."

"Do we not have copies of this document?" Solomon asked.

"Nathan would certainly know."

"I never read it." Solomon lightly touched the dried lettering.

"It is an incomplete document, my lord," Gad said.

"How so?" asked Solomon.

"The family history." Gad pointed to the bottom of the scroll. "The two main characters of this love story are a Moabite woman and a direct descendant from Judah's line, the fourth son of Jacob, the son of Isaac and the grandson of Abraham.

"So, who is missing?" asked Solomon.

"You, my lord." Gad tapped his finger on the bottom letters. "Samuel anointed your father in the home Jesse, your grandfather. The writing stops there."

"What are you saying, Master?" Solomon cast his wary eyes upon the prophet.

"Samuel did not know who would follow your father. The one the people call 'the Lion of Judah' occupies the throne, but not forever," Gad asserted. "An heir will come forth, a successor will be chosen and anointed, but who will the Almighty choose?"

"I do not like what you are implying, Master," Solomon said. "There are too many brothers in line before me. Only Amnon is no more, and the natural order is for the oldest to assume the throne."

"That is the natural order of man, but what might Yahweh desire? Your great grandparents, Ruth and Boaz were not a pure line. Who can know the mind of Yahweh?"

"Why do you and Master Nathan keep implying that I might be king?" Solomon moved away from Gad, stopping before the large hole cut out of the floor. Torchlight flickered from the chamber below. The light seemed to beckon Solomon to come down and enter the empty cave. His father had done so and was overcome with wonder and awe. "I chose to leave behind the palace and pursue scholarship and country living. It suits me."

"You have acclimated well to this new lifestyle, my lord, but we both know you came here out of fear," Gad said, his eyes boring into Solomon. "You confessed as much when you learned Absalom was returning to Jerusalem after his long exile in Geshur."

"I did not want to face him. I cannot deny it. Amnon's murder still haunts me."

"I understand, my lord." Gad turned Solomon to face him. "That was a terrible moment. I have been witness to many horrific moments and the cruelties haunt me, but in spite of these terrible incidents, the divine will of Yahweh prevailed."

"It is not that I just cannot face him, Master. I do not trust Absalom or my father. Why would the king give his blessing for my brother to return in the first place?" Solomon asked. "He should know Absalom is not to be trusted."

"The king has his reasons," Gad said.

"I do not have such faith in my father whatever his reasons." Solomon pulled away from Gad.

"You have never forgiven your father, have you?" Gad asked. "For what he did to your mother."

Solomon whirled and glared at Gad.

It did not frighten the prophet. "Forgiveness comes at a bitter price, my lord," Gad said gently.

"It is not the bitter price of forgiveness, Master. It is the bitter consequences of the king's choice that holds back my forgiveness."

"I understand, my son, but the choice not to forgive becomes a heavy weight for our mortal hearts to carry." Gad turned to the desk and began to carefully roll up the gevil scroll. "Nathan and I have been discussing a plan to record all the family generations. We would start with the first family in the Book of the Beginnings and carry through the genealogies of Abraham and beyond. All the descendants, the tribes, the clans, even the Levites, perhaps more groups of people if we are so inspired. A record of all the branches of the tree of the chosen people of Yahweh."

"That is not a family tree, Master. That is a forest."

"Tedious work, indeed." Gad tied a leather strap around the scroll.

"Even more tedious to read," Solomon added. "A cure for the sleep deprived."

"It would include the kings and their children and their children after them, my lord. All would be chronicled."

"Any chance I might escape your recordkeeping?" Solomon grinned.

"Your birth gives you no chance to avoid a mention in the archive, but as to the extent of what might be written, that is in the hands of the Almighty."

"And to me," Solomon interjected. "Should I choose, that is."

"Yes, my lord. Should you choose to participate. Yahweh invites us into the streams of his purposes, then gives us the freedom to take part. I believe Yahweh has a purpose for all of us in every turn and twist of life, and our character is revealed and refined by our choices."

"Master, I cannot pretend to have the wisdom to see or understand the unfolding will of the Almighty. It frightens me to even ponder such mysteries."

"I know, my lord, but you must not attempt to hide. You must pay attention. Yahweh's choice of your father, not the firstborn, but the eighth son of Jesse, was plucked from the hills of Bethlehem to rule the chosen. It was no accident, and your father chose to enter into the divine will of Yahweh. As frightening as it may be, you hide or run from the Almighty at your peril."

Gad turned when he heard his name being called. He stretched out the window for a better look. Solomon joined him, and they saw Jashar waving from the road.

"I cannot hear what he is saying." Solomon dashed out of Nathan's office, through the lecture hall, and onto the top landing of his newly installed staircase. He cupped his hands around his mouth and shouted, "What is it, Jashar?"

Gad stepped out the entry door and stood next to Solomon.

"Nathan and Benaiah have arrived from Jerusalem," shouted Jashar. "Your mother has come with them. They wait for you at the house. Hurry."

"Why would my mother leave the palace? What could this mean, Master?"

Gad grabbed Solomon by his arm. "This is a purposeful visit, my lord, not one of whimsy."

Solomon pulled away from the prophet's grip and bolted down the stairs.

Chapter 31

SOLOMON GRABBED HIS TUNIC HANGING OVER THE RAILING AT the bottom of the stairs and jogged down the hill to the road toward Jashar.

"I have set a table of refreshments on the roof," Jashar said as Solomon raced by. "They wait for you there."

Without breaking stride, Solomon slipped his head through his tunic and his arms through the sleeves still damp from the earlier dosing with water from the bucket.

This has to be about Absalom. What else could it be?

After murdering Amnon, Absalom's last words to Solomon had been watch over his sister. Solomon had been faithful to that request, visiting Tamar regularly and seeing to her every need, often taking his mother. However, during Absalom's exile, neither Solomon nor Bathsheba had seen much improvement in Tamar's demeanor.

Enough time had passed for the king to give his blessing for Absalom to come home. Tamar immediately brightened when she learned of her brother's return. Her appetite increased and she took more care with her appearance. When Bathsheba told her that Absalom had married and would be bringing home a daughter, a son, and a pregnant wife, Tamar's spirits soared.

"Your brother named his daughter after you," Bathsheba told her.

"Then I shall thoroughly spoil her," Tamar said.

Solomon found it easy to avoid direct contact with Absalom once he returned. Even his father had not warmed to his brother. The king made it clear that while Absalom was welcome to return to Jerusalem, he would not be allowed to "see the king's face." Absalom would not stand in the presence of the king, would never be invited to family meals, would never sit with in the imperial stalls during festivals and holy days.

It could have been a half-measured punishment for the murder of Amnon, but Solomon believed his father was afraid of Absalom. And why not? Solomon was afraid of him. If one son had murdered another son, might he not murder his father as well or another son or all the rest of his sons? It was the way of the despot.

Absalom and his family chose to live on his country estate, the scene of Amnon's murder, and a place Solomon vowed never to visit. For a length of time this arrangement worked, until Absalom became vexed with the king's refusal to grant him an audience and took the rash measure of setting ablaze the barley field adjacent to his own to demand his father's attention. The neighboring field just happened to be on Joab's property, and Absalom secured his hearing with the king.

The day Solomon was summoned to the palace to witness the reunion between Absalom and their father he was listening to Gad at the prophet's school give a lecture from the writings of Moses on the qualities of good leadership. Solomon and the other students were copying down the admonition given to Moses by his father-in-law: "Choose capable men from all the people—leaders who revere Yahweh, are trustworthy, and hate dishonest gain—and appointment them—"

That was as far as he got when Nathan dashed into the classroom waving for Solomon to come with him.

Nathan explained the urgency once they were on the way to the palace. "Your brother Absalom is coming to the palace to stand before the king," Nathan said as they hastily moved through the city streets. "We must bear witness."

The Hall of the Lion was crammed with counselors and advisers, priests and Levites, courtiers and military leaders, along with the special security detail Benaiah had assigned to the king. No one wanted to miss this moment. A father would sit in judgment of his son, something the king had avoided for years.

Solomon caught his mother's eye as she took her place beside her husband. Her face appeared rigid, fraught with worry, but she offered him a faint smile.

Absalom had brought his whole family. They had grown in number. His firstborn, Tamar, was a striking child. Solomon could see that she would blossom into the same beauty as her aunt. His sons nestled into the sides of their very pregnant mother, cowed by the attention from a hall filled with strangers.

Absalom had taken a risk in presenting himself to the king. The outcome was in no way predetermined. It could be a long-delayed sentence of death. It could be reconciliation.

When Joab moved onto the raised platform where the king and Solomon's mother sat, the great hall fell silent. "My sovereign lord," Joab began as he took a knee before the king. "After a long absence, your son Absalom has returned and seeks the face of his father, the face of the king. You, my lord, tasked me, the commander of your army, to fetch him home. Many years have passed. Much sorrow has been expressed. May the arms of father and son no longer be resistant to accord, but flexible enough to embrace."

Joab stepped off the platform, and Solomon watched his father cast his eyes toward Absalom. His brother had been the darling of the people before his exile. Since his return, he had become even more popular. The crowds of young men and women who once strived for his attention, continued to vie for his affection. Were father and son to be publicly reconciled, the whole kingdom would rejoice.

Absalom was remarkably handsome. Along with his captivating personality, it was obvious to Solomon that the years had only enhanced his brother's rugged appeal and aura.

Who would not fall under his spell once they moved into the shadow of his presence?

The king motioned for Absalom to approach his throne. The wordless drama played out in silence. The only sound in the great hall was a collective gasp from the onlookers as Absalom drew his sword.

Benaiah and the soldiers lurched forward to protect the king.

But the son knelt at his father's feet. Absalom did not extend the sword to his father. He held onto the blade with his gloved right hand then stretched out facedown upon the platform. The hilt of the sword beckoned for the king to grasp it. It was an offering. The sword of execution if guilty, or the sword of mercy if there was to be hope for amity. The fate of the son lay in the hands of the king.

The king rose from his throne. The moment he grasped the hilt of the sword, Absalom released his hold of the blade. The king raised the sword but not in a threatening manner. After handing the sword to Joab, the king bent and lifted Absalom to his feet. The king tucked a finger beneath Absalom's chin lifting his face, then he leaned forward and kissed his son.

When the great hall erupted with cheers, Solomon shouted into Nathan's ear. "I want to move out of the palace. I want to be near the prophet's school."

With his mother's blessing, Solomon moved into a small apartment close to the prophet's school. He visited the palace from time to time, always careful to avoid direct contact with Absalom. But when his brother began to parade through the streets of the city in his chariot with an honor guard of fifty armed men clearing the streets ahead of him and shouting his praises, it became impossible for Solomon to ignore Absalom's growing influence over the people. Day after day, his brother positioned himself at the city gates giving speeches, listening to people's complaints, sympathizing with their disputes, and claiming that if he were king, they would get justice.

Solomon reached a breaking point and voiced his concern to his parents.

The king only shrugged, and his mother sighed, shaking her head in dismay.

Why will my father not defend himself and silence the fomenting of sedition?

When Solomon could no longer bear watching his brother speak openly against the king, stealing the hearts of the men of Israel away from his father, he had fled to Ramah and taken refuge at the prophet's sanctuary.

Solomon paused at the entrance into the courtyard gardens in front of the house to catch his breath. Jashar had not mentioned the cadre of bodyguards who accompanied Bathsheba and Nathan to Ramah. This was no doubt at Benaiah's insistence.

Gad was right. This is not a trivial visit.

The armed guards greeted the prince as he walked through the gardens toward the outside steps. He feared the turmoil he had escaped in Jerusalem had only grown worse since leaving the city and had now caught up with him. He climbed the steps to the rooftop and stood before his mother, his master, and the captain of the king's bodyguard. Their combined presence was not a good sign.

"My clothes are filthy, Ima, and I smell," he said as his mother approached.

Bathsheba ignored her son's warning and threw her arms around him squeezing him tight. Her embrace felt desperate.

It took a moment for Solomon to recover from the shock of this surprise visit, of the armed escort in the courtyard below, of the grave faces this trio all shared, and the vigorous clasp of his mother's arms around his waist.

"Ima. Ima, why are you here? What is the trouble?"

"Evil lurks at the gates, my son," Bathsheba said. "The city is upside down. The king is lost and helpless. I have never seen him in this condition."

"Nor have I," Benaiah added. "I have served at the king's side all my life. He has allowed his age to creep into his bones and hunch his shoulders. I fear he may lose the kingdom."

"It is true, my son." Bathsheba pulled away from his embrace. "He wanes before my eyes. When I appeal to him to take action, he waves me off as if he hopes that by ignoring the danger, it will not come to pass."

"What counsel does he take and who from?" asked Solomon.

"He listens only to those who say to appease Absalom," Benaiah said. "They tell the king he should accept what is coming and abdicate the throne before it is too late. These so-called advisors are plucking the teeth from the Lion of Judah one by one."

"Has Absalom lost all reason? Would he indeed mount an armed rebellion against the king?" The thought of such evil caused Solomon to shudder.

"The plot is in motion, my lord," Benaiah answered.

"When I left Jerusalem, he was only parading through the city befriending those who already adored him. He has been engaged in such self-puffery long before now."

"Parades have now become speeches of sedition, my lord," offered Benaiah. "The speeches have become rallying cries, and the cries grow louder each day."

"And you, Master." Solomon turned to Nathan. "Does he not heed your advice?"

"The king has not called for my counsel since…since the day of his marriage to your mother." Nathan lowered his head before mother and son.

When his mother raised her hand to stifle a cry, Solomon extended his arm and drew her to his side. No matter the years, the wounded memory was not fully healed.

"I understand." Solomon tenderly embraced his mother. "Why did you come, Ima, and put yourself in danger? Captain Benaiah and Master Nathan could have easily delivered this terrible news."

"I risked the danger because I believe you are in danger," Bathsheba said. "And to persuade you."

"Persuade me of what?" Solomon cast his eyes on each of them, but no one answered him. "Captain, of what must I be persuaded?"

"My lady Bathsheba speaks the truth, my lord. The evil lurking at the gates of the City of David is indisputable," Benaiah said. "It does not come from without, but from within. We have not seen war in such a long time, but when it came, I expected an attack from the Philistines or other Canaanite peoples. But this is rebellion rising within our own nation, from within the tribe of Judah, from within the household of the king."

"Is this more of the calamity you wrote about, Master?" Solomon whispered. "Falling upon my father."

"I cannot say, my lord. I pray it is not so," Nathan replied. "But I fear the Destroyer is about to be unleashed upon our people by the hands of our own people."

"But what am I to do?" Solomon asked. "I cannot reason with Absalom to come to his senses. I cannot stop this…this disaster. Only Yahweh can."

"None of us knows the will of the Almighty, my son," Nathan said as he approached Solomon. "What I do know is that you are not safe here. That you and your mother, the king and all his family must be prepared to flee the looming danger."

Solomon had to compose himself. He sat on the stone parapet that encompassed the roof of the house. Would he be forced to flee the pastoral beauty of hills and valley, the prophet's sanctuary with its barns and corrals, its gardens and retreat center? Flee such a place of tranquility?

He remembered his father telling him how he had, in the long ago, sought refuge in this place. Of how he studied the sacred writings upon this roof while eating the delicious meals prepared by Shira. Of how he had come to a deeper knowledge and love for the Almighty as Samuel taught him. Even though he had been hiding from the wrath of King Saul, his father had spoken of his time in this location as one of respite from the outside world. This was his father's sanctuary long before Solomon had arrived.

"Does my father want me at his side?" Solomon asked, gazing at the idyllic scene. When no one spoke, he turned to his mother. "Ima, does father want me to come home?"

"Your father is so indecisive, I do not believe he knows what he wants," she said. "He is in distress and bewildered at how the people are swayed by Absalom's outrageous claims that he has become an incompetent king. He is disheartened by the brazen attempts to turn the people of Israel against him."

"What is worse is to see how so many are swayed by Absalom," Benaiah added. "They are intoxicated by his lies. He even has his own standard now, a banner with him riding a mule, his braided hair flowing behind him. His followers carry it every time he parades through the streets in his showy chariot. It is disgusting."

"But has my father bidden me?" Solomon could not explain why he insisted on an answer. There was a hollowness inside that he had tried to fill by pouring his mind into scholastic study, into writing his own meditations and observations of the world, of the creative edifices he designed, but nothing he pursued had filled the vacancy in his heart.

"No, my son. Your father has not asked for you." His mother knelt beside him and rested her hand upon his knee. "He has not asked for any of his sons or his wives. He has not asked for me. His heart is in turmoil, and he does not know how to ask anything of those closest to him. He asks only of the Almighty. I have heard him repeat a prayer to lure the notice of the Almighty. 'Hear my cry, O Yahweh; listen to my prayer. From the ends of the earth I call to You, I call as my heart grows faint; lead me to the rock that is higher than I,' he says, then the words fade, and his heart becomes weary. He does not ask of you, my son, because he fears he has lost connection to Yahweh and his soul aimlessly wanders. I ask you to come home and help your father find his soul before it is too late."

Solomon took his mother's hand and stood lifting her to her feet and tucking her into his side. "Captain, what outcome do you foresee under the circumstances?"

"Seven days ago, Absalom came to the king and requested his blessing to go to Hebron to fulfill a vow he claims to have made to Yahweh while in exile in Geshur," Benaiah began. "I believe this vow is a pretext for the marshalling of his troops. I made known my thoughts to the king, but in spite of my protests, the king gave his blessing to Absalom, and he departed for Hebron with two hundred men."

"Benaiah, in all fairness, I do not believe all of these men were privy to what the prince might be plotting," Nathan interjected.

"Whether in ignorance or subservience, to a man they all marched in Absalom's parade bearing his banner," Benaiah responded without concealing his contempt.

"I stood at your father's side on the balcony as Absalom and his men marched through the street in front of the palace," Bathsheba said. "I agree with Benaiah. This claim of fulfilling a vow to Yahweh was not an act of contrition but an excuse to take his followers to another city for a nefarious purpose."

"This is confirmed by a message of Absalom's intent intercepted by one of my spies." Benaiah withdrew a scroll from his carryall and handed it to Solomon.

Solomon opened the small scroll and read the terse message aloud, "As soon as you hear the sound of the trumpets, then say, 'Absalom is king in Hebron.'"

Solomon then turned to Benaiah. "How is this cryptic message to be interpreted?"

"The trumpets in Hebron are the signal for Absalom's men to disperse throughout the kingdom, carry his standard, and rally all those in opposition to the Lion of Judah."

"It is symbolic, my lord," Nathan said. "Hebron is the capital city in the heart of the tribe of Judah. There, I anointed your father a second time, and Abiathar placed the crown upon his head. Regardless of how many men are truly aligned with your brother, he is endeavoring to usurp the throne from your father."

"I fear that should Absalom succeed in this attempt, that not only will he kill his father but all of his male offspring," Bathsheba said.

"Benaiah, do you have the latest reports from Hebron?" Solomon asked.

"While Absalom offers sacrifices in his false show of piety, he is gathering political and military counselors. This conspiracy gains strength, my lord. We must act."

"Come home. Help us protect your father."

Come home. Home to protect his father. A father who once doted on him when he was but a boy, but when he became a young man, his father had become distracted by the demands of being king and no longer offered his son the affection he craved. The father who had allowed Solomon's older brother to get away with murder was now in dire need of his aid to protect him from the very same treasonous murderer. The Lion of Judah did not lift a hand to stop the evil within his own house. Other hands must take up the task.

"I shall gather my belongings," Solomon said, then kissed his mother's forehead.

Chapter 32

DAVID FOLLOWED BENAIAH THROUGH THE PRIVATE PASSAGE-way from the king's chambers to the Hall of the Lion. Bathsheba and Solomon walked beside him. The rest of the king's family were safely ensconced at the family dwellings under heavy guard. The military and political counselors had assembled and waited inside the great hall.

Benaiah paused before opening the door from the passageway into the anteroom outside the Hall of the Lion. "My lord, I have summoned old companions," Benaiah said. "From long ago."

It was out of character for Benaiah not to have informed him before now, nor had he requested David's permission for a private meeting at this critical hour. "What have you done, Benaiah? Who have you called to my court without my consent?"

"I believe you will approve, my lord. Once your eyes behold them." Benaiah pushed open the door and led the way.

The rumbling of the voices in the great hall was heard just outside the anteroom.

David stepped into the room, and Benaiah pointed toward two old men sitting on a wooden bench.

Both of them rose when they saw David and ambled toward him. Their faces were wrinkled, their teeth stained, and their hair salted with gray, yet they did not shuffle like old men. There was a strength to their gait and a smile on their faces. They stopped in front of David and together they locked arms to help the other as they took a knee.

David felt lightheaded and reached out to Bathsheba, then looked at Benaiah. Not with a look of puzzlement as to the identity of these two men kneeling before him. David knew who they were the instant he laid eyes on them. Regardless of what the years had done to alter their faces and forms, David would always recognize them.

Still, how had Benaiah succeeded in bringing them to Jerusalem after so much time had passed and after the brutal reason that had caused such a bitter parting?

"Benaiah?" David said, searching for an answer.

Benaiah knelt beside the others. All subjects kneeling before the king, but not just any subjects.

David pulled his hand from Bathsheba and dropped to his knees in front of this trio. Had they stopped cursing him in their hearts for what he had done? Had they come to curse him now?

"Have you forgiven me?" David looked from gaunt face to gaunt face. "Can you ever forgive me?"

The last David had seen of these two was at the burial of their friend. After laying Uriah inside the tomb in Hebron where Abner was laid to rest, these two had bowed their heads, spoken a terse farewell, and departed. David expected Benaiah to follow their example and quietly disappear, but he remained faithful even after the murder of Uriah.

"I forgive you, my lord," Eleazar said, his voice raspy with emotion.

"As do I, my lord," Jozabad offered, tears welling in his eyes.

"And I, my lord. I forgive you," Benaiah said.

It was impossible to restrain the gratitude that engulfed David's heart.

"O Yahweh, my rock and redeemer. O Yahweh, what is man that You care for him, the son of man that You think of him? I am like a breath; my days are like a fleeting shadow. And yet, You are gracious and merciful to me," David cried, and then he kissed each man and pressed them into his chest. "How good and pleasant it is when brothers live together in unity. It is like precious oil poured on my head, running down on my beard. For there, Yahweh bestows His blessing, even life forevermore."

David turned to find Bathsheba leaning against Solomon's side. He beckoned, and she knelt beside the king and his companions of old. Every man bowed his head and whispered, "My lady" as Bathsheba placed her hand upon the cheek of each one.

More than a touch of kindness. More than a touch of forgiveness. It was a touch of healing. The wound in David's heart had only been covered with a thin membrane of defense against the sharp arrows of his stricken conscience. With the wife of Uriah touching each face, only then could each man begin to know reconciliation was possible.

"I am so sorry for what I have done to each of you, so sorry for what I did to our dear companion," David said as he opened the palms of his hands, offering them to his friends. "I lift up my hands to you. I set my prayer before you like incense. May the lifting of my hands be to you like the evening sacrifice."

Benaiah was the first to take David's hands. Benaiah folded them together placing them against his heart. Then Benaiah offered the king's hands to Jozabad, and he too placed them against his chest. Followed by Eleazar who did the same. When Eleazar offered the king's hands to Bathsheba, she looked into David's eyes before taking them. It had all begun with her, yet she bore no blame. The blame was David's to bear. It had always been David's to bear.

Now, his wife completed the circle of forgiveness. She grasped David's hands and placed them upon her heart. "The king's blessing is like precious oil that flows into our hearts filling us with mercy and forgiveness."

"Oh, my dear wife," David exclaimed, lifting his hands into the air. "Oh, my friends. You are the righteous ones. You rebuke with your kind forgiveness. You anoint my head with the oil of mercy, and my heart overflows."

David wrapped his arms around Bathsheba and looked at his friends. Jozabad was the first to chuckle. His mild laughter was contagious, and the others joined in, though David had no idea what Jozabad found so humorous. None of them could stop laughing. Even Bathsheba began to laugh, and whatever was the cause for this infection, the joyous sound reverberated in the anteroom.

"This is like the old days," David said. "We laugh and cannot explain why."

"Oh no, my lord. I know why," Jozabad said, his hand raised with the answer, but then he choked with his own laughter and had to rest his hand upon Eleazar's shoulder.

Eleazar slapped Jozabad upon his back, which momentarily arrested his choking. Eleazar wheezed, "We need help to stand on our feet."

It took another few moments for all five to regain control.

"Help us to stand." David motioned to Solomon. Then the king looked back at his old friends. "Jozabad. Eleazar, meet our son, Solomon."

Benaiah was first through the door into the Hall of the Lion and announced the king. Solomon followed David, leading his mother through the door, then Jozabad and Eleazar came after. All who had been with David in the anteroom stood off to the side.

David sat upon his throne and looked back at this group of friends standing with his wife and son. Bathsheba smiled and wove one arm around her son and the other around Eleazar. David's heart was lighter than it had been in years. His mind was clear and prepared to discuss the life and death business that could not wait. David viewed the somber faces before him. He would listen to each argument for the right course ahead then make his final decision.

"Commander Joab, what are the latest reports of this rebellion?"

"Absalom has spent years fomenting descent against the king and kingdom," Joab said in undisguised anger. "Under our very noses, and we have done nothing."

"Commander, I did not ask for a history lesson. I am well aware of what my son has been doing in the city and throughout the country. I chose to ignore it in hopes that his heart would change toward us, but it appears it has not. I alone bear the responsibility for the consequences. Now, proceed with Absalom's recent actions."

"My lord, Absalom has succeeded in capturing the hearts of the men of Israel," Joab said. "There is no kind way to say it."

"I do not ever remember you saying much of anything with kindness, but this is why you have been successful as my commander, and I am grateful." David flavored his dig with a compliment.

No warmth existed between them, but David knew Joab had, without question, carried out his order to place Uriah in the front lines of the fighting in the war against the Ammonites to assure his death. However, with this recent reconciliation to those closest to him, David felt he was out from under any debt he might owe to Joab.

"What is the current location of my son, and what is the strength of his forces?"

"My lord, the word of this rebellion has spread to the four corners of the kingdom," Joab said. "At this moment, Absalom is in the city of Hebron. He is bringing to a close the days of his sacrifices to Yahweh for the vow he claimed to have made to the Almighty while in exile. His false piety is all for show, but it has allowed him time to organize his forces in Hebron and for the other tribal divisions from the north and west to join him there. These rebels have sworn an oath to crown Absalom king once you have been dispatched. All these military units are fully armed and will be prepared to attack the city once the order has been given to march on Jerusalem."

This was the inevitable outcome of David's inability to bring Amnon to a just penalty for the rape of Tamar. He ignored and waited and even denied the truth of his firstborn's reprehensible action. Absalom had wanted his father to act morally for this crime against his sister, but he did not. David could not.

Absalom had turned his vengeance against his family. First with Amnon, and now with his father. The years Absalom had spent turning the hearts of the people against him were paying off. The moral retribution David should have extended to Amnon was about to fall upon his own head.

"My lord, may I interject a word of possible conciliation?"

David was happy to hear an idea that could be hopeful, one that might not involve a civil war. His gaze fell upon Hushai standing between Gad and Nathan with his hand raised. This young man was educated at the prophet's school and had been appointed to the court with Nathan's commendation to become a counselor to the king. Hushai and his friend Ahithophel, also educated at the prophet's school during the same time period, had wisdom well beyond their years. Both young men had conducted successful negotiations with dignitaries from foreign countries establishing accords and trade compacts. This potential civil war would put those treaties, indeed the very survival of the nation, in grave peril. If either Hushai or Ahithophel had a good proposal, David would listen.

"Where is Ahithophel?" asked David. "I was hoping the both of you would be present. You two are my Urim and Thummim of wise counselors."

"My lord, forgive me," Hushai replied. "I do not know where my friend is at present. I have not seen him for several days, though I have sent inquiries."

"Very well, what are your thoughts, Hushai?"

"My lord, is it possible there might be an appeasement between the king and his son?" Hushai offered.

"What sort of appeasement are you suggesting?" Joab chose to answer for the king, which David did not take kindly but decided to ignore.

"Perhaps if you offer your son a governorship, say, of the tribe of Judah."

That suggestion met with loud grumbling from everyone but David. He raised his hand for quiet. "What is your thinking behind this suggestion, Hushai?"

"I believe the king desires to avoid bloodshed, which we all desire." Hushai said, waving his arm around the room.

No one offered a verbal agreement or nodded. If he looked for encouragement from the others, it was not extended.

Hushai continued. "Were the king to go out to meet his son not in battle array but with an olive branch, then there might be a chance for a peaceful resolution."

"The Lion of Judah should never concede one tribe or one city or one cubit of land to this rebel, prince and son though he is," declared Abishai, standing next to Joab his brother.

This received a more heated response in opposition to any idea of concession.

"And who says this is concession?" David rose from his throne. "Who says giving up some territory to my rebellious son is not an excellent idea were it to prevent bloodshed? I am a man of blood. It is why I cannot build a temple for the Almighty. Is this not so, Nathan?"

"Yes, my lord," Nathan answered. "Yahweh has spoken thus, 'You shall not build a house for My Name because you are a man of war and shed much blood.'"

Nathan's pronouncement of the word of Yahweh silenced the room.

David raised his hands before the crowd then looked at his friends and his wife and son standing off to the side of his throne.

"I have shed blood in just wars and for just causes," David said. "I have also shed innocent blood that has left an invisible stain on my hands and my heart. I do not wish to smear myself again with the color of blood. I do not wish to add to my account lives taken—guilty or innocent—especially if those lives would be the citizens of our nation. If there is the least chance to avoid bloodshed, should I not consider Hushai's proposal?"

The hall was not filled with the usual cast of courtiers and wealthy merchants, secretaries and historians, Levites and musicians, servants and trades-men, or just regular citizens of the kingdom come to sightsee in the City of David. The small crowd of advisors consisted only of military personnel, prophets Gad and Nathan, the High Priests Zadok and Abiathar, and Hushai, and their one topic to discuss was war.

David was king over all of Israel, anointed by Yahweh, but he could not deny that at this moment he wished it was not so. His scalp began to perspire underneath his crown. He was king over all, even over a rebellious son whose blood he would never shed, and the weight of such a position felt heavier than ever.

"My lord, I do not advise you go out to meet Absalom with an offer for peace," Joab said, his voice subdued though his position contrasted that of Hushai.

"Why not, Commander?" asked David.

"I believe Absalom is not vying for any offer of peace," Joab said. "I believe he has broken with the king and the opportunity for any appeasement or treaty, or shared power is no longer an option. I believe your son desires your throne and your head."

"Always clear and brutal with your assessments." David rubbed his hand beneath his neck at the thought of its possible separation from his head.

"And honest, my sovereign king," Joab said.

"Yes, honest, always," David murmured. "Then what do you advise, Joab?"

"We might take a stand here in Jerusalem. We are well-fortified."

"A siege could last for weeks or months." Benaiah stepped away from the group.

"But a long siege would give time for Absalom's followers to see his folly and turn against him," argued Abishai. "Less chance of bloodshed as the king expressed."

"Or a long blockade could have a similar effect on the citizens of the city," Benaiah countered. "Starvation within the walls of Jerusalem can drive one to surrender or revolt against the king."

"Or?" David responded.

"My lord, it pains me to suggest this, but I believe we should flee the city," Benaiah said. "Let Absalom have Jerusalem and crown himself king and give him what he desires. He spews his lies disguised as affection for the people and that he will make a better king than my sovereign lord. Too many of our people have fallen under his spell and follow him. I say, let him have his chance to rule. I do not believe it will last."

"None of us will last, my friend. We are all like a vapor over the water, soon to disappear in the heat of the sun." David's pensive thought silenced the room.

He returned to his throne but did not take his seat. He stared at the emptiness. Anyone could take a seat within its vacancy.

The throne was beautifully carved with lion's paws for the feet and lion's claws at the end of the armrests. The embossed face of a lion was carved into the back of the chair. It had a cushioned seat of goat hair dyed purple and embroidered in gold. It was meant for a king, designed just for him. It was meant to bear the sovereign weight of the nation.

Now, it was threatened by usurpation, to be stolen from him by his son. And untold numbers of citizens, the chosen of Yahweh, could possibly die to defend it and attempt to take it, just so he might continue to sit in this royal chair.

"Gad, tell me. When was the last time our nation experienced civil war?" David turned to face the group.

"My lord, we have had civil unrest in our country, but civil war with Israelites fighting other Israelites? Not since all the tribes marshaled their forces against the tribe of Benjamin have we known such turmoil."

"Remind us now what happened." David motioned for Gad to continue. "What was the result of our fighting against ourselves?"

"The loss of life for the Benjamite troops exceeded twenty-five thousand. When the other tribes realized the carnage inflicted upon their fellow countrymen, and that all of the male population that remained within the tribe of Benjamin was only six hundred strong, the other tribes were filled with remorse and ceased the slaughter. The thought of exterminating one of the tribes was unthinkable."

"'Filled with remorse and ceased the slaughter.'" David repeated Gad's words. "I do not believe I would be able to live with myself should such a massacre take place within our nation just so I can occupy a wooden chair. That too is unthinkable."

David removed his crown and wiped his brow with the sleeve of his robe. Then he wiped down the interior of the golden band but did not immediately put it back upon his head. David raised it and looked through its open circle scanning the faces of those in front of him finally stopping with Bathsheba and Solomon.

"Each one of you has pressed your life into my heart, leaving an indelible impression I carry with me as long as I live. I see your faces through the orb of my crown, and the thought of losing any of you is unthinkable to me." David lowered his crown. "While I wish I could offer the olive branch to my son as Hushai has suggested, I agree with Joab and Abishai that Absalom will refuse it, choosing war over peace. A siege is also a great risk. I do not like the possibility of any of us, especially our citizens, being cooped up inside the walls of this city regardless of its excellent fortifications.

"And, while the thought of once again being forced to flee and live on the run…" David choked as he gazed upon his audience. Except for his wife and son and Hushai, everyone had been a fugitive with him at some point. He had to clear this throat before he could continue. "The thought of being on the run fills my soul with torment, but it is better than risking the possibility of great bloodshed. Let us prepare to take flight."

Zadok raised his arms toward the ceiling and offered the prayer of Aaron, the first High Priest of the nation. "May Yahweh bless us and keep us. May Yahweh make His face to shine upon us and be gracious to us. May Yahweh turn His face toward us and give us peace."

Chapter 33

DAVID WANTED TO DEPART JERUSALEM UNNOTICED. HE IN-structed the household not to overburden the wagons with personal belongings. The traveling would be arduous, the weather unpredictable, food rations would be meager. This would be a hard, comfortless march, so no finery. Wherever they might settle, life would no longer be normal.

Only the wives and children would make up the family party, and there were not enough wagons for everyone, so many would be traveling on foot. Too much uncertainty lay ahead for David, his family, and all those loyal subjects who chose to fall in with him.

Under these trying conditions, Mephibosheth chose to remain in the city. David did not wish to uproot everyone from the family dwellings, and it would be less of a burden not to have them counted among the travelers. In the absence of the royal family, Mephibosheth was given the responsibility of helping to maintain the palace along with David's concubines and servants. Surely, Absalom would respect their relationship to the king. They all would prove useful in the care of the palace under its new occupancy.

There was no standing army for David to muster. He would not command Joab to call for troops loyal to the king. Pitting brother against brother was unacceptable. He did not order the palace guard to escort him in the streets and out through the gates of the city. They were to remain at their posts, awaiting the arrival of the new king.

David gave his servants the option to remain and serve his son if they chose to do so, which most did. The royal cooks remained behind as well, too accustomed to well-furnished kitchens and ready access to the butcher and farmer and winegrower with the finest selection of livestock and produce for the asking. He was leaving it all behind, comforts and luxuries.

David and his party would be at the mercy of the Almighty. Long ago he had lived such a life. Would he possess the stamina now for such a grueling journey, or had he grown soft?

Though it had been many years since David lived in fear and distress from an enemy bent on killing him, he had not forgotten the perilous nature of such a nomadic existence. Back then, he was fleeing the mad king who wished him dead. Now, his son, who was not mad but furious with his father, was bent on revenge.

The revenge Absalom sought was David's destruction, something he never expected. The danger and discomfort ahead was one thing. The outright hatred of his favored son was something else entirely. Even if he could go back to repair the damage, his soul was so broken, he would not know where to begin to set all things new.

In the early light of dawn as David tramped through the streets of Jerusalem, leading his caravan of family and followers, memories of his life on the run came flooding back. Sleeping on the ground, in caves, under trees, inclement weather, lack of food, constant threat of danger, and the weight of the responsibility of all those in his care. It all came back, and he began to groan as the aches in his muscles rose, his breathing became strained, his joints popped and cracked, his pours gushed with sweat.

Can I live like this again?

He could see the east gate from the main street. Once he passed through it, there was no going back. He had not even departed, and his legs began to buckle.

The days of his splendor were over. The days of his defeat were at hand.

David would exit the city, not as he had entered years ago driving his chariot with Mikal at his side, waving to the adoring populace. The perilous uncertainty of the journey was ahead, and he could do nothing to change this new course. It was set. But within the physical agonies and the self-doubt was also the familiar, and within the familiar his poetic voice awakened.

It startled him when the impulse emerged from his gut, but he was unable to restrain it. The lament was impossible to hold back.

> *"I cry aloud to the Almighty;*
> *I lift up my voice to the Almighty for mercy.*
> *I pour out my complaint before Yahweh;*
> *Before Yahweh I tell my trouble.*
> *When my spirit grows faint within me,*
> *It is Yahweh who knows my way.*
> *In the path where I walk men have hidden a snare for me.*
> *Look to my right and see; no one is concerned for me.*
> *I have no refuge; no one cares for my life.*
> *I cry to You, O Yahweh; I say, 'You are my refuge,*
> *My portion in the land of the living.'*
> *Listen to my cry, for I am in desperate need;*
> *Rescue me from those who pursue me,*
> *For they are too strong for me.*
> *Set me free from my prison, that I may praise Your name.*
> *Then the righteous will gather about me*
> *Because of Your goodness to me.*
> *O Yahweh, hear my prayer, listen to my cry for mercy."*

David was gently pulled out of his expression of grief when Bathsheba took his arm and pulled him into her side. "Look, my love," she whispered. "Look about you."

He could not believe his eyes. He had been in a trance during his prayer, and he awoke to a new vision, one that bolstered his heart with a tenderness he never thought possible.

The citizens of Jerusalem were emerging from their houses, out of the alleyways and side streets, standing on their rooftops, moving into the procession beside David, some weeping, some praying, some offering blessing for this most ignoble exodus of their king. The sight of the people, who had risen before dawn to be present at his parting, arrested David's heart. He had to stop and bow his head.

> *"Yahweh. Yahweh. Yahweh. You keep me safe, O Yahweh.*
> *For in You I take refuge.*
> *I said to the Lord, 'You are my Lord;*
> *Apart from You I have no good thing.'*
> *As for the righteous who are in the land,*
> *They are the glorious ones in whom is all my delight."*

David lifted his head and took in the sight of those he proclaimed were glorious ones. A multitude surrounded him. As David proceeded toward the east gate, the citizens began to make way for him to pass among them. Some touched his robe, some touched his arm and shoulder, many weeping and bemoaning his departure. Then a chorus of the glorious ones began to sing a hymn of praise to their king.

> *"You are the most excellent of men*
> *And your lips have been anointed with grace.*
> *May the Almighty anoint the king with His oil of gladness.*
> *May the king walk the land in peace.*
> *May his memory be kept alive through all generations."*

David could not feel his feet or legs. He was near collapse, and Solomon and Benaiah stepped on either side to help him make his exit. While they passed beneath the gates, it was as if he walked on air. He had no strength. He had no firm foundation on which to plant his legs. It was like a dream, passing into the open country. He was being carried and finally set down on the Kidron Valley road at the foot of the Hill of Olives.

"My lord, here is Ittai," Benaiah spoke into David's ear. "I dismissed him and your bodyguard as you requested, but he and the men refuse to go home to Gath."

The last moment David remembered was the sound of voices singing to him. One moment he had been inside the walls of the city, now he found himself outside looking into the face of the person in command of his elite forces, his "Mighty Men," David called them.

One dream had ended. Another had begun.

"Ittai," David said, his voice hollow and weak as if questioning this reality. "Here we are again."

"Indeed, my lord. Here we are again." Ittai began to take a knee.

David gripped Ittai's shoulders, preventing him from showing such respect. David did not need the honor of a reverent pose. He needed the upright flesh and blood vigor of kinship.

"Ittai, you have served me for so long, through hardship and abundance," he said. "It seems only yesterday we were on the run together, being pursued, danger at every turn. I cannot ask you to do this again, wander about with me when I do not know where I am going and what dangers lie ahead."

"My lord, in the long ago, when we lived off the land fleeing the mad king, six hundred of us joined you from Gath," Ittai began. "When you came to your throne in the City of David, six hundred came with you. While the ebb and flow of our numbers varied throughout the years, six hundred remain devoted to you now."

Then Ittai slipped free of David's grip and took a knee. Since David was not wearing a robe, only leggings and a tunic for the ease of rugged travel, Ittai laid his hands upon David's sandaled feet.

"My lord, as surely as Yahweh lives, as surely as my lord the king lives, wherever you may go, wherever you may be, whether it means life or death, there I will be, I and the others, to a man. I am your servant."

The bitter fruit of his choices had brought him to this moment in the road. Before this humble man kneeling at his feet, David was not a king. He was not a warrior. He was not a poet or psalmist. He was unmanned. He was not worthy of such loyalty. He was not worthy of this man's life-pledge to him, a foreigner, a Philistine who had left his people and turned his back on his gods, for him. David should be the one to have knelt down and placed his hands upon the feet of Ittai in grateful thanks.

David laid his hands upon Ittai's gray head. "This is my darkest hour. That you and your men have chosen to remain at my side gives me strength. Please rise."

"Benaiah, what is our destination?" Ittai asked as he came to his feet.

"Mahanaim, beyond the Jordan River."

"Half of us will march ahead then," Ittai said. "I will deploy the rest to the rear."

"We must move with haste, my friend," Benaiah said.

"As always," Ittai said with a slight chuckle, then bowed his head and began barking orders to his men.

The men under Ittai's command stepped aside, so David could make his way up the Kidron Valley road. As David passed through the gauntlet of burly warriors, old loyal friends and some the progeny of those who had gone before, many wept aloud as he passed. There was no restraining them.

The smoke from the burning fires and the sweet smell of incense took David by surprise as he emerged from the phalanx of Ittai's men. On the northern slope of Mount Moriah, outside the Levitical compound, Abiathar and other priests had set up makeshift altars and were offering sacrifices. Zadok scrambled down the slope ahead of the cadre of Levites carrying the Ark of the Covenant on their muscular shoulders with the acacia wood poles coated in gold.

The last time David saw the Ark was years ago when he had it transported to Jerusalem. It had been hidden inside the Holy of Holies of the Tabernacle. The sight of its approach filled his heart with dread.

"My lord," Zadok said as he dropped to his knees before David. "May the Almighty be with you. Wherever Yahweh will lead you, may the Presence be at your side. You are Yahweh's anointed, and the Ark of the Covenant belongs wherever the rightful king may be."

"No, Zadok." David quickly lifted Zadok off the ground. "This can never be."

"Abiathar and I wish to go with you," Zadok insisted. "As do many of our Levitical brothers. If you are to be driven from the city and Tabernacle, then the Ark should accompany you, so you will know Yahweh is with you."

David raised his hand toward the Ark. "I am not worthy, Zadok. Return it."

"My lord, I wish for you the favor and protection of the Presence." Zadok pointed back to the Ark suspended above the ground.

"It shall remain in its proper place in the sanctuary. I do not gain Yahweh's favor by trusting in a sacred object. I suffer the consequences of Nathan's pronouncement upon me. The hands of Yahweh are righteous in judgment. If the justice of the Almighty is true, I can also trust His mercy. If I find favor in the eyes of Yahweh, perhaps the Almighty will bring me back that I may worship the Presence in its rightful place. Return with the Ark, dear friend. I am ready to allow Yahweh to do with me as only He sees fit."

"But how can we serve you, my lord?" Zadok asked.

David laid his arm over Zadok's shoulders, and they walked together up the road. "You and Abiathar serve me by serving Yahweh. Do everything you can to maintain the worship and sacrifices and ceremonies Yahweh has ascribed. Even if I am not on the throne, I will know Yahweh is being honored by His anointed priests."

They came to a spur trail leading up to the crest of the Hill of Olives. David paused and shielded his eyes from the sun's light rising in the east as he gazed upon the grove of trees at the top.

"Long ago, I remember us worshipping once at the summit of that hill in the midst of the olive trees."

"Yes, my lord. Until you brought the Ark to Jerusalem."

"That is how I will worship Yahweh," David said, his eyes fixed on the hilltop. "For as long as I am cast away from Jerusalem, from the throne, I shall worship Yahweh in the spacious firmament of His creation."

David waved for Abiathar to join them.

When the priest came down the slope, he dropped to his knees before the king.

"Abiathar, you came to me in the wilderness." David lifted Abiathar to his feet. "Yahweh brought you to me after the death of your father and all the priests of Nob. We endured many perils together. Now, it seems I am to face yet another. I need you both to return to the city and serve the new king for as long as you are able."

David wrapped his arms around the two priests drawing them into a tight circle. He placed his hands on the backs of their heads gently pushing them forward, so what he whispered could not be overheard. "You must be alert to all the plans and strategies of the new king. I leave behind no trusted friend."

"What of Gad and Nathan, my lord?" asked Abiathar.

"They insist on going with me, though I tried to dissuade them. Listen carefully. I know each of you has a son."

"Yes, my lord, Ahimaaz is my son," Zadok answered.

"And Jonathan is my son," Abiathar responded.

"Good men, I know, because they have you as fathers. It will not take long for the new king to organize his troops to pursue me. When you learn of the plans, you must send your sons to me with the report. We are marching to the fords of the Jordan and will stop there for a much-needed rest. Your sons will find us camped there."

"Yahweh be with you, my lord," Abiathar said.

Zadok and Abiathar walked up the slope toward the Tabernacle. Zadok waved for the Levites carrying the Ark to follow them back into the Levitical compound.

David turned back in the opposite direction of the grove of olive trees on the hill overlooking the city.

Benaiah came to stand beside him. "My lord, shall we continue?"

"Benaiah, I intend to ascend the hill of the olive trees." David took a step forward onto the spur trail.

"This trail continues on the downside of the hill that will reconnect with the road to the village of Bahurim," Benaiah said.

"Never retrace your steps," David said with a chuckle. "Yes, I remember."

"Should anyone escort you, my lord?"

"No, Benaiah. I will go alone."

"My lord, I have learned the reason for Ahithophel's absence at our last council assembly."

"What have your spies told you?"

"Ahithophel has gone with the conspirators," Benaiah said. "He has sided with your son, and so the conspiracy gains strength and Absalom's following increases."

He did not expect this news, an added shock to his present ruin. The young man Ahithophel had chosen to be a counselor to the house of David but had transferred his allegiance from the sitting king to the usurper.

David had misjudged the loyalty of this trusted advisor. "Even my close friend, whom I trusted, who sat at my table and shared my bread, has lifted up his heel against me." David shook his head. "I used to believe the young man spoke as one who hears from Yahweh. And now...now, may Yahweh turn his counsel into foolishness."

The moment David finished his prayer he felt the sting to his conscience. The road filled with his followers, all refugees fleeing the fury of his son, and all because of his foolishness. Who was he to pray this prayer against the counsel of Ahithophel?

"I will meet you on the road to Bahurim." David left his friend and began the ascent up the Hill of Olives.

Chapter 34

DAVID PAUSED TO CATCH HIS BREATH. IT HAD BEEN TOO LONG since he expended such physical energy. Barely halfway up the Hill of Olives and he was winded and lightheaded. Sitting on a throne required his mind and his heart, not a strapping body. Now, he needed a leather binding to support his middle. He loosened the knot of the cords wrapped around him and took a deep breath. It was not just the exertion that strained him. Absalom's revolt overburdened both body and soul to the breaking point.

He looked downhill at the stream of people making their way along the Kidron Valley road. His family and loyal friends. His guardians and supporters. He might be forced from his throne and driven out of his city, but he was not abandoned.

Yet, his heart was consumed with loneliness. Trudging up this hill tore his soul asunder.

This could be his last vision of the City of David. He may have conquered this city, but he would not try to hold onto it. He may not live to see his city ever again, but he would not be the cause of its destruction. Death lay ahead, but whose death was not yet determined. If he should die in the wilderness, so be it. If he should be brought back to Jerusalem it would not be in triumph, but under the veil of grief.

He placed his hood over his head and felt the gold band of his crown. He removed it and ran his fingers across the embossed head of a lion. This token of his sovereignty was the only object he brought. He left behind all the accoutrements of his royal reign. None of those things mattered, including this crown, but he chose not to part with it. If Yahweh smiled, his head might be made worthy again to wear this noble diadem. He slipped the leather belt through the crown and secured it with a double knot.

David groaned as he sat on a rock to remove his sandals. He tried digging his toes into the ground, but it was too hard. He then scraped the soles of his feet along the surface of the crusty earth. The tenderness of his skin needed to adjust to the granular soil. This would prove a painful ascent, a king in defeat leaving behind his beloved city, a king beset and overcome by rebellious forces, a king who had to accept the terrible consequences of sin—his sin.

He tied his sandals onto the leather belt beside his crown and slung the strap over his shoulders as he got to his feet. He looked up toward the crest of the hill, a hallowed spot with a grove of olive trees, one of the high places where Yahweh had once been worshipped. He grabbed the ends of the strap in his hands and continued to climb.

"Listen to my prayer, O Yahweh, do not ignore my plea;
Hear me and answer me.
My thoughts trouble me and I am distraught;
My heart is in anguish within me;
The terrors of death assail me.
Fear and trembling have beset me;
Horror has overwhelmed me.
I said, 'Oh, that I had the wings of a dove!
I would fly away and be at rest—
I would flee far away and stay in the desert;
I would hurry to my place of shelter,
Far from the tempest and storm.'
I cry aloud to Yahweh.
I lift up my voice to the Almighty for mercy.
When my spirit grows faint within me,
It is Yahweh who knows my way.
In the path where I walk snares are hidden from me.
I have no refuge; no one cares for my life.
I cry to You, O Yahweh
I say, 'You are my refuge,
My portion in the land of the living.

Listen to my cry, for I am in desperate need;
Rescue me from those who pursue me,
For they are too strong for me.
Because of Your goodness, gather the righteous around me.'"

Once he reached the crest, David collapsed upon his hands and knees, heaving from exhaustion, from sobbing, and the pouring out of his heart. His tunic was soaked in sweat. His face and head burned inside the oven of his hood. He tried to swallow, but there was no moisture in his mouth.

"My lord, my sovereign lord," came a voice nearby, and then the bearer of the voice knelt beside him, lifting him to his knees.

David looked into Hushai's face, pinched and curled inward. The young man's head and beard were covered in dust and grime, the outward sign of affliction. His undergarment exposed and torn, a sign of deeper sorrow.

"I have been watching you, my lord, from behind the olive trees." Hushai pointed to the grove behind him. "Let me help you to their shade."

Hushai carefully lifted David to his feet and guided him into the olive grove. David cried out with each painful step until Hushai lowered him between the exposed roots of an ancient olive tree.

"My lord. My lord," Hushai sobbed as he offered David his waterskin.

David drank the skin dry, gasping between swallows. When he finished, he leaned his back into the gnarls of the tree's massive trunk.

"Oh, my lord. My lord," Hushai mumbled. He stretched out David's legs and looked at the soles of his feet, bleeding and torn and caked in dirt.

"I never expected to see you, Hushai," David gasped. "You are a beautiful sight."

"I want to come with you, my lord." Hushai removed his satchel from his shoulder. "I spent last night here in the olive grove. I have packed light for swift travel."

"No speedy traveling for me after the damage done to my feet," David said.

Hushai took out a vial of oil and clean strips of cloth from his satchel. He propped David's feet upon his knees and removed as much dirt and blood from the tender soles as he could with a dry cloth.

David winced and groaned each time Hushai pressed hard upon the wounds.

"I am so sorry, my lord."

"You are a much better counselor than you are a physician," David gasped then began to chuckle.

"I want to continue to serve you as counselor, my lord, no matter where you are." Hushai soaked a cloth in the oil and rubbed the ointment into David's feet.

"I believe I know the best way for you to serve me." David stiffened his legs each time Hushai rubbed the liniment into his wounds. "The company traveling with me is large, more than anticipated, and each additional person would add its own burden."

"But my lord, I will not eat much, and I can keep up."

"Hear my plan and see if you do not agree if this might be the best use of your skills." David raised his hand for Hushai to listen. "Before I began my ascent up the hill, Benaiah informed me that Ahithophel has forsaken me and gone over to Absalom. It is why he was not at our last council meeting. He was in Hebron lending his support to my son's conspiracy."

"I did not know, my lord," Hushai said. "How could he betray you so?"

"We humans are easily deceived," David answered. "He fell prey to the lies of my son, and he will attempt to do more harm with his wisdom and counsel than the full force of any army. I need you to return to the city and wait for the arrival of the new king. Once he comes to the palace, greet him with respect saying, 'Let the king live.'"

"I have faithfully served you all this time, my lord. Will Absalom not be suspicious why I remained behind?"

"I expect he shall, but you swore to serve the house of David, and Absalom is of that house," David replied. "You can say he is now the rightful king, the one chosen by the Almighty and by all of Israel. You served the father. Now, you will serve the son."

"But he has usurped your throne, my lord. You know he will do all he can to destroy you."

"That is why you must remain in court and learn his intentions. Ahithophel will offer his counsel and support to the rebellion, and you, my friend, must do all you can to impede and frustrate these plots."

Hushai stopped applying the salve and became silent.

David had asked Hushai to do something that might require more of him than was possible. To meet the treachery of his son with a treachery of his own. To create a falsehood, a dangerous tactic of pretense, in order to thwart a rebellion. Such a ruse would not come naturally for his trusted advisor who always gave him honest counsel.

"Is this too much to ask?" David placed a hand upon Hushai's forearm. "Be truthful."

"My lord, you task me with a great charge, to act with deception. I am not sure I know how to do such a thing."

"It is why you are the only one I can trust with such a furtive undertaking," David said. "And you are not alone in this purpose. Zadok and Abiathar are also my secret observers within the court, as well as their two sons, Ahimaaz and Jonathan. They are swift runners and will bring reports to me. Relay any information you may hear to those two young men, and I will be sure to receive it."

"I have never done anything so dangerous, my lord. I have no experience with such risks."

"You are not alone. You share the dangers with other good men." David squeezed Hushai's arm before releasing it.

He then looked above into the branches of the great olive tree. "I must be off." David pointed to a low-hanging branch. "I believe that branch looks perfect for a staff. Would you break it off and strip the leaves."

"Can you walk, my lord?" Hushai asked.

"I have no choice," David replied. "May I have two of those pieces of linen? I want to wrap my feet before I strap on my sandals."

Hushai handed David the cuts of linen. While he broke off the olive branch and stripped it, David carefully bound each foot with a cloth then snugly tied the leather straps of his sandals around his ankles.

When Hushai presented him with the makeshift staff, David extended his hand. "Now, help me stand."

Hushai gently pulled David to his feet.

David took the staff and bounced it in his hand feeling for the rough spots. Then he took a few hobbling steps in a circle to test its strength against the tenderness of his feet. "I believe this will do. Thank you."

"My lord, we live in dangerous times," Hushai said. "I am looking at the rightful king of Israel, the true anointed king, chosen and approved of Yahweh. All others, whether blood kin or stranger, are imposters and should not be allowed to succeed. I will play the falsehood and do all I can to spoil the evil designs of the usurper."

"Yahweh be with you, my friend," David said, and then he hobbled through the grove of olive trees and descended the other side of the hill.

The downward slope merged onto the main road heading north to Bahurim. Before David joined the long line of travelers in his company, he sat on a rock at the bottom of the hill to catch his breath and examine his feet. He was careful in the descent using the aid of his new staff, but blood had seeped through to the edges of the cloth. He tightened the leather straps around his ankles where they had come loose. Years ago, his feet could have taken this punishment. From head to toe, his body had yielded to inertia and royal luxuries. David grunted in disgust at how he had allowed himself to become complacent throughout the years. But time never stopped. Time never aged. Time only moved forward, leaving behind life's ravages done to the body and mind.

Surrounded by a special protection detail, the family wagons rumbled by where the trail merged with the road. The line neared its end, and the last of the rear guard was not far behind.

David gingerly tested his feet and sandals. There was less pain, but his feet would not heal if he was forced to march the long distance ahead. He spotted Solomon behind the last family wagon and blew a sharp whistle through his teeth and waved to Solomon.

His son trotted back toward him. "What happened to your feet, Abba?" Solomon's eyes widened at the sight of his father's banded and bloodied feet.

"I ascended the hill of olive groves unshod." David elevated one of his legs. "This is a reminder to never allow yourself to grow soft."

Benaiah and Abishai broke ranks from the rear guard and rushed along the trail to join David and Solomon.

"He has damaged his feet," Solomon announced, holding his father's arm.

"It is not as bad as it looks, my son," David insisted.

"Shall I fetch you a mount, my lord?" Abishai asked.

"I can walk," David replied. "Where is your brother?"

"Joab is leading the procession. By now they are beyond Nob and entering Bahurim. Shall I send a runner ahead with a message to stop?"

"No, no," David said. "We need to keep moving."

David took a couple of steps and stumbled, wincing in pain.

"Let me fetch a mule, my lord," Benaiah said.

"Spare the mule, Benaiah. I shall walk."

"What if we ride together in the family wagon, Abba," Solomon suggested.

"I can walk," David said. "I need to walk. Where are Jozabad and Eleazar?"

"Among the rear guard, my lord," Benaiah answered.

"I need my companions," David said. "And the prophets? Where are they?"

"I believe Gad and Nathan are in front of the family wagons," Abishai answered.

"Good, fetch them as well. I want the fellowship of my comrades."

Benaiah and Abishai dashed away to fulfill David's request to gather his friends. He had trudged up and down the Hill of Olives alone, not as a king but as a man, broken, penitent, damaged in body and soul. Now, he needed close companions and his son.

"Do you wish to wear your crown, Abba?" Solomon pointed to his father's crown strapped to his waist.

"Not now." David pulled down the hood of his robe to allow his head to breathe. "Its weight is burdensome at present."

With his son on one side and the use of his staff in his other hand, David was able to maintain a steady pace behind the family wagons. They kept a little distance between them. David did not want the attention from his wives and children, nor did he want to taste the dust and grime stirred up from the ox-drawn wagons. When his friends formed rank around him, a trickle of strength revived his legs which helped him temporarily forget the pain in his feet.

From the road, they could see the village of Nob nestled into the eastern hills. It was no longer known as a priestly city. David never returned to Nob after his one fateful visit. The memory of what King Saul had done to the city was too bitter. He was escaping the wrath of the mad king at the time, and the High Priest had offered him succor. Now, he was in flight once again, from another bent on harming him, but Nob did not offer the sustenance he needed. The village was inhabited by an assortment of displaced people and never regained a thriving populace after the carnage inflicted upon it.

"You know the story of the city of Nob, son? Have I told you what happened?"

"I have read the story in the scrolls, Abba. It was destroyed by the mad king."

"The citizens were slain and the village put to the torch," David said. "The scrolls are a reliable source how the incidents unfolded in the story, but they do not adequately describe the horror, the sounds of human screams, the smells of death, the visions of butchery. Words are inadequate in describing the human cost of the evil we are capable of. There was a time when I too left waves of such destruction behind. I pray you will never know such darkness."

"Is such darkness not upon us now, Abba?"

"I fear it is. I hope my decision to leave reduces the risk of bloodshed. By leaving in peace, perhaps your brother will come to his senses and lives will be spared."

"But what of the will of the Almighty, Abba? Was it not Yahweh's will for you to reign as the anointed king? It is recorded as such."

David looked over his shoulder at Nathan and Gad walking arm in arm as they lagged behind. These two prophets had devoted themselves to serving the Almighty, and, at the same time, remained loyal servants of both kings of Israel.

"You may fully trust what these prophets of Yahweh and others have recorded in their scrolls, Solomon. But I doubt either understands fully the will of Yahweh."

An inhuman piercing scream came out of nowhere, not a squeal of a child or the cry of a woman, but the shriek of an animal or disembodied spirit.

"You man of blood. You dog. Get out. Get out!"

Stones rained upon him, but David did not flinch. He did not duck his head or raise his arm to block them. When Solomon moved to protect his father from the barrage of flying stones, David held firmly onto his arm keeping him from exchanging places.

"You are now repaid. You bled the house of Saul of its heirs," the voice shouted. "You took the kingdom. You usurped the throne from Saul, and Yahweh has yanked the kingdom from you and given it to your son, Absalom. You are overtaken by your own evil and come to ruin, you dog. You have come to ruin because you are a man of blood."

"Who are you who dares to curse the king," shouted Abishai, raising a fist at the attacker standing on a mound of earth above the road.

"Shimei, son of Gera, of the tribe of Benjamin and the household of Saul, the first king of Israel. You killed all his heirs and stole the throne, you man of blood."

Shimei did not back down from Abishai's threats but continued to pelt David and Solomon and those gathered around him with stones and curses.

"My lord, why should this dead dog curse you?" Abishai removed his sword from its sheath. "Let me go cut off his head."

"Return your sword in its sheath, nephew," David replied. "You are not a part of this. Keep walking."

David never looked at Shimei. He tightened his grip on Solomon's arm and kept his steady, limping pace. His feet were injured. His exposed head had been scratched by the glancing stones. From head to foot, he was a walking damaged soul.

"Learn from this, my son," David spoke into his son's ear, yet loud enough for those nearest to hear. If anyone could learn from this moment it was Solomon. "What this man says is true. A son from my own loins is trying to take my life. Can the insults and stones cast by this Benjamite be more harmful than that? If Yahweh commands, then let this man revile me. I submit myself to the will of the Almighty. Perhaps Yahweh will see my affliction and someday restore goodness to me. Keep walking."

Solomon pulled away from David's firm grip and stepped to his opposite side. The others drew beside and behind David to serve as a human shield as they marched onward, a fixed rank together.

Their actions were a comfort against the curses, yet deep in his soul, David knew he would never be fully clean from the stain of all the blood he had shed.

Chapter 35

HUSHAI STUMBLED DOWN THE OUTSIDE STEPS THAT LED TO the roof of the palace, his hand braced along the wall to help maintain his balance. He could no longer control himself, but he did not want to break down in front of the others. When he pitched onto the first landing of the staircase, he gave over to the anguish of his heart. What he had witnessed was not a dream from slumber, not a vision to be treasured, but unbridled licentiousness playing out before his very eyes, before the eyes of all of Israel. This was the horrors of rebellion, and now the horrors were despoiling the nation.

Hushai had come to the palace to welcome Absalom and hail him as the new king, to establish himself in the new court, but when he arrived, the courtyard was crammed with revelers drinking and eating and celebrating. Hushai did not recognize any of these people. These must be Absalom's followers who had entered the city with him along with his military retinue. When the trumpets blared and the drums were beaten from the palace rooftop, the revels ceased, and everyone cast their eyes up to the roof where Absalom stood dressed in a short purple robe loosely tied with a golden sash.

With outstretched arms, Absalom motioned for silence. "Jerusalem has been taken. The city belongs to us." He could not continue for the uproar of the crowd below. He kept waving his arms for them to quiet down. "The former king is deposed and on the run. His crown, his city, his lands, and his property belong to the victor."

Absalom beckoned to the guards behind him, and they brought forward the ten concubines David had left in charge of the palace and lined them along the edge of rooftop, five concubines placed on one side of Absalom and five on the other side. None of these women bore any expression of excitement or pleasure. Each face looked pained by the public humiliation, and when the jeering crowd began hurling their lewd insults, several burst into tears.

"All the spoils of the defeated monarch are to be enjoyed by the new king," Absalom shouted with lecherous triumph. "All of Israel will bear witness that the Lion of Judah is crushed and his disgrace complete. There will be no turning back. The City of David belongs to the victorious son."

Hushai came undone when Ahithophel appeared from behind Absalom holding the long-woven mane of the new king in both hands. As Ahithophel raised the thick tresses, decorated with flowers, golden threads, and purple ribbons, the people went into a frenzy. What Absalom was most famous for was once again on full display.

Hushai now knew where his friend had been all this time and where he placed his loyalty. Ahithophel had thrown in his lot with the usurper and his place beside Absalom meant only one thing, Ahithophel was the king's chief counselor.

Could he stop it? If Hushai could reason with Absalom and keep him from this outrage against David's concubines, then there might be a chance for a father to come to terms with his son. That the son might beg forgiveness of his father and resubmit himself to the rightful king, Yahweh's anointed.

So, Hushai had raced through the courtyard, pushing aside the revelers, running past the guards stationed at the bottom of the outside staircase, and leaping up the stairs until he reached the top where he was stopped by two guards who crossed their spears in front of him. He curled his fingers around the wooden javelins preventing further progress, struggling for breath, and watched as Absalom's loyal soldiers pulled back the flaps of the family tent and revealed five cushioned pallets. The first five concubines were led into the tent, the same tent where David and his family had enjoyed their meals on cool evenings, gazing at the sun setting over the city.

Hushai screamed for them to stop this folly, but his pleas were not heard above the roar of the crowd, the blare of the trumpets, and the pounding drums.

He waved frantically, hoping to catch the attention of Ahithophel, but his friend was preoccupied with the virile spectacle performed by the new king and the reaction of the crowd below. Ahithophel gave the braided strand of Absalom's hair to the king and then removed the king's robe. If the crowd had not lost its mind before, it now became a hysteria of mob madness restrained only by the desire to witness the lewd behavior of the new king. Ahithophel stepped back, robe in hand, and that was when Hushai caught his eye, but his friend ignored him. He led Absalom into the tent closing the flaps after him.

Hushai could no longer watch the depraved exhibition and began his staggered descent of the outside staircase. His strength had vanished when he stumbled onto the staircase landing. He fell onto all fours, panting and weeping. How could he now pretend to serve this imposter king? How could he say to this fraud, "Long live the king," and not have the words burn out his tongue? How would he play the hypocrite, even if it was as an insurgent for the true king?

He must flee the city, find King David, and confess his failure.

"Hushai. Hushai." He heard his name shouted above the landing and then the sound of hurried footsteps descending. He was too slow to react, and two arms wrapped around his midsection and lifted him to his feet. When he was spun around, he looked into Ahithophel's excited face.

"I wondered where you were," Ahithophel said, drawing Hushai into his embrace. "Where were you when we entered the city? I looked for you, but no matter, you are here now, in time to present yourself to the new king. My friend, we have taken the kingdom. The old man is gone, and the new king is staking his claim at this very moment."

Ahithophel indulged a lewd chuckle at the activity above them on the palace roof.

Hushai stepped back and wiped his eyes with his sleeve. To his amazement, Ahithophel no longer wore the robes of a scholar and counselor but was dressed in warrior's garb with a leather breastplate and sword and sheath belted around his middle.

"Do you even know how to wield that weapon?" Hushai point to the sword.

"You mean like this?" Ahithophel yanked out his sword and made a playful swipe toward Hushai's neck. He burst out laughing when Hushai slammed his back against the palace wall. "I have put away the books and scrolls, my friend, to become the chief counselor for King Absalom. This is just decoration." He slid the sword back into its sheath. "Still, I like wearing it."

"Did you counsel the king to carry on like this on the palace roof?" Hushai asked, finally coming to himself to form a coherent thought.

"Oh, the genius of it, my friend," Ahithophel exclaimed, unable to resist the self-evaluation of his counsel. "Lie with your father's concubines in the sight of all Israel, and the breach between you and your father is complete."

"And irreconcilable," Hushai cried, pushing away from the wall. "There is no going back from this."

"Which is exactly what we desire," Ahithophel countered. "You saw the people in the courtyard. You heard the roar of their elation. All of Israel will see the impossibility for the son to secure a pardon from his father. There is no going back for Absalom, for his followers, for me. The end for us is clear."

"And what is this end that is so clear to you?" asked Hushai.

"The head of the old king on a spike," Ahithophel answered without hesitation. "We have created a new destiny, our destiny. We have overthrown the old kingdom and brought in the new, and it will be glorious."

Hushai closed his eyes. He had to shut out the proud, ecstatic face of Ahithophel rejoicing in his moment of triumph. He had to clear his mind and think, imagine what this meant and where he stood in this man-made destiny of which Ahithophel boasted. If he chose personal ambition and betrayal, there was a place for him here, a place to serve and be greatly rewarded for the counsel he could provide. Hushai had proven himself valuable to King David and established his reputation as someone with wisdom and prescience. Ahithophel knew this, and these two friends could work together to serve the new king. Absalom could wear the crown, but Ahithophel and Hushai could come to prominence as the true powers in Israel.

"May I have an audience with the king?" Hushai opened his eyes.

"Come with me." Ahithophel took the stairs to the roof two at a time.

Hushai watched his friend bound up the staircase. Once he ascended those stairs and was ushered into the presence of King Absalom there was no going back. The guards on the rooftop, who had blocked Hushai's first attempt to get on the palace roof, snapped to attention with lances at their sides and not crossed to prevent intrusion. The path was cleared by Ahithophel.

Just follow him and the way will be clear to the king.

His friend stood between the two guards and waved for Hushai to follow, and like his friend before him, Hushai bound up the steps two at a time.

"Quickly now, he is coming out of the tent." Ahithophel led Hushai across the roof. "He will need refreshment before the next round."

Absalom emerged from the tent with a large woolen blanket wrapped around his broad shoulders covering him. Only his lower legs and feet were exposed. The drums began a slow cadence that built in tempo as Absalom staggered toward the edge of the roof wearing an exhausted, haggard expression, but it was only a part of the show. As soon as the crowd saw him from the courtyard below, they erupted with bawdy praise. Absalom took his braided hair and waved it like a rope above his head prancing in a circle with the pounding rhythms of the drums to the delight of the throng.

The first group of concubines were ordered out of the tent and hastily escorted to the staircase. Hushai turned his head away as the guards rushed the women away. He did not wish to be recognized or that he was leering at their shame.

Servants took the paddings off the five palettes and tossed them off the roof and into the courtyard. A near riot broke out as the people fought for the soiled cushions.

"Come. The king will meet us here." Ahithophel pointed to a throne and a table set off to the side of the tent. The table was covered in a small feast of meats, cheeses, fruit, and breads with a large pitcher of wine and a single goblet.

Hushai was shocked that the throne designed and constructed for King David had been removed from the Hall of the Lion and brought to the roof.

Absalom strutted over and plopped onto his father's throne. The humiliating takeover was complete. Every action designed to show the prince had dethroned the king.

"This tupping is an exhausting business," Absalom mumbled as he crammed cheese and mutton into his mouth before filling his goblet with wine from the pitcher. "The crowd certainly enjoys it though. Good advice, Ahithophel."

"Thank you, my lord." Ahithophel bowed his head.

"Long live the king. Long live the king!" Hushai exclaimed with purposeful repetition designed to commend Absalom, so he would know Hushai was assenting to the authority of the new king. But when he moved to take his bow, Hushai was cut short.

"Who is your companion here?" Absalom held up his greasy fingers, stopping Hushai's approach. Before Hushai answered, Absalom guffawed with laughter. "I only jest with you," he said with a dismissive wave. "But I am puzzled by your presence, Hushai. I never expected to see you here. I thought you would run away with the old man. Is this your way of showing kindness? I thought he was your friend."

"On the contrary, my lord. I serve the house of David of which you are the rightful heir," Hushai said. "You have been chosen, my lord, by the army, by all of Israel. I am yours to command, and with you I shall remain."

Absalom slumped back onto the throne and stared at Hushai.

Hushai prayed that the veracity of his words and the commitment he had spoken would stand up under the scrutiny of the disbelief he saw on Absalom's face. He had spoken words of loyalty to the usurper, but the stab of pain in his belly by speaking such words was a piercing reminder that he could never betray, he could never yield to even the slightest temptation for personal power that could be achieved with such allegiance to a supplanted kingdom.

Absalom took another swallow from his goblet and sloshed the wine around inside his mouth before spitting it out onto the roof.

"Good then. Thank you for recognizing me as king," Absalom reached for a piece of bread, tore off a bite with his teeth and continued. "Two things, a request and some counsel. First, the request. I want a shrine built in my name. My sons died quite young, this last one in childbirth that took his mother with him. My only child, a daughter named for her aunt, will live with my sister for a time until I am settled in my kingdom. I want this monument placed in the Valley of Shaveh south of the Kidron Valley, so everyone will see it as they enter and leave the city."

"Easily done, my lord," Ahithophel said.

"Not a pile of stones," Absalom said. "The monument must be a thing a beauty."

"No expense will be spared, my lord," Ahithophel said. "A column will be carved that will proudly bear your name for the ages. I shall assign the best artisans to the task."

"And second is…," Absalom paused and settled back in his throne. He stirred the wine in his goblet with his finger as if something might be divined in the childlike action.

"What is the second desire you have, my lord?" asked Ahithophel.

"I need the counsel from two of the wisest men I know," Absalom responded, his voice soft and pensive, his eyes still staring into the goblet.

"We shall gladly give the king our best counsel, my lord." Hushai looked at his friend standing next to him. "Please tell us."

Absalom did not take another drink but licked his moist finger before setting the goblet back onto the table. Then he leaned forward, tucking his folded hands beneath his chin, and shifted his eyes back and forth from Hushai to Ahithophel.

"The king, the old king, what am I to do with him?" Absalom asked. "He may have fled Jerusalem, but still his presence is deeply felt among the people."

His voice was sober. His eyes were sober. His question, sober.

Hushai knew not to answer with haste. He would allow his friend to offer his advice first, it was the honorable thing to do. Were it not for Ahithophel, Hushai would not have this audience with Absalom or the opportunity to advise and guide the new king.

"My lord, we must strike an immediate blow," Ahithophel began, stepping in front of Hushai to command Absalom's full attention. "With the king's permission, I would select a sizable body of troops, twelve thousand at least, and I will lead them. I believe we should set out tonight in pursuit."

"Tonight." Absalom sat up straight with a look of surprise.

"My lord, the old king is in distress. He must be exhausted as are those who travel with him. None could resist the sudden onset of an attack. Now is the time to strike."

"A quick strike, you say." Absalom appeared to mull over the prospect.

"Quick and decisive, my lord," Ahithophel continued. "So as to terrorize the old king and send those who follow him into a panic. They will flee like frightened sheep."

"Leave him alone and helpless then," Absalom said, following the line of reason.

"Exactly where we want him," Ahithophel said, his body becoming more animated in response to Absalom's quick grasp of his plan. "Then, my lord, I would strike the fatal blow upon the old king. None of the other exiles need perish. I shall bring them home, back to Jerusalem, back to their rightful king."

"I want no parade, no open celebration of my father's...of the king's death."

"The safe possession of the kingdom can only be assured by the old king's death, but I agree, my lord, no public display of triumph," Ahithophel concurred. "That is wise and compassionate of you."

The content and mood of Ahithophel's counsel was now clear to Hushai.

The brief and urgent presentation was as quick and decisive as his plan to attack and kill King David. This was excellent counsel on the part of his friend. Everything he said was true and were Absalom to agree with this course of action, then David's doom was almost assured. There was not a moment to lose for Ahithophel to have success, yet while Absalom did appear to be giving serious consideration to the plan, he was not quite ready to decide in Ahithophel's favor.

Absalom looked behind the throne. The other five concubines were placed at the edge of the rooftop for a last taunting from the crowd below. He turned back, leaned his head against the throne, and sighed as if reluctant to carry out this second round.

"You have given this much thought, Ahithophel," Absalom said. "You seem confident. I like that."

"Thank you, my lord." Ahithophel stepped back beside Hushai. There was no disguising the satisfied look on the face of Ahithophel.

"And you, Hushai," Absalom said. "What are your thoughts on the matter? Does this plan seem good to you?"

"I am no military strategist as my friend here," Hushai began. "The counsel of Ahithophel is always well thought out and succinctly declared. I find no fault with it."

Hushai paused to give himself another few heartbeats to think, but his heart was beating so fast, and Absalom had detected his hesitancy and pressed him.

"Well thought out, you say, and you find no fault in it, but…" Absalom motioned for Hushai to continue.

"But, my lord, the counsel of my good friend neglects one vital consideration." Hushai placed his hand upon Ahithophel's shoulder hoping to ease his distress, but he felt the muscles in Ahithophel's shoulder contract with tension.

"And that would be?" asked Absalom.

"The strategy is brilliant, my lord, but the timing is not. You know your father and his men. You know what fierce warriors they are. In every battle, he and his men fight like wild she-bears robbed of her whelps."

"This is true," Absalom acknowledged. "I have read the stories."

"The eyewitness accounts are true, my lord. Your father is a fighter, and after decades of combat, you know he will never spend a night with his troops, nor sleep out in the open fields. He will find a cave or some other well-fortified location. If the purpose is to kill him and spare the rest, you must spend more time preparing for multiple situations. What if Ahithophel and his men are ambushed in the wilderness? What if they are drawn into a trap? It will only mean a great slaughter for Ahithophel and his men."

"That would never happen, my lord," blurted Ahithophel, his face giving up its earlier confidence.

"It certainly is possible that Ahithophel could succeed with his surprise attack," Hushai conceded. "But your father merits his title of the Lion of Judah. He is the bravest of warriors as are those who fight beside him. Should they turn the tide on Ahithophel, even the hearts of the bravest of his troops would melt with fear, and there would be a great slaughter among the twelve thousand of your troops."

Hushai paused to let his words settle on the son of the true king. He did not cast his eyes upon Ahithophel who remained beside him, but he could hear the raspy breath of discontent and frustration and the deep groan of a coming rejection.

"So, Hushai, what might be an alternative plan?" asked Absalom.

"My lord, all of Israel is at your feet," Hushai said. "Send word throughout the nation, to all the tribes, from Dan to Beersheba, marshaling the number of troops that will be like the sand on the seashore. With you leading them into battle with such an overpowering force, you shall fall upon him like the dew that saturates the ground so that neither he nor his men will be left alive."

"And what if he withdraws into a city?" exclaimed Ahithophel in desperation.

"My friend makes a good point, my lord," Hushai said, hoping to alleviate the growing anxiety his friend expressed. "Should that happen, then all Israel shall bring ropes and attack the city dragging it down to the ground, leaving no stone upon another."

Before Absalom was able to respond, a captain of the palace guard called to him. "My lord, we are ready to proceed."

Absalom peered around his throne. The concubines were being herded into the tent, the drums summoning his presence, but Absalom looked back at his two counselors.

"I must get back to it." He chuckled as he stood. "I doubt I will feel like leaving tonight, Ahithophel. Your counsel to despoil the old king's concubines was good, but my energy will be spent. I believe Hushai has the better plan. Prepare a summons to arms and send it to all the tribes. I shall lead the army against my father."

Hushai and Ahithophel bowed as Absalom began to dance to the edge of the rooftop waving his coiled and braided hair above his head, inciting the rapturous crowd.

"I am sorry, my friend." Hushai turned to Ahithophel.

His friend's joy and confidence had vanished. The color drained from his face. His eyes were blunted and vacant as if focused on some far distant image.

"Absalom has gone mad," Ahithophel said, his voice breathy with wonder.

"No, no, friend." Hushai grabbed Ahithophel by his shoulders and pulled him close. "Do not see this as a rejection of your counsel."

"Mine was the better counsel," Ahithophel insisted. "We both know it. Now, his doom is assured, and I will be marked as a traitor. I can see how this will unfold."

"No, never," Hushai asserted. "This would not be the case."

"I must go home now. I must put my house in order."

Ahithophel's calm demeaner upset Hushai, but his friend pulled free from his grip. He crossed the roof, stopping at the top of the staircase. "It was good advice," he shouted at Hushai. "Only the Almighty could frustrate my counsel. Disaster is certain."

Then he disappeared down the staircase.

Hushai started to run after him but stopped when Absalom shouted his name. He turned back and saw the apostate king waving his hair as he disappeared into the tent.

"I must find the High Priests," Hushai whispered to himself. "I must get a message to David at once."

Chapter 36

BATHSHEBA WADED UPSTREAM IN THE KNEE-HIGH WATERS while her husband sat on a ledge protruding from the shoreline, soaking his feet. She had needed to get out of the city of Mahanaim and take this respite from the family.

She stood still and turned her face upward into the light. The warmth of the morning sun and the cool water rushing around her feet and legs was a blessed twinkling of peace after the relentless days of forced marches, living on meager rations and depending on kindness from people she did not know.

The stream fed into the Jabbok River that flowed into the Forest of Ephraim. The water was crystal clear, and Bathsheba dug her toes into the sandy bottom. The terrain around the city was rugged and wooded.

She had become the informal caretaker of the family. The children were plentiful, but the number of wives had been reduced. Some had died. Others made different choices. The first wife had returned to her home in Gibeah years ago. The mother of Tamar and Absalom chose to stay in Jerusalem to be with her children and granddaughter. Haggith, Abital, and Bathsheba were the only wives who remained.

When they all lived in the palace, servants carried out the household duties and the concubines acted as nurses and caretakers of the king's children. Without the servants or concubines, the familial duties fell to her. Bathsheba had argued for taking everyone including concubines. She warned her husband and believed the women would not be safe if they remained in Jerusalem, but she did not prevail. The logistical wrangling of all the children was challenging enough, but it became a lamentation when messengers arrived with word of Absalom's repulsive treatment of the ten concubines at the palace.

The king grieved openly, as did she and all of the family, when they heard the terrible story, but Bathsheba took the news hard. She struggled with the bitterness that streamed through her heart like the waters flowing around her legs. It took all she had to stand against the hard current.

Her husband never mentioned the obvious. Gad and Nathan never mentioned the obvious. Bathsheba was loath to discuss it. The news of what had happened to the concubines was a harsh fulfillment of the prophesy Nathan delivered on her wedding day. The consequences of what the king had done to her in secret and to her husband Uriah, had rolled down upon him in such a brutal fashion like a landslide, but others suffered as well. Her husband was a great king, his dominion thoroughly established, his city a beacon on a hill, he was beloved by the people and esteemed by neighboring countries. But his secret behaviors were brought to light and his shame made public, while others were assaulted or died for his crimes.

Nathan's words were true. The man after Yahweh's own heart had broken the heart of the Almighty, and a reckoning was expected. But when and where would it end?

Bathsheba must be prepared for whatever might lie ahead. She must prepare her heart. She must prepare her family. She must prepare her husband.

She could not foresee the conclusion of this retribution. The untimely death of her firstborn son was only the beginning. Whatever the ending of Nathan's prophesy, it was at hand. Reports were that Absalom was marching north intent on killing the king with an army three times the size of those who protected her husband. If this was the final end of the prophesy, how many would die in battle for the sake of one man's unbridled lust?

The battle in her heart was constant. Bathsheba had to fight against despising her husband for the consequences of his action inflicted upon her and the family. She might have forgiven him these brutal consequences were it not for the stream of painful reminders of righteous justice. She had done nothing to deserve any of this, and yet she was married to the perpetrator of all this pain, fleeing for her life with him, hiding out in a foreign city, herself a fugitive with an uncertain future that could end in death.

She looked back at her husband stretched out on the rock, his legs hanging off the ledge, feet in the water. She was the youngest wife and the most dedicated to David. She tended to the wounds of the one who had brought this grief and guilt on himself and countless others. Yet, it was a battle to forgive. A battle to replace resentment with love. A battle to hold any hope of survival.

Bathsheba splashed back downstream and climbed out of the water onto the rock. She had rolled up her leggings while wading, so she sat beside her husband and stretched out her legs for them to dry in the sun. Then she lifted one of David's ankles propping it upon her knee to inspect the sole of his foot. She ignored his groaning as she touched the wounds on the bottom before drying them with a towel.

"You are torturing me," David complained.

"No, my love, you tortured yourself walking barefoot up the Hill of Olives." Bathsheba did not conceal her impatience with her husband as she dried the moisture around his ankle and foot. "What were you thinking?"

"Guilt and grief make me do unusual penance." David winced from Bathsheba's touch. "Be gentle, please."

"Your feet must be completely dry for the ointment to work. Now, move back up on the rock. I need more room."

David did as requested, scooting up onto the ledge, so Bathsheba could finish drying both feet.

"The swelling is down, the cuts are mending, and the discoloration is going away," she said. "All good signs."

"The soaking helps," David said. "The cold water has a nice numbing effect."

"We must keep them well-oiled and wrapped." Bathsheba reached into the satchel she brought on their outing and pulled out the vial of liniment and fresh strips of cloth. "It is best if you spent more time off your feet than on them."

"Impossible," he said. "Absalom is on the march. We have little time to prepare."

Since coming to Mahanaim, a steady arrival of powerful chieftains in the surrounding region brought wagons full of supplies for David and his company. While Mahanaim was a well-fortified city with gates and walls and high citadels for the lookouts, it did not have the provisions in its storehouses to feed such an influx of people traveling with the king.

Bathsheba had seen the family had proper housing inside the city walls, but as for her husband and the rest of his company, they camped outside the walls at the edge of the Forest of Ephraim and along the Jabbok River. David insisted that he and his men be a buffer of protection against attack. He did not want to hide inside the walls and risk the city being overrun by his son's army.

"I believe I now understand how King Saul might have felt." David braced himself on his elbows and propped up his foot for Bathsheba to anoint and wrap.

"How so?" Bathsheba rubbed the ointment into the sole of David's foot and then began to wrap the linen cloth around it.

"Jonathan always defended me, stood with me against his father, and the king felt himself a fool, misled by his own son. It drove him mad. I now know a son's betrayal and feel I have fallen into the mire of madness."

Bathsheba tied off the bandage and reached for his other foot, but David winced and pulled his leg away. He fell back and crossed his arms over his eyes and wept.

She laid her head upon his chest and listened to his rapid heartbeat.

He struggled for breath, but his words could not be stopped.

> *"O Yahweh, hear my prayer, listen to my cry for mercy;*
> *In Your faithfulness and righteousness come to my relief.*
> *Do not bring Your servant into judgment,*
> *For no one living is righteous before You.*
> *The enemy pursues me, he crushes me to the ground;*
> *He makes me dwell in darkness like those long dead.*
> *My spirit grows faint within me;*
> *My heart within me is dismayed.*
> *I spread out my hands to You;*
> *My soul thirsts for You like a parched land.*
> *Answer me quickly, O Yahweh; my spirit fails.*
> *Do not hide Your face from me*
> *Or I will be like those who go down to the pit.*
> *Rescue me from my enemies, O Yahweh,*
> *For I hide myself in You."*

This rush of words from her broken husband surprised her. She had been preoccupied with her agonizing thoughts, with the despair of their shared circumstances, and her husband's entreaty for Yahweh's tender mercies echoed her own plea.

"Whatever happens in the coming days, I want you and the family to be safe inside the city walls," David said, his voice raspy with grieving. "Whatever happens to me…should I fall into the hands of my enemies…"

"You will not die," Bathsheba said firmly. "Others may, but not you."

"Others have died because of me." David removed his arms from covering his eyes and enclosed her inside of them. "Amnon, my firstborn. Our firstborn."

"Hush now." Bathsheba lifted her arm and lay her hand upon her husband's lips. There was no need to be reminded of the past, for the past was all too present and the future foreboding. "This does you no good. It does us no good. Whatever comes, you will live. We will live. And we will make the best of all the days that Yahweh gives us."

"You are a wonder and a comfort," he said. "Yahweh be praised for you."

"Let me wrap your other foot," Bathsheba said as she pulled away from her husband's embrace. She was determined they would survive. She believed being strong-minded and shouldering through these troubles was the only way to bleed the bitterness from her heart.

David rubbed his face then tucked his arms beneath his head and raised his other leg for Bathsheba.

"My lord. My lady."

David and Bathsheba looked up to see Gad approaching from the opposite side of the stream.

"What are you doing out here, Gad?" David asked. "You should not be alone. Where are Nathan and the others?"

"They have gathered at the king's tent, reviewing the scouting reports and discussing strategy. I am useless in such matters."

"You will not be setting aside the scrolls and taking up the sword?" David teased.

Though faint, Bathsheba was happy to see a smile appear on her husband's face. She finished her linen wraps on David's other foot and tied them off.

"My lord, I come with encouragement mightier than any sword." Gad removed a scroll from his satchel. "May I approach?"

"This I must hear." David motioned for Gad to cross the stream.

As Gad waded through the water, Bathsheba gave David his footwear.

"We are on the sacred landscape that your ancestor Jacob trod when coming home to his brother Esau after being gone for twenty years," Gad said once he reached the bank.

Bathsheba finished tying off the leather straps around her heels and rose before David. She and Gad took David's arms helping him to stand. Her husband had the strength, but his feet were still tender.

After testing the snugness of the fit, David was ready to give Gad his full attention. "Tell me more, Gad."

"In the Book of the Beginnings, from the stories of our ancient fathers, when Jacob and his household arrived at the Jabbok River flowing along here, he was greeted by angels of the Almighty." Gad waved his hand over the landscape to include the tributary feeding the Jabbok River and the Forest of Ephraim beyond.

"Met by Yahweh's angels?" David asked in wonder. "In this area here?"

"Yes, my lord. Before Jacob reunited with Esau, he camped here."

"That was in the long ago," Bathsheba said.

"Seven centuries from our time, the forefather of the king camped at these waters. Jacob named this place 'Mahanaim,' the 'Two Camps.' One for his family—"

"The other for a camp of angels," David said, interrupting the prophet.

"Jacob was terrified of meeting his brother, and Yahweh must have sent His angels to encourage him." Gad waved the scroll in his hand.

David did not take the scroll. "There are no angels for me today." He shielded his eyes from the glare of the sun as he scanned the surrounding landscape. "Was this the same place where my forefather wrestled with Yahweh?"

"Yes, my lord, he wrestled with Yahweh all night, and at daybreak, the Almighty wrenched Jacob's hip and changed his name to Israel."

"This is too much for me." David marveled at the thought. "Too much to take in."

Bathsheba felt David going limp, so she looped one of his arms over her shoulder to lend support against his slumping weight. If the prophet's word was meant to encourage her husband, it appeared to have the opposite effect.

"My lord, do not be dismayed." Gad grabbed David's other arm. "You are the son of Judah, the son of Jacob. You are the Lion of Judah, who crouches and no one dares to rouse him. The scepter will not depart from Judah. You may not see angels, my lord, but you are the anointed of Yahweh. The one who seeks your life will not take the scepter from you. It will pass peacefully to the rightful heir."

"Abba, is something the matter?" Solomon called, quickening his pace as he approached the rock ledge.

"My son. My son," David said taking his arm from Gad and extending it to Solomon. "Nothing is the matter. My soul is overcome by the prophet's word and the wonder of Yahweh's splendor."

Gad stepped back, so Solomon could move beside his father.

Bathsheba was surprised to see her son dressed for battle.

"I was sent to fetch you, Abba." Solomon placed his hand upon his father's back. "A scout has come with the latest report."

"Why are you dressed in a warrior's garb?" Bathsheba tried to hide her alarm at the sight of her son attired in a leather skirt and breastplate with a sword and sheath strapped to his side. She had not seen him in anything other than royal robes.

"I wish to be at my father's side not as a scholar, but as a protector," Solomon replied. "It is time to set aside the scrolls."

David smiled at his son's bold statement.

"You are not to encourage him," Bathsheba said openly for everyone's ears.

"What is the news, my son? Your ima has finished with her healings," David said.

"Our scouts report that Absalom has arrived in Gilead and the army has pitched their tents west of the Jordan River," Solomon replied. "Commander Joab and the others believe that, once the army is fully mustered and organized, they will cross the Jordan and march on Mahanaim."

"We have the Forest of Ephraim, the deep ravines, and the Jabbok River between us," David said. "They can be used to our advantage."

"How best to use the landscape is now being debated, Abba."

"Son, Gad has just told us our ancestor Jacob and his family camped here in the long ago." David gingerly stepped off the ledge and onto the sandy soil. "Tell him, Gad, as we walk to join the others. We will follow behind."

Bathsheba waited for Gad and Solomon to move toward the main encampment.

"How are the bandages?" She watched David shift his feet inside his sandals. "Any slipping?"

"No, my love. Perfect as usual." David offered his hand to her.

Bathsheba did not take it but looked him in the eye. She witnessed his breakdown. She knew his soul was curving inward from the strain of impending battle, that while he still may have the spirit of a warrior, his body was not keeping pace.

"Do you take heart from Gad's words?" she asked. "You need not pretend."

"I am not sure I know how to pretend anymore," David answered. "Not with you, and especially not with Yahweh. The Almighty knows me, to the depths of my heart to my anxious thoughts. Where can I go to escape the Almighty? It liberates my spirit to no longer try and hide from the consequences of my transgressions. That truth and your presence is balm for my soul."

She took his hand and stepped off the ledge. Together, they walked toward the king's tent in the center of the encampment. However the righteous verdicts of Yahweh may unfold, whatever additional sorrow she may experience, she would keep the poison of bitterness from overwhelming her heart. She would remain faithful.

She would walk by the side of the king to the end.

David slowly moved around the large table studying the drawings of the terrain and defensive positions of his army. When he was uncertain of a detail on a specific sketch, he tapped his finger on the parchment and looked to his commander to explain.

"A ravine," Joab would answer then give the dimensions of the gorge. "A grove of wild olive trees, a clearing, winding paths, uneven ground, terebinth trees with thick boughs hanging low to the ground."

Joab, Abishai, and Ittai had explored the face of the landscape from Mahanaim to the crossing at the Jordan River. David was impressed, and when he glanced at Benaiah, Jozabad, and Eleazar, they too nodded their approval.

"You like fighting in this terrain?" David looked at his three oldest friends.

"We have fought in worse, my lord," Eleazar answered with a chuckle.

"You remember when we chased the Amalekites who had pillaged our homes in Ziklag?" Jozabad pointed to the table of sketches. "When we finally caught up with them, they were spread out everywhere, and this landscape looks just as bad."

"But we used the countryside to our advantage and beat them," Joab said.

"That we did. That we did," David said, still scrutinizing the drawings.

"That is our intention now, my lord," Joab continued. "We are outnumbered, but we have knowledge of the terrain. We have used our time to learn every ravine, every grove of trees, every outcropping of rock, every cliff and bald. We used the landscape to rescue our loved ones from the Amalekites, we will do the same to protect the king."

"Just like back then, I will march out with you to battle." David glanced at Joab before returning to the drawings of the lay of the land. He did not ignore the silence inside the tent at his announcement, but he did not give anyone time to respond. He tapped the drawing. "I see what appears to be a large clearing on our side of the Jordan."

"Correct, my lord," Joab replied. "We will draw the enemy into this clearing, attack from three sides and disperse them into the Forest of Ephraim."

"Surprise and panic, my lord," Ittai said. "Invisible weapons that are lethal."

"When we scatter the enemy over the rough ground, then, if the Almighty is with us, the landscape and forest might claim more than the sword," Abishai added.

"If Yahweh wills it so," David mumbled under his breath. "So, a center with two wings. How will you divide these three-fold positions?"

"Abishai will hide his division in the cliffs and outcroppings north of the clearing, while my division is concealed in the forest south of the clearing," Joab explained.

When Joab did not finish his explanation of where all three divisions would be positioned, David looked at his nephew. Whoever took the clearing would be the most vulnerable. They would be exposed to the enemy in hopes of drawing them into the deadly landscape.

"My lord, I will be leading my men into the clearing."

David looked at Ittai and smiled. "You cast a bad lot, my friend."

"I volunteered, my lord." Ittai nodded toward Joab and Abishai. "Besides, you Hebrews do not want to fight under a Philistine banner, and my boys do not want to fight under the command of your nephews. We must keep our honorable reputation."

"Ah, keeping an honorable reputation, is it?" David winked at Ittai. "Well, Yahweh forbid we lose face before superior forces who are more likely to win the day than are we. But if we are going to die this day, I doubt the earth will care whose blood it soaks up, Philistine or Israelite. It is all the color of crimson. Ittai, you are an honorable man. I shall be proud to march out with you."

David ignored the clearing throats and the raspy grumbling among his men, and gripped Ittai's shoulders giving the Philistine commander a firm shake of appreciation.

"May I speak honestly, my lord?" Ittai asked.

"Of course you may." David released Ittai and took a step back.

"You must not go out with us," Ittai said. "We number in the thousands, but we may be forced to flee. Even if half of us die, the enemy will not care. They only want you. There is no one like you, my lord. Do not do this."

When Ittai finished, he bowed his head in honor of the king.

David never considered not going into battle with these men. He was the only reason they were preparing for a battle that could potentially destroy them all. David felt flush and off balance. He leaned against the table to keep from falling. His surety was unraveling, and he did not know what to do.

"What then do you suggest I do?" David tried to control his voice.

"My lord, I agree with all that Ittai has spoken," Joab replied. "As commander of the king's army, it would be better if you remained in the city. It would give your men a steadiness to know that so experienced a warrior king stood within the walls watching the fight, prepared to aid any of the three divisions that might be overrun with danger."

"Remain in the city," David repeated, wanting to be sure of what Joab was saying.

"Yes, my lord, along with a force of three hundred men. I have asked Benaiah, Jozabad, and Eleazar to be your commanders each of them leading one hundred men."

David looked again at his three friends smiling at him. This was enough for David to feel strength in his legs, so he pushed off from the table.

"Whatever is good in your sight," he said. "When do you take your positions?"

"We muster within the hour while there is still plenty of sunlight," Joab said. "The supply wagons and the men must be in place before the enemy crosses the Jordan."

"We have already captured several enemy spies sent to scout our positions, my lord," Abishai added. "We cannot risk delay."

"I will stand at the city gates so the men will know I am with them heart and soul," David offered.

"The sight of the king will fortify the spirits of the men, my lord," Joab said, then he addressed the others. "To your tents, collect your things and prepare to depart."

Once again David placed his hand upon Ittai's shoulders. "Thank you, my friend."

"A father should never be forced to fight against his son," Ittai said. "My heart is pained that it has come to this, my lord."

David received Ittai's words like a shower of arrows piercing his body. A life-or-death outcome was upon them. A rebel son had traveled a great distance with a massive army for the sole purpose of killing him. It was so incomprehensible David felt his soul had caught fire, as if Absalom's loathing was consuming him in the flames of his hate. His son was driven to see his father dead, to steal the throne from his father, to defy the Almighty for the sake of revenge. The madness of revenge had descended upon him, and he and countless others might die, yet David could only think of Absalom. The thought of seeing his beautiful son dead could bring upon him an unstoppable grief.

"Absalom. Do not harm him." David's voice faltered as he spoke. "Be gentle with the young man, for my sake."

"But my lord, you forget what he has done," Joab blurted as if David had asked they not strike down the Destroyer should it appear outside the tent.

"Joab." David raised his tightly balled fist. "I know what he has done. I know what he is doing. Tell your troops, deal gently with the young man for my sake."

Joab did not answer.

No one responded.

Was it an order or a plea? Had David begged, or had he commanded? He was not sure. In such a battle, under such circumstances, in such difficult terrain, how could he expect anyone to obey such an order?

Yet, David hoped his words might give pause to anyone who had the chance to strike a death blow upon his son. Except for the rustling of parchments, maps, and drawings and the shuffling of feet, everyone departed the king's tent in silence.

Chapter 37

SOLOMON LEANED BACK AGAINST THE TRUNK OF A TEREBINTH tree. The long, low branches extended into the surrounding trees fashioned a compact weaving of bough and branch creating a leafy canopy. In the growing darkness, he could only see the outline of the supply wagon and Gad standing behind it.

Solomon and Gad had been assigned to drive one of the supply wagons for Joab's division positioned in the Forest of Ephraim. By afternoon, all three divisions had taken their assigned locations. The terrain surrounding Mahanaim was alive with warriors yet hidden in the landscape.

A thick cloud cover had moved in before sunset concealing the moon and stars. With no natural illumination from above, it was assumed Absalom would not attempt a sneak attack but wait until daylight to march forward to Mahanaim. Yet, Joab's orders were strict. The troops would spend the night in complete darkness. There would be no campfires or noisy movement, and voices kept low. They must not reveal their positions.

"I do not need to close my eyes," Gad whispered as he inched his way from the supply wagon toward the tree. "There is slack difference between the darkness behind my lids to what little I can see around us."

"Be careful of the exposed roots," Solomon said.

Gad grunted and sucked in a painful breath through his teeth.

"Like I said, be careful of the roots." Solomon tried to stifle a laugh.

"Somewhere in Israel a shoemaker must design footwear that will better protect the toes," Gad grumbled as he hobbled the last steps to the base of the tree.

"When we get back, have my ima give you some of the ointment she uses on my father's feet." Solomon took the blanket Gad handed to him.

"Age no longer creeps up on me." Gad groaned as he eased to the ground next to Solomon. "It has arrived in full force. My bones and muscles bray like an angry donkey."

"Is this what life was like when the mad king pursued my father?" Solomon asked as he covered himself with the blanket.

"Worse," Gad replied then exhaled a breath of exhaustion.

"How so?"

"Well, your father and his men were always outnumbered by Saul's army, so that has not changed. Though if the estimation of Absalom's troops is accurate, this is worse."

"You did not always travel with him, did you?"

"No. Jashar traveled with your father for most of his years on the run," Gad said. "You have read the scrolls of those days. Samuel remained in Ramah until he died, and Nathan served the great prophet until joining your father in Jerusalem."

"Why did you remain with King Saul?" Solomon asked. "It seemed clear that the Almighty was no longer with him, and he remained an enemy of my father until the end."

"So it would seem," Gad replied. "While my heart was torn, I believed then and now that Yahweh wished for me to serve in the court of King Saul, if for no other reason than to bear witness and keep the chronicles as best I could under such duress."

"You were loyal," Solomon said.

"I was obedient." Gad bent over and began massaging his stubbed toes. "I cannot explain all that came to pass in my life. As my days increase in number, the more mysterious life seems. Nathan and I came to study in Ramah when we were boys with little direction as to what our futures might become. The prophet Samuel saw something in us that we could never identify in ourselves. One thing was for certain. There was the grip of Yahweh on our hearts, and I, for one, have never questioned it, though the journey has been fraught with danger and, oftentimes, I was despairing."

Gad ceased rubbing his foot and leaned back against the tree.

"And our present moment? Are you despairing now?"

Gad remained silent.

When the prophet did not answer, Solomon continued, "Earlier this morning as we left the tributary, you expressed confidence my father would survive," Solomon said. "At least it is what I gleaned from your tale of Father Jacob and the angels, that the scepter would pass to a rightful heir of the tribe of Judah."

"And who is the rightful heir?" Gad whispered his question more as a personal reflection. "I want to believe your father will survive. I want to join with your father in hoping Absalom might be stopped, reasoned with, and reconciliation come about. I believe it is why he asked Joab and the others to be gentle with Absalom. But only the Almighty knows the outcome of our lives."

Gad removed the leather pouch from his shoulder and opened the flap. "I have cold roasted mutton wrapped in unleavened bread."

"I am starving." Solomon pulled his hand from beneath his blanket like a hungry beggar. "We left in such haste I forgot to pack anything to eat."

"No matter the hardship, I always have an appetite." Gad handed Solomon his mutton. "Not like the royal cookery, but it will fill the crevices in your belly."

"It tastes delicious, thank you," Solomon garbled while chewing his first bite. "Thank you again for helping me with my ima."

"She wants no harm to come to her son, nor do I." Gad pinched off a bite from his wrap. "We are safer with the supply wagon."

"My father believes I need to face an enemy, though I never thought the enemy would be my brother."

"Your father has known many enemies from his father-in-law to the sovereigns of other nations. They all wanted his head. But it is another thing entirely to have a son intent on killing you. It has broken the king's heart."

"I do not know what to make of it all, Gad." Solomon paused from wolfing down his food. "I am perplexed how the human heart can be deceived and cause one to take such fatal action. The murder of Amnon at the hand of Absalom and his assassins is a memory that forever haunts me."

"Nothing has changed. In the Book of the Beginnings, Cain murdered his brother Abel," Gad said. "I have no wisdom or insight into the way the human heart is deceived or can deceive itself. I only know the painful cost when one loses sight of the truth."

"I pray for wisdom, Gad. I pray the Almighty gives me wisdom to understand how to be a good man and lead a quiet, productive life."

"I do not know your future, my lord. I am confident it will be a productive life, but I doubt it will be a quiet one. All we do now is survive tomorrow."

"Yes, survive tomorrow," Solomon said. "A future is built one day at a time."

Solomon leaned his head back against the tree. His once ravenous appetite had vanished after only a few bites. It was impossible to think of food and drink or a future beyond this moment, sitting in near blackness with his mentor. Gad had faithfully served two kings. The prophet had scribed copies of the sacred books and taught their truths to student prophets and Levites and kings. He had taught Solomon as had Nathan. He could not overestimate the importance of both men in his life.

The privilege of being born a prince in a royal household, enjoying the life of a student and scholar, able to devote himself to learning the deep ways of the Almighty and write his personal musings, he had accepted without much self-reflection. It had been a quiet and productive life, as he preferred, but his world turned over the night Tamar came to his room. He and Gad were sitting in darkness waiting until first light for a battle, all because of Amnon's brutal assault. Even now, Solomon felt the grief flowing from Tamar's wounded heart. Then he had to face a starker truth and admit to an even deeper pain once he learned how his father had treated his mother in a similar fashion.

The truth had no conscience. The truth was clear. The truth cut deep into his soul. He could not hide in the comfort of scholarly robes. He could not bury his mind in the scrolls of the Almighty. He could not travel to the outer reaches of Israel and avoid the truth of his own reality and his place in the family of the king. The truth was inescapable and hostile and must be lived through to its bitter end.

Perhaps he slept. Perhaps in his pondering and remembering he had drifted into sleep. In the darkness beneath the terebinth tree, his mind was flying through memory after memory, reliving each poignant detail, feeling the shock and marvel of each episode, deepening his grasp of the world's unpredictable turning.

He could not tell which came first to his consciousness, the bright sunlight, the trembling ground, the blaring shofars, or the bloody screams. All burst at once, for in an instant he cast off his blanket and scrambled to his feet. The whirling and howling of man and beast rushing by blurred his sight and muddled his mind as to who was friend or foe.

His name was called, shouted, then screamed. Gad was not beside him at the base of the tree.

Solomon saw the prophet, his arms straining and bending from the force of keeping Joab and Ittai apart. The two men were at each other's throats.

Had Absalom's forces overrun his father's army, and the generals were now turning on one another?

"Solomon, help me," Gad screamed.

He dashed over and grabbed Joab pressing him against the back of the wagon.

"You could have killed him when you had the chance," Joab yelled. "You left him hanging there and did not plunge your sword into his heart?"

"You heard the king," Ittai responded with the same intensity. "You heard his command not to harm—"

"You are a fool, Ittai," Joab cried. "Absalom would have killed the king had we not routed him. You would have been rich, a warrior's belt and ten shekels of silver."

"You could have poured a thousand shekels into my hands, and I would not have lifted my sword against Absalom." Ittai gripped Gad's arms but did not push him aside. "You heard the king. He told us to protect the young man for his sake. You just want him dead and someone else accused. You would never have defended me if I had killed Absalom. You would have executed me on the spot."

"I am wasting my time with you," Joab growled. He pushed Solomon away with such force he fell to the ground.

"Where is he?" shouted Gad as he shook Ittai's arms. "Where did you leave him?"

"Joab, there is no need to do violence against the young man," Ittai said. He paid no attention to Gad or his question, his eyes riveted upon Joab. "The day is ours. The battle is won. Allow the king and his son the chance to reconcile."

Joab ignored Ittai's pleas and barked an order to his captains and armor-bearers. When he broke into a run, ten of his men fell in behind, following their commander through the forest.

"Where is he?" Gad yelled, again shaking Ittai as if he were a withered man inside the husk of his warrior's gear.

"At the eastern edge of the forest, hanging between heaven and earth." Ittai dropped to his knees. "Absalom and his men pursued us into the forest.

When his mule went under the branches of a large oak, his hair became entangled in the limbs."

"Run!" Gad yanked Solomon to his feet. "Go save your brother."

Solomon raced through the grove of trees, following Joab and his men. The forest was so thick he could not see them until he came into the clearing.

As Ittai had said, his brother hung from the limbs of an oak trying to hold himself up with his arms and at the same time kicking his legs and feet at Joab's men who had surrounded him. One soldier had climbed upon the shoulders of another and was using his sword to try to cut the limb that ensnared the braided hair.

Absalom kicked the soldier in the chest toppling both of them to the ground.

Just as Solomon reached the tree, Joab yanked a javelin from one of his men and jammed the blunt end into Absalom's belly.

He gave out a bestial grunt as the blow knocked the wind out of him.

Joab struck him twice more.

The air and the fight gushed out of his brother. The blows were not meant to kill but disable. Absalom swayed under the boughs gasping for breath, barely able to hold on.

Two-man teams, one on the shoulders of another, encircled Absalom. The top soldiers began hacking the limbs with their swords until they gave way. When Absalom dropped to the ground, a soldier on the ground raised his sword above his head to strike.

Solomon rushed forward but, at Joab's command, was stopped by other soldiers.

When Solomon screamed, he startled the soldier with his raised sword, and instead of severing Absalom's neck, he cut the long plait of hair disconnecting it from the severed tree limb. The soldiers hurled Solomon to the ground.

He landed on his stomach but began to crawl toward Absalom.

Joab slammed his foot onto Solomon's back flattening him into the hard ground.

Solomon lost the air in his lungs and was barely able to speak his brother's name.

Absalom turned his head to Solomon just as the ten armor-bearers fell upon his rebel brother without mercy.

The sight of Absalom's face vanished inside the ten pairs of legs all vying for position to strike. Solomon buried his face in the ground and covered his head with his arms. He could feel the vibrations in the earth, hear the trampling of legs, hear the grunts of killing and the groans of death, but he would not look. He would not record the sight of his brother's mangled body in his memory.

"Blow the shofars," Joab ordered. "The supplanter is dead. The rebellion ended. Let those who remain flee to their tents."

The shofars pierced the air with their harsh blasts, and within the broad landscape of clearing and forest, hilltop and stony cliff, sounded the elated shouts and cries of Solomon's father's victorious warriors.

"Take the body to the deep pit at the far edge of the clearing. Heap stones upon him," Joab said. "Let the cairn be a remembrance of judgment."

Solomon did not have the strength to move, nor could he as long as Joab held him to the ground with his foot. When the shofars went silent and the soldiers bore away his brother's body, Joab lifted his foot off Solomon's back. He gulped down a deep breath the moment the weight was gone and rolled onto his side panting.

"I will send a runner to Mahanaim to tell the king of our victory," Joab said as he looked down upon Solomon. "You and the prophet drive the wagon back to the city."

Joab did not wait for Solomon to respond. The commander and his armor-bearers jogged in the direction of the ravine where his men had tossed his brother's body.

Solomon would not follow. He did not want to see his brother's final resting place or bear witness to any more scenes of death.

Solomon rolled onto his hands and knees and crawled to where his brother had dropped to the ground. The earth, indented and scarred, was still warm from the blood spilled upon it. The limb with the braid of his brother's hair had been kicked to the side during the frenzied execution, and Solomon edged his way to it.

The length of the remaining hair was longer than Solomon's extended arm. The hair that had once brought the crowds of Jerusalem to their feet and filled the king's coffers with donations of treasure lay on the ground, a nest of twigs and leaves, moistened with blood. The braids and leather wrappings around and through his brother's glorious hair had unraveled.

His hands and fingers trembled as he retied the loose tresses and leather straps. Then he withdrew his sword and carefully cut away the cruel limb that had yanked his brother off his mule and suspended him between heaven and earth until the jaws of Sheol swallowed him.

Solomon rose to his feet cradling the thick strand, and then stumbled back to the supply wagon.

Chapter 38

SOLOMON COULD NOT DRIVE THE SUPPLY WAGON. HE WAS LIKE an exhausted infant, baffled by the swift pace of killing.

That morning, he had been startled awake by the prophet's cry for help. He had been yanked from one dreamscape and thrust into another. He had lost the sense of reality. All the terrible moments of the morning were a blur. His heart still pounded at these fresh memories, and Solomon questioned their accuracy. He was present for each moment. He could still taste and smell the foul aromas of blood and sweat and offal, hear the grunts and groans and screams of carnage. Yet, he doubted his senses. He could not trust the reliability of his recall. The only evidence that validated what he had witnessed was the copious locks of his dead brother's hair. He cradled the thick, matted strand in his arms as if holding a woodland creature.

Gad drove the mule team into the encampment outside Mahanaim. Solomon expected sounds of great rejoicing. Joab had sounded the victory and sent word of Absalom's death well ahead of the returning warriors of the king's army. It had taken longer for Gad and Solomon to arrive with the supply wagon. The city should be alive with celebrations, but Mahanaim was quiet. None of the soldiers in his father's army acted as if they were preparing to revel in triumph. The warriors were sullen and vexed, ready to decamp as though ashamed of giving the king his victory.

"This is puzzling," Gad said as he drove toward the gates of the city. "The king should know of his victory long before now."

"The soldiers are huddled around their tents," Solomon observed.

"They should be singing and lighting up the city with torches," added Gad.

"There is Ima with Adonijah standing at the gates." Solomon pointed at the entrance of the city. "Why is Father not with them?"

Gad drove them through the city gates, and Solomon began to hear faint sounds of wailing above the rumbling of the wheels and rattle and clack of a wagon full of weapons, medical supplies, and provisions of food and drink.

"Do you hear that, Gad? Is that howling? It sounds inhuman."

When Gad brought the wagon to a stop, Solomon became distracted by his mother and older brother. He dropped the coil of hair behind the seat of the wagon before hopping to the ground.

"Thank Yahweh." Bathsheba threw her arms around her son and gave him a forceful embrace before looking for cuts or bruises. "Are you hurt? Did anyone strike—"

"Ima. Ima, stop." Solomon took her shoulders and pulled her into his embrace, embarrassed by his doting mother.

"Brother, did you see what happened?" Adonijah asked. "We have been told very little about the battle."

"Where is everyone?" asked Gad as he came around from behind the wagon.

"Since the runners came to announce the victory, the soldiers have gone to their tents," Adonijah explained. "Many are slinking out of the city, intending to leave."

"But why?" Solomon asked.

"Listen." Adonijah pointed to the open chamber of the guard tower.

The howling, now distinct and from a single source, emanated from within a human soul as if funneled up from a deep cavern. Solomon's whole body begin to tremble. The sound was so unnatural it was difficult to control his impulse to respond with his own cry of agony. A sound leapt out of his gut, a sound he had never uttered, a sound he could never imagine uttering, and it came forth as if casting out a vile demon lodged in his soul.

"This is like the howling of the Egyptians the night the Destroyer came for their firstborn." Gad clutched the wagon wheel to keep from falling to the ground.

Solomon felt his legs begin to buckle.

"Your father has not stopped mourning since he learned of your brother's death."

"Ima, I watched him die. I saw his face. He recognized me," Solomon mumbled barely able to speak the words. "I must see my father."

Solomon ran for the steps leading up to the tower above the gates where Jozabad, Benaniah, and Eleazar were standing.

"The king is grieving," Jozabad said, placing his hand on Solomon's chest preventing him from climbing the staircase.

"The victory has turned to mourning." Benaiah cast his eyes to the tower.

"O Absalom, my son! If only I had died instead of you," his father howled. "O Absalom, my son, my son."

His father's haunting words floated out of the chamber, a cry from a solitary heart. One man in such profound misery, his entire being was captured by a single howl, the ripping out of human sorrow buried so deep that the only vocal response was one of pain and torment. More than a father's expression of heartache at the death of his son, it was grief for a kingdom torn asunder, for a nation that had suffered under the affliction of a king's unrestrained passions.

"I must see him." Solomon made a motion to pass.

"He has been up there since the runners arrived with word of your brother's death," Eleazar said. "The prophet Nathan has been with him the whole time."

"Joab is with him now," Benaiah added. "He pushed right past us."

"He was furious." Jozabad removed his hand from Solomon's chest.

Solomon was free to ascend. He could not explain his compulsion to see his father. He did not know what he might do or say to bring comfort. He could go back to his mother and wait for it to pass, but the drive to climb the stairs had taken control of his legs. He could not be stopped.

He was met by Joab once he reached the top steps. If the commander had been furious when he blew by his father's dear companions at the bottom of the staircase, he now appeared apoplectic. His face was contorted with rage, red and creased with color and lines, a fearsome mask.

"He has lost his mind," Joab yelled, no concealing his anger or softening his tone.

"Joab, please," Solomon dropped his voice in counter to Joab. "Go join the others at the bottom of the steps. I will speak with him."

"Look in the village square." Joab waved his arm over the near-empty town center. "And the encampment. Do you see any of the men? No, they are stealing away in shame at the king's lament of the death of a wicked fanatic."

"Joab, can you lower your voice. The whole village and camp can hear you."

"They should all hear. Everyone has had to listen to him weeping," Joab shouted, no diminishment of his tone. "He humiliates himself and all the brave men who fought to save the king's life. He makes it clear that we mean nothing to him."

"That is not true, Joab, and you know it," Solomon retorted.

"You cannot defend him," Joab said. "We would not be standing here if we had been defeated. The king's head would be mounted on a pike, as would yours and mine."

"He is grieving the loss of his son," Solomon pleaded. "You cannot understand."

"Here is what I *can* understand," Joab said. "If your father does not stop his wailing and go out and encourage his men, thank them for their loyalty and bravery, then I swear by the Almighty the men will leave. It will be worse for him than all the calamities that have fallen on him since the days of his youth."

Joab threw up his hands in disgust and stomped down the staircase ignoring the three companions at the base.

Solomon watched Joab storm out of the gate and disappear into the encampment then turned his eyes to the chamber of the watchtower. The howling had ceased. Perhaps Joab's fierce tirade had silenced his father, but Solomon was sure it had done nothing to heal his father's grief. He eased over to the entrance of the room. No light shone inside the chamber, and the afternoon sun provided little illumination. Solomon moved into the threshold and allowed his eyes to adjust to the shadows.

Nathan sat on a stool with his back against the wall. His father lay crumpled on the floor leaning into the prophet's embrace. The breath of the prophet and the king harmonized in saturated grief. His father's eyes were vacant, staring at some image on the far horizon only he could see, his face so drawn it looked like a dried and withered fruit. Were it not for the crown on his head, Solomon would have taken him for a beggar.

"Abba. Father," Solomon whispered, and he knelt upon the floor.

The king of Israel flinched at his son's voice, a sign of life.

"Abba, would you come outside with me?" Solomon inched across the room on his hands and knees. He forced a faint smile at the broken man sprawled before him cradled in the arms of the prophet. "Come outside with me and greet the men. Then, Abba, I will take you home."

Solomon extended his hand to his father. "Take my hand, Abba."

The eyes of the king came back from its vacant stare and focused on Solomon. He raised his trembling hand.

Solomon could not be sure if his father recognized him, but the arm was raised and the hand extended in honor of his request. Solomon took his father's hand. The fingers were dry and limp, the hand chafed from rubbing across the hard floor of the room. This hand had no power. This hand could wield no sword—or scepter. His father's hand was a child's hand, lost, dependent, helpless, yet extended in hope of being grasped by someone of strength.

Solomon brought his father's hand to his lips and kissed it.

At the touch of his lips, there was a tremor, a spark, and as the king's fingers found life and began to curl into Solomon's hand, it was all the proof he needed that his father's heart had awakened and sought hope and healing.

SOLOMON WAVED FROM THE BALCONY OF THE COURTYARD TO the citizens gathered to honor him. People scrambled onto rooftops and stretched out of the windows of private residences and buildings. The streets leading to the palace were so crowded it was impossible to find a way through the dense humanity.

All eyes were on Solomon. All voices hailed him. Musicians played their trumpets and shofars, drums and symbols, lyres and harps. The Levitical choirs sang their choruses extoling the Almighty, Creator of heaven and earth. The harmonies of voice and instrument hovered over the city like an invisible layer of melodic sound. The atmosphere was alive, pulsating with worship.

Solomon's soul soared.

He had just returned from the springs of Gihon outside the city with Benaiah, Zadok the High Priest, and Nathan. The location of the springs was the main water source for the Levitical compound and Tabernacle and chosen by his father for his public anointing because of the significance of the wellspring of cleansing waters. Solomon had ridden the royal mule from Gihon back to the palace.

Solomon turned around and reached for his mother, standing behind him next to Benaiah. She took his hand, and Solomon raised them in the air, which elicited another uproar of approval from the crowd.

Then Benaiah stepped up to Solomon's opposite side, withdrew his sword, and raised it into the air to silence the crowd. "Just as the Lord, the Almighty, has been with the king, the Lion of Judah, may Yahweh, the Almighty, be with Solomon, his son, and make his throne even greater than the throne of King David."

There was time enough for Benaiah's booming declaration to echo off the walls of the palace before it was overwhelmed by the eruption of chanting, "Long live King Solomon! Long live King Solomon!"

Benaiah returned his sword to its sheath, and Solomon embraced the old warrior.

"You must beside me as you were my father," Solomon shouted into Benaiah's ear to be heard above the throng.

Benaiah knelt and kissed the hem of Solomon's robe.

Solomon placed his hand upon Benaiah's head then lifted him to his feet.

"Son. Son," shouted Bathsheba.

His mother tugged on his arm and pointed for Solomon to look at the citadel built upon the palace roof. It was the highest point in the city with openings on all sides. From the height of the citadel, the entire landscape of city and countryside could be seen. Solomon smiled when he saw his father standing in the window. He waved and his father waved in return, then disappeared from view. Once they returned from Mahanaim his father had requested to move into the tower chamber. He wanted to live out his days having a full view of the landscape from the City of David to the south to the Levitical compound and Tabernacle to the north.

"He will want to see you now," his mother said.

"He will want to see us both," Solomon replied.

Once again Solomon gave a vigorous wave to the multitudes then signaled to Benaiah that he was going to the citadel. He took his mother's arm and led her away from the palace balcony.

"I need you to grant me a request," Bathsheba said as they moved through the courtyard to the stairs leading up to the citadel.

"Name it, Ima," Solomon said.

"I do not wish for Tamar to live out her days in isolation."

"Nor do I. Invite her to return to the palace."

"You will make a great king, my son," Bathsheba said.

When they reached the top of the stairs, Gad emerged from the tower chambers, his glum expression only slightly brightening when he saw the king and his mother approaching. Solomon could tell from Gad's countenance all might not be well.

"Ah, just the people he wants to see." Gad extended his hands to them. Then he stopped and knelt instead. "I no longer greet you as a prince," he said, after kissing the hem of Solomon's robe. "My lord and my king."

Solomon was unnerved by this humble response from his teacher and dear friend. He had always loved Gad, felt the prophet had been more like a father to him than the one he was about to see.

"Please, Gad, I am not ready to be treated this way, especially by you," Solomon said, and then he got down on his knees and put his hands upon Gad's shoulders. "We must always be able to look each other in the eye and see love and trust. I need your wisdom for the days ahead."

"For the rest of my days I will serve you as I have served your father," Gad said. "Now, he is anxious to see you both."

Solomon stood, but when Gad remained on his knees, he said, "Please rise."

"I would love to, my lord, but my knees are locked."

The three of them could not help being amused as Solomon took Gad by his hands and helped him to his feet.

"How is the king?" Bathsheba asked.

Gad became somber, and he sighed before he spoke. "My lady, he struggles to breathe, and there is constant pain in his chest. He moves about slowly, but his mind is strong and his speech clear."

"Good. Good," Bathsheba said. "And the chills?"

"They come and go," Gad replied. "He spends much of the time sitting by the fire wrapped in blankets."

"What of the young virgin we brought from Shunam to keep him warm?" Bathsheba asked. "Is she not able to provide heat and comfort?"

"I am sure she does, but he asked for time alone with you. Now, hurry inside. He is waiting."

The two windows facing south and north were open allowing a breeze to flow through the king's chambers and some natural light to illuminate the large room. The other windows had been covered by wooden shutters.

When Solomon entered, he felt the stifling heat. He whispered to his mother, "How can he stand it in here?"

She did not answer, for she was making her way to the bundle of fur sitting in the throne of the Lion of Judah.

Solomon was surprised to see his father's legs and bare feet protruding from the heavy blankets, yet more surprised that his feet were moving, not stamping with impatience or frustration, but lightly tapping the floor as if gamboling on air. When his mother knelt before her husband, the feet ceased their graceful dancing. His father reached out to stroke his mother's face.

Solomon had only ever witnessed affection between them. Even after learning the dreadful story of their union, he had never heard his mother speak ill of his father or withdraw from him.

Would Solomon ever know such love as his mother gave to his father? Would he ever love someone in return?

He approached the throne and stood beside his mother, who remained on her knees. His father's scraggly beard and disheveled hair merged with a mound of fur wrapped around his frail body. Were it not for the crown atop his head, the old king would appear as some mythical, wild creature, half-human, half-beast.

"I apologize for the temperature," his father said. "Between the fire and my blankets, I am able to keep warm."

"What of the young woman we provided?" asked Solomon.

"Abishag, you mean? One would think sleeping beside a beautiful young woman would keep any man warm. Not me." He chuckled as he continued to caress Bathsheba's face. "I barely stay above freezing."

His mother took his father's hand and gently rubbed it.

"So, it is done then," David said, but as he leaned forward, he winced in pain, so he eased back into the throne.

"It is done, Abba," Solomon answered, choosing to ignore his father's pained expression. He did not want to accept the physical signs of the inevitable.

"I smell the aroma of Yahweh upon you." David withdrew his hand and massaged his chest. "The myrrh, cinnamon, cassia, and cane, mixed together in olive oil. You are consecrated like the vessels in the Tabernacle. You are now holy unto Yahweh."

His father extended his hand to Solomon. "Come, both of you. I have something for each of you."

Bathsheba rose as Solomon stepped in front of the throne and took his father's hands. He was surprised by the strength of his grip, but he was still careful in bringing him to his feet.

"I want to move to the table under the window looking over the Tabernacle," he said, extending his elbows out so they could aid him. "I am a little wobbly."

His father had never fully recovered from the ordeal of Mahanaim. Solomon, along with Hushai and Joab, had to negotiate with the tribal leaders to get them to accept the king. When they returned to Jerusalem, the chieftains still argued among themselves as to who had the greater claim on the king.

"This is what it is like to be king of such unruly people," his father had told him on their journey home. "At your throat one moment, singing your praises the next."

Once back in Jerusalem, more threats of rebellion followed even among Solomon's brothers vying for the throne. Solomon did not seek the throne, would have preferred the life of a scholar studying with the prophets and Levites, but this was not to be. All these events contributed to his father's rapid decline.

"I will need to sit on that stool." David nodded to the highbacked chair at the side of the table.

Solomon braced his father against the table while he fetched the stool and lowered him into the seat.

David pressed his hands upon the table covered with parchment and scrolls and struggled to inhale, but it caught in his throat, and he put his hand against his chest.

Bathsheba took the pitcher on the table and poured wine into a goblet. She held it up for David to drink.

After a few light sips, he waved it away. "Thank you, dear. I want a clear head."

David unfurled the scrolls revealing detailed plans for the Temple of Yahweh.

Solomon's eyes widened as he looked upon the sketches and drafts for the portico of the Temple, its buildings, its storerooms, the upper parts, the inner rooms, and the sacred place for the Ark of Yahweh, the room of atonement.

"I have been dreaming on these plans for a long time. This is everything the Almighty put in my mind for the Temple of Yahweh," David said, and then he looked out the window onto the Tabernacle. "I can see this Temple in my mind's eye, its glorious beauty shimmering in the sunlight, a beacon on the mount to draw the nations of the world to its sanctuary. Yahweh gave me the understanding of all the details of the plan, but I can only imagine it. You, my son, will bring it into being."

"Abba, I knew you had been working on these with the Levitical designers, but I did not realize so much had been drawn out."

"I approved the final designs with the draftsmen and engineers before we took flight to Mahanaim. They worked in secret while we were gone. Now, they are for you."

"And the treasury to pay for all this?" Solomon asked.

"One hundred thousand talents of gold and ten times as much in silver," David answered. "The skilled craftsmen are in place and ready once you give the command."

"Abba, this is overwhelming," Solomon said as he began shuffling through the documents. "I do not know what to say. Can I even do this?"

David lifted up his cupped hands with their bent fingers. "I know who I am, Solomon. I am a man of bloodshed. I have fought many wars and shed much blood upon the earth. Such hands cannot build the Temple of Yahweh. But you are the son promised of Yahweh. You are the son who will have rest from our enemies on every side and peace in Israel throughout his reign. You will make a great king, my son, and you will build a temple worthy of the name of the Almighty."

David gasped and clutched his chest with both hands.

"Abba, we must get you back into bed." Solomon reached for his father.

Bathsheba held onto his other side to keep him from falling off the stool.

"No. No," David said, struggling for breath. "I have more to say."

Once David steadied his breathing, he removed the crown from his head placing it upon the stack of designs for the Temple. "In the Book of the Beginnings, our forefather, Jacob blessed our father Judah comparing him to a lion. I am unworthy of such a title. That is for another, someone Yahweh will raise up, a true Lion of Judah. I lay my crown before him. I wish only to dwell in the Temple of Yahweh and gaze upon the beauty of the Almighty."

"Come, my love, let me get you to bed," Bathsheba said. Her voice trembled with concern. "You have exerted yourself too much."

"I have something for you as well, my dear." David reach across the table and retrieved a bound collection of parchments. "I had Gad make these copies just for you. I lost count of the number."

Solomon placed his arm across his father's shoulders, so his mother might take the collection with both hands.

"I knew Yahweh had given me a poetic gift, since my days tending sheep," David said. "I knew then there was no escaping the Presence, the hand of Yahweh was upon me. These psalms are a lifetime of my open heart to the

Lord. My fear, my distress, my poverty of soul, my hope and joy in the shadow of the Almighty. All has been written."

His mother embraced the manuscript to her heart as she shook her head to dispel the sorrow that threatened to overwhelm her.

"Do not weep, my dear." David reached to wipe the tears spilling from her eyes. "I am going the way of all the earth. Let these psalms of mine be a sweet whisper in your ear and a caress for your heart."

"Your words will never depart from me," Bathsheba said. "They will live forever in my heart."

David dropped his hands back onto the table and panted. "Now, I need to return to my bed," he said hoarsely.

Solomon lifted his father from the stool while his mother lay the manuscript on the table, so she might help her husband.

"Your mother will be a great help to you, my son," David said as the three of them shuffled toward the bed. "Pay attention to her."

"I always do, Abba." Solomon looked over his father's stooped head and smiled at his mother.

Bathsheba stretched over the bed and fluffed the cushions before Solomon helped his father onto the mattress covered in thick linen.

"Get in beside me, my dear," David said, reaching up to Bathsheba.

She slipped into the bed, and Solomon lay the heavy fur blankets over his parents.

"Son, come to my other side," David gasped. "I want the warmth of you both."

Solomon went to the other side and lay beside his father but remained on top of the covers.

"My son, you are still a young man, but already beyond your years in experience and wisdom." David lifted his hand for Solomon to clasp.

"Abba, I am fearful of what lies ahead." Solomon took his father's hand.

"I know. I know. I too was frightened by such a prospect when the great prophet Samuel came to Bethlehem to anoint me," David said. "But you must be strong and keep the charge of Yahweh. Walk in the ways and commands of the Almighty, and you will prosper. When a man rules men in righteousness and in reverence of Yahweh, he is like the light of morning at sunrise, like the brightness after a rain."

Solomon felt the strength of his father's grip fading, and he pressed his hand against his chest.

David nestled his head beneath Bathsheba's shoulder. His breathing became calm, no longer labored gasps. His feet began to move beneath the blankets.

"Are you dancing, my love?" Bathsheba asked.

"I want to dance into the gates of the Temple of Yahweh," he said.

"Dance, my love," Bathsheba said. "Dance into the Presence of the Almighty."

"Yes. Yes. Blessed is he whose transgression is forgiven, whose sin is covered. Blessed is the man whose sin the Lord does not count against him."

Every word he spoke floated on a sigh.

Solomon breathed every breath with his father until the duet became a solo. He held onto his father's hand even when the spirit had flown from his body. And he watched his father's feet dancing beneath the blankets until they became still.

The dance on earth had ended. The dance in the courts of the Almighty had begun.

READING GROUP GUIDE
Discussion Questions for *Lion of Judah*

1. Before David is anointed and assumes the throne, he experiences a crisis of confidence. He knows he is walking the chosen path of Yahweh's calling, yet he has his doubts and fear. He turns to his closest companions for encouragement. Have you ever experienced a similar situation where you were unsure of the future course of your life? When has it been difficult for you to make a decision to move out in faith?

2. Mikal has been reunited with David, the one true love of her life. Yet early in the story she is blindsided by the harsh reality of death in her immediate family. She was able to reach out to the one true friend she had who could understand her grief. Recount a time in your life where you have been surprised by dramatic circumstances that you never expected. What was your emotional response? And who was there to offer comfort?

3. David is first anointed king by Samuel in a private ceremony. When he is anointed in Hebron it is very public. It is a great honor to receive such recognition. What is like to be recognized for one's accomplishments and what sort of expectations does that place upon the one who receives the honor?

4. Friendship is a key component of this story. In our modern world it can be difficult to establish close relationships with people. In the Bible, it appears that David is not close to his blood family. He does have a close bond with Jonathan, King Saul's firstborn son, and a circle of friends he calls his "mighty men." What does a bond of friendship mean to you today? What form does the commitment take? How has life shaped your life?

5. Back in the time of this story marriages were normally arranged between families. The modern experience of "falling in love" was just not the norm. But it is clearly stated that Mikal, King Saul's second daughter, was "in love" with David. However, once they were married it was not a smooth path. There were many conflicts between them that eventually causes them to separate. While the historical context of the circumstances for David and Mikal are unique to them, what have you observed in other people's romantic relationship or personally experienced that might be similar?

6. Once David establishes his throne in Jerusalem he becomes obsessed with

a creative project that involved bringing the Ark of the Covenant into the city. How can you relate to this attachment to a creative endeavor? What has been the outcome of your effort?

7. As time passed David found himself with less and less to do. Others were in place to run things. As St. Jerome (347-420 AD) said, "an idle mind or brain is a devil's workshop." So, when David no longer gave his attention to ruling or creative projects he is beset by his own folly, which then leads to dire consequences. What might be a cautionary tale from this account?

8. It can be difficult to relate to the female characters in *Lion of Judah*. A few receive a lot of "coverage" in the Bible, but most have little description about their lives. To make them more "modern" and thus more accessible to the reader, they have been presented in the novel as having more influence than what might be true in that culture and time period. What aspects of these female characters in the story that may not be found in the Bible? Is there anything about the characters that strikes you as unusual, even modern? And does the way these women are presented humanize them more?

9. Except for Moses, there is more written about David's life than any other character in the Old Testament. He was a complex human being with many flaws on full display. Yet he had a heart that was both tender and courageous, and displayed many character traits that modern society would consider admirable. What does it mean for a man to possess both these admirable traits? How may we encourage these qualities in us?

10. There are instances in the story where many of the characters are given an opportunity to acknowledge God as one who is the "living" God, one who is an active participant in a person's life and then move out in faith based on who God is. Can you identify those moments in the story? Can you also cite some examples in your own life when you were met with similar challenges and how did you respond?

11. In every story there is the protagonist and antagonist. Sometimes there is more than one. What character did you identify with the most and why? Were you able to empathize with all the characters, even the ones who might be considered as an antagonist?

12. What were some of your favorite themes in the story? Identify some ways these themes resonated with you.

ACKNOWLEDGMENTS

Gratitude begins with my parents, Henry and Bernie, and ends with my wife Kay, daughters, Kristin and Lauren, husbands, Derek and Erik, and grandkids, John Erik, Clara Larie, and Patton Blair.

Michael Blanton, Steve Brallier, Michael W. Smith, Jim Davis, and John Brewer. These men of God gave of themselves to me for decades. They sacrificed their time and treasure on my behalf just because they loved me and believed in me even when I didn't believe in myself.

Brian Mitchell and Dave Schroeder, formerly with WTA/Media. These two eternal optimists brought my multi-volume *The Song of Prophets and Kings* historical fiction series across the finish line. And now to Jenaye Merida who took the baton from Brian and Dave and runs the race of the literary agent with excellence.

Jillian LaFave/Robotic Fox for her fabulous web design work.

Jim Thomas, senior pastor of The Village Chapel in Nashville, for his inspired teaching on *1st* and *2nd Samuel*.

Publicist extraordinaire, Jeane Wynn of Tall Oak Media and Marisa Stokely Deshaies, the brilliant marketing guru for WhiteFire Publishing.

Jim Reyland and the studio team at Audio Productions, Inc./Nashville for making my audio book sound terrific.

All my theatre and film artist collaborators and friends who inspire me to be a better storyteller.

David and Roseanna White of WhiteFire Publishing for taking the risk on an unknown. To Roseanna for her beautiful book cover designs. To Janelle Leonard, Wendy Chorot, and Kim Peterson for their insightful editorial guidance. This series has achieved a higher level of literary craft because of them.

And finally, to God…I have been carried between His shoulders all my life.

HENRY O. ARNOLD

Henry O. Arnold has co-authored a work of fiction, *Hometown Favorite*, with Bill Barton, and nonfiction, *KABUL24*, with Ben Pearson. He also co-wrote and produced with Steve Taylor (director) and Ben Pearson the film *The Second Chance* starring Michael W. Smith, the screenplay for the authorized film documentary on evangelist Billy Graham, *God's Ambassador*, and the documentary film *KABUL24*, based on the book which is the story of western and Afghani hostages held captive by the Taliban for 105 days. He lives on a farm in Tennessee with his lovely wife Kay. They have two beautiful daughters married to two handsome men with three above-average grandchildren. For more information please visit: www.henryoarnold.com